Forever: London

Kristina Frankel

Library of Congress Cataloging-in-Publication Data

Names: Frankel, Kristina, author.
Title: Forever London/Kristina Frankel
Description: First Edition
Identifiers: ISBN 979-8-9888825-0-3 (paperback)
            ISBN 979-8-9888825-1-0 (ebook)

First Edition: August 2023

Cover Design by Haley McMillian

Dedicated to TAS

Episode 1- Nothing Ever Happens

Madison Stevens stepped out of the terminal, her first flight in her 22-year-old life behind her. She smoothed out her skirt, pulling her large purple suitcase topped with a duffle bag behind her as she entered the terminal. The weight of the stress from the last 48 hours weighed heavy on her shoulders. Just two mornings ago she was sitting on her surfboard in the Pacific Ocean watching the waves come in and out, feeling the mist of freedom on her face. Now she was halfway across the world, with what she could shove of her whole life into two suitcases and a backpack, searching the crowds of the Heathrow Airport for a man holding a piece of paper with her name on it.

"Ms. Stevens?" he asked as she approached a tall man in the back of the crowds.

"Yeah, I mean, yes, I'm Ms. Stevens," she replied. She wasn't sure how polite she needed to be in this situation.

"Is this all you have?" he asked, motioning towards her purple hard-shell suitcase. It had seen better days, but she hadn't had time to buy a new one before her flight.

"I have one more bag," she said with a slight smile. She wanted to roll her eyes at his question. Of course, she had more clothing than would fit in this small carry-on sized suitcase. She was moving to London, not just visiting for a weekend. He nodded and turned towards a sign pointing to baggage claim.

Madison followed him, taking in the new sounds and accents around her. LAX was always a busy airport, full of international travelers and the like, but never had she heard so many English accents around her. She followed the driver to a carousel with bags coming out. After spotting her own bag, she heaved it off the platform and they headed out towards the car. The air was wet and humid like home, except here, the sky was gray unlike the blue sunny California skies.

"I was told to drop you off at the office and take your bags to the hotel," the driver said opening her car door. Madison slid into the seat, her eyes growing heavy.

"Yes, that is correct," she replied fidgeting with the edge of her skirt.

"Nervous?" he asked looking up at her in the rearview mirror.

"Extremely," she sighed looking out the window at the old timey houses and the green vegetation everywhere.

****

Ryan looked at his watch. "Twenty minutes and she'll be here," he muttered to himself. Of course, the woman who stole this job from him, could arrive two weeks after he had done all the hiring and set up of the office. And while yes, he had help, it would have been nice for the American princess to have been here to do her share of the heavy lifting. Maybe she was sleeping with the old guy who owned the publishing company. Maybe that's how she got the job. Ryan clicked through some emails, watching the clock in the corner of the computer as the minutes moved closer and closer towards her arrival time.

Relaunching a magazine when magazine sales in general were on the decline and everything was now moving to the internet was not going to be the easiest thing to do. Yet, Brad Garrison, the CEO and owner of Garrison Publishing, was a risk taker who jumped at any opportunity to defeat the odds, even if that meant he might lose some money in the process. So here they were, in the heart of London, ready to relaunch Forever London, the failing sister of the popular Forever Los Angeles and Forever New York. Each city's magazine catered to the wants, passions, trends, dreams, and news of that city. The concept had been risky back when Garrison turned his eyes away from just publishing books, but in about a year and with the growing hipster trends of both LA and New York, both magazines took off in both print and eventually started to grow a presence online. Now Garrison was ready to relaunch this concept internationally and this time add a social media spin.

Ryan jumped at the chance to lead the relaunch and to help cultivate it in a city he called home since the age of 16, yet, after two months of schmoozing and interviews, Ryan received an email thanking him for his interest as Editor-in-Chief and offering him a lesser job as the Creative Director instead. The news that an American who never once ran a magazine, led a business, or from what he could tell from searching her on the internet, worked a day in her life, now running this magazine, shocked Ryan. And, any minute from now, she was about to step off the elevator as the head of Forever London and his boss.

****

"You can do this. You got this. It's just a job," Madison muttered to herself in the backseat of the car.

"You have to get out at some point," the driver said, looking at her from the rear-view mirror, after sitting parked next to the curb for ten minutes.

"Right," she replied.

"Let's do it now, I have other places to go," he said politely.

"Okay," Madison said quickly, finally exiting the car.

Garrison Publishing UK was in an old grandiose building near Piccadilly Circus in London. Madison sauntered up to the huge glass doors with large gold handles. Drawing a deep breath, she pulled open the door and entered the lobby. The lobby was buzzing with people hustling to an exit or through security and up the elevators. Madison looked around taking it all in. She scanned the lobby for the security desk to get her security badge for the elevators per the email she read and re-read at least 85 times on the plane.

As she looked around, she noticed a group of posh looking English women hovering in a circle chatting. Each one of them looked as if they walked straight out of a fashion magazine with perfect make-up and every single strand of hair perfectly pulled back into a high ponytail, tight bun, or classy bouffant. Madison's dark green pencil skirt started to feel a little too tight and a little too drab as she examined each woman's outfit. Each outfit tailored and color coordinated to perfectly fit their bodies and skin complexions. Madison let her shoulder drop as she re-tucked the bottom of her top into her skirt, trying to regain the confidence she felt when she put the outfit on in the airplane restroom before they landed.

"Madison Stevens?" a female voice from behind suddenly asked. Madison slowly turned around to acknowledge the voice. There walking up to her was Allison Davis. Back home, Allison was the well-known daughter of a huge Hollywood director. She

3

was constantly in the news romping around with numerous actors or models, and always found having a scandalous time at all the top celebrity parties. Seeing her in person, dressed professionally, during the day was a rare occurrence. In this light she was even prettier than any magazine had ever portrayed her before. Allison looked like the other women in the lobby. She wore a highly tailored cranberry suit with a tight black blouse and black high heels.

"You're Madison Stevens, right?" Allison asked.

"Oh yeah, I mean yes, I'm Madison," Madison replied hurriedly approaching Allison.

"I thought so. I'm Allison Davis, your new boss. You can call me Allie," Allie said, reaching out her hand. Madison could feel her arm shaking and her hand starting to sweat. She quickly shook the hand of the tall, beautiful, blue-eyed woman in front of her and diverted her eyes down to her own two feet covered in a pair of brown oxfords she thought would look cute and very British for her first day of work. She now regretted every piece of her outfit. How could she ever compare to these gorgeous statuesque women in the lobby.

"Nervous?" Allison asked, looking concerningly at Madison.

"A little. Is it obvious? I've been trying really hard to hide it," Madison grimaced.

"It's okay. Honestly, I'm a little nervous too," Allie replied offering a calming smile. "Let's do this, let's grab our security badges and head out to this cute little café nearby and grab a coffee. We can get to know each other a little. And it's not like the office won't still be there in an hour or so. Plus, then we can really make our grand entrance when people least expect it. Sound good?" Allie asked.

Madison nodded in reply, her throat feeling like she just swallowed a mouthful of sand.

After getting their badges, Allie led Madison to a little café down the street. As they walked inside, Madison noticed the deep crimson walls cluttered with paintings in no particular order or theme and the furniture didn't match the walls in a variety of yellow and green fabrics or wicker. To the naked eye the room looked chaotic in detail, but something about it felt cozy and welcoming. Madison let her eyes wander all over before settling on a large bar area with espresso machines and other coffee contraptions looking for a menu.

"Some things never change," Allie whispered. Madison followed Allie over the counter, finally spotting the handwritten menu in chalk with a variety of teas and very plain coffee drinks.

"Let me guess, you are a small vanilla latte, extra shot of espresso sort of girl?" Allison said.

"What gave it away?" Madison replied.

"Let's just say I have a knack for this kind of thing. Why don't I order and pay, the magazine's treat, and you find us the perfect spot near a window?" Allie said nodding towards the café seating.

Madison smiled politely and headed over to the seating area. Allie was nice so far, but she was also pretty odd. Sure, Allie was Madison's boss, but she didn't come across as all that authoritative. Madison took a seat in a green chair near the window and watched Allie order. Everything about Allie was in place, yet something still felt off. Allie seemed perfect, almost too perfect.

Allie laughed with the girl behind the counter as the girl handed her two plates with scones. Suddenly a short man with gray hair emerged from a door at the end of the counter.

"Allison!" he exclaimed with his arms wide open. Allie put down the plates and her purse before giving the small man a huge hug. After about five minutes of talking Allie retrieved her items from the counter and headed towards Madison.

"I hope it's okay that I got you a scone. You must get a scone when you come here. They are so good," Allie said, setting the plates down on the small table in front of Madison.

"I take it you've been here before," Madison replied, taking a mug from the male barista who also came over to hug Allie.

"Sorry, I used to work here," Allie said, finally taking a seat. "It's been a few years, but everything seems to be the same."

"You lived here before?" Madison asked, taking a sip of her latte.

"Yeah, it was for a short time while in college. I'm originally from Malibu, California, but I've lived in a couple of places since my time out here which I'm sure you know about since every gossip magazine out there seems to like to cover my life," she said pulling apart her scone. "How about you? Where are you from?" Allie asked, relaxing in her seat a bit.

"I'm from Santa Barbara," Madison replied, taking a small sip of her latte.

"Ah, I thought you might share the California mindset! Where'd you go to college? USC? UCLA? Somewhere up north?" Allie asked.

Madison paused; she could feel her heart start to race a bit. "I went to UCLA," Madison said avoiding eye contact.

Allie could tell Madison was nervous. Why wouldn't she be? Allie swooped into the lobby and took the poor girl out to coffee before she could even get into the office. "Are you liking London so far?" Allie asked, changing the subject.

"I haven't seen too much of it just yet. But what I've seen looks cool," Madison replied. She took a sip of her latte, her eyes glued on Allie. She couldn't be too much older than Madison, but she acted so mature and powerful. Strength exuded from every part of her. She sat up straight, her legs perfectly crossed at the ankles and tucked to the side, her coffee cup perfectly balancing on a plate in her left hand. This wasn't the Allison Davis, party girl from California that Madison heard about regularly, no this was a different, too grown up, too proper version of that girl. Madison listened as Allison talked about the various things to see and do in London, nodding occasionally.

I can do this. I can do this. I'm not a total fraud. I can do this. Madison thought to herself over and over until it was time to head back to the office.

****

Ryan paced back and forth in front of the elevator doors. She was over an hour late and cutting it close for the meeting she was to lead in another 30 minutes. Ryan paced back and forth in front of the lobby elevators. He looked at his watch as he took another lap around the lobby.

6

"Before we get up to the offices, I want to warn you about Ryan Eliot. He's a little upset that he didn't get my job and I can guarantee that he will do whatever it takes to undermine me here," Allie told Madison as they stepped into the elevator from the lobby. "He is very charming which can be dangerous, so keep your guard up. He's not a good person."

Madison nodded as the elevator dinged and the two women stepped out, into the lobby. Ryan instantly recognized Allison Davis, the Californian party girl Brad Garrison pulled out of the party circuit and put into this prominent position She looked like every other west coast American Ryan saw in the media. Her hair blonde, her outfit overly chic, and her make-up bland. The girl next to her, however, looked different. Her hair a shoulder length curtain of brunette, her outfit a green pencil skirt paired with a long black sleeve shirt, her skin tan and her make-up minimally assisting her natural beauty.

"Hi, I'm –"

"Ryan Eliot. I know who you are," Allison interrupted. "Let's not make a habit of meeting me at the elevator instead of doing work, okay?"

Madison looked at Allison, her eyebrows raised in surprise. This was not the same woman Madison was just having coffee with. No, this was a stern, cold, Meryl Streep in 'The Devil Wears Prada' of a woman. Madison felt a little bad for Ryan, however it was odd to her that he was waiting for Allison at the elevator, so maybe Allison had a point. Madison looked back at him, her brown eyes meeting his piercing green eyes. Her cheeks suddenly felt hot.

Madison gave him a once over. He had dark brown hair. It looked messy, but still put together. A slight but well-manicured beard covered his square jaw. Of course, like Allie, he wore a suit. It was blue and looked expensive, but he wasn't wearing a tie. He wore brown loafers, which Madison knew cost him more than she would ever be able to make in a year. He looked young, almost too young to be working here in a power of position.

Ryan furrowed his brow. "Noted," he replied. "The conference room is set-up for our meeting in about 20 minutes. Let me know if you want a tour of the office before. Sort of a chance to get to know everyone before you lead the meeting."

Ryan flashed Madison a small smile, accompanied with a tiny wink, noticing her staring at him.

"I think a tour is unnecessary. Please make sure to send me a list of all the positions left to fill. See you in 20 minutes for the meeting," Allie said, starting to walk past Ryan.

Madison followed Allison out of the lobby.

"Too harsh?" Allison whispered.

"Maybe a little," Madison replied, looking back at Ryan who was standing in the same place.

"Hmmm… Ryan? Give Madison a tour of the office please," Allison requested without turning back to look him in the eye.

"My pleasure," Ryan replied shaking his head.

"Thanks!" Allison called back, disappearing down the hall.

Madison felt a small bead of sweat roll down the back of her neck, as she turned around slowly, her eyes meeting Ryan's again.

"So, this is the lobby," Ryan laughed motioning around the room they were currently standing in. Madison chuckled, as the tensions in the room left by Allison started to dissipate.

"Shall we?" Ryan asked, motioning towards the hall, Allie just disappeared down.

Madison nodded following Ryan out of the lobby and into a giant office space. The office was breathtaking. Instead of traditional cubicles, there were long wooden tables with three workspaces on each side. Nice large plants stood at the end of each table area. Huge wooden box light fixtures hung above each table. Around the large office space were other offices and small conference rooms. Every piece of the office felt meticulously thought out, including the wall in the far corner made of plants. Everything was in white and dark green: the Forever Magazine colors. Madison looked around taking it all in.

"This is the main work area. A lot of our interns and staff writers will work at these stations. Around the corner that way," he pointed ahead of them to the left, "is where some of the editorial team works, mainly my creative team and the layout team led by Clarissa Hayes. It's also where Allison's office is. And around the other corner is where the fashion editors and their teams work. It's also where the closet is."

"Interesting." Madison replied. Maybe it was just the first day jitters still, but she felt even more nervous around Ryan. She could hear her heart pounding as she maneuvered around him on the very short tour around the offices. She didn't want to come off too naïve, but also not too strong either, a dilemma she rarely dealt with since college. *God don't think about that right now. You'll ruin this all.*

"How old are you, Madison?" Ryan asked, his eyes on the room ahead of them.

"I'm not sure that personal questions are part of the tour," Madison replied, immediately regretting her answer.

"It's called getting to know you," Ryan retorted, his eyes still forward.

"I'm 22," Madison answered. "My turn, what is your accent?"

Ryan chuckled. "Good question, I grew up in the States until I was about 16, then I moved here."

"Makes sense I guess," Madison replied, looking over at Ryan's profile. Growing in California, namely the L.A. area, meant seeing and interacting with gorgeous men everywhere. Well for the most part. Madison usually just took their drink or food orders when she had a job. None of them ever took an interest in getting to know her and none of them spoke like Ryan.

"Shall we continue? I can show you more of where my team works," Ryan asked.

Madison nodded, following Ryan back towards his office. Ryan's office was a corner office with large glass windows instead of a wall. He could see everything happening in the areas around him from his desk.

"What is your title exactly?" Madison asked, looking into the small conference room near Ryan's office.

"Creative Director," Ryan replied. Madison looked at him, her eyebrows scrunched down taking in the title. "I'm responsible for the conception, design, and on-brand execution of all visual print and digital materials for the Forever London brand. Though I wanted your boss's job."

"So, I gathered from her icy interaction with you earlier," Madison said.

"Yeah. Well, right over there is your desk and Allison's office." Ryan replied, pointing to a desk outside of a large corner office.

Madison smiled. "Thank you for the tour."

Ryan nodded. "Anytime Madison. Let me know if you ever want a tour of the other offices, we have a large chunk of real estate here and I am more than happy to show you around."

"Will do," Madison replied, walking away with a smile.

Allie stood at the window of her office looking over Piccadilly Circus. A small chuckle of excitement escaped her lips. This was it. This was what everything else led her to. She reached into her coat pocket pulling out her phone. She needed to document this moment, not only herself, but her 1million+ followers on social media. One year ago, Allie decided to stop fighting the urge to join the social media world and let people into her life. Well as much of her life as she wanted to give them with the hopes that the tabloids and other gossip magazines would stop writing about her and she could fix her public image a bit after damaging it over the past five years.

Allie snapped the picture, added a filter and a quick caption (*Started from the beach and now we are here…<3… first day in the new office of @ForeverLondon as the new Editor in Chief…wish me luck!*) before posting the photo and leaving the window. Allie removed her jacket, tossing it on a chair nearby. Her desk was filled with flowers and mail. A giant vase of white peonies sat in the middle of the desk. Smiling, Allie reached for the card.

Als-
Take it all in, you did it! You did it all on your own and I couldn't be prouder. Give me a call later! The beach house is lonely without you!

Love and miss you,
Nick

He always knew how to make her smile. Allie repositioned the vase of flowers on the windowsill behind her. She'd snap a photo later to post in the days to come. Returning to her desk, she started to go through the mail, which included numerous cards from people welcoming and congratulating her on the new role and magazine. Allie flipped through them quickly, making a mental note of which ones to open later and which ones she would have Madison open and send a thank you note. She kept flipping until ... *Mitch McGowan.* Allie felt fear start to rise in her. Without even thinking, she tossed the unopened envelope in the trash. Her body sunk deep into her desk chair. The rest of the mail would wait until later. Her heart was racing, she could feel the anxiety, hate, and disgust pulsing through her. How did he know she was here? Did that mean Myles knew too? Allie's brain started racing with what-ifs. She needed to find a way to numb the anxiety, to stop the rush of thoughts.

At that moment, her phone started to buzz on the desk. Nick's goofy smile flashing onto the screen. Allie drew in a deep breath, forcing a smile onto her face, before clicking the little green phone icon to answer.

"Hello?" she answered.

"Uh oh, what's wrong Als?" Nick's voice rang out from the other side.

"Nothing, sorry I was slightly distracted! There are these amazing peonies sitting in my office. They are quite mesmerizing," Allie answered.

"Glad you liked them. How is your first day going?" Nick asked.

"Just getting started. I took my assistant out for a coffee. She's totally nervous and really young. She's a fellow Californian, which is nice," Allie replied, her eyes fixating on the piece of mail in her trash can. "Wait, speaking of California, isn't it like 2am there? What are you doing up?"

Nick laughed, "Don't worry about me. I've just been working on a script for your dad. He wanted to see a lot of edits before tomorrow."

"Don't let him work you to death Nick. You know he will if you don't set boundaries. Remember the last movie he roped you in on? You had to be on set in Thailand for six months. It was… horrible," Allie replied, her eyes glued to the trash can.

"You sound distracted still. Are you sure things are okay? I'm worried that you going back to London is going to cause you to relapse," Nick said, his voice getting lower. Allie heard him yawn.

"I'm fine, I swear! Get to bed! The rest of my dad's edits can be done in the morning after at least six hours of sleep, a run on the beach, and maybe two cups of coffee. Love you, miss you."

"Yeah, yeah, yeah. Love and miss you too. Text me if something comes up or you are ready to talk about whatever is on your mind. Bye." Nick said before his voice disappeared from Allie's ear, leaving her to find something to focus on other than the envelope mocking her from her wastebin. Allie turned to her emails and calendar. If anything would distract her it would be the work to be done and the meeting in about 10 minutes that she needed to prepare for.

Allie drew in a deep breath, looking up to see Madison heading to her desk outside Allie's office, a huge smile on her face. Allie knew that smile well: someone had a crush. A crush that Allie couldn't let flourish into something more.

Episode 2- Big Girls Don't Cry

"How was the tour?" Allie asked, emerging in the doorway to her office as Madison settled in at her desk.

"It was alright, not too informative, but at least I know where the closet is," Madison replied, her smile disappearing as she noticed the stern look on Allie's face. "What do we need to do to get ready for the meeting? I'm assuming you need me to take notes. Anything else?"

"There's a box of padfolios behind you on that table. Can you please make sure everyone gets one?" Allie requested. Madison nodded, getting up from her desk to retrieve the box.

"Question," Allie started, moving closer to Madison. "What do you think of Ryan?"

"He seems nice, I guess," Madison replied, sweat starting to pool in awkward places. "Why?"

Allie watched Madison closely searching for any hint of a crush or amusement by Ryan cross her expressions. Madison shrugged uncomfortably trying to break the tension.

"I'd just be careful if I was you, men like him tend to use young pretty girls like you for his own games," Allie paused watching Madison start to fidget with the ends of her hair. "I guess what I'm trying to say is don't trust him," Allie finished.

"Makes sense," Madison replied getting up to grab the padfolios. "I'll see you in the conference room."

Allie nodded, heading back into her office as Madison disappeared down the nearby hallway.

As Madison set the box down, her phone dinged notifying her of one new follower: **Ryan.Eliot**. Madison quickly clicked on the notification smiling as she followed him back. Madison slid her phone back into her pocket, as people started to file in.

Allie waited an extra couple of minutes past the meeting start time before entering the conference room. Tucking her hair behind her ears, rolling her shoulders back and standing up straighter than normal, she left her office heading straight into the conference room.

"Good morning, everyone," Allie said upon entering the room. Everyone immediately straightened up in their chairs around the large mahogany table. Allie spotted Madison in the corner, a note pad in her lap. Allie scanned the faces at the table when her eyes landed on an empty chair. Her eyes did another lap around the room. Ryan was nowhere to be found.

"Looks like we are just missing one person. But let's go ahead and get started. Clarissa, please make sure to update Ryan on whatever he misses," Allie instructed, knowing deep down his tardiness wasn't on accident.

"No need for that. Phone call ran over but I am here," Ryan said appearing in the doorway. Slowly he made his way to his seat making sure his eyes caught Madison's on the way. Madison's cheeks turning a deep shade of pink, as she looked down, trying hard to keep a straight face.

"Noted, but let's also not make this a habit," Allie replied, her voice and posture stern like an unforgiving boarding school headmistress.

"Let's get started," Allie continued. "As you all may already know I am Allison Davis, your inaugural editor-in-chief. I am excited to work with all of you on the first re-launch issue of Forever London which will be launching in a little over two months from now. We have a few more vacancies on the staff to fill, including a few staff photographers, is that correct?"

"Yes, we were waiting for you to come aboard before hiring any photographers," Ryan replied.

"Alright then. I know some galleries in town and will see if there is any talent out there, we could use them on a trial basis and bring in more seasoned photographers as we go. How are we looking on advertising? Have we secured any ad companies to help fill our ad space?" Allie immediately regretted asking this question, thinking back to the envelope she quickly tossed in her garbage earlier.

"I have a meeting set-up with McGowan Advertising at lunch today. Mitch McGowan is good friends with Mr. Garrison, which I'm sure you know. McGowan Marketing is one of the top advertising agencies in the UK," Ryan replied, leaning back in his chair, his eyes dead set on Allie's face.

Madison looked up, as Allie paused before responding. Allie's face was turning a deep shade of red, as she nodded and quickly looked down at her notes in front of her. "Um… I'd still like it if we could ex-explore some other options," Allie stuttered.

"I am quite positive that will not be necessary," Ryan retorted, a sly grin crossing his face.

"Nevertheless, I am asking for you to pursue it!" Allie snapped. Everyone looked up at Allie, but all she could see was Ryan raising his eyebrows and shaking his head. Allie's hands started to tremble.

"No need to shout. I will have my assistant contact some other agencies and set up meetings," Ryan replied.

"Moving on, let's hear your pitches for articles and photoshoots," Allie said, regaining her composure.

After about an hour of pitches and new assignments from Allison, the meeting ended, and people started to file out of the room. Madison stuck around, pushing in any lingering chairs as she grabbed any pens left behind.

"Ryan, a moment please?" Allie asked, her eyes glued to the notepad in front of her. Ryan nodded, waving off the staff member he was speaking to.

"Do you have more yelling to do?" he asked, approaching Allie. Madison looked at Allie, her eyes questioning whether she needed to stay or go.

"Ryan, Madison will be joining you at your meeting with McGowan Marketing today. I would like to have some honest notes about the potential collaboration between McGowan and our magazine," Allie said, her voice stern and quiet.

Madison stood off to the side of the room as they discussed her lunch plans in front of her. A pit started to form in her stomach. She didn't know the first thing about advertising.

"Why don't you just come yourself then? I'm sure Mitch would love to meet you," Ryan replied.

"I have more important things to do, and I think you and Madison are more than equipped to handle getting the details of the proposed collaboration back to me," Allie said.

"Is that the only reason? It might be good to meet Mr. McGowan since we are more than likely going to be working with him. Unless you've met him already," Ryan said, buttoning his suit jacket.

Madison looked to the floor, trying to hide her reaction to the power struggle unraveling in front of her. She wanted to interact and say something, but her brain couldn't form words through the static noise quickly filling every inch of her head.

"Excuse me?" Allie snapped. "What the hell is that supposed to mean? Actually, you know what, I don't give a shit about what it means. Madison is going with you, and I get the final say on whether we use McGowan Marketing or not. That's all, you can go."

"Whatever makes you feel like you have some control here," Ryan replied, turning to leave the room. Madison stood awkwardly by the door, her hands full of pens and empty padfolios.

"Be ready at 12:30," he whispered to Madison, as he brushed by her and through the door.

****

"Any new leads?" Myles asked, walking into the brightly lit white and yellow painted gallery.

"Not since yesterday," Patrick answered from behind a huge portrait he was installing in the corner of the room.

"You didn't even peek out from behind the picture to see who it was," Myles retorted, checking out some of the large photos leaning against the walls waiting to either be put away or hung up, as the gallery switched over its installation.

"Didn't need to, you come in every day at the same time, wearing the same suit, on your way to your father's firm and you ask me the same question. And unfortunately, I always have the same answer," Patrick replied, leaning out from behind the picture to face Myles, and to ensure things were straight. "Does that look straight to you?"

"It's a little off on the left," Myles answered.

"Thank you. I told you yesterday and the day before that, let me use your old photos, let me display them, send them out to potential buyers, to ad agencies, and to magazines and then the sales and leads will come," Patrick explained, fixing the picture, and stepping down the ladder to join Myles on the floor.

16

Myles thought for a second. "Not today mate. I'll work on something new this coming weekend and check back in with you next week," he said walking towards the door back onto the street.

"You must let the past go at some point. Just let me send those photos out!" Patrick called out as the door began to close behind Myles. Myles simply waved acknowledging Patrick through the window as he disappeared down the block.

Patrick shook his head. "Impossible," he muttered to himself. The man had so much talent taking photos but stifled himself with drinking and a career at his father's office. If only he could let the past go, the girl in his best pictures, his muse, would never come back, something Myles just couldn't accept still after five years.

****

Allie immediately pulled out her cellphone dialing Brad Garrison's number the second she reentered her office.

"He will have nothing to do with this magazine," she said.

"Good morning to you too, Ms. Davis," Brad replied.

"I mean it," Allie said.

"Look, we already have a contract in place with his firm and the UK branch of Garrison Publishing. I'm not firing his firm due to your personal issues with him," Brad explained.

Allie sighed, "Fine, but if I can find a better advertising firm, I'm going to contract my magazine with it."

"Allison, your name may be on that office door, but my name is on the whole damn company. I understand that you have personal problems with Mitch McGowan, for reasons I don't frankly care about, but until I have a reason to fire a firm that is bringing us in a lot of money, you will use his firm and you will knock off this ridiculous behavior. I took a chance on you with this job, don't make me regret it," he said before abruptly hanging up. Allie tossed her phone into the chair currently housing her jacket and purse.

"We will not work with that firm if it's the last thing I do here," she muttered to herself waking up her computer. "I won't let him ruin this for me."

"Bad time?" Madison asked softly, opening the door slowly.

"No, it's probably for the best we discuss the information I need you to get at this lunch," Allie sighed pausing her angry driven search for a new firm to work with.

"About that…do you think it's best that I go? I have no idea what we need in an advertising firm. I barely know how to turn on my computer here, which I have yet to do this morning," Madison started rambling.

"It will be fine. I just need you to let me know what Mitch McGowan and Ryan discuss over lunch. Hopefully it will all be business and there will only be the terms of our business arrangement to report on. But I doubt it and that's why I need you there," Allie replied. "Also, just make sure to steer the conversation to something else anytime my name comes up please."

Madison nodded, opening her mouth to ask Allie about her issues with Mr. McGowan, but stopping before a word could come out.

"Alright, when you get back, I do need you to actually do work today and turn on that computer. We need to first find a venue for our relaunch party that will take place the Saturday before our anticipated launch date. Second, I need you to also start researching advertising firms in London, as a back-up to McGowan's firm," Allie directed, her eyes darting to her computer screen. "While you are gone, I am going to reach out to a few connections to find a few photographers. We will need to set up time to go through their portfolios with Ryan and Clarissa later this week. Please work with Ryan's assistant to figure out a time that works for him. I'll connect with Clarissa."

Madison nodded, looking down at her watch. It was almost 12:30 and time to go meet Ryan in the lobby.

Ryan stood impatiently by the elevator waiting for Madison yet again. Ryan checked his watch: 12:29pm. He let out a frustrated sigh as he ran his fingers through the top of his hair. He prided himself on the fact that he was never late to anything these days. In his university years he would arrive late to every class, every family meal, every meeting or appointment, every rugby match, but now, now he was sophisticated, an adult no longer weighed down by childish inhibitions. Now, he didn't have time to wait around for an assistant sent by her boss to ruin his lunch. Ryan looked at his watch again: 12:31.

Annoyed, he pressed the elevator button. If Allie wanted Madison at this lunch, she would have to find another means of transportation for her. The elevator doors opened, letting out a few members of the styling department. Ryan nodded, forcing a fake smile at the two women who passed him as he stepped onto the elevator, hitting the ground floor button. The doors of the elevator started to shut, as Madison's hand slid in between them triggering them to reopen.

"You're late," Ryan said keeping his eyes forward.

"By like a minute," Madison replied, untangling her hair from her purse strap.

"Two minutes to be exact. You really should pride yourself on being on time when people give you an exact time to meet them somewhere. Actually, you should really be 15 minutes early. To be early is to be on time, to be on time is to be late," Ryan rattled off as the elevator made its descent.

"Oh god, who drilled that into your head? You sound like an old man," Madison retorted chuckling.

"I'm serious," Ryan said, looking at the elevator doors. She looked over at him. He was standoffish and cold now, extremely different than he looked on the tour of the office.

"Wait, you seriously wanted me to stand in our lobby for fifteen minutes, just in order to meet you to go to lunch? That's such a waste of time." Madison said rolling her eyes.

"It would have been the polite thing to do instead of keeping me waiting," Ryan answered as the elevator doors opened to the ground floor. "Let's go, the car is already here."

Madison followed Ryan to the car. They sat in silence for the entire car ride. As the car slowly pulled up to the restaurant, Ryan turned to Madison, finally looking her in the eye.

"Try not to say anything stupid. Mitch McGowan does not tend to take kindly to people who waste his time. If he asks you a question you answer with something short and sweet. Do not make small talk, and do not interrupt any conversation at the table. If you can manage that, we will both be able to survive this lunch with minimal embarrassment. Understand?" Ryan asked, his voice deep and low, his eyes darting into hers like daggers.

Madison slowly nodded, getting out of the car, following Ryan. The butterflies in her stomach turning into fire breathing dragons. Ryan opened the door to the restaurant, allowing her to enter before him. Tables of cream and white cloths were surrounded by rich people all over the room. The air felt stuffy, as if the money of each patron sucked all the oxygen from it. Madison hated these types of restaurants back home. The restaurants where the subsect of old money rich people would go to subtly flaunt their wealth and look down on the others around them who came from new money or fame. Madison took a step closer to Ryan as he spoke with the hostess. His voice was different again, smooth and charming this time. The hostess smiled and laughed at a joke that made Madison roll her eyes before promptly leading them outside to the patio and their table.

A tall, strongly built man stood up at the sight of Ryan and Madison. His hair was a blonde grey, his eyes a piercing blue, and his jawline perfectly outlining the hardness of his face. He extended his hand to Madison who shook it without a word. Madison felt her hand start to ache in his grip. Ryan introduced her as he pulled out her chair for her, "Madison Stevens, assistant to the editor in chief."

"Nice to meet you, Madison. I am Mitch McGowan, the head of McGowan Marketing and a member of the board for Garrison Publishing. I'm not sure Ryan mentioned that you would be joining us today at lunch," Mitch replied, giving Ryan a curious look.

"It was a last-minute request by Allison," Ryan answered rolling his eyes as he unbuttoned his suit jacket and took his seat.

Madison felt her heart trying to escape her chest, causing her breath to become shallow. She didn't want to be here just as much as it seemed that Mitch McGowan wanted her here. She could feel the daggers of his piercing eyes narrowing in on her. Could he tell she was panicking deep down? Could he tell she was so out of place, out of her element, too far from home?

"Where are you from Madison? You look very familiar," Mitch asked.

"Um, I'm from California. It's- It's my first time in London," she managed to get out.

"I take it this is your first business lunch?" he asked. Madison looked at Ryan who gave her a small encouraging smile.

"Yes, sir," Madison answered. The dragons were starting to turn back into butterflies.

"No need to call me sir, please call me Mitch. Please order whatever you would like for lunch, though the salads here are quite exquisite, you may want to take a look at that portion of the menu," he said. Madison nodded, looking down at the menu.

Mitch turned his attention to Ryan. "How are things shaping up at the magazine?"

"Things are just getting started. Allison is looking for some staff photographers. Our team pitched ideas for the first issue, and the relaunch party is scheduled for about eight weeks out," Ryan answered as the waitress brought some red wine to the table. Mitch took a sip and nodded to the waitress to pour the rest of the table a glass.

"Eight weeks. Does she think she can actually get this first issue and website done in time? It's a bit ambitious," Mitch retorted, his eyes flickering to Madison's face and then back to Ryan.

Madison watched Ryan as he answered, discussing the timelines he was going to set up with Allison and his plans on the creative side. He was different once again. Softer almost, excited about his work, and totally different than the man who defiantly stood in front of Allison in the conference room, different than the man who annoyingly scolded Madison in the elevator, and different than the man telling ridiculously flirty jokes with the hostess. He seemed eager to share with Mitch all he was working on, as if he needed Mitch's praise. Madison listened to Mitch negate Ryan's plans and Ryan calmly, and disappointedly, agree with Mitch.

The waitress came back around a few minutes later to take orders. Mitch ordered for himself and Ryan before looking at Madison and telling the waitress, "I think Madison is looking at a salad to eat. Did you find one?"

Taken aback by Mitch's pointed comment Madison nodded ordering a simple cobb salad, the first one on the menu. She could feel her cheeks turning red. Needing a distraction, she reached for the glass of red wine in front of her. She hated red wine, but took a swig, hoping it would help calm her nerves.

"So, Madison, where did you go to university?" Mitch asked, breaking the silence on her side of the table.

"Um…I haven't decided to go to school yet," she replied.

"Interesting," Mitch replied, raising his eyebrows as he took a sip of wine.

"No schooling at all yet?" Ryan questioned, scrunching his eyebrows a bit.

"Correct. I- I just haven't found a school I like or a major I want to pursue," Madison replied. The dragons were back.

"You have no ambition or future is what you mean," Mitch retorted shaking his head.

Madison felt herself sink in her chair a bit as she fought back tears. She could feel Ryan's eyes on her, but she couldn't muster up the strength to meet his gaze.

"Mitch, I would not go as far to say that she has no ambition or future. I'm sure Madison is taking her time to make the right decision before spending a couple hundred thousand on classes," Ryan interceded on Madison's behalf.

"Ryan, while I appreciate you standing up for an employee of the magazine, I mean it's quite chivalrous and all, I quite think that any young woman who has yet to settle down or select a method in which she can busy herself with a career or building a family by the age of eighteen is in fact telling the world that she holds no ambition or drive for the future. No offence if the opposite is true, but at this point in time she seems to have nothing going for her, especially in working as the assistant of someone like Allison Davis," Mr. McGowan said smoothly, as if the words simply slid out of his mouth without a thought.

Madison kept her eyes focused on the wine glass, now empty, in front of her. She knew this lunch would be horrible. Mitch McGowan obliterated her before the entrees even arrived. She felt Ryan's hand give her knee a squeeze under the table. She looked up at him giving a slight smile of acceptance and he let go.

"Well then, what business should we discuss? Advertising space maybe?" Ryan asked, changing the conversation.

"How's Allison doing so far?" Mitch asked.

"So far, she's doing fine. She's not 100% sure on the direction of the first issue. As I mentioned earlier, we heard pitches from the staff today. I think we should really showcase the upcoming pop culture in society, the mix of cultures, Brits meet Americans, fashion meets music and so forth. Allison feels that it's a little too all over the place for the Forever brand, but I really think I can change her mind," Ryan replied.

"You will need to find a way to make her listen," Mitch suggested as the waitress returned with food. Madison stared at her plate. If there was one thing, she hated more than anything else on the planet it was salad. Well, actually now it was Mitch McGowan and then salad.

"Ken Davis has always talked about how his daughter's mind can be easily swayed as long as there's something in it for her," Mitch continued. "Allison comes from a long line of Hollywood royalty, which means she's used to doing as she's told. Her grandfather was all about controlling the narrative of his family, and now Ken is too. Maybe I can get the board to vote to oversee the relaunch of magazine and help nudge Allison in the right direction."

Madison looked up from her salad putting down her fork softly. She opened her mouth to say something, remembering Allie's instructions before she left, but stopped as her eyes met Ryan's and simply shook his head trying to dissuade her from saying anything. Madison picked up her fork again, rolling a tomato back and forth on the edge of the salad.

"I don't think that is necessary. Plus, now that Madison knows your plan, Allison will too," Ryan answered.

Mitch laughed. "Well then maybe Madison can make herself useful to us."

Madison finally made eye contact with Mitch again, setting down her fork. "I would rather not."

"At least your loyal, uneducated, but loyal. Use that loyalty the right way and the education piece will not matter, you'll be able to ride on the coattails of someone else eventually," Mitch replied, checking his watch. "I need to head to another meeting. Ryan, lunch has already been paid for. Madison, good luck."

Ryan nodded, and Mitch departed. Madison pushed around the lettuce on her plate. Ryan shook Mitch's hand and slid back into the seat next to her.

"Not hungry?" Ryan asked, his voice calm and low.

"Can we just go back to the office now?" Madison asked, her voice trembling. All she wanted to do was escape this horrible lunch and hide in the bathroom to cry for a while.

"Sure, let's go," Ryan agreed.

****

"Hey Patrick, it's Allison Davis." Allie said, closing her office door, when Madison returned. Madison sat down at her desk. She still felt sick to her stomach. She didn't want to be here. She turned on her computer, still fighting the urge to cry. As the computer took its time turning on, Madison looked at the ground. Her stomach churned. She couldn't tell if it was hunger or stress causing this churning, but she did know that she couldn't do this. Opening her email, she began a new message, her resignation.

"Hey, how was lunch?" Allie asked, suddenly appearing in front of Madison's desk.

"It was fine," Madison said, her eyes glued to the words on the screen: *I am sorry to do this on the first day, but I quit.*

"Are you okay?" Allie asked. Madison looked pale and upset. Allie could see the tears forming in Madison's eyes.

"I'm fine," Madison replied, her voice cracking.

"Come into my office," Allie replied kindly. Madison got up and followed her into the office.

"Now tell me what happened at lunch," Allie demanded gently, motioning Madison towards a cushioned set of chairs in the corner of the room.

"Honestly Allie, I just think it's best if I leave. I'm not made for this job. I don't know anything about this world. I don't fit in here, I think I'm just going to quit and let you find someone more equipped and educated to assist you," Madison blurted out, letting a tear roll down her cheek. Allie stared at Madison letting silence fall between them leaving Madison feeling even more anxious.

"Well," Allie began pausing to collect her thoughts. "If that's what you want to do, then I wish you the best of luck."

Madison looked at her confused.

"Look Madison if you came in here for a pep talk, I'm sorry to inform you that I don't have one for you. I'm not going to fight for you to stay. I'm not going to beg you to change your mind. I can only imagine what was said at that lunch. Mitch McGowan is one of the biggest pricks I know, but if you can't find a way to deal with men like that, then you are right, you aren't cut out for this business. Hell, you probably aren't cut out for a lot of businesses. There are pricks all over the place, people looking to tear you down from every direction. If you can't learn to shield yourself from their attacks, you are going to end up running from every fight and never get what you really want in life. So, if you want to quit now, I'm not going to stop you. But if you want to stand up with your head high, if you want to fight the Mitchs of the world, if you want to grow and become someone you've always dreamed of becoming then make the decision to stay and keep coming back here every day to help get this magazine off the ground and running," Allie said, leaning back in her chair.

"Madison if you want to quit at least finish the work I gave to you today and then tomorrow if you aren't in that chair and there isn't a coffee on my desk by nine then I will accept your resignation and hire someone new. Deal?" Allie asked.

Madison nodded, getting up to head back to her desk.

"Madison," she heard as she passed through the door. Ryan was standing outside Allie's office holding a Forever branded padfolio, waiting to meet with Allie.

"No," Madison replied. "Please just leave me alone."

Ryan sighed, chuckling a little, as she pushed past him.

"Ryan are you ready?" Allie called out. Ryan looked back at Madison, fighting the urge to say something to her to try and make things better. He tried numerous times in the car ride back to the office from lunch but could never find the words. Not wanting to keep Allison waiting he headed into her office shaking his head as Madison avoided eye contact with him.

****

Madison printed a list of potential venues and a list of advertising firms and set them on top of her keyboard. Everyone in the office was gone, except Allie, Ryan, and herself. Madison powered down her computer, packing her limited items back into her bag.

"I'm going to head out," Madison said to Allie who was deep in a set of photographer portfolios brought by messenger an hour ago. Allie looked up and waved her off.

"Think about what I said, Madison," Allie said without looking up. Madison nodded and turned to leave.

She knew she had until tomorrow morning to decide whether to stay or leave, but how could she stay now? Even if she could muster up the strength to stay, she literally just sat in her boss's office seconds away from a panic attack. Madison made her way to the elevator, passing Ryan's office from afar. She could see him in there excitedly talking on the phone. She took a mental picture of his smile just in case she never saw it again.

Allie flipped through her tenth photographer portfolio sent over to her by Patrick, a local studio owner and someone she trusted. Out of the ten portfolios she had already flipped through, only about three of them were even contenders for a staff position and this one was by far the worst one. There were pictures of dogs from odd angles, nothing graphic or weird, just what looked to be amateur photos of dogs. There were also a couple of human faces included in the stack, all of them stoic and uncomfortable looking people. Allie sighed closing the book.

Her phone buzzed on the corner of her desk lighting up with a notification of another like on her earlier photo and a few more follows, nothing more. Allie looked over at the peonies on the windowsill. Today had been a long day, and with her assistant already trying to quit, Allie knew that the week ahead of her was only going to get worse. Pulling her hair up into a messy bun, she opened the next portfolio.

"These are alright, okay, okay," she thought flipping through the book of people sitting in chairs in empty rooms. Every photo looked the same, a boring collage of people doing boring things. Allie continued to flip through the book until she recognized a very familiar face: her own.

Allie slammed the book shut as if she found a bug in the middle of the portfolio. Snatching her phone up off the desk, she stood up and began to pace back and forth.

"What the hell? Did he… no…he wouldn't dare," Allie muttered, selecting Patrick's number from her recent call list.

"I was starting to wonder when I would get another call from you," Patrick answered.

"Is he seriously using these photos in his portfolio?! Don't lie to me Patrick!" Allie snapped. "He can't be seriously using these. I told him never to use them!"

Ryan headed to Madison's desk to leave the name of a potential venue, pausing outside Allison's office door, as he heard Allison's voice ring out in anger. Eavesdropping wasn't his favorite way to get information, but he'd make an exception this time. Allie's door was open a crack, allowing him to hear her side of the conversation. If he leaned against Madison's desk writing her a quick note and just happened to listen in on Allie's conversation there would be no harm in that and if his phone just happened to record the conversation by accident, well, he couldn't stop an accident from happening.

"You act like these are some risqué nude photos of you Allie," Patrick replied calmly from the other side of the phone.

"Regardless, he has no right to use them!" Allie continued to furiously storm back and forth between the sides of her office.

"Allie, he's not using these photos. He would kill me if he knew I sent them to anyone, especially you. Did you see the rest of his portfolio?" Patrick asked. Allie sat down. Her anger subsided, as she reopened the portfolio.

"Yeah," she sighed. "They suck."

"Myles has lost his touch. It's been that way for quite some time. He refuses to let me showcase the photos of you, his best work. So, he never books a job. He never has a showing at the gallery. He simply comes in here every week, almost every day, inquiring as to whether I have any new leads for him," Patrick explained.

"Patrick, I can't hire Myles," Allie replied, her voice cracking as years of suppressed emotions started to boil up.

Ryan smiled, stopping his phone from recording. "Welcome to the team Myles," he whispered.

Episode 3- Anxiety

Allie walked through the frosted doors of Forever with one mission in mind- to see if Madison decided to stay or go. She was already exhausted today and since she woke up late, she didn't have time to go get coffee before her first meeting. After talking to Patrick about the potential photographers and Myles in particular, she went to her new London townhouse and could barely sleep. Allie avoided making eye contact with anyone as she made a beeline for her office.

Madison was nowhere to be seen. Allie shook her head at and tossed her bag in the cushioned chair in the corner of her office. Allie slumped down in her desk chair, staring at a painting on the wall. In just one day she managed to lose her assistant, get in an argument with not only her creative director but her boss, Mitch McGowan would be involved in her magazine, and Myles' photos were burned at the forefront of her mind again.

"Rough night?" Madison asked, walking in with a very large hot cup of coffee. "Looks like my idea to get you an extra shot was smart."

Allie perked up, suppressing a smile, nodding in gratitude as she took the coffee cup. "Didn't think I would see you this morning after I came in and saw your desk empty," Allie said before taking a sip of the warm coffee and milk.

"Sorry about that. The line for coffee was extremely long today. I would have been here earlier otherwise," Madison explained. "Look about yester—"

"Better late than never. Do you have the lists I asked you to put together yesterday?" Allie interrupted.

"Yes, of course, let me grab those for you," Madison replied, quickly walking to her desk to set down her bag and her own coffee. A bright yellow post-it note on top of the papers she left on her keyboard last night caught her eye.

Madison-

Sorry for what happened at lunch. As a gesture of goodwill, here's a great venue you should pitch to Allie for the launch party. She'll love it.   -Ryan

Madison removed the yellow sticky note. The paper underneath had only an address and the name "Altitude360." Madison set it aside, grabbing the other papers Allie requested.

"Here," she said as she handed Allie the printed pages.

"Thanks. Oh, and please take those," Allie said, gesturing towards three photographer portfolios on the table across the room. I will need three copies of each resume and the interview schedule written on the top page. We have three interviews for photographers scheduled from LifeColor Studios this afternoon. Ryan, Clarissa, and I will be handling the interview part, but I would like you there to take notes."

Madison nodded. "Is there anything else you need me to do? Do you want me to get rid of those portfolios over there?"

"Not right this second. I am going to review these lists and then we can meet later to discuss next steps," Allie replied. Madison turned to leave Allie's office with the portfolios in hand. "Oh, and Madison?" Madison stopped before leaving the doorway and looked back.

"You made the right decision showing up this morning," Allie said with a slight smile.

****

Patrick heard the door ding from the backroom. He sighed shaking his head. He was sure it was Myles coming to check in again today. No matter what Patrick said last night, Allie refused to give Myles a chance. If anyone knew his capabilities it was Allison Davis, and yet, even she passed. Now, Patrick had to go out there and chip away another piece of the hope that kept Myles held together.

"Look I know I said I wouldn't come in until next week, but any luck?" Myles asked, jumping at the sight of Patrick. Patrick shook his head in response. Myles looked overly excited today, not in a suit and tie, his hair slightly disheveled.

"Sorry for the bad news," Patrick managed to say.

"No, I understand. Maybe I will manage to take some worthwhile photos today," Myles replied.

"Do you not have to go into the office?" Patrick asked.

"Not today. My father called and told me to take the day off. So, I am off to go take photos, just thought I'd stop by," Myles

29

chuckled. "One of these days, I will get some positive news out of you Patrick."

****

Madison knocked on Ryan's open door. "What can I do for you Madison?" he asked.

"Here," she replied handing him back the paper he put on her desk. Ryan took it, setting it down on his desk, cocking his head to the right confused.

"May I inquire into why you are handing this back to me?" Ryan asked, staring at her. She looked extremely nice today, nicer than she looked yesterday. She wore a navy-blue midi skirt with a white button down. Her hair could still use some work, as it sat limp on her shoulders without any styling or volume, but the simple-girl-look worked for her.

"I don't need your charity. I don't need an apology for yesterday's lunch. And I don't need you to feel sorry for me," Madison asserted.

Ryan smiled. "Madison, I don't feel sorry for you. Though I am curious as to why you lied to Mitch at lunch. That's something we can discuss later. I put this piece of paper on your desk because Altitude360 is a great venue and if you are not from London, then you can easily miss it. I've attended quite a few parties there, and I think Allison will approve of this venue. However, if you feel like you have found better options, then I will just keep this venue in mind for a later event," Ryan replied.

"What lie?" Madison asked, dismissing his condescending tone, and fixating only on Ryan's accusation.

"About not going to college. I have it on good authority you at least finished a year at UCLA, yet yesterday you said you had yet to decide on a college to attend," Ryan replied. Madison looked down to the carpet and then back at Ryan.

"I have work to do," she murmured as she turned to leave. Ryan watched her walk away as he tossed the paper, she handed back to him in the trash.

Madison sat back at her desk in a huff. She had about thirty minutes before she needed to meet with Allie and then order lunch. She opened her text messages, scrolling down to her mom's name. Five text messages in a row from Madison graced her screen, left unanswered by her mom. Madison typed a few questions marks and sent them in yet another text to her mom, knowing full well she wouldn't answer for at least another week. Trying to pass the time, Madison typed 'Altitude 360' into a search bar, pulling up photos of the venue.

****

Patrick could hear the phone ringing in the front of the gallery, he finished wiping down the edge of a frame before wandering over to the cordless phone on the reception desk.

"Hello, LifeColor Gallery, this is Patrick," he answered.

"Hello Patrick, this is Ryan Eliot from Forever London calling to set up an interview this afternoon with one of your photographers," Ryan replied.

"Which one?" Patrick asked confused by the phone call, all of the photographer interviews were already set up by Allison last night.

"Myles. He was just added to our list this morning by Allison Davis. We are very impressed by some of the photos in his portfolio and would like to meet him in person. Is he available?" Ryan explained.

"Wow, well that's quite the change in tone from my conversation with Allison last night! Um, I will give him a call, I'm sure he will be quite excited. What time should he be at the offices?" Patrick asked elatedly.

"4PM," Ryan answered. "I'm sure you already have the address and information from Allison. We look forward to meeting Myles later today."

****

"Madison?" Allie called out from her office desk. "Ready to meet?"

Madison stood up, straightening out her outfit and sliding her feet back into her cream heels. She looked back at the pictures on her computer of Altitude 360 once more before heading into Allie's office.

"Ah, Madison, awesome. Go ahead and close the door behind you and have a seat there," Allie directed, looking up from her computer to point to a pair of white and gold chairs in front of the window behind her. Madison sat down feeling slightly nervous. Not even 24 hours ago she sat in this very room on the brink of tears, quitting this job, and yet here she was again about to get feedback on her first assignment. Allie continued to stare at her computer.

Madison thought to herself, letting the awkwardness of sitting alone settle in her mind. Another minute passed, before Allie moved from her desk to the chair across from Madison.

"So, I reviewed these lists. Thank you for creating them," Allie started. Madison swallowed as she felt a but coming. "I can't help but wonder though if these are the best venues out there for our event."

Madison nodded taking in the feedback.

"I mean don't get me wrong, it's not a bad list of places. Just half of these venues are too small, and the other ones are not fancy enough for the party I am envisioning," Allie continued.

"What exactly are you envisioning?" Madison asked, gearing her pen up to write down this grand plan.

"I want this party to feel young and hip, while still giving our board members the classy vibes of old Hollywood parties," Allie described. "We will have a red carpet going into the venue, which we should be able to do at any place really. Make a note to get the proper permits for the press outside of whatever place we pick. The venue should have an outside area or at least a ton of windows to make it feel less crowded, so this one venue you listed that is really just an old warehouse is out."

Madison jotted down as many buzzwords as she could while Allie continued to describe her ideas for the party and give reasons why the venues on Madison's list wouldn't work. After about 45 minutes Madison felt defeated. Not a single venue on the list would work for Allie's launch party.

"I have one more option. Look up Altitude 360 on your computer. I found it last night when I couldn't sleep. I think it might be the perfect place for the party actually," Madison admitted.

"This place is perfect. Why didn't you mention it earlier or add it to the list this morning?" Allie asked.

"I wasn't sure if it had the right vibe," Madison replied. "I probably should have asked more questions as to what you were looking for. I'll make a mental note to do that in the future soooo," Allie raised her hand cutting off Madison's nervous spiral.

"Just set up a walkthrough," Allie said as Ryan appeared in the doorway.

"Our first photographer is here for her interview. Are you both ready?" he asked.

"Madison, go ahead, I need another minute," Allie replied, turning to reapply her lipstick and smooth down her hair. Madison grabbed the interview packets off her desk before following Ryan to the conference room.

"So did you both choose a venue for the party?" Ryan asked nonchalantly.

Madison rolled her eyes and the smirk on his face. "We did," she replied.

"And?" Ryan asked, the smirk turning into a smile.

"We are scheduling a walk through at Altitude 360," Madison stated reluctantly. "If it can hold the party Allie is envisioning then we will book the space."

"So, you pitched it to her after all?" Ryan asked coyly. Madison rolled her eyes at him, pushing open the door of the conference room. "What? I can't help that I have great ideas and the fact that it actually helped you makes us even."

"Even?" Madison asked, setting the interview packets individually on one side of the table.

"I mean, you did use my suggestion meaning you've accepted my apologies and that I don't owe you anything," Ryan explained, placing his hands on the back of one of the chairs. Madison let out a laugh. "What?" he asked.

"Ryan, you didn't owe me anything to begin with. I only used your suggestion because it fit all the criteria Allie seemed to be looking for," Madison replied, taking a seat in the corner.

"Understood. Anyways, about yesterday. I hope you know that there are going to be plenty more people in this business commenting on your weight or experience," Ryan replied.

"What is that supposed to mean Ryan?" Madison asked annoyed, feeling anger and shame rising in her chest. Sure, she wasn't a size double zero like her boss or half of the women walking around this office, but that sure as hell didn't open the door for anyone to comment on her weight.

"What are you a size 6 or 8? I'm just saying that it might help to lose a little weight if you want to be taken seriously in this industry. I'm not trying to be offensive, just giving a pointer. You'll either need to lose some weight or grow some thicker skin to deal with people like Mitch" Ryan answered.

"Stop, I don't need your advice on how to deal with Mitch McGowan," Madison replied.

"Now don't get defensive Madison," Ryan said feeling the tension pulsing throughout the room.

"Let's just sit in silence until the interviews start," Madison replied, her voice monotone and cold.

"Madison, come on, it's just a suggestion. I'm just trying to hel—"

"Enough," Madison interrupted, spotting Allie walking down the hallway with Clarissa.

Allie walked in, followed by Clarissa, a gorgeous woman on two stilts for legs complete with a tiny waist, long brunette hair and piercing green eyes. She could pull off any outfit, especially the high waisted flowy white slacks she currently had on matched with a very chic dark green sleeveless top which tied around her neck. Clarissa worked in the layout department but was someone on the staff that Allie knew well and trusted. Madison knew they partied together here and there over the past few years. They were some of the early "It Girls" of the party circuits in Hollywood. Clarissa nodded to Madison giving her a polite half smile as she took her seat.

Madison looked down at her skirt, smoothing it a bit. She crossed her legs and uncrossed them at the thought of how fat her one calf smooshed up against the other would look to others. Her face felt hot thinking about the other clothes she brough to London with her. None of them would ever make her look like Clarissa did, so effortlessly put together. Her mind was spinning trying to figure out how to get some new clothes but also how to lose weight. She couldn't get the thoughts to stop coming at her faster and faster, until her eyes met Ryan's calming blue eyes. For a moment, the waves of intrusive thoughts crashing over her stopped. He looked sincere, softer than before.

"Sorry," Ryan mouthed from across the room. Madison nodded in acceptance; their eyes glued to one another. The whole room started to fade around him, until all she could see in color was Ryan.

"Ryan are you ready?" Allie asked, following his gaze to where Madison sat on the other side of the room.

"Ryan? Earth to Ryan," Clarissa said waving her hand in front of his face. Ryan shook his head, focusing in on Clarissa. Madison looked down at her notepad, her cheeks fully red now.

"Um, yes. Sorry, I zoned out for a moment. Who is our first candidate?" Ryan asked, straightening the papers in front of him.

"It's Brynn Jacobs," Clarissa replied with a smile and a slight cock of her head.

Madison watched Clarissa flirt with Ryan. "*Gross*," she thought as she grimaced at the sight of Clarissa's hand on Ryan's arm. Madison let out a large sigh from the corner. Ryan looking over at her, pulled his arm away from Clarissa's touch. Allie made eye contact with Madison who raised her eyebrows in response, acting as if nothing happened.

"Very well then, Madison please go get Ms. Jacobs from reception," Allie directed.

****

"Is that the last one?" Clarissa asked two hours later, leaning back in her chair.

"I think so," Allie answered. "I liked that last candidate. She had some spunk that could be very useful in some of our more advantageous pieces down the line."

Ryan was silent, checking his phone and watch. Madison, curious, watched him tap his pen on the table. He was acting strange. He almost seemed uncharacteristically nervous. Allie and Clarissa continued to chat about the three candidates for another minute or so. As the conversation ended, Allie stood up.

"Ryan, let me know your thoughts in an email and we will make an offer to at least two of them tomorrow," she said collecting her items. Ryan jolted out of his seat.

"Wait! We have one more candidate I found. Don't go anywhere," he said, buttoning his suit jacket and exiting the room.

"Did you know about this?" Clarissa asked.

"I did not," Allie replied, looking to Madison for confirmation. Madison shrugged her shoulders as she shook her head.

"Myles?" Ryan asked, entering the lobby.

Myles knew that voice without having to turn around to see the face of its owner. "Of course," he said turning to see Ryan Eliot standing near the receptionist desk. "Did my father put you up to this? That would make sense. He gave me today off without a reason. I should have guessed you two would be up to something."

"He has no idea. Shall we?" Ryan asked, gesturing Myles towards the office and out of the lobby. Myles nodded, following Ryan to a conference room. Myles could feel the uneasiness rising in his stomach with each step. As they drew near the conference room. Ryan opened the conference room door without a word to Myles.

"Ladies may I present our fourth candidate, Myles McGowan," Ryan announced as Myles stepped into the room behind him.

Allie dropped her pen. Every hair on her body stood up straight at the sound of his name. She could feel her hands starting to shake. Drawing in a deep breath, she turned her head to see his face. There he was, standing in her conference room. He looked exactly the same as he did five years ago.

Neither of them spoke, letting the tension rise as three other people sat in the sea of awkwardness flooding the room. Myles couldn't believe his eyes, there sat Allison Davis.

"Hi Myles, nice to meet you," Clarissa grinned, standing up to extend her hand to him.

"I'll be right back," Allie said, getting up and hurriedly leaving the room as Myles shook Clarissa's hand. Ryan pointed Myles to a seat on the other side of the table and turned to follow Allie out of the room.

"Do you want some water?" Madison asked trying to diffuse the tension.

Episode 4- Don't Start Now

"Allie, it's highly unprofessional to just leave an interview. I hope it was for an urgent issue," Ryan said, lingering in Allie's doorway.

"Mitch put you up to this?" Allie asked, sitting down at her desk.

"He has the best portfolio out of everyone," Ryan replied crossing his arms as he leaned against the door frame. "Don't let a personal situation rob the magazine of the relaunch it deserves."

"Don't lecture me on what the magazine deserves!" Allie snapped. "I know this is just a game to you, but this is my life you are playing with."

"Actually, this isn't a game at all. It's business and you would rather throw a little fit over this photographer than do your damn bloody job. You know that if you were to set your emotions aside and be rational for a minute you would be able to admit that Myles is the best prospect we have," Ryan said.

"There were better candidates," Allie replied.

"Like hell there were. That second candidate took pictures like he was some teen girl on social media. I could find better pictures taken by hundreds of other people than what he submitted. Myles tells stories with his photos. Hell, for a second he made me believe you weren't some Hollywood party girl who got this job solely based on who her daddy is," Ryan explained.

"Not fair," Allie said crossing her arms and leaning back in her chair. "You have no idea what I went through to get this job."

"Tell me, honestly, that he didn't have the best portfolio of them all and I'll go cancel the interview," Ryan replied.

Allie looked back at the flowers from Nick, slowly wilting on the table. Ryan was right. Myles did have the best pictures out of the bunch. "Fine," Allie muttered getting up from her chair. "But this isn't over."

"Glad to hear it," Ryan replied.

Myles watched Allie walk the length of the conference room to the door, Ryan following behind her. She looked more beautiful than ever before, even with a slight scowl on her face. Myles looked down at the table, his heart sinking in his chest.

"So, Myles, what makes you think you are cut out for this job?" Allie asked, jumping right in. Clarissa and Ryan sat back in their chairs letting Allie take the lead. Madison watched Ryan's face light up as he leaned back, covering his mouth with his hand, undoubtedly enjoying this.

"Well, as I'm sure you've seen from my portfolio, I can take a wide range of photos. While I have never photographed an editorial campaign, I have some experience in the design of advertising campaigns, so I do understand the industry," Myles replied.

Allie straightened up in her chair. "To be honest, your portfolio lacked a lot of quality photography that we look for in the industry. It's easy to take artistic photos void of any emotion or spark. It's not easy to take photos of models who are modeling clothes and trying to pull a theme together. I'm not sure this is the right fit for you."

Myles nodded, unsure what he could say to change her mind.

"Well, there were a few photos of our Allison here that were very much what we are looking for," Ryan interjected sliding some photos from Myles portfolio, the photos of Allie, to Clarissa. Myles looked over to Allie for any reaction to the photos.

"Interesting," Clarissa muttered.

"A few photos that showcase a talent are hardly indicative of whether or not he can produce photos at the quality we need," Allie said bluntly.

"Ah, but at least there were a few photos showcasing talent, we can teach you all you need to know Myles. You have a great foundation to build from," Ryan replied.

"Allie, these are the EXACT photos that we need," Clarissa interjected, her eyes glued to the photos in front of her.

"Myles, thank you for coming in today but I think it's best if we go ahead and pass," Allie said ignoring Clarissa. She quickly packed up the photos on the table and made her way to the door. "Ryan, please show Mr. McGowan back out to the lobby."

"I believe what Allison means is that we will let you know our decision in a few days. Thank you so much for coming in," Ryan said standing up.

"I said what I said," Allie retorted before leaving the conference room in a huff.

Myles stood up, too embarrassed to speak. He nodded to Clarissa who thanked him for coming in before following Ryan out of the room back towards the lobby. He looked back to see Allie disappear around a corner.

"Well, like I said, we will let you know our decision in a few days," Ryan said.

"I don't know what game you are playing Ryan, but that was unnecessary and not to mention humiliating for not only me but Allie," Myles replied.

"I'm not playing any games. I simply think you have the talent we are looking for and wanted to give you a chance to showcase those talents. She wasn't going to give you a fair shot no matter what, but Clarissa and I are two of the three people making this decision, we can and will overrule her," Ryan explained.

"If she doesn't want me here then I don't want to be here. Period," Myles said as the elevator dinged.

"You shouldn't let your past dictate your future. You'll regret it," Ryan replied as Myles stepped onto the elevator.

"That's for me to decide," Myles said as the elevator doors closed.

"Well, that was interesting to say the least," Madison said walking into Allie's office. Allie was flippant, tossing random items off her desk into her large purse.

"I need to get out of here. I need a drink. You're coming with me. Let's go," Allie demanded as she shut off the lights to her office.

"Where are we going?" Madison asked.

"Anywhere I can get about four glasses of wine or margaritas or martinis… anything that will erase this day," Allie answered. "Come on."

Myles waited outside the building hoping to catch Allie on her way out. Of course, his first ever interview for a photography job had to be with the one woman in the world who hated his guts.

He stood against a wall at the edge of the building. A black car with tinted windows pulled up as Allie stepped through the huge glass doors, followed closely by Madison.

"Allie!" Myles called out. Allie paused, looking over her shoulder.

"Should we-" Madison started.

"I'll be just a second, go ahead," Allie interjected, walking over to Myles. Madison headed to the car.

"Allie, what are you doing here?" Myles asked, running his hand through his hair.

"Clearly, I'm working," Allie replied shaking her head annoyed.

"Clearly, but you know what I'm asking. Why are you here in London and not in California?" Myles asked.

"Why the hell not?" Allie snapped readjusting the bag hanging off her arm.

"A heads up would have been nice, so I didn't just randomly bump into you like just now," Myles retorted shaking his head. "After all this time, it would have been nice to know you were in town."

"Myles, you lost the right to know when I was in town when you made me leave town. The day I left was the last day I ever owed you anything," Allie snickered.

Madison watched from the car as a few people walking past Allie and Myles turned to look at them.

"Allie, calm down. You don't need to be rude. I can't apologize enough about the past, but I wasn't waiting out here to rehash the whole ordeal. I get it, you are still angry five years later, but I was waiting out here to ask you to give me a chance at this job. I need it, Allie. Please," Myles begged. Madison watched as Allie's shoulders dropped and she shook her head.

"No," Allie said without an explanation before disappearing into the car.

Madison slid over to the other side of the backseat as Allie got in. "Now I really need a drink."

"Where to?" Madison asked.

"Let's just head to my place, I have a full bar cart and don't want to risk running into another ghost of my past in this god-forsaken city," Allie suggested.

About twenty minutes later the car stopped in front of a row of townhouses. Allie thanked the driver as she stepped outside of the car. Madison followed her towards the garden gate. She could see the remnants of green climbing vines cascading down over white bricks. Allie pushed through the garden gate leading to a red brick path up to a black front door. Madison looked around the small garden, softly tucked under a light layer of spring snow. She could only imagine how wonderful this area would look a few months from now full of life.

"Are you coming in?" Allie asked as she effortlessly grabbed her keys from the pocket of her coat and opened the door.

Madison nodded following Allie in. The interior was even more breathtaking than the exterior. As they stepped into the foyer, they were greeted by a long hallway. A staircase on the left that led up to the next floor and a room on the right with huge glass French doors leading outside. Everything was bright and cheery from the wooden floors to the blank white walls. Madison removed her coat and draped it over her arm.

"Allie, this place is gorgeous," she blurted out. Allie laughed in agreement, watching Madison spin around trying to take in every detail.

"Follow me, it gets better," Allie teased, disappearing into the next room. Madison followed, her eyes widening at the sight of a large room complete with two white couches on one side, a fireplace on the other, two huge windows peering into a dimly lit garden at the back of the house, and an elaborate chandelier pulling it all together. Everything was done in the Forever color motif of green and white.

"What will you have?" Allie asked as she tossed her coat on one of the couches and headed to the bar cart in the corner.

"Whatever you are having is fine with me," Madison replied dropping her coat over the back of one of the couches.

"Vodka martinis it is!" Allie declared. "Go ahead and make yourself comfortable. Kick off those heels and let down your hair, after today we deserve a drink or two. We deserve a good time."

Madison shrugged, nodding her head at Allie's statement. Slowly she slid off her heels, setting them nicely at the end of the couch. Allie was different again, her demeanor light and joyful. She no longer paused to formulate the perfect response, instead she laughed and called out whatever thoughts came to her. Everything about her changed the second they entered the house, her home. Madison smiled, taking a seat on the couch.

After about another five minutes Allie turned around from the bar cart carrying a pitcher of martinis and two martini glasses. She kicked her shoes off as she set everything onto the coffee table. She poured a very full glass and handed it to Madison, who was now sitting with her legs tucked up under her. After pouring herself a full glass Allie sat cross legged on the floor facing Madison, her back to the fireplace.

"I meant to tell you this earlier today... I really like that skirt on you. It's very flattering," Allie said taking a sip of her drink.

"Thanks, that's nice to hear after Ryan pretty much told me to lose weight earlier," Madison replied.

"Fuck him. I swear he pulled that stunt with Myles on purpose today. He was most likely going to work out the logistics yesterday at lunch and then when I sent you Mitch attacked you because I ruined their plans. You know what, fuck 'em both," Allie said lifting her drink in a cheering motion before downing her drink.

"Are you going to tell me what happened between you and Myles or is that going to remain a mystery?" Madison asked nursing her drink. Allison Davis did not play around with her cocktails; these were some strong drinks.

"What is there to tell? Myles and I dated for a little over a year. I moved in with him and about two months later he sent me packing without an explanation," Allie told Madison as she poured herself another drink.

"How did you two meet? Were you already in London when he met you?" Madison asked.

"No. This might sound strange, but we started off as pen pals in high school. It was this weird assignment from my junior year English class. Our school partnered up with Myles' school and we were to send letters to the person the teachers matched us up with. I was matched up with Myles. We were only supposed to write to each other for a semester, but that one semester turned into four years of letters," Allie reminisced. Madison watched as a slight smile started to cross Allie's face at the memory.

"I still have every letter back home. We got each other through some pretty rough times. I helped him cope with his father's third marriage to some random lady he hated, and he helped me cope with my parents' near divorce. We became great friends and so for my last year of college I decided to study abroad out here in London. I thought he was the one, we started dating the second I moved to the city and then one day he just was done with me I guess," Allie disclosed, her voice trailing off as she raised her glass to her lips again. "I can't believe he showed up there today and then after all was said and done waited to bombard me outside of the building."

"What did he want?" Madison asked sipping on her drink.

"He had the audacity to ask me why I was in London without telling him and then he pathetically begged me for the job," Allie answered downing her drink.

"Are you going to give him a chance?"

"Probably not," Allie shrugged. "Madison, you are falling behind. Drink up! Also, we need music, let's turn on some music." Allie got up and wandered over to a record player in the corner. Madison finished her drink, setting the glass down on the table, as the liquid burned her throat. She watched Allie select a record and place it on the record player. The sweet tunes of Otis Redding started playing, singing out into the living room. Allie swayed to the music singing along as she walked back over to the couches.

"Guess we need another pitcher of this," Allie laughed setting down the empty picture. "So, what do you really think of Ryan? I feel like yesterday you gave me a very basic response."

Madison took a long slow sip of her drink. "Um, he's interesting."

"Interesting? How so?"

"I mean, he's hard to read. One minute he's nice and the next he's a smug jerk. I just don't even know what to think about him to be honest," Madison replied, downing the rest of her drink. She could feel her cheeks starting to tingle.

"Do you like him?" Allie asked, getting up off the floor to make another pitcher of martinis.

"Um, what?" Madison asked, letting out a small cough from choking on some spit.

"Do you like him? Like do you have a crush on him? I see how you smile when he's around. I've seen you go to his office. Do you like him? It's not a complicated question," Allie said, her back to Madison.

"No. Definitely not," Madison lied. "He literally told me I was fat. I would never go for someone like that, ever. Like never ever."

Allie laughed. "Good. Make sure to keep it that way. Can't have you falling in love with him when I need you to keep tabs on him for me."

****

The next morning Madison's head pounded so hard her eyeballs felt like they might explode out of their sockets. Her mouth and throat felt dry and every sound around her felt like a personal attack. Somehow, she convinced herself out of bed and mustered up enough energy to look halfway decent for the office, knowing that she looked like hell.

"Well don't we look bright eyed, and bushy tailed today," Ryan teased Madison as the elevator doors opened. He pushed back from the reception desk where he was obviously flirting with the dark haired, thin, petite, dark lipstick wearing receptionist that greeted everyone with a disapproving look when they entered the lobby. The receptionist looked Madison up and down as Ryan came around the desk.

"Not today, Ryan, I beg of you," Madison replied, her head pounding.

"Here, take two of these. I saw Allison come in with a similar look a couple hours ago, or well she was at least trying to cover it up with more make-up than usual. I can only imagine what the two of you got into last night," Ryan said offering her two small pills.

"I'm good," Madison replied pushing past him and through the lobby doors.

"Morning Madison!" Allie called out, seeing Madison walk by her open office door. "I left a coffee on your desk. Grab it and come here."

Madison looked over on her desk, seeing a coffee tucked safely between the keyboard and monitors. Grabbing it she meandered into Allie's office.

"You look pretty dead inside," Allie noted as Madison took a seat and sip of the coffee to help her swallow the ibuprofen.

"And you look perfectly fine," Madison retorted.

"Yes and no. It's easier to sober up when you find out what I did after I called a car to come and get you," Allie said. Madison motioned for Allie to continue as she took a sip coffee.

"Well, I called and left a voicemail for Mr. Myles McGowan, offering him the job," Allie said shaking her head. Madison set her coffee down on the corner of Allie's desk, forcing the coffee in her mouth down her throat before letting out a huge groan.

"Oh, it gets better. You might be wondering just how I know I did this, well, I also called Ryan and let him know that I offered Myles the job, which he so graciously played my voicemail back for me today before I could even make it to my office," Allie continued.

"Let me guess, he was standing there in the lobby ready to pounce on you," Madison replied. Her head was spinning trying to process all the information Allie was throwing at her.

"Yeah, also, why is he always in the lobby when I get here?" Allie sighed.

"One word…boobs," Madison replied picking the coffee back up. Allie stifled a laugh.

"So, since I did all of that last night, I am going to need you to go in my place to check out the potential venue for the launch party with Ryan. I don't think I can be alone with him right now without saying some other choice things to him," Allie continued.

"I don't know Allie, maybe we should just reschedule the venue walkthrough until you can go," Madison replied, feeling slightly queasy.

"No, I've already told Ryan you were going with him," Allie replied slowly rubbing her forehead. "Take some photos on your phone, get the pricing, see how many people it can fit, the drink menu and catering options and bring it all back to me. If you and Ryan like the venue in person, we'll probably book it. The walkthrough is soon, so you might want to chipper up and head out."

Madison nodded reluctantly, leaving Allie's office to go and meet Ryan who was making his way over to her desk.

"Give me the pills," she said to him.

"Atta girl. And don't worry, it's just headache medicine, I swear," Ryan teased.

20 minutes later, Ryan and Madison walked into Altitude 360. The venue was amazing. It was one giant circular room with large glass windows all around and a double-sided bar in the middle. Madison was still feeling nauseous as they walked around looking for someone named Charlie to give them a tour and the details.

"You okay there Mads?" Ryan asked.

"What did you just call me?" Madison scrunched her eyebrows wondering if she heard him wrong.

"Nevermind. That must be Charlie," Ryan said nodding towards a man walking into the room. Madison spun around slowly to see a man in dark jeans and a t-shirt. His hair was jet black, his skin olive, and his eyes a mesmerizing green.

"Hi, name's Charlie, sorry to keep you waiting," Charlie greeted them both with a handshake. Madison forced a smile even though she felt like throwing up.

Ryan took Charlie's hand introducing himself while Madison continued looking around. The views of the city from here were beautiful. On one side of the room, she could see the Tower of London, not too far away sat the Globe Theater and as she made it around the circular room, she could see Buckingham Palace and Big Ben. In the past few days Madison had only seen the city through the window of the car.

"The city is the best from up here," Charlie said appearing beside her.

"It really is. I thought the closest I would ever get to London was through television or books. I still can't believe that I'm here. Now, if I could only have a moment to explore this city," Madison exhaled, her headache slowly starting to dissipate.

"Well, if you ever want a tour, stop by, I'm sure I can manage to recommend or show you all the best places." Charlie smiled.

Madison tucked her hair behind her ear smiling as she nodded. "That would be nice."

Ryan looked up from the contract to see Madison smile over at Charlie. She laughed at something Charlie said, turning towards him. Ryan looked back down at the paperwork, until he heard Charlie ask Madison for her number. Hearing this Ryan abandoned the contract walking over to where Madison and Charlie stood together.

"Hey, Mads, you want to take a look at this contract and make sure it's what Allie would like?" Ryan asked, his hand grazing her lower back. Madison tensed at his touch.

"Um, we can just bring it to her. She actually asked that we do that," Madison replied uncomfortably.

"Just give it a look over before we do. If you'll excuse us Charlie," Ryan said leading her over to the bar, leaving Charlie at the far window. Madison shot Ryan a scowl.

"That was unnecessary," she hissed.

"Stop flirting and do your job. It's really unprofessional to give a potential vendor your number," Ryan retorted with a fake smile in case Charlie was watching.

Madison looked down at her phone. "Are we almost done here?"

"Charlie! Let's talk about this contract. Is this really the price?" Ryan yelled out his eyes glued on Madison who didn't look up.

Ryan let stale air fall between them in the car. "You know you were acting extremely unprofessional in there."

"Yes, you've now said that twice. But how was giving him my contact information unprofessional? I gave him my number in case he needed to call me directly about the venue. Now the way you acted did up there was the true unprofessional thing that happened," Madison replied.

"I heard him offer to show you around the town. I'm not sure what rock you've lived under, but that's flirting," Ryan snickered.

"That's called being nice. Why do you even care? It's not like you were jonesing to take me out around town. Weren't you flirting with the receptionist when I got to work today?" Madison replied.

"I don't care, I just don't want you to make the company look bad," Ryan said.

"Of course, you just want to do that on your own," Madison sighed.

Ryan snickered. "Don't forget who left you the name of this place and who negotiated the price just now. You owe me."

Madison rolled her eyes. "You're so full of yourself. As you said, we're even," she groaned.

"It'll grow on you," he replied, looking out the window.

"I highly doubt it will," Madison said, looking out her own window. She smiled remembering the touch of his hand on her lower back.

****

Allie slouched down in her chair, closing her eyes, her head still pounding. Allie let out a small groan as someone knocked at the door. "Come in."

Myles opened the door slowly, stepping inside. "Let me guess, you made martinis last night?"

Allie groaned shrugging. "Some things never change. What can I do for Myles?"

Myles took a seat. "I think you know why I am here."

Allie straightened up in her chair. "Myles, I'm not in the mood. If this is about the phone call last night, yes, you have the job. You'll start in a few days, with everyone else," Allie sighed.

"Are you sure? I could tell by the sound of your voice last night that you weren't exactly lucid. I don't need your charity."

"It's not charity. Just accept the offer and let's discuss whatever else it is that brought you all the way down here in that horrible suit later. I have a headache and a lot to get done," Allie sighed, looking back to her computer screen.

"Just one more thing before I accept the offer. Please accept my apology for accosting you outside yesterday. That was uncalled for. Seeing you in the interview made me lose my head. It was just unexpected," Myles explained.

"It's fine."

"I guess I will see you in a few days."

"No, you'll see Ryan. He will be leading your orientation and such."

Myles frowned. "Alright. See you around I guess."

"Myles, look, I'm sorry to be rude, I just…"

"Yeah?"

"I just, can't show you any favoritism given our past."

"Noted."

Episode 5- Bad Liar

Madison's alarm went off at 5AM. Her eyes shot open to the hotel room ceiling. For two weeks now, her eyes traced the ceiling every morning as a deep desire to hear the ocean filled her mind. For ten minutes she would let the sounds and smells of home flutter into her imagination erasing any drama for the previous day. As her mind drifted off to the sounds of home, a ding pulled her back to reality.

>**Allie:** Hope you are up! It's photo shoot day!
>**Madison:** You know it! See you soon with your coffee order :)

Allie was always wide awake early in the morning, returning from a long run around the city. Madison grumbled, removing the blanket from her body. Every morning was the same. She'd leave the bed unmade for a housekeeper to come and make later. She would go through her limited wardrobe and try to put something together that seemed high fashion enough to get her by for the day. After a quick shower she would change and head out to grab Allie's coffee and get herself something to eat for breakfast. Living in a hotel was the worst, Madison ate every meal out and her bed became a one stop shop for watching tv, reading, working, and sleeping.

****

An hour later she met Allie outside the office building, coffee in hand, ready to face the day. Allie was uncannily dressed in a pair of dark blue jeans with a navy and white striped sweater peeking out from under a blue peacoat and a white pair of loafers on her feet.

"I didn't think you owned a pair of jeans," Madison joked, handing Allie her coffee.

"I figured since we will be on location today, I'd dress down a little. I see you are wearing the dress from last week again," Allie commented.

"Yeah," Madison replied smoothing out the bottom of her dress. "I don't have many outfits here and even if I went shopping there's not a ton of closet space in my hotel room."

"That's right, we have yet to get you a proper place to live. Anyways, I figured we would split up today. You can be my eyes and ears with Ryan at the photoshoot with Myles and I will oversee the other shoot," Allie instructed.

Madison tucked her hair behind her ear. Things were still weird between Ryan and Madison ever since she gave her number to Charlie at Altitude 360. He avoided her in the office, bypassing her to go directly to Allie or by using his assistant to ask Madison questions.

"Yeah, sure that works. Anything you want me to watch out for?" Madison asked, feeling the butterflies of having to be near Ryan without the distraction of the office or Allie to intervene start to flutter around in her stomach.

"Just make sure that Myles stays relaxed. If he starts to get flustered, you'll see it in his photos. Also, keep Ryan in check. I'm still not sure what his game is here with Myles but call me if things get weird and I can try to walk you through it," Allie said as Ryan's car pulled up.

"Aw, ladies you didn't have to wait for me outside today. I hear the boss doesn't like it when you wait around instead of getting work done instead," Ryan greeted them sarcastically.

"Good morning, Ryan. Nice of you to join us on time today. I was just telling Madison that I would like her to accompany you to today's photoshoot with Myles on my behalf," Allie replied.

"Lovely. It's always nice to know I'm being babysat by someone with way less experience," Ryan said smirking. "Well Madison, I just need to grab something from my office, and we can head out if that's okay with you and Allie here."

Allie rolled her eyes and Madison nodded as Ryan gave her an annoyed look as he stepped inside the lobby of Garrison Publishing.

"Remember what I said, be careful around him. He thinks his charm can get him out of everything. Stay on guard Madison," Allie warned. "Oh, there's Brynn, I'm going to grab her and head out to the site. Remember to make sure Myles stays relaxed!" Allie called out walking away from Madison.

As Allie walked away, Madison spotted Myles walking up from the opposite direction. She waved to him as he approached. "How's it going Myles?"

"I'm nervous as hell. Where did Allie go?" Myles asked, looking around Madison.

"She's working on Brynn's set today. You are with Ryan and well, me, I guess," Madison answered. Madison glanced through the glass doors, searching for Ryan. "Ryan should be down any minute now. He said he needed to run up to the office."

Myles kept staring straight ahead searching for Allie. Madison looked through the glass waiting for Ryan to return. Awkward silence filled the space between Madison and Myles as the minutes ticked away.

"Ready?" Ryan asked, finally emerging from the building holding only a belt in his hand. Madison looked at him puzzled.

"Yes, let's get this over with," Myles muttered.

"Here, put this on," Ryan whispered handing Madison the belt as Myles got into the car.

"I don't need a belt Ryan," Madison hissed. "Is that really what you went upstairs for?"

"You wore that dress recently. People are going to notice. Throwing an accessory on will not only make it less noticeable but it will also give you more of a waist. Just put it on," Ryan whispered, putting the belt in her hand.

"Are you two done? Can we go now?" Myles asked impatiently.

"Fine, but if you make one more comment about my waist, I swear," Madison angrily whispered at Ryan, putting the belt around her waist, and tightening it a bit.

"Now see, that looks great," Ryan replied. "Let me get a picture of you getting into the car."

"No," Madison said pointedly as she slid next to Myles in the back seat.

"You know eventually, you are going to have to be on our social media pages, which I help run and need your picture for the website. It's part of the job. Everyone will be spotlighted on the page. I'm imagining it to be sort of like a reality show feature, where we spotlight an employee of the magazine, follow them around for the day snapping pictures as we go and getting video footage. I think it will help build up our presence as a new and improved version of the magazine," Ryan rambled as they headed to their destination cramped in the backseat of the car.

"Why do we need to build a weird social media reality television feature like presence or whatever the hell you just said? We are a magazine, not a tv show. And aren't there already reality shows and movies where people work at magazines out there? I don't understand how you plan on revolutionizing the presence those already have in mainstream media," Madison retorted sandwiched in between Ryan and Myles as the car started their journey to the countryside.

"That's because you aren't a visionary like some of us. And it's not about revolutionizing anything. It's about making sure we are on the cutting edge of social media now, so we are on the cutting edge of it later when it takes over how people communicate. Right now, nobody knows who we are, but they will," Ryan replied.

"You sound like Mitch. In my opinion social media is a fad that will eventually die out when everyone realizes how vapid you must be to post pictures of yourself to get attention. Plus, who the hell sells anything but a false dream life on social media presently?" Myles answered.

"Good thing your opinion on this doesn't matter," Ryan replied. "And mind you, your job is to take really good photos of other people to sell things. Who is to say that one day people won't be doing the same on social media?"

Madison shook her head as the two continued to argue over her like brothers who grew up arguing for years. She could feel Ryan's leg against hers. The more passionate he got about the subject the more his arm brushed hers. Madison sat silently letting the two go at it for what felt like an eternity before the car pulled up to a field outside of London near a small pond. Small tents filled with models, designers, and assistants were buzzing with chatter and laughter as Madison, Ryan and Myles exited the car and headed towards the photoshoot area. Myles wandered off ahead of Ryan and Madison, excited to get away from Ryan for a moment.

"The belt looks great and really shows off—" Ryan started.

"Don't finish that thought. I really don't want to have to murder you out here in broad daylight," Madison fumed.

"It really shows off the beauty of the dress. I wasn't going to say anything about you," Ryan replied with a wink. Madison drew in a deep breath, letting it out slowly.

"I'm sorry, it's just that the other day you made a comment about my weight that was so unnecessary, and I know this dress is plain and that I've worn it already, I just don't have anything else to wear at this point. I'd just really like it if people stopped talking about my clothes or my body and just let me sort of fade into the crowd of beautiful people here," Madison admitted, kicking at the grass below them.

"Wow. That's a lot to unpack," Ryan said processing Madison's confessional. "Well, if anything I apologize for my comment about your weight. I didn't mean to offend. I was certainly just offering up a piece of advice from the industry."

"It's fine. Let's just drop it all. Where'd Myles go?" Madison asked to change the subject. "Oh, there he is. I'm going to make sure he gets all set up."

Ryan nodded, watching as Madison walked away from him a small smile starting to spread across his face before he turned to head into models' tent. "Ladies!" he called out as he entered, his arms wide open.

"Hey, this place is stunning. What a cool place to have your first big photoshoot," Madison said walking up to Myles. Myles looked up from his camera bag, nodding.

"England is so beautiful," Madison continued trying to fill in the silence. "Do you ever get bored looking at it? I mean how could you?"

"Did Allie tell you to come talk to me and keep me calm?" Myles asked, standing up with his camera in his hand, leaving his bag at his feet.

"I mean, I'm just checking in on you. I'm kind of nervous about today. I would think if anyone would understand that it'd be you," Madison replied.

Myles looked off into the pond. "You know I sort of like to mentally prep alone."

"Oh, okay. I get it," Madison said backing up a bit. "Let me know if you need anything. I'll be around."

"Thanks," Myles replied drawing in a deep breath. He turned back towards the pond, his shoulders dropping as his heart and mind started racing.

Madison watched Myles shake his head, running his hands through his hair. There was a deep sadness in the way he stood at the edge of the pond alone. There was a deep melancholy to his voice and mannerisms mirroring the pond and the small group of trees on the other side. Madison could hear the models laughing behind her, Ryan's voice loudly telling a flirty story. There she stood stuck between two worlds. She didn't belong to either of them, not the one of deep sadness nor the other filled with immense happiness. Madison turned looking back at the model tent, catching the eye of one girl stepping out. Madison forced a weak smile as Ryan emerged from the tent walking arms linked with two other big industry name models.

She looked back at Myles, her heart beginning to fill with the same melancholy she saw. Suddenly, as if lightning struck him, he turned around his shoulders back and head held high. He directed the lighting tech to move one of the lights over as he began discussing some of the mechanics of his shots and ideas with Clarissa. Clarissa would sit through the whole shoot behind the makeshift desk, housing the computer screens where his photos would show up as he took them. As the models approached Myles began to stage them one by one for a group shot.

Ryan now stood over near Clarissa, every now and then looking Madison's direction. Madison felt herself awkwardly standing away from everyone, just watching from the outside as the two worlds she stood between earlier melted into one another, still leaving her on the outside. Madison switched between picking at her fingernails and playing with the ends of her hair, her eyes focused on the back of Myles's neck.

"Hey Myles, come here for a second," Ryan beckoned after 20 minutes of shooting. "Ladies, take a break. Go grab some water in the tent."

As the models scurried off, Myles walked over slowly to Ryan. Madison stood up from where she sat in the grass heading down to rejoin the group.

"Hey Myles, I want to sho-" Clarissa started.

"What's up with these photos? Everyone looks so stiff, and you have them grouped awkwardly. Honestly, the clothes and concept aren't coming across at all," Ryan interrupted, stepping in front of Clarissa and the computer screens. "I get this is your first professional shoot for a magazine, but these are really just missing the mark."

"We're just getting started, I'm sure the photos are not all bad," Myles defended himself. "Clarissa?"

"Well, there may be a fe—"

"That's generous Clarissa but lying to him is going to solve any issues. The photos are rubbish, and we will not be able to use any of them," Ryan continued, his voice low and mean.

"Well, what in the bloody hell do you think I should do to fix that Ryan?" Myles snapped back.

"For starters you can lose the attitude, I am only trying to be of assistance," Ryan said in a lighter tone.

"Who the hell picked this location, you or Mitch?" Myles asked, shifting his weight back onto his heels.

"He may have mentioned it when I asked for ideas, but I had my team scope it out and decided it was the perfect fit for this shoot," Ryan answered.

"Fuck off!" Myles exclaimed before storming off in the opposite direction.

"Ryan, what the hell!" Madison snapped. "Did you need to provoke him like that?"

"I'm just telling the truth here. These photos are not good." Ryan shrugged. "It's not my fault he doesn't take critiques very well and let's be honest, I'm a bad liar so sugar coating it just wasn't going to happen."

"You better go and get him back here, so we can get this done and over with," Madison demanded.

"I think my name is being called over in the tent. Since you are Allie's stand in today why don't you handle this? That's why she had you tag along right?" Ryan retorted. Madison bit her lip holding in her anger.

"That's what I thought, now if you'll excuse me, I think I hear that someone is stuck in a dress and needs my expertise in removing dresses with broken zippers," Ryan said, jogging off to the tent in the distance.

Madison looked over to Clarissa who simply shrugged her shoulders in response. Myles was halfway up a small hill in the distance now. Madison pulled out her phone, only one person could fix this mess at this point.

"Hey Madison, how's it going over there? Brynn is killing it over here, absolutely killing it, I think she may have even gotten the cover shot. Honestly," Allie answered with a fever of excitement in her voice.

"That's great news," Madison muttered.

"Yes, I'm very pleased with everything over here. How is Myles doing?" Allie asked, her voice dropping a bit.

"See, the thing is, I'm not sure we've really gotten any good photos. If I'm being honest, I..." Madison let her voice trail off as she looked over at Myles getting smaller in the distance.

"Madison? Are you still there?" Allie asked.

"Um, I don't think this is working."

"Madison, what did I tell you? Did you keep Myles calm? What's Myles doing right now?" Allie asked.

"Well, he sort of just stormed off set. I'm not quite sure where he's going. He's like halfway up a hill in the distance. I tried to keep him calm and talk to him before the shoot and he asked me to go away. Then Ryan said something about his photos being crap and something about Mitch picking the place, all which caused him to storm off," Madison replied grimacing.

"Madison, your job is now to get Myles off that hill and back to the shoot. Fuck!" Allison yelled through the phone.

"Allie, I'm in over my head. I'm sorry but I," Madison paused, she could feel the tears coming. Allie was silent on the other side of the phone. Madison sighed. "I don't think I can fix this."

"Fine. Send me the address. I'll be there soon to supervise the rest of the shoot, just go get Myles off that hill and back on set before I get there," Allie said before hanging up.

Madison stood at the edge of the pond staring out at the stillness of the water. After three attempts, Myles still wouldn't come back down. Allison was pissed and surely, Madison being unsuccessful would make it worse. Madison could see Myles off in the distance alone, sitting on a hill. She tossed a small pebble into the water, watching the sun glisten on top of the ripples.

"Come on, this is the perfect spot for a picture. Indulge me while we wait," Ryan begged Madison as he approached.

"Allie will be here any minute to fix the mess you've made. I really don't think we should worry about your weird photo gathering expedition right now. Plus, don't you have to finalize your dinner plans with a few of those models? Taking them out in shifts tonight or as just one big group?" Madison scoffed.

"Are you jealous?" Ryan asked smirking.

"Are you kidding me? Like I'd ever be jealous of one of those girls who will surely end up at a nearby clinic the next morning because of some sort of burning sensation down there," Madison scoffed, motioning towards her lower regions.

"Most people cannot pull off the whole jealous girl act but it's becoming of you. Better watch out, you might actually make me like you if you keep it up," Ryan teased.

"Ryan, honestly, why would I be jealous? You are nothing more than an arrogant, ass kissing, womanizing, jerk who is hell bent on ruining Allie's chance at succeeding, all because you didn't get her job in the first place," Madison replied.

"Nice to meet the feisty side of you finally. I thought she might be hiding in there. But also, you don't know me at all," Ryan replied calmly. "All I asked for was a picture for our social media campaign. Nothing more."

"Just go Ryan. Leave me alone so I can figure out how I'm going to fix this situation when Allie, who is extremely pissed at me, gets here," Madison replied turning back to look at the water. Ryan nodded and took a couple steps back towards the tents of models. Stopping a few steps away, he reached for the digital camera in his pocket, snapping a quick photo of Madison's profile as she tossed another pebble into the water watching the sun dance across the top of the pond. He smiled as he looked at the photo.

Allie stepped out of the car. Madison stood nearby ready to assist in any way she could. As Madison approached Allie waved her off. She could see Myles sitting on the hill. Bypassing the tents of models and Ryan, Allie headed up the hill. This place was familiar. The pond down below and the rolling green hills ahead of her made her heart race. She stopped before getting too close to Myles and looked around at the view. It wasn't a big hill, but from it you could see the grass stretching towards the horizon, interrupted only slightly by a smaller hill here and there. The view was gorgeous and yet filled with immense sadness.

"This is our spot, isn't it?" Allie asked, approaching Myles from behind.

"I figured that's why you chose it but then realized my father had a hand in this," Myles replied without turning around.

"No this is my fault. I didn't ask where the shoot was planned and if I had, I would have never assigned it you." Allie stood a few feet behind him, nervous about getting any closer. "Why are you up here and not down there taking pictures?"

"I always wanted to do a photo shoot here. I wanted to capture the ocean of green grass rolling through these hills. I wanted to catch the sun reflecting off the pond with the various tiny insects hovering right over it as if they were dancing in the reflecting light," Myles replied still looking off into the distance.

"Well, here's your chance. Get down there and do it," Allie replied, finally sitting down next to him. "It's kind of what we are paying you to do."

"I don't care about the money Allie. It's not that easy to just go down there and create magic, when—" Myles shook his head, letting out a small chuckle.

"When what Myles?" Allie asked impatiently.

"You wouldn't understand," Myles replied, turning to look at Allie.

"I knew you weren't ready for this." Allie whispered shaking her head.

"That's not the issue either."

"Then what is the issue?"

Myles stood up, brushing loose pieces of grass off his pants. "I was going to ask you to marry me here. At this spot. Those were the photos I wanted to capture of that moment."

Allie froze. Myles turned to face her and for the first time since her return she let herself study his face. Not that long ago it was filled with joy and happiness and now there was a haunting shadow in his eyes. The joy was replaced with sorrow. Allie longed to hug him, to let herself imagine what life would be now if he had asked her to marry him here, but she knew better. He didn't ask her to marry him. No, he asked something very different from her all those years ago.

"That's not fair. You broke up with me. You sent me packing. Then you begged me for this job all these years later and now you are telling me you had some plan to ask me to marry you here and that's why you can't do the job you begged me for?" Allie replied, her voice low with anger.

"Let me explain it all. Let's get dinner and let me explain, please," Myles begged. "I'll do the damn shoot as long as you just promise to let me explain it all."

"Myles," Allie sighed, closing her eyes to stop her mind from racing. "Myles, I need you to do the shoot either way. Contractually it's what you are out here to do. If it helps, I'll stay. I'll help stage, you can take test shots using me if it helps."

"What about dinner?" Myles asked.

"I'll think about it. No promises."

Myles smiled a half smile. "At least it's a step closer to yes. I'll take it."

"Can we take pictures now?" Allie asked, forcing a half smile as her insides twisted in around each other.

Myles nodded.

"Well, it looks like they are returning and just in time, my special guest just arrived," Ryan whispered in Madison's ear. Madison shrugged him off, turning to see a well-known American pop star emerge from a black car.

"How the hell did you pull that off?" Madison gasped.

"I know some people," Ryan replied. "Don't fret, I'll snag you an autograph before the end of the day."

With a wink and squeeze of Madison's arm, he headed off towards the car to greet his surprise guest.

"Well, I'll be damned, look who Ryan is talking to. I wonder how he pulled that one off," Allie said approaching Madison.

"Apparently, he knows someone. I'm not sure. How mad are you still?" Madison asked timidly.

"To be honest I was ready to fire you, and well, Myles and half of the staff here, until I you sent me the address and I got up on that hill. I'm the only one who could fix this, so I don't blame you for calling me," Allie answered. "But now, now we have our fucking work cut out for us to pull off this cast change and keep Myles calm. Let's go relieve the models and discuss a new approach to this shoot. I have a good feeling about this."

Episode 6- Quick Question

"Alright, the day has come to pick our cover," Allie announced exiting her office. "Come on, we are meeting with Clarissa and Ryan over in Clarissa's office."

Madison followed Allie across the office over to a small fishbowl like room with a medium size table in the middle. On the far-right wall four monitors hung above a small desk with two more monitors. In the back, giant lightboxes adorned a dark green wall. Madison surveyed the room for the perfect out of the way spot to take notes. She could see Clarissa diligently attaching the ancillary photoshoot pictures on the lightboxes before turning on the lights and Ryan already sitting at the table.

"Who do you want to start with?" Clarissa asked as Allie and Madison entered.

"Let's start with Brynn's photos," Ryan answered. Clarissa nodded, putting the photos up in the monitors in front of her. Madison stood in the far corner of the room as Allison took a seat next to Ryan. Brynn's photos were breathtaking, full of color and capturing life in downtown London.

"I love the colors of the photos. They really pop and bring a lot of life to the whole scene. It's like you are in London with Tom, which what woman wouldn't want to be exploring London with a big movie star?" Clarissa added.

"I agree. I think these photos really will draw our readers in. Every woman will want a copy. Tom's a cool guy and I think the interview will be phenomenal for the relaunch of the magazine," Ryan replied.

Madison looked over at Allie, who was staring intently at the photos on the screen. She shook her head slightly, letting it rest into a tilt as she squinted her eyes, letting her mind go into a deep thought. The room fell silent as everyone waited for Allie to speak.

"I'm not sure I agree," Allie finally muttered with a sigh. "Don't get me wrong, I think Brynn did a fantastic job on these photos, but there's something missing. Can you pull up Myles' set?"

Clarissa nodded, switching out the photos. There was a stark difference between the two sets. Part of this due to the two different settings: Myles' in nature and Brynn's in the city. Allie stood up walking over to the monitors displaying the photos.

"Clarissa, pull up the third photo from Brynn's shoot and the fourth one from Myles' on the screens over here," Allie requested, standing in front of the monitors. The two images could not appear more different. Madison studied Allie as she stood there silently taking in the photos. The first photo was Tom, standing in front of a classic London red bus, in a bright blue suit. The second photo was Taylor, sitting in a field of green grass, in a big white sweater and black pants.

"If we are going off these two photos, I say Brynn's all the way," Ryan inserted. Allie continued to stare at the screen in silence, her arms crossed.

"Taylor's found love," Allie said, her gaze still on the photo. "She's got that twinkle in her eye. It's a secret all of her own, but it's also so obvious. That's our cover story and our cover is the first photo of her getting out of the car. That's what's going to sell the first issue of the magazine. Good idea bringing her in Ryan." Allie turned around and gave Ryan a nod before taking her seat again.

"Wait, what? These photos are not nearly as good as Brynn's photos. There's very little dimension in these. I mean Taylor is gorgeous, she always is, but there's nothing special about these photos," Ryan replied with fervor.

"Push Tom's cover to the following month. I want the car photo on the cover and the rest, I want to go alongside an interview with her," Allie demanded.

"Look, with all due respect, Taylor is an American, Tom is British. The young women want to date Tom and the older women find him cute and charming. Men everywhere want to dress like him, to be him. I say we flip what you're suggesting," Ryan answered.

"I wonder who she's dating," Clarissa interjected, looking at Myles' photos closer.

"I hear he's British," Madison blurted out to Clarissa.

"I rest my case," Allie said to Ryan, tipping the brim of her invisible hat.

"Madison, what do you think? You're new to the business and don't know much about the sales and marketing portions of the magazine. Which cover would you buy?" Ryan asked. Everyone turned to face Madison. She could feel her heart start racing and her cheeks turning red. She didn't want to disappoint either Brynn or Myles by not picking their photos. She knew they both worked hard to snag the first cover photo and spread, but she had to hand it to Myles, he captured a magic in Taylor's face that Brynn failed to capture with Tom.

"I agree with Allie," Madison replied. "The pictures of Taylor draw me in. She's been quiet for a while working on a new album and now looks happier than ever before. I want to know what's going on."

"Then that's that!" Allie exclaimed. "Clarissa, get these photos printed and ready to be placed in the book. I know we are waiting for a couple more photoshoots to be finished, but I would like the first mock-up done by tonight. Madison will wait around for the book and deliver it to me. I am heading to California tomorrow morning and will take the book with me and send comments via email while I'm gone. Good job everyone."

Madison made eye contact with Ryan who smirked and winked as Madison followed Allie out of the room. Things were still weird between them since the photo shoot. Anytime they encountered each other in the hallway or lobby, Ryan walked the opposite direction or hurried past her without a word. Today was the first time he spoke directly to her in days. And while it was a nice reprieve to not have to combat his every comment, him avoiding her struck a nerve. Madison hated the silent treatment and lack of attention from him and here he was finally giving her a wink of acknowledgement causing her to lose her breath.

"Are you ready Madison?" Allie asked Madison as she turned back to the fishbowl. "We have a lot of work to do."

"Oh, and I'll let Myles know that his photos were chosen. Be gentle when you let Brynn know that her photos will be in the next issue," Allie said turning back to Ryan.

"Fantastic," Ryan replied watching Allie and Madison leave the room and head down the hallway.

"So, the book, I need you to wait around tonight and take it straight from here to my townhouse. You can just leave it on the kitchen table. I don't want to forget it in the morning when I leave for my trip. The flight should give me enough time to review it and come up with some ideas before I spend the weekend picking out table arrangements and flowers with Nick," Allie explained as they entered her office.

"Got it. Question thought, what exactly goes in the book?" Madison asked, taking a seat across from Allie.

"It's our layout of the issue. So far it should have at least a few of the minor articles, with or without photos, some mock-up sketches of photo shoots that are in progress or planned to shoot next week, the cover photo and cover photo spread, and some advertising. It's pretty much going to be bare bones right, but it will be enough to figure out what needs to be pulled or shifted around."

"What time do you think it will be done by?" Madison asked.

"Who knows with Ryan at the helm," Allie said, rolling her eyes. "Why, do you have a hot date tonight?"

"Me? Date? Please," Madison scoffed.

"You never know, London can be a magical place if you play your cards right," Allie said with a smile. "Anyways, I leave tomorrow, extremely early and I will return on Thursday. I've made a list of everything that needs to be done while I'm gone. When I come back, I'll give the book back to Ryan to update. That should give you all enough time to finish up some photoshoots, get the interview with Taylor done and finalize some more ad space," Allie responded. "Also, we need to meet with the party planner to finalize the décor for the launch party when I get back. We will be about a month out at that point and the workdays are going to get longer, so be ready."

Madison jotted it all down in her notebook. Tomorrow started almost a week of no Allie in the office. She hoped that meant that Ryan would actually speak to her again and that maybe she could apologize for snapping at him at the photoshoot.

"Alright, I need to call Myles to set up a dinner to tell him the news," Allie said, grabbing her phone.

"A dinner? Why not just tell him over the phone?" Madison asked, leaning forward.

"The only way I got him down off that hill to take photos was the promise of a dinner. No time like the present to kill two birds with one stone. I can get the dinner out of the way and tell him the exciting news all at once!" Allie exclaimed.

Madison nodded. "Well, I'll leave you to it," she replied before leaving the office, shutting the door.

"You could have at least agreed with me in the cover shot choice," a deep hushed voice said startling Madison.

"What the hell Ryan?" she snapped as she turned around. "Don't just sneak up on people like that."

"I was clearly standing here, it's not like it was a secret," Ryan retorted rolling his eyes. "Anyways, I came to tell you that I would have the book ready for you by 8pm tonight. I'm sure that means Allie is expecting you to wait around for it, so I would plan on either skipping dinner or just ordering something."

"Unnecessary comment number 500."

"Excuse me?"

"The comment about skipping dinner was unnecessary. You've gotten your thoughts about my body across already. You don't need to keep making comments about it," Madison replied, grabbing a stack of belts off her desk to take back to the closet.

"That's not what I meant," Ryan replied softly. "Look, I'm sorry if I offended you at the photoshoot by giving you a belt to put on. I get it, it takes a while to build up a wardrobe for a job like this. I didn't mean anything by it."

Madison didn't say anything, stepping around him. While his apology seemed sincere, she wasn't ready to be wrong if it wasn't.

"So…8pm then. I'll drop the book off by your desk." Ryan called out behind her as she made her way to the closet.

"What can I do for you today, Allie?" Myles asked, picking up the phone.

"Well, I was hoping you could grab dinner tonight. I'm heading out to California tomorrow and was hoping we could talk before I left," Allie replied. Silence fell between, Allie's dinner request lingering between the phones.

"Look, you don't have to take pity on me and set-up a dinner just because I brought it up on the hill. I get caught up in the moment and frankly looked like a total wanker. Go to

California and have a great time. Have Ryan call me with the results of the cover shoot later," Myles replied.

"Myles, I want to go to dinner with you tonight. It's not a pity dinner," Allie sighed. "I think it's important that we catch up, set some ground rules if we are going to be working together."

"Allie, I don't have to work there if it's going to cause issues."

"Who said it was causing issues?"

"Why else would you need to call me to set-up a dinner to 'set some ground rules?' I've been contemplating quitting anyways," Myles said.

"Myles McGowan, you are not going to quit before talking with me tonight. After your outburst at the photoshoot, you owe me at least that. I have reservations at our favorite spot. Meet me there at 7pm and if you still want to quit after dinner, then you can, but cannot quit until we have dinner. Understood?" Allie slid down in her desk chair shaking her head.

"I'll see you at 7," Myles muttered.

"Great. I'll see you then," Allie replied before ending the call. Looking for a distraction she opened Instagram. Ryan and his team oversaw Forever London's social media pages and until now she had yet to actually make sure he was doing his job. She searched for the magazine's Instagram handle to see how the page was beginning to look. The creative team decided that they would spotlight a different staff member every Thursday with a headshot and bio on the magazine's various social media pages. Allie knew she wouldn't be in the spotlight until right before the launch party, but she was curious to see who this week's staff member was.

"Interesting," Allie whispered as her eyes fell on a candid photo of Madison by the lake from Myles' photo shoot. Madison looked gorgeous, the sunlight bringing out the various shades of brown and small golden highlights of her hair. She was looking out and away from the camera. Her skin radiated with joy as her eyes were filled with a melancholy look of bewilderment. She wore a half smile filled with a mix of forced happiness and loneliness.

"Madison Stevens, Assistant to the Editor-n-Chief. California native. Favorite book: The Great Gatsby. Favorite Movie: She's the Man. Favorite Song: All Too Well. Dream Role at Forever Creative Director," Allie read out loud. Allie looked up to see Ryan leaving Madison's desk through the tiny window next to the door. "Not into him…yeah right," she whispered to herself.

****

Myles stood up as Allie approached the table. She looked dazzling in a little black dress, her hair pulled up in a bun, a pearl earring in each ear.

"I was worried you weren't going to show up," Myles admitted as they both sat down.

"I thought about it, but I'm actually just running late because I have some great news," Allie smiled.

"What?" Myles replied.

"What can we get you to drink?" the waiter interrupted.

"Just water for me, thank you," Myles answered. Allie looked at him quizzically before ordering a chardonnay.

"What was that expression for?" Myles asked.

"It's just not your normal beverage option," Allie replied folding her hands in her lap.

"Things can change. What is your news?" Myles answered.

"I think you might want a different drink after I tell you," Allie teased.

"Go on," Myles said.

"I'm sure you know that the cover photo spot is a very coveted spot, and everyone wants to be the photographer who shot the cover," Allie explained. Myles nodded. "Going into it we figured it would be Brynn's cover because her photoshoot had a big buzz name in it, and then things changed. And well, we've chosen our cover for the inaugural issue."

"Here are your drinks," the waiter interrupted. "Are we ready to order?"

"Not quite," Myles responded, looking back at Allie as the waiter politely walked away. "Let me guess Brynn got it. You really did not have to tell me at dinner."

"Myles, it's you," Allie interjected. "The photo we chose is one of your photos."

Myles sat back in his chair placing his hand over his mouth in disbelief. "Well, I be damned."

68

"Congratulations Myles. It's a really big deal. I mean, the photos we got from the photoshoot are amazing. You should really be proud of yourself," Allie said.

Myles sat across from Allie in shock. "You did not have to throw me a pity cover Allie. I know Brynn had some way better photos and the credentials to back it up."

"Myles," Allie said reaching for his arm across the table, her voice soft. "This wasn't a pity cover. You had the best photos, even Taylor was in love with them when we sent her the photos today."

Myles searched Allie's face for a sense of doubt, a gotcha moment coming to life, anything that would tell him that this was all a big joke, a revenge plot to get back at him for breaking her heart. Yet, Allie looked at him sincerely, like she used to when they would lay on the couch together listening to her favorite records. She looked at him with a soft smile and encouraging eyes.

"You mean it?" Myles asked, his voice low and his eyes locked on hers.

"I mean it," Allie chuckled unleashing a huge smile.

"I think I do need that drink," Myles laughed.

"Order whatever you want, it's on the magazine tonight." Allie nodded, pulling back her hand to straighten out the napkin on her lap. Her nerves started to build as their conversation on the hill flashed back into her mind. As happy as she was to see Myles succeed, part of her longed for the life they could have built together had he proposed instead of making her leave. She watched him order a drink, an overwhelmed look of disbelief still on his face.

"We should go out for waffles after this," Myles said. "You know the normal celebratory treat."

Allie chuckled, "Whatever you want to do. This is your night."

"Waffles it is!" Myles said lifting his glass up toasting his triumph. For the first time in five years, Myles finally let himself feel a tinge of joy.

****

Madison looked down at her watch. *7:55*. Ryan said he would deliver the book to her by eight. Madison played through

69

another game of solitaire as she waited. Allie left hours ago to get ready and head to dinner with Myles. After she left, Madison ordered dinner to eat at her desk and attempted to wade through Allie's notes on the décor for the launch party. After an hour she opened solitaire as she watched the office slowly empty.

After winning a few more games, she looked at the clock again. 8:10PM. Madison pushed her chair back from the desk, sliding her feet back into her shoes before standing up. The office was quiet and dimly lit as she made her way over to Ryan's office. His lights were off and the door closed. Madison drew in a deep breath of frustration when she noticed a sticky note on the door.

Mads-Meet me at 923 Bond Street. I'll give you the book. - Ryan

"Are you freaking kidding me?" Madison muttered. "How long has he been gone?" Madison stormed over to her desk grabbing her purse. "I could have freaking left probably an hour ago with the book in tow and been back in my hotel room by now enjoying some trashy tv, but nooooooo here the hell I am chasing Ryan around town for the damn book."

Madison stomped over to the lobby still talking to herself, typing the address into her phone. "I'm going to kill him for this."

"Hey," Madison said walking up to Ryan seated at the end of the bar.

"I'm glad you made it," Ryan replied standing up to pull the barstool next to him out a bit motioning for Madison to sit. Madison furrowed her eyebrows inquisitively at this. Why was he being so polite?

"Hand over the book," she demanded.

"Take a seat," he replied, gesturing to a barstool.

"Ryan, I don't have time."

"One drink or no book," he said, shrugging his shoulders.

Madison sighed, weighing her options. "Fine."

"What can I order you, a margarita? Something girly and fruity?" he asked, motioning for the bartender to come over, as Madison slid onto the barstool next to Ryan.

"I'll take an old fashioned, thank you," Madison ordered directly from the bartender.

"Alright then, color me surprised I wouldn't have pinned you as a whiskey drinker," Ryan said, his eyes set on Madison's face.

"I prefer whiskey to 'something girly and fruity' as you so misogynistically put it." Madison looked at the bartender as she spoke. She could feel Ryan's eyes on her face. Did he think this was a date? All she wanted was to get the book and head home, but from the looks of it, he didn't even bring the book with him.

"Fair. How are you liking London so far?" Ryan asked, nodding a thank you to the bartender as he set Madison's drink down in front of her.

"I haven't seen much of it still. Allison's schedule has us going non-stop all day, every day of the week. But from what I've managed to see from the car window, it's a cool city," Madison replied, taking a sip of her drink. She felt it sting as it went down her throat and warmed her chest. She looked over, her eyes meeting Ryan's gaze. A cold shiver went down her spine. He was gorgeous, even in the dimmed lighting of the bar. He had that dangerous bad boy look tied together with a good guy smile.

"We could change that," he replied, his blue eyes sparkling as his lips turned into a mischievous smile. "What do you want to see the most?"

Madison felt her hands start to get sweaty not only from the condensation of her glass, but also from the way he was looking at her. "I'm not sure I want to tell you. You are just going to roll your eyes at me."

"Tell me." He laughed.

Madison took a hearty swig of her drink. "Nah, I'm good. Do you have the look book with you? I should head out soon, I have to get up early."

"Lies. And if you won't tell me, then I am going to guess," he replied, ignoring her question.

"Ryan, come on, I don't want to play any games," Madison groaned rolling her eyes.

"Guess number one: you want to see the whole city from the top of the London Eye?"

Madison didn't reply.

"Okay, so not the London Eye. Let's see, you want a photo with the guards at Buckingham Palace?" His eyes narrowed in on Madison's face. She was staring at him clearly annoyed. She pursed her lips and furrowed her eyebrows as she slowly shook her head in response. He watched as she drew in a deep breath, her nostrils flaring ever so slightly.

"Okay, okay, I know, you want a photo in one of the telephone booths whist wearing a union jack hat and scarf?"

Madison started laughing. "No. Though something tells me you've had many girls wanting to do that come through your life."

"You'd be surprised how many times I've managed to bring a girl home after taking that photo," Ryan chuckled. He watched as Madison took another sip of her drink. As she set the glass down, she reached up tucking her hair behind her ear.

"Well, I definitely am not looking to be one of those girls. It's a little too tacky for my liking and I prefer sleeping alone," Madison replied. Her heart started to race as Ryan ran his hand through his hair trying to think of something else to suggest.

She didn't want to get pulled into his world. Did she? She knew his type well. He would hit and quit it, another conquest of his in the office. Another girl he could say he slept with and left broken-hearted. She didn't want to be another girl on his list, but she could feel herself being pulled in by his magnetic personality.

She watched as he downed the rest of his drink and set the glass back down. Suddenly, a sense of excitement spread over his face. "Bradley, here's some cash it should cover both of our drinks! Madison, either leave the drink or down it and follow me!" He shouted jumping up from his barstool.

Madison watched as he headed towards the door. Noticing she wasn't right behind him, he spun around, frantically motioning her to come with him before disappearing out the door. Madison finished the rest of her drink and scurried out the door behind him.

"Ryan, stop! I need the book and then I'm going," she said catching up with him.

"Look I'll give you the book if you get in this car right now and come with me, no questions asked," Ryan said, opening the back door of a taxicab.

"Ryan," Madison replied sternly.

"Madison, look, I know you don't trust me. You think of me like every other girl in the world does. I'm a pretty face, a guy with a reputation that is well deserved. I'm the sort of guy Taylor Swift writes songs about. But what if right now, right in this moment, there was a chance I wasn't being that guy at all. What if I was genuinely being a good guy, someone you could be friends with? What if I was the opposite of who you think I am?"

Madison looked at him in disgust. "You know that's not something to be proud of, right? Making girls cry and hurting them for sport or so they'll write a song about you?"

"Sure," Ryan replied with a smile. "Not the point I was trying to make, but okay. You getting in?"

"Ryan, I-I," Madison paused. What was the worst that could happen tonight? "Okay. But you better have that book hidden wherever we are going."

"Don't worry, I'll get you the book before her highness Allison leaves tomorrow," he replied with a grin, motioning Madison into the car.

"I better not regret this," Madison mumbled to Ryan as she slid by him into the back of the car.

Within a few blocks the car stopped. Madison looked out the window. She laughed knowing exactly where they were. "Well, are you going to get out of the car or just stare at it from the car window like usual?" Ryan asked, opening her door. Madison shook her head in disbelief and tried to suppress her smile. She slid out of the taxi, staring straight ahead.

"Madison Stevens, welcome to Kings Cross Station, the home of the famous Platform 9 and ¾!" Ryan exclaimed, throwing his hands in the air gesturing at the huge brick building with arching windows lit up from the inside.

"I hate you," Madison said with a small chuckle. Ryan started to jog backwards toward the building.

"I guess I know you better than you think. Shall we then? What are you waiting for? The train leaves soon!" Ryan yelled, still jogging away from her. Madison shook her head, walking swiftly after him.

"You're gonna miss the train and have to take the flying car!" Ryan yelled.

Madison ran to catch up to him. "Stop causing a scene!" she yell-whispered at him as she caught up.

Within minutes Madison and Ryan stood in a small line to get a photo with the small luggage cart sticking out of the wall dubbed Platform 9 and ¾. Madison felt silly having Ryan take her picture, but he was right, this was the thing she wanted to see the most. He snapped a few photos of her on her phone, and then a selfie of the two of them.

"Would you like me to take your picture together?" someone decked out in a yellow and red scarf with a lightning bolt on their head asked.

"Um…I…" Madison stuttered looking over at Ryan.

"That'd be great. Thanks!" Ryan replied, handing over his phone instead of Madison's phone.

"Smile!"

"More like say Expecto Patronum on three!" Ryan replied.

Madison couldn't help but smile at the extremely handsome but surprisingly nerdy man standing next to her.

"Ready?" he asked, putting his arm across her back, and pulling her in.

Madison smiled as Ryan yelled his magical spell and broke out into a laugh. She felt goosebumps spread all over her body at the warmth of his arm around her. This feeling she felt was dangerous. She knew this could never be anything more than two work associates hanging out. She wouldn't let it be.

"Too bad the wizarding store here isn't open right now. We could buy some wands," Ryan said as they walked towards the exit.

"How many girls do you put this act on for?" Madison asked as they pushed through the large glass doors and back outside.

"I've never brough another woman here," Ryan replied. "You're the first and honestly, probably the last."

"How'd you guess that I would want to come here?" Madison asked, her eyes glued forward to the doors.

"It just seemed right," Ryan replied. "You know what else seems right? Ice cream and a walk by the Thames. What do you say?"

"Ryan, I can't, and you promised me the book if I came with you here," Madison replied. She could see his expression drop from excited and full of light back to his normal moody look.

"Fine, the book was delivered to your hotel room before you met me at the bar. Let me get you a car," he said, his voice defeated.

He waved down a taxi and opened the door for Madison to get in. "Thanks," she said, getting in the taxi. "Hey, question, what was this all about? Lately you've not said anything to me other than I'm fat and need a new wardrobe and then tonight you're a totally different person."

"Figured I need to make it up to you somehow and to show you that I'm not the villain you think I am. Hopefully it worked and even if it didn't, I'll see you tomorrow. Good night, Mads," he replied shutting the door.

"Good night, Ryan," she whispered to herself as the taxi headed out towards her hotel.

Episode 7- Gold Rush

Allie scrolled through her feed to see the latest post from the magazine as she sat in the airport waiting to board her flight. "Maybe it's too early," she whispered to herself refreshing her feed once again. As she released her thumb from the screen, a picture of Madison and Ryan at Kings Cross Station popped up on with the caption: *The Forever London staff is here to create some magic*. Ryan was standing with one arm in the air and the other around a smiling Madison looking up at him. They were getting close, dangerously close. Allie closed Instagram, opening her contacts to call Madison.

"You came in pretty late last night," Allie said as Madison answered, her voice groggy with sleep.

"I know, there was a bit of a delay getting the book in general," Madison replied, trying to suppress a smile at the memory of last night.

"What sort of delay?" Allie asked.

"Ryan, he told me to meet him at a bar to get the book and then it turns out he didn't have it and long story short he had delivered it to my hotel room earlier that evening. It was very frustrating," Madison answered.

"So, he left the office with the book and you left the office without the book, going against my instructions? He had you meet him at a bar, and had someone else deliver the book to your room at the hotel while you had drinks with him? Allie asked.

"I mean I don't know the logistics, but yeah, it seemed like a little game for him. I tried everything I could to get him to give me the book, but he wouldn't unless I met him at the bar and then got in a taxi to Kings Cross Station. Well, he wouldn't tell me where we were going, just told me to get into the car," Madison explained.

"Wait, we still have you in a hotel?" Allie asked.

"Yeah, but it's okay. I don't mind. It's nicer than my mom's house at least," Madison admitted.

"I think it's time we find you something a little more permanent. I know it's not ideal, but I have a couple of extra rooms in my townhouse. I'm gone for the next week, meeting with the L.A. offices, and you already have a key. I'm going to go ahead and cancel your hotel room, pack your stuff, head over to my place, pick a room, and get settled in. You'll have the place to yourself for the week to get accustomed to everything. After that we can talk about finding you a flat or something near the offices. For now, move in," Allie said, her voice trailing off a bit at the end.

"Allie, I couldn't. I don't want to impede on your space," Madison replied nervously as Allie went silent.

"Too late, you have nowhere else to go. Check out is at 11 today. Get to packing and I will see you in a week. Oh, got to run, my flight is boarding," Allie replied hurriedly.

"Shit." Madison rubbed her eyes and looked around the room.

****

"You're late," a deep voice said as Madison stepped off the elevator. Madison looked up from her phone to see Ryan standing in front of her.

"Yeah, I spent the morning moving my stuff over to Allie's townhouse where I will now reside for the time being, all thanks to you," Madison replied, taking a step around Ryan. She could smell his cologne as she side-stepped him.

Ryan chuckled. "How is that my fault?" he asked, stepping back into her path. Madison's breath caught on a twinkle in his eye, the flash of a memory from the night before.

"Your little shenanigans last night made me late with the book and Allie was already asleep and packed by the time I got there," Madison replied trying to get around him.

"Interesting. I thought it might have been caused by the picture I posted of the two of us on the magazine's account this morning," Ryan replied.

"What photo?" Madison asked, taking a step back towards the wall between the elevators as she scrambled for her phone.

"Well, I was going to invite you to lunch today but seeing that it is now past noon and you haven't even been to your desk yet, I think it's safe to say you are going to be busy with work for the rest of the day," Ryan said avoiding her question as he stepped back in her way and leaned in close, reaching to press the elevator door button behind her. He felt her tense up, holding her breath, until he stepped back.

"Ummm. I'm not hungry anyways," Madison said, slowly letting out a long breath and distractedly looking for the photo. Ryan smirked at Madison, stepping around her and into the now open elevator.

"Well, I am out for the rest of the day, enjoy your weekend and I will see you on Monday," Ryan said, rebuttoning his blazer as the doors began to close.

"See you on Monday," Madison whispered lingering in the lobby for a second more. Her body tingled and her face felt hot. She took a few deep breaths trying to calm herself back down before heading to her desk. As she approached her desk, she noticed a small green envelope lying on the keyboard. Madison sat down, opening the envelope to see a picture of her and Ryan standing at Platform 9 and ¾ from the night before. She flipped it over to see the words: "A magical beginning…" written in Ryan's handwriting on the back.

Madison shook her head. Ryan was the most confusing and yet charming guy she had ever met. Last night he was different, kinder, sweeter, and almost someone she could see herself being with. Madison smiled at the thought of them sipping coffee on the couch as Ryan read the newspaper and she listened to a record, basking in the sunlight sneaking in the window. She could see it now, Ryan dressed down in a t-shirt and sweatpants, his hair mussed from sleeping in, her legs draped over his lap, the perfect weekend morning. And just as she imagined him looking over to smile at her, the sound of a text message pulled her back to reality.

Unknown Number: Hey, it's Charlie from Altitude. How about that tour of London this weekend?

Madison felt her anxiety start to build. The idea of spending a Saturday morning with Ryan began to fade from her thoughts as a pit settled in her stomach. Charlie seemed like a nice enough guy. She did want a friend in London, and a cute, nice, international boyfriend could work too.

Madison: Hey Charlie, sounds good. How about tomorrow? Where should we meet?

Madison slid the picture of her and Ryan back into the envelope, letting it and the memory of last night fade to the back of her mind.

****

"It's so good to be back in Cali. I don't even know what I was thinking, saying I would relocate to London full-time. I miss the sunshine and the ocean," Allie said, stretching out on a lounge chair in an all-black bikini on her balcony in Malibu. Nick nodded leaning against the balcony edge, facing Allie while drinking a beer. His back to the sun and ocean. Allie loved her house right on the beach. After returning from London years ago, she took money from her trust fund and purchased this house. Nick moved in a year later and it never felt more like home. It was her haven, a place to escape from the rest of the world and reconnect with herself and boy did she need a chance to reconnect with herself after the first few weeks in London.

"You should have never left. California is way less fun with you halfway across the world," Nick laughed. Allie smiled studying Nick's dark brown hair always perfectly parted on the right, his chiseled chin always slightly hidden behind a five 'o'clock shadow, and his bright green eyes, currently hidden behind a pair of sunglasses, always pierced into your soul. He was a gorgeous man, though he would never believe you if you told him. Being out on the balcony with Nick felt calm and yet made the world an exciting place full of opportunity and moments to seize.

"Oh, I'm sure you get along plenty well without me here. Plus, you get this whole place to yourself when I am gone," Allie teased scrunching her nose at him. "How many times have the guys been over since I left?"

"I don't think that matters," Nick answered walking towards Allie. "Scoot over."

Allie slid over, giving Nick room to lay beside her. "Missed having my partner in crime here," he said, kissing her on the forehead before taking another sip of his beer. "Not to ruin this moment, but I do have to ask, have you seen him since being in London?” he asked staring straight ahead.

Allie slowly took off her sunglasses, sitting up. “In an interesting turn of events, he’s on staff as a photographer for the magazine,” she said, biting her lower lip waiting for Nick’s reaction.

“Are you shitting me? I can’t believe you would hire him after everything. What the hell are you doing?” Nick said, standing back up. “I don’t think I’m comfortable with you two working together.”

“Nick, it’s not going to be like the last time I was in London. I’m not in love with him. I’m his boss and I’m only doing it because he has some real talent. I’ll show you the photos he took and it will change your mind about him being on staff,” Allie assured him. “Give me a second. I’ll go get the book and show you.”

Allie got up, stepping past Nick. “I don’t need to see the book, Allie. I could care less about his skills. I care more about the effect he has on you,” Nick said. Allie stopped in the doorway to turn back and look at Nick. His eyes were visible now, bearing a deep sadness she didn’t see before.

“Nick,” she said, stepping back towards him.

“Just promise you won’t fall in love with him again,” Nick said, reaching out to pull Allie back over him. Allie obliged, taking his hand. Nick pulled her into a deep hug and Allie wrapped her arms around his neck.

“Nick,” Allie whispered. “I promise.”

He nodded his head, letting her go, and took another sip of beer. “By the way, you are losing your tan.”

Allie laughed sighting a beer pong ball lodged under the stack of folded lounge chairs in the corner. “And once again, I ask how many guys nights you have hosted here since I left?” she teased retrieving the ball.

“The world may never know,” Nick said, rolling his eyes.

“Oh, it knows,” Allie said, grabbing her phone to check the time. “And it also knows that we are going to be late to the cake tasting if we don’t get ready and leave in the next ten minutes.”

****

The next day, Madison waited outside the Tower of London for Charlie. The fortress behind her matched her mood. Everything about today felt cold and dreary. The cool morning air touched her face as she leaned up against a small wall along the River Thames. Madison looked down at her high-top black sneakers. She wanted to keep it simple today, her hair in a high ponytail, a pair of skinny blue jeans and a navy and white striped t-shirt with her army green jacket to top it off. Charlie was cute, very cute and flirty from what she remembered. Madison felt a smile start to cross her face at the thought of today turning into a movie romance. Girl starts a job in London, meets a cute guy at a bar for work, he offers to take her on a tour of the city, they laugh and hit it off, maybe get caught in a rainstorm and then he walks her home and ends the day with a nice kiss.

"Hey, ready to start this tour?" Charlie asked approaching Madison from the left. He looked just as charming as Madison remembered.

"Let's do it!" Madison chirped back, immediately regretting her perky voice.

"Someone is in a cheery mood today," Charlie replied, flashing a smile and pushing his hair back.

"Just excited to see London from the eyes of someone who lives here," Madison lied feeling butterflies growing and flapping wildly in her stomach.

"Right, well this might seem a little touristy, but starting here is the Tower of London. It is a place where you can drop a lot of quid to see some old royal jewels. Not really a place I would recommend, but it felt like a good place to meet up. I have never really seen the appeal of this old place, but I do like the River Thames here. Shall we walk along it a bit?" Charlie asked motioning Madison along. Madison nodded.

"How is 'jolly ole London' treating you anyhow?" Charlie asked as they began to stroll away from the Tower.

"So far so good. I do miss the sunshine a bit, well that and the ocean and beaches back home, but I honestly can't complain. Though it's a bit lonely for me here," Madison babbled on, stealing a quick glance of Charlie as he looked ahead.

"Haven't made many friends I take it?" Charlie asked, motioning to Madison to cross the street with him.

"Not particularly. I mean that's not uncommon for me. I don't have many friends at home either. I tend to stick to myself, but at least at home I had my mom to hang out with," Madison paused. "God that sounded pathetic, didn't it?"

Charlie chuckled. "A little. So, no boyfriend back home?"

"Nope. Why? You know any single available Londoners?" Madison teased.

"Maybe," Charlie replied coyly, motioning Madison along toward Neal's Yard. Madison turned the corner to see rows of brightly colored shops. "Welcome to Neal's Yard. It's nothing special, but has some great shops, some quirky colors and a great coffee shop. Shall we?"

Madison nodded. "Let's do it." Charlie led the way pointing out his favorite shops as they walked over to grab a cup of coffee. "I could get used to this," Madison thought watching Charlie animatedly talk about a shop where he liked to buy clothes.

****

"Fancy running into you two here," Ryan said appearing next to Madison and Charlie at the counter.

"No models this weekend mate?" Charlie asked shaking Ryan's hand.

"Not every weekend is filled with models, sometimes a man has to come down to earth and see what the regular women look like for a moment. It can't be models all the time," Ryan replied.

"You are not serious, are you?" Charlie scoffed. "No bloke would date a 'regular woman' as you put it if they could date any supermodel they wanted. I would kill to be in your shoes."

Madison felt her heart drop as the words left Charlie's mouth. Ryan's eyes flickered in her direction and Madison felt her expression tense up as her eyes met his. He looked sincere, slightly worried about her. Madison forced a smile, awkwardly raising her eyebrows.

"I mean look, supermodels are overrated and typically only good to hang out with for a night or two. Eventually, I wouldn't mind settling down with someone who has a brain and personality," Ryan replied, his eyes glued on Madison as he spoke. Madison rolled her eyes, turning to face the espresso machine in front of her.

"I haven't found a woman worth my extended time just yet, if you know what I mean," Ryan continued, turning to Charlie, who shrugged.

"I don't know. Sleeping with a new model every night must be fun though," Charlie replied.

"It's not a bad life, I will give you that much," Ryan laughed.

Madison rolled her eyes again. "I'm sure there are plenty of supermodels who have gone on one date with you Ryan and found you extremely superficial and boring. And I'm sure all those women aren't as daft as you make them out to be. You'd be lucky to end up with a model who would want to be the 'one' for you," she finally said.

Ryan's eyes narrowed in on Madison. "Maybe you're right, but if you find a girl who is equally gorgeous and smart, be sure to point her out," he replied with a wink.

"It sounds like she's calling your name," Madison said directly, gesturing over to the end of the counter where the barista stood, sliding a to go cup across the counter.

"Well, I hope the two of you enjoy the rest of your date. Madison, I'll see you Monday," Ryan said before heading to gather his coffee and out the door.

"Well, that was bloody awkward," Charlie muttered.

"Just ignore him, he's always like that. And don't worry, I know this isn't a date. You wouldn't want to date a girl like me if you could get supermodels, which I'm sure you are around all the time at Altitude," Madison blurted out as her name was called signaling her drink being ready.

"You aren't completely wrong," Charlie chuckled, following Madison. Madison scoffed, shaking her head as she hustled towards the door and out onto the busy sidewalk. She felt stupid and embarrassed for all the flirting with Charlie she put effort into today. All she wanted to do now was retreat to Allie's townhouse and never come out again.

"Hey wait!" Charlie yelled, chasing after her. Madison stormed off down the road only stopping when Charlie grabbed her arm.

"Madison, stop, let me explain," Charlie said a little out of breath.

"You don't need to explain, I was stupid for thinking that maybe you might like me. I guess I did think that maybe this could be a date," Madison replied hastily.

"Look don't get me wrong, you're gorgeous. I know you don't see it, but you are, I just prefer men a bit more than I prefer women. It's not that I would never date you, I just like men a whole hell of a lot more," Charlie replied.

"Wait, so you are bi-sexual then?" Madison asked, relaxing a bit.

"Yes, while I find women attractive and have spent plenty of nights in the company of a woman, I prefer men. Call it a 70/30 split," Charlie said with a shrug. "I've just gotten accustomed to pretending to like these avantgarde models who walk into the club on the arms of arrogant men like Ryan. Men who view themselves as these sorts of gods who need to feed off the admiration of those men they deem lesser than them. It's all a game if you know what I mean," Charlie explained.

Madison nodded, looking down at her feet.

"I'm sorry if you think I led you on at all. If you want to stop the tour now, we can, but at least let me take you to one more spot. I promise you'll love it," Charlie suggested, giving Madison a slight nudge.

"Okay, lead the way," Madison sighed.

"Atta girl."

****

"What would you say about being part of a documentary about your life?" Nick asked as they left the cake shop and began walking up the street towards their next stop.

"I'd say people would be bored to tears. Who wants to watch a documentary about growing up rich?" Allie replied, slowing down her pace, eyeing the outside of an old-fashioned ice cream shop. "How does ice cream sound to you?"

84

"How can you even want sweets after all the cake we just tried? Plus, don't you have a dress fitting tomorrow?"

"How dare you say something like that?" Allie laughed pretending to be offended. "Do you want some or not?"

"I'm going to go with not," Nick replied crossing his arms. "I'll wait for you out here."

Allie shrugged her shoulders, turning away to step inside. Nick watched Allie through the shop window. She lit up every room she walked into since their first day in kindergarten. Nick could see Allie interacting with the kid behind the counter, undoubtedly ordering a double scoop of rocky road ice cream in a waffle cone. Every summer it was the same. She would make them stop by some ice cream shop and grab a cone. She used to flirt with the various ice cream scooping boys to get herself some free toppings or an extra scoop at no charge. Every time it was the same, she'd come barreling out of the shop carrying a cone for her and a cone for Nick and would have some sort of phone number scribbled on her forearm. They would then head to the beach and people watch while ice cream dripped down Allie's arm, ruining the digits belonging to this week's ice cream boy. Everything changed when Allie moved away to London for the first time. She was no longer the wistful girl of their youth with sun-kissed skin and a carefree attitude. She was guarded now, every move she made was calculated as to keep her from ever feeling the pain of lost love again.

"Shall we continue our walk?" Allie asked, emerging from the shop with a double scoop of rocky road in a cone, starting to drip down her arm as it melted in the sun.

"Some things never change with you," Nick commented.

"I mean I didn't get his number. That's a change." Allie joked, liking the ice cream already starting to melt down the side of her hand.

"Well, I hope not, it wouldn't be very appropriate these days since he's probably a minor," Nick teased.

"Seriously!" Allie exclaimed. "Though, that might make for juicy documentary topic."

"That it would. About the documentary, what if it was a new take on a documentary? Like a series of social media posts and confessional videos made by you documenting your life. You telling stories about your childhood up until now? Like ten-minute videos over the course of a year strung together to make a television series or a short film even. Hell, it could just be a series of short videos posted regularly for people to consume daily," Nick asked as they headed up the street to a small venue where numerous table settings waited for their critiques inside.

"I just don't see the appeal. I run a magazine in London. My wealth comes from my father's Hollywood job and my grandfather's old-world money. I don't party anymore or do anything remotely noteworthy. I'm not self-made or exciting. Why? Are you trying to start a new project? Is my father behind it? I thought you were working on a script for him," Allie asked, licking the ice cream off her arm.

"It was something I was just tossing out there to see if it would stick. Reality television is getting boring and overrun by stupid dating shows, this could be a fresh take" Nick replied, opening the door for Allie.

"Well, maybe if you find someone more interesting it could work. It sounds like the type of documentary people might enjoy on their way to and from work, or even on a break. The format sounds interesting," Allie replied. "But for now, let's go pick out the perfect table setting for the big day!"

****

"Ryan, what is the plan for the launch party?" Mitch asked over the phone. Ryan watched Madison and Charlie leave the coffee shop in a huff from afar, leaning on a wall out of sight just enough that Madison wouldn't be able to spot him.

"I've told you all I know at this point. It's going to be held at Charlie's bar, as requested. Other than that, I don't have the plans for anything else. Madison and Allison are keeping them hush hush," Ryan replied. His eyes stayed on Madison who turned around to face Charlie.

"Did you set-up lunch with the girl?" Mitch asked. Ryan sighed as he saw Madison and Charlie come together and walk out of sight. "Ryan?"

"I'm working on it," he replied. "Don't worry, I'll make sure to get more information from her, though she's a lot stronger willed than we may have thought. Plus, she is very loyal to Allison."

"Well, keep getting her alone and posting photos of the two of you on social media. That's sure to drive a wedge between the two of them. From what I've heard, the photo you posted from the other night caused Allie to cancel Madison's hotel room and make her move into the townhouse. Seems like things are going according to plan, so far," Mitch responded.

"I really don't appreciate having to babysit Madison," Ryan replied, watching Charlie nudge Madison.

"Just get the fucking job done," Mitch said coldly before hanging up. Ryan shoved his phone back in his pocket. Madison and Charlie disappeared into the crowd. Ryan shook his head, turned away from the coffee shop, heading back to his flat, alone.

"So let me guess, you came to London, hoping that you would find love?" Charlie asked, walking alongside Madison towards Hyde Park.

"What?" Madison asked embarrassed, nervously sipping her coffee.

"Look, it's okay, a lot of people move to a new city because their hometown or old city didn't give them the wants and desires of their hearts. Your desire seems to be a desire to be loved by someone. It's not a bad desire but based on your reaction to my conversation with Ryan, you are desperately looking for love and attention," Charlie laid out.

Madison could feel tears building behind her eyes. "I wouldn't call me desperate. Maybe I should just head home. I think I've had enough adventures for today."

"Madison, look, I don't say this to hurt your feelings. I would just be careful if I was you. Don't get too attached to anyone here too quickly. Get to know them first. First impressions, second impressions, hell even third impressions can be deceiving in a new city, especially one with dreamy accents. Just be careful," Charlie reassured Madison.

"I'm not desperate for love. Sure, I'm a bit of a romantic, but what's wrong with that?" Madison asked, continuing to follow Charlie down the busy streets of London towards Hyde Park.

"Let me ask you something, do you meet a guy and immediately imagine what your weekends would look like together?"

"I mean not immediately, maybe after I've gone out with them at least once," Madison replied. Charlie chuckled.

"That's the issue. You don't give yourself enough time to get to know someone before imagining a life with them and getting your hopes up. It changes how you approach them, how you interact with them," Charlie explained.

"It doesn't change anything. I'm just being me no matter what," Madison retorted.

"I could see the shift from the first time I met you and this morning. You were shyer and a little flirtier than before," Charlie replied. "In your imagined weekend, did we at least do something cool?"

"I don't know what you are talking about. I didn't imagine anything with you," Madison lied, knowing that this morning as she got ready, she imagined them eating croissants on the floor of Attitude 360 looking over the city.

"Sure," Charlie teased. "Look, next time you meet a nice guy, and I mean a nice guy, not a guy like Ryan, he will ruin your life. I've seen it happen before. Anyways, the next time you meet a nice guy, approach it like you may never see that guy again. I guarantee you will get a second date, maybe even a third or fourth."

"I guess we will have to wait and see," Madison replied defeated from this conversation. They stopped in front of a large brick wall covered in vines. Charlie motioned Madison towards an opening down the street a bit.

"Are you ready?" Charlie asked.

"You know we have parks in California," Madison replied, finishing off her coffee and tossing the cup into a nearby bin.

"Not like this. Just you wait," Charlie answered as Madison turned the corner to see rows of large trees filling in a huge grassy area. Everything was green and luscious. A large path made its way winding through the trees. Madison stepped inside the large brick walls, feeling a sense of magic rush through her body.

"It's breathtaking, isn't it?" Charlie asked, watching Madison's eyes fill with a sparkle. She had never seen anything like it. There was magic hanging in the air, unlike anything else she had ever experienced before. A small breeze tickled the ends of her hair and the tip of her nose. For a moment, every other interaction she had today faded away. She felt as free here as she did at home on her surfboard in the middle of the ocean.

"I don't even know how to explain it. I know it's just a park, but it feels like so much more," Madison sighed, her eyes scanning the pathway ahead of them.

"You haven't even seen the best of it yet, let's head over to the lake," Charlie urged her along. "The park was originally used as hunting grounds for King Henry VIII back in the 1500s. It used to also contain the land on the other side of the lake, Kensington Gardens, but one of our Queens of the past separated it out with the lake. I enjoy walking through the park and getting lost."

Madison followed Charlie around nodding politely at his fun facts while dreaming about what it would be like to get lost in this park with Ryan.

Episode 8- Green Light

"Do you want to go to lunch?" Ryan asked approaching Madison's desk. Madison looked up over a stack of binders, her dangling earrings clinking as she swung her head up to see Ryan. He was a bit dressed down today wearing dark pants, a light blue dress shirt and a dark grey cardigan over top.

"As long as wherever we go doesn't require us to look extremely nice like the lunch with Mitch McGowan," Madison said standing up. She was wearing a pair of dark distressed skinny jeans, with a black sleeveless shirt tied in a bow at the side of her neck. A pair of bright teal heels finished off the outfit. Her hair was pulled up into a messy bun allowing her earrings to freely swing without getting stuck.

"I see you either bought some new clothes or finally decided to wear something different from your current wardrobe," Ryan teased with a smile.

"I went shopping this weekend for some new pieces," Madison replied rolling her eyes.

"Well, I think you'll be fine in this outfit. How do you feel about Indian food?" Ryan asked.

"Sounds great to me. Let me just grab my bag," Madison answered squatting down to grab her purse from under her desk, her elbow hitting the side of one of the binders on her desk, causing them all to fall over. Ryan lunged forward in an attempt to catch them, missing the toppling stack by a second.

Madison stood up frantically at the sound of the binders hitting the floor. "Dammit!" she exclaimed, setting her purse on top of the desk now as she bent over to pick up the mess.

"Why do you have so many binders on your desk anyways?" Ryan asked, squatting down to help.

"It's partial party planning and partial wedding planning," Madison replied.

"Whose wedding?" Ryan asked, his left eyebrow lifting inquisitively.

"It's a side project I'm helping Allie with," Madison replied, straightening out some of the pages in the wedding planning binder that were now slightly crinkled from the fall.

"I didn't know she was engaged," Ryan replied trying to dig information out of Madison.

"She's very private about her life. All I know is that she wanted me to print a whole bunch of information and pictures, three-hole punch them and put them in this binder. She sends a new email almost hourly with stuff to go in here," Madison replied, picking up the last binder and placing it on the stack. "Are you ready to go?"

"Let's do it," Ryan said cheerfully.

****

"Nick, get up," Allie said nudging Nick slightly. "Niiiiiiiiiiiiiiiiick!"

"What? What's wrong?" Nick whispered half awake.

"Nothing's wrong, just get up I want to show you something," Allie replied. "Come on… I know you will like it!"

"Allie it's 5AM," Nick groaned. "Can it wait?"

"Nope nope! Get up buttercup or you will miss out," Allie laughed nudging Nick again. "Meet me downstairs in five minutes, sweats, running shoes, and a smile."

Nick groaned again as Allie left the room. Begrudgingly he slid his legs over the side of the bed following her instructions and heading downstairs. "Okay, what is the surprise?"

Allie jumped up off the barstool. "It's out on the beach! And we sort of have to run there just a little bit."

"Alllllllllllllllllls, really? A 5AM run is what you got me up for?" Nick complained, dropping his head down and sighing.

"Come on Nick. It's worth it, I promise!" Allie exclaimed, bouncing over to Nick, grabbing his hand. "Please come with me. Please? Please? Pleeeeeease?"

Nick laughed, shaking his head. "Fine. Let's go."

Allie smiled pulling her hair up into a ponytail, leading Nick out the back door. Smiling Nick followed her down the beach. The air was crisp, as the sun began to rise behind them, burning off the morning fog. After ten minutes of running, Nick saw Allie run towards some rocks grabbing something from behind them.

"Allie what are you grabbing?" Nick yelled out.

"The surprise! Stay right there!" Allie called back.

91

Nick stared out at the ocean taking in the calming sounds of the waves crashing in and out. Allie walked up slowly carrying a blanket rolled up under her arm and a basket in the other arm.

"I should have guessed. Our anniversary is coming up next week. Beach breakfast tradition?" Nick asked.

"Beach breakfast tradition! Did you really think I was going to leave here before doing it?" Allie replied, setting the basket down and laying down the blanket.

"You never cease to amaze," Nick chuckled. "Croissants from Marco's?"

"You know it! Let's dig in!" Allie unpacked a variety of croissants, fresh fruit, champagne, and orange juice on the blanket. Nick smiled, grabbing the two champagne flutes from the basket.

"So, when do you leave?" Nick asked, popping the bottle of champagne open.

"Well, the plan is to spend the next few days in Los Angeles with Brad Garrison and the Forever Los Angeles team and then I will be heading back to London," Allie replied chewing on a chocolate croissant.

"You aren't going to visit your mom and dad while you are here?" Nick asked, sipping on his mimosa.

"Nah, you know how my dad gets, you work for him. When he is working on a film, he's too busy to even remember to sleep or eat. I'd rather not bother him. I'm sure he'll come out to London with my mom at some point," Allie replied stretching out on the blanket. "You're coming out for the launch party, right?"

"Yeah, at least I think that's the plan right now, that is if you don't get fired for anything beforehand," Nick joked.

"When's Kara due back from her assignment?" Allie asked.

"In a couple weeks. She doesn't have a definite date yet, but things in the village she's helping are going well and they are wrapping up," Nick answered.

"Well, she's more than welcome to come out to London too. Please let her know, my treat!" Allie said, scrunching her nose up as she smiled at Nick.

"I'll let her know the next time I talk to her. But are you sure you have to go back to London? Do they even have beaches to do beach breakfast tradition at?" Nick teased grabbing another croissant.

"Even if it did, it definitely doesn't have you to do beach breakfast tradition with. I will give London a year or two and then hopefully Garrison will trust me enough to let me take over the L.A. or New York offices and then I'll be back here full-time or at least closer. In the meantime, you could always move to London with me," Allie suggested.

"You know I'll never leave the beach behind. Plus, someone's got to take care of the beach house," Nick replied.

"A girl can dream right?" Allie sighed sitting up to down her mimosa. Nick nodding as the sun started to glisten off the waves.

****

"So how was the rest of your date with Charlie?" Ryan asked as they waited for their food to come to the table.

"It wasn't a date. He was simply showing me around London," Madison retorted rolling her eyes. "Why do you care so much anyways?"

"Just wondering how it went. You two look good together," Ryan lied.

"I still don't understand why it matters to you. Charlie showed me around the city, that's all that happened," Madison replied.

"And bought you some new clothes?" Ryan questioned.

"No, I bought me some new clothes. It was time, I haven't gone shopping in quite some time and most of my wardrobe is back in California," Madison snapped as the food approached the table. "But again, why do you care so much as to whether I had a good time with Charlie?"

"I don't care, I was just trying to make small talk," Ryan replied. "I see it's a testy subject, so I'll drop it. How are things for the launch party going?"

Madison shrugged. "Things are going well. Allie sends me a daily to do list with items she would like done before she returns. We should have everything in line and ready to go in the next two weeks. Then it will be smooth sailing from there."

"Sounds like you and Allison have it under control. Do you know the theme of the party?" Ryan asked, tearing a piece of naan.

"I don't think I am allowed to announce it just yet. Allie will be back in a couple of days and then she will make the announcement," Madison answered before taking a bite of curry.

"You can't even give me a hint or color scheme, so we can start planning the social media campaign?" Ryan asked.

"I mean, it's going to be in Forever colors, but I'm not saying anything beyond that. Allie will murder me," Madison said firmly before taking a sip of water. "Now what I want to know is, who is your favorite Harry Potter character?"

"Ohhh, Draco no doubt in my mind. He's handsome, rich, and very confident. All traits that I enjoy in character or person," Ryan replied arrogantly. Madison rolled her eyes.

"I mean he's an alright character, but there's no way he's the best!" Madison exclaimed.

"He surely is the best. He's the antithesis of Harry. I mean think about it, they have the same start: both are tossed into situations because of their parents, Draco is on the path to darkness because of his parents and Harry the chosen one due to his parents' decisions. Neither of them has a choice about their life paths. The key difference is that Harry spends so much of his time whining and putting himself and others in harm's way in order to prove himself, while Draco has to make tough decisions to follow in his father's footsteps and go dark. Draco ends up being redeemable in the end, his character arc is complete. Harry on the other hand never learns and continues to just get lucky in his actions. Sure, there's the whole he has to die thing, but honestly, who cares?" Ryan explained. Madison nodded her head impressed by Ryan's answer.

"So, you are like a secret nerd then?" Madison asked, taking a sip of her chai.

"I'm not a nerd," Ryan replied. "I'm just answering your question."

"Sure, you are! You just gave me a 2-minute explanation as to why a fictional character was the best of an entire series and you used the word antithesis. Only nerds do that," Madison teased.

"I can't help but enjoy reading in my spare time. It's a hobby, but it does not make me a nerd," Ryan countered.

"You are such a nerd, just admit it." Madison chuckled.

"I will never," Ryan answered with an uncontrollable smile on his face.

"We'll see about that," Madison replied.

****

"Ugh! Work you stupid thing!" Madison whispered harshly, kicking the bottom of the copier as another warning came across the screen.

"You know kicking it isn't going to help it work better," Ryan said appearing behind her. "Do you need help?"

Madison scoffed, tossing her papers on top of the copier. "I just need to get these out to Charlie today. It's the final paperwork for booking Altitude. But this stupid thing keeps jamming or saying it's an invalid email address," Madison replied, giving the machine another kick.

Ryan chuckled behind her. "Let me assist."

"No, Allie said that these papers cannot be out of my hands," Madison replied, letting her shoulders sink down. "Why won't this thing work? I have about a hundred other things to do for Allie today."

"Trust me, okay? Allie doesn't have to know who sent them. I'll get the copier to work, and you go get started on whatever else you need done today. I'll bring you the confirmation page and this stack when it's done," Ryan assured.

"I don't know," Madison said, feeling a pit form in her stomach.

"Or you can stand here for the next hour trying to get these to send and not get anything on your to do list done today. It's up to you really," Ryan replied. Madison turned around to face him.

"I hate when you give me that look," Madison replied.

"What look?" Ryan smirked.

"The one where you smirk like that, knowing that you're right," Madison teased, feeling the tension from moments earlier leave her body. She would never admit it to him, but over the past week Ryan time and time again proved that he had a way of calming her when things felt out of control. He showed her a

95

different side of him in the past week, one that made her almost start to like him.

"So, we agree then, I'm right? You are going to let me send these forms to Charlie, while you go and work on your tasks for the afternoon?" Ryan asked.

"Fine, but Allie never finds out," Madison warned sternly. "I cannot afford to lose this job."

"Deal, the ice queen will never find out" Ryan replied sticking out his hand to shake on it. Madison looked at Ran's hand and then his face as she slowly reached out to shake his hand. As their skin touched, she felt a spark of electricity pulsate through her body and pulled away quickly.

"Thanks. The email address is on the sticky note there," Madison said, stepping around Ryan and scurrying off to her desk.

****

"Hey Allie," Madison said answering her phone as she put away her dinner dishes. The afternoon flew by as she managed to get the florist, caterer, and venue in line for the launch party.

"How's everything in the office?" Allie asked, juggling a coffee, her purse, the book, and her car keys as she tried to open the car door.

"Things are going well. I've sent your notes on the book to the various teams. Taylor's interview wrapped today and is being edited tomorrow. And I sent the final paperwork for the launch party venue earlier today. How are the L.A. offices?" Madison replied, pouring herself a cup of tea.

"A bit of a mess to be honest. Brad Garrison is in the office so everyone is in a panic. I think he is going to fire the creative director out here. The magazine numbers are down, and they aren't getting any traction on social media. The creative director, Shirley, refuses to do things differently so I'm pretty sure her job is at stake," Allie explained as she drove back towards the office from lunch.

"Bummer," Madison replied.

"Maybe you'll be interested in applying for her job?" Allie asked.

"What do you mean?" Madison chuckled nervously.

96

"Your bio on our social media says your dream job is being a creative director."

"What bio?" Madison asked, putting Allie on speaker so she could pull up Instagram, searching for the magazine's profile.

"You were last week's featured employee. Didn't you know? Don't you follow us on social media?"

"To be honest I don't normally check my social media," Madison replied distractedly looking for her photo. She slowly scrolled through this week's photos, only stopping to look at the picture of her and Ryan together at King's Cross Station before moving on to the photo Allie was talking about. She looked soft yet strong at the same time in the photo. The perfect balance of traits she wished she always carried with her. She remembered declining to have her picture taken, but Ryan must have snapped something anyways.

"Well, you better start. Everything is moving to social media platforms and everyone on staff is going to need to start posting more and more over the next few weeks," Allie directed.

"Why didn't Ryan's team tell me about this photo? I don't even remember it being taken," Madison said as she read the bio captioning her photo.

"You two seem to be spending a lot of time together. You both went to the Harry Potter train station thing together and lunch this week from what I can tell," Allie replied, pulling into the parking garage at Garrison Publishing.

"How?"

"It's all there or on his page. Madison, I'm going to lose service pulling into this parking garage, but when I get back, I want to talk to you about this all. Oh, and please start using your social media. I'll be checking. Talk to you soon!" Allie exclaimed before hanging up.

Madison looked at the other photos on the Forever London profile. Pausing again on photo snapped of her and Ryan at Platform 9 and ¾. Every other photo was of just one staff member or a quick behind the scenes picture except their photo. They did look cute together in the photo.

"No wonder Allie made me move in here," Madison muttered to herself setting down her phone. Taking a sip of her tea she leaned back a little in the chair trying to imagine what sort of social media content Allie would require of her. Madison didn't have many photos of herself or of London at this point and the thought of having to create content on top of working her normal job was exhausting.

****

"Here," Ryan said handing an herbal hot tea to Madison who was ferociously typing at her computer early in the morning.

"What's this for?" Madison asked, looking away from the computer screen for a moment.

"You seemed stressed yesterday, I thought this lavender tea might help," Ryan replied, leaning up against the wall near her desk.

"Thanks," Madison replied staring at her screen again.

"Anything I can help with?" Ryan asked, walking around Madison's desk.

Madison spun around in her chair. "Nah, but I'm sure you can snap a photo of me working, add a quick fake bio and toss it on the internet."

Ryan gave Madison a confused look. "Explain?"

"Don't play dumb, why did you post a photo of me from the photoshoot day, one that you didn't ask my permission to take, and then you added a bio which included information that I didn't provide. Like what makes you think I want your job? And why didn't you ask me? Allie is pissed thinking I okayed that," Madison replied.

"Well, someone slept on the wrong side of the bed and woke up feisty today. I wrote that because you would be good at it and I took the photo of you because you looked good that day," Ryan replied coolly.

"I'm pretty sure you didn't approve of my outfit or weight at that point, so there's no way that is true," Madison said rolling her eyes.

"I'm never going to live down one moment of douchery am I?" Ryan laughed.

"One moment? Surrrrrrrre. Anyways, why did you do it?" Madison asked again.

"What? Post the photo? It was a great photo, but I know you wouldn't approve of it. You don't seem to like to be in the

98

spotlight. If you knew I took the photo and wanted to post it, you would have immediately told me to delete it and gotten Allison involved. You were up next in the employee spotlighting cycle, and I needed a photo and bio," Ryan answered.

"You could have at least given me the chance to at least answer the questions honestly and you didn't need to post the picture of us at Kings Cross Station without asking me. I don't need people making assumptions about me, especially when it comes to you," Madison said, turning back to her computer.

"Well, I sincerely apologize." Ryan walked back around to the front of her desk. "I'll leave you to your work."

Madison let Ryan start walking away as she contemplated her next move. Over the past week, Ryan proved himself time and time again to be a friend and an ally at work. He was confusing still, but Madison chopped it up to Ryan having layers that he rarely let anyone else see. She knew with Allie's return to the office her guard would have to go back up.

"It's fine, but you better watch out, word is out that I'm looking at taking your job," she said wanting to savor the moments of having a friend in London a little longer.

"I look forward to the moment you try. See you for dinner later? Last chance to hangout before Allie's back," he said flashing her a smile.

Madison smiled back shaking her head playfully. "See you then."

****

Allie checked her email while waiting for her flight. "Madison, Madison, Ryan, Brad, Madison, Madison…" Allie whispered to herself scrolling through searching for an email from Myles. Myles hadn't reached out since their dinner a week ago. She thought for sure he would text or email about the magazine at least, but there was nothing but silence between them. Allie closed her laptop as her flight started to board.

Gathering her items, she felt her phone vibrate.

Nick: Go get 'em Als. I hope you have a safe trip. Call me when you land.

Allie smiled. Spending the last few days with Nick felt refreshing, but also left Allie feeling more confused about London. Allie typed a smiley face and "Will do!" before putting her phone into airplane mode. "Back to the old city we go," she whispered.

****

"You're late," Ryan teased, getting up as Madison approached the table. He could see tears in her eyes as she sat down. "What's wrong?"

"Allie is going to fire me. I lost our venue for the launch party," Madison muttered trying to suppress the rising urge to ugly cry. She kept her gaze on the table, not wanting to admit her mistake to Ryan. Unfolding her napkin, she drew in deep breath. Ryan watched her struggling to stay composed.

"Do you want to eat somewhere else? I can make us dinner at my place if you'd rather not be in public. Or we can grab dinner another time," Ryan suggested.

"I'd rather not be alone and if this is going to be my last dinner in London, it might as well be here," Madison replied, forcing a smile as she avoided looking at Ryan.

"Alright then, my treat. Order anything you want," Ryan replied trying to comfort her.

"Thanks, I'm honestly fine with whatever. Hell, I'll even eat a salad and nothing else at this point," Madison answered. Ryan chuckled.

"Don't laugh at my pathetic mess of a life," Madison said, as the waiter approached the table.

"Alright, I'll order my favorites and we can split them." As Ryan began to order Madison heard her phone beep. She slowly reached behind her into her purse hanging from the chair, retrieving the phone to see a text from Charlie on the screen. Opening it she saw a picture of the paperwork Forever submitted for Altitude showing the correct month and day for the launch party, but the wrong year.

"I swear I put the right year down on both sets of paperwork. I double checked it a hundred times," Madison whispered to herself, scanning the photo again.

100

"Do you want to talk about what happened with the venue?" Ryan asked as he finished ordering.

"Apparently, I put the date down for next year and not this one. I could have sworn that I-" Madison paused, narrowing in on the date. Madison felt her heart drop into her stomach. Her eyes traced the familiar yet foreign curves of each number in the year as her mind searched through its files to figure out where she recognized the swirl of the 2 and the swish of the 3 before.

"What is it?" Ryan asked as the waiter poured them each a glass of wine.

"It was you," Madison said swallowing the truth hard as the sticky note with the address of a bar from a week ago shined bright at the front of her brain.

"Who? Madison, what's going on?" Ryan asked feeling slightly panicked.

Madison scoffed. "I left you with both sets of documents for Altitude. Once at the venue and then again at the copier. I trusted you! You changed the date. God. I'm an idiot. And to think I was so quick to forgive you this morning about the pictures. So stupid."

"Madison, slow down, what are you talking about? I didn't change anything. Let me see the picture," Ryan asked, reaching his hand out for her phone.

"What the hell kind of game is this, Ryan? You've spent the last week being nice to me. Going to lunch, grabbing me coffee, this dinner… and for what? To get me fired? To get Allie fired? What in the actual fuck?" Madison exclaimed, standing up from her chair.

"Madison stop, where are you going? I didn't do this. I didn't change the date. I know you are upset that we lost the venue, but we will figure something out. Just take a breath," Ryan said in a hushed tone as he leaned in. People were starting to stare at the commotion rising between them.

"Stop the charade. I should have listened to Charlie when he said not to trust people so willingly. Enjoy your dinner Ryan," Madison replied grabbing her bag and storming out of the restaurant.

"Good job Ryan," Mitch said walking up behind him.

"I should have known you had something to do with this," Ryan replied, his eyes on the front door.

"I'm not sure what you are insinuating here, but I had nothing to do with that outburst. It was just fun to watch," Mitch replied stepping around the table. "Like she said, enjoy your dinner. Oh, and make sure to call my office in the morning, we need to talk about the next steps."

Episode 9- Don't be so hard on yourself

Madison woke up to the smell of coffee the next morning. Confused, she slid out of bed tossing on a solid black dress that pulled snuggly across her hips. She threw on a long copper cardigan and slid her feet into a pair of booties. She was uncertain of the actual time but felt certain she was late for work. She threw her hair into a messy bun and grabbed her purse to head downstairs.

"You look nice today, new outfit?" Allie said looking up from behind the newspaper. Allie was dressed casually, wearing a pair of dark green joggers and a grey t-shirt, her hair in a ponytail and a hint of lip gloss on her lips.

"What time is it?" Madison asked, pouring herself a cup of coffee. "I'm assuming I'm not late for work since you are still dressed like you just got off the plane."

"You have plenty of time," Allie replied taking a sip of coffee from an oversized mug. "Plus, once you put your make-up on, I want to hear about what's been going on this past week, all the juicy details."

Madison felt her shoulders tense up. She knew she needed to tell Allie that a month out from their inaugural issue launch party that they lost the venue.

"Allie looks calm this morning, and a bit tan, so the trip must have gone well. Maybe if I tell her now...or is it best that I wait until we get to work," Madison thought, watching Allie quietly reading the paper.

"I'll get you all caught up once we get to the office. I'm going to head upstairs and finish getting ready now that I know I have time. Don't want to give Ryan the fuel to ridicule me today," Madison chuckled nervously.

"Ugh, don't mind him. He's a misogynistic schmuck," Allie replied, setting the newspaper down. "Plus, your outfit looks great today. A little light shimmer of eyeshadow, some mascara, and a little lipstick should do the trick."

Madison smiled as Allie stretched back in the chair with a big yawn. Allie could literally wear her streetwear to the office seconds after getting off a plane and the world would still tell her she's perfect.

"How do you do it?" Madison asked, leaning against the kitchen counter.

"Do what?" Allie asked, setting down the newspaper.

"Make all of this," Madison motioned to Allie. "Make it look so effortlessly good?"

Allie laughed. "By putting in a lot of effort. It's not effortless you know. Facials, expensive creams, hired stylists and specialists who decide what looks good and what doesn't. Years of being told not to trust myself when it comes to what to wear and to let others pick out my clothes just in case I go somewhere and get photographed," Allie explained. "It all became second nature to me over time and if you live in this world long enough, you'll understand what I mean."

"Sounds exhausting," Madison replied.

"It is. And on that note, I better start the process and get dressed for work. Give me about 30 minutes and we will head to the office?" Allie asked, getting up from the table.

"Take your time," Madison insisted trying to buy herself more time to figure out how to tell Allie the devastating news.

****

"Let's make this quick. I have a job to do," Ryan said, unbuttoning his blazer as she sat down in a chair across from Mitch McGowan.

"A job that you only have because I put you there, so let's not forget manners," Mitch replied, sitting up straighter in his chair. "Now that Madison and Allison have lost their venue, you need to make sure that Garrison knows before Allison has the chance to come up with a new plan. I want you to post about it on social media enough that news outlets pick up on it but subtle enough it flies under Allison's radar but that some of our big-name attendees who already have save the dates will see it and start asking about it."

Ryan sighed. "And why do we need to do this? They already don't have a venue. Allie is going fire Madison and when she does that she'll never catch up and get the party finished."

"Ryan, do I need to remind you the terms of our agreement?" Mitch asked rhetorically, standing up and walking to the window, no longer facing Ryan.

104

Ryan felt his jaw clench. "No. Fine, I'll post about it. Is that all?"

"No, we need to find a way to get Myles more involved with the magazine. I've seen him in his office too many days this week which means he's not connecting with Allison like we need him to," Mitch continued.

"Allison has been out of town this week. I believe most of her trip was spent with Brad Garrison in Los Angeles, hence why you've seen Myles, though I will work on a plan to get him in the Forever office more," Ryan replied. "Now if that's all, I need to go." Ryan stood up, rebuttoning his blazer.

"Let me know when Allison fires her assistant. I have some girls lined up to take her place on the off chance that Allison isn't fired first," Mitch said, turning back to face Ryan. "You may go."

Ryan nodded, leaving Mitch's office. He relaxed his shoulders as he made his way to the lobby of the building and out the front doors. He hated Mitch was every morsel of his being, but they had a deal that Ryan couldn't go back on now.

****

"Alright, get me up to date. Where are we on the plans?" Allie asked, sliding into the back of the car next to Madison.

"It's easier to explain at the office," Madison replied, rubbing her hands together to keep them from visibly shaking in front of Allie. Madison could feel the pit in her stomach widening.

"Alright, so how has the office been? Anything gossip worthy?" Allie asked excitedly.

Madison shook her head no, unable to get a word out and risk crying from the rising anxiety of having to tell Allie her big mistake.

"Okaaaaay? Madison, are you okay? You look like you are going to be sick," Allie said concerned. Madison nodded, giving Allie an encouraging look.

"Well then, I had a thought on the plane. What if Myles also did my headshots for my letter from the editor this month? I mean he did so well with the cover shoot, I'd hate to have his work squandered by a bad headshot earlier in the magazine," Allie explained.

"That sounds like a plan," Madison responded as they pulled up to their building in Piccadilly Circus. Madison drew in a deep breath feeling her lungs expand for what could be the last time, as Allie would kill her in less than ten minutes.

"Alright, just tell me, what did Ryan do while I was gone that has you all nervous and acting weird towards me?" Allie asked, turning to Madison.

"He didn't do anything really," Madison replied.

"Did you kiss him?" Allison pried. "You can tell me. I know you two have been hanging out."

"No, I didn't kiss him," Madison said quickly pretending to shutter at the thought.

"Okay, so what is it? You've been acting weird all morning. I don't want to blindly walk in there without knowing what is going on," Allie said. "We aren't getting out of the car until you tell me."

"We lost the venue!" Madison blurted out. Allie sat back in her seat, her eyes wide and eyebrows raised. "I don't know how it happened, I swear I checked the date on the paperwork one hundred times, but somehow, I put next year on there instead of this year. I'm so sorry Allie."

Allie sat in silence seething in anger and panic. "Did you leave the paperwork with anyone else?"

"Allie, I swear this is my fault," Madison replied.

"That's not what I asked. Did you, or did you not, leave the paperwork with anyone else before sending it to Altitude?" Allie repeated coldly.

"I left both sets with Ryan, but only for a few seconds each time," Madison sighed. "I couldn't get the copier to work and had a million other things that needed to get done. He offered to help send the paperwork off. I know you don't trust him, but he's been really helpful this week, and I really didn't think he would do something like this."

"I explicitly told you to not let that paperwork out of your sight and I also told you to not get attached to Ryan, to not trust him. You went and disobeyed me on both. I warned you and I think we both know what that means," Allie said, reaching for the door handle.

"Allie, you can't be serious. We will figure it out. Don't fire me over this, please. I really need this job," Madison begged.

"And I need someone who I can trust to do this job. So, you can either go upstairs now and pack your stuff, or go when no one else is in the office," Allie said, getting out of the car. Madison paused, a tear rolling down her cheek. "Enjoy your last day in London, Madison."

Madison broke into a cry as Allie shut the door and the car pulled away. Allie headed inside never looking back.

"Good morning," she heard from behind her as she waited for the elevator to open in front of her.

"Hello Ryan," Allie muttered.

"How was your trip?" Ryan asked, looking around hoping to see Madison nearby.

"I would really like to skip the unnecessary small talk today. Apparently, we have a lot more work to do for the first issue and launch party than I thought, but you should know all about that," Allie snapped, pressing the elevator call button again.

"So, she told you that we lost the venue, and by the looks of it you fired her on the spot," Ryan retorted.

"You're lucky I can't fire you," Allie replied as the elevator door opened. "How about you grab the next elevator."

Ryan nodded, taking a step back. As the doors of Allie's elevator closed, Ryan walked away from the elevators pulling out his phone to call Madison.

"I asked you to leave me alone," Madison answered the phone sniffling.

"Where are you?" Ryan asked sympathetically.

"Why do you even care? You got what you wanted. Allie fired me, she doesn't have a venue for the launch party, and you can now step up, secure a venue, rescue the magazine, and get promoted to Allie's job. Just leave me alone." Ryan shook his head as Madison hung up on him.

****

Madison made it back to Allie's townhouse just as it was starting to rain outside. She paused on her way up to the front door letting herself get soaked as she took in the garden around her. It was starting to turn green and come to life, just in time for her London adventure to die. She would never see the vibrant colors bloom in the bushes or discover what beautiful flowers were laying dormant waiting for their chance to come and wow anyone who walked through the garden. Time stood still as the rain penetrated Madison's cardigan and dress and melted away the small traces of make-up she managed to put on. Madison sat down on the brick path near the front door, letting the water continue to wash over her. She took her phone out to text her mom the bad news, knowing that when she returned home, a failure, her mom would remind her of their deal. As she started to piece the words together, an email notification with her flight itinerary flashed across the top of the screen.

"Tomorrow morning this all ends," Madison whispered to herself, clicking off her phone and heading into the house, and up the stairs to her room. Luckily, her shopping trip over the weekend wasn't too extravagant, allowing everything to simply fit back into her suitcases. After about ten minutes of packing everything away, still soak and wet from the rain, Madison stripped off her wet clothes, grabbed a towel and sat down on the bed, pulling her phone back out.

"Well, at least I don't have to post pictures on social media anymore," Madison muttered, opening Instagram. She scrolled through the photos of her feed, barely looking at any photos along the way. She just needed to numb herself, let her brain shut off and forget that in less than 24 hours she would be heading back home, a failure, an unemployed, fired nobody. Madison stood up suddenly as her eyes and fingers stopped on Forever London's latest post.

****

"Ryan! What in the hell is this!?" Allie yelled, storming into Ryan's office letting the door slam behind her as she held her phone out.

"It's today's post about the launch party. We said we would announce more details today, and since you told Clarissa the theme of the party, I figured we would follow through and post some more details for our attendees who follow us," Ryan said calmly, leaning back in his chair. "Is there a problem?"

"Is there a problem!? Are you fucking kidding me? You know what the problem is," Allie continued to yell.

"Allie, please refrain from yelling at me in the office. It's tacky," Ryan replied. "Also, no, I don't know what the problem is."

"Forever London is proud to announce more details regarding the Launch Party. Theme: Old Hollywood; Date and Time…blah blah blah…" Allie read aloud. "Location: Still to be determined. Not top secret, not information in your DMs, nope, 'Still to be determined.' Are you trying to tank the relaunch of this magazine before we even get it off the ground?"

"Allie, I am just reporting the actual details. I doubt anyone is going to read into like you are," Ryan answered keeping his cool. "Maybe you should take the day off. You seem tired."

Allie scoffed. "You asshole, I swear, if Mitch McGowan didn't have such a say in you working here, for whatever fucked up reason he does, I would fire your two-faced, privileged ass so fast. Do not test me."

"Talk about double standards," Ryan chuckled, leaning forward towards his desk.

"What does that mean?" Allie snapped.

"Did you or did you not just head to LA for a week, so you could run around with your fiancé planning a wedding, instead of being here to oversee your assistant who was well in over her head planning a party that 'Ms. American Hollywood Party Girl' should have been planning herself? Then again, you can just run to daddy to fix your problems and buy you another house in Malibu when things don't work out in London this time.

I hate to break it to you Allison, I'm not here because of Mitch McGowan, I am here because I worked my so called two-faced, privileged ass off to get to where I am. Now if you could please leave my office so that I can get to work on helping fix the mess you and Madison have made and get us a location for the party that would be splendid," Ryan said, motioning towards the door.

"You know nothing about me. Don't waste your time, I already have a location for the party," Allie lied, before exiting Ryan's office, all eyes on her as she walked back to her office.

****

Madison walked in and sat down at the bar ordering an old-fashioned from the bartender.

"Drinking alone this evening?" the bartender asked, pouring her a drink. "No Ryan tonight?"

Madison looked at him confused. "Just me."

"Ryan's a regular, usually comes in alone, except the time he met you here," the bartender continued, sliding Madison the glass.

"Yeah, I doubt we'll see Ryan again. I only came here because it's the only bar I actually know and since it's my last night in London figured it was a good enough time to drink. Tomorrow, I head back to the States and back to living under a rock on my mom's couch," Madison babbled before downing her drink.

"Sounds like London hasn't been so kind to you," the bartender answered, taking her glass back, starting a new drink.

"More like the people of London haven't been so good to me," Madison sighed, looking around at the empty seats around her.

"Maybe you just didn't find the right people. There are plenty of great people around," the bartender continued, passing Madison another drink as the front door opened. "And it looks like you were wrong about not seeing Ryan."

"Shit," Madison whispered as Ryan walked over to her.

"Well, well, well, if I didn't know better, I'd say you were waiting for me here," Ryan teased as he sat down next to Madison.

"I was actually just getting ready to leave," Madison said, pulling out her wallet.

"Madison, one more drink with me, that's it," Ryan requested, motioning to the bartender.

"Ryan, I don't want to hear anything you have to say," Madison replied.

"Just hear me out, I swear I didn't have anything to do with changing the dates on those documents. I don't know how it happened, but either way, I wanted to let you know that if you need a recommendation for any future job feel free to put down my name and information. I think Allie acted rashly today," Ryan said, taking a sip of the drink placed in front of him.

110

"The way she looked at me was like I just told her that I killed her best friend and hid the body in her townhome," Madison chuckled. "London just wasn't the place for me."

"I don't think you've spent enough time in London to know whether or not it was the place for you," Ryan replied.

"I mean it's just another city. Maybe I should try a small town, you know, like the ones you see on tv where everyone knows everyone, and the town does wacky festivals together all the time. Those places seem way nicer than big cities like this," Madison continued, sipping on her third drink. She could feel her cheeks starting to burn and her head starting to get lighter. In all of the drama from the day she realized she forgot to eat. She did remember to have coffee and make a couple of drinks from Allie's bar cart before coming here for a few drinks that were all starting to catch up to her.

"Oh, come on, London has so much more to offer than that," Ryan laughed, scooching closer to Madison.

"Stop being so nice to me," Madison replied, sliding off the barstool and stumbling a bit.

"Whoa, looks like you could use some air," Ryan said, reaching out to steady Madison. Madison shook him off, grabbing her drink and finishing it off.

"I can take care of myself," Madison said, pushing Ryan away. Ryan laughed, shaking his head as he took a step back from Madison.

"Put the drinks on my tab," he said to the bartender who nodded in reply. "Madison let's get you home."

"I don't want to go home. I want to go to the one place that made me feel good this whole time. I want to go to the park," Madison said, heading towards the door.

"Which park?" Ryan asked, walking behind her.

"Hyde Park," Madison responded with excitement, her head feeling light and airy, all of her cares starting to fade away.

"Sure, it's your last night in London, whatever you want to do, we can do," Ryan laughed, guiding her out of the bar. "Should we take my car?"

"No, I want to take the Tube. I haven't had a chance to take it yet," Madison replied.

"Well, then it's a good thing I ran into you. There's no way you can navigate it alone like this," Ryan said, linking his arm with hers and guiding her to the nearest tube station.

After about thirty minutes of travelling and walking, Madison and Ryan stood outside the gates to Hyde Park. Madison felt a surge of drunken glee pulsate through her as the magic she first felt swirled together with the whiskey in her system. Ryan watched as Madison started down a dirt path lined with giant trees. She was smiling and giggling. For once she was carefree and unguarded, not worrying about her outfit, how people looked at her, or whether she would have a job at the end of this escapade. She was more beautiful to Ryan now than ever before.

"How can you live in a place like London and not want to spend all of your time here?" Madison called out to him shaking her head.

"It's been quite some time since I've even been over here," Ryan admitted, jogging to catch up to her. "I forgot how beautiful it can be."

"And magical. Don't you just feel magic when you are in those gates?" Madison asked, her eyes sparkling with wonder. "Do you want to see my favorite part of the park?"

"Lead the way," Ryan insisted. Madison nodded with a giant smile plastered on her face. They walked around for about an hour, as the sun began to set, they took a seat in the grass to watch the sky turn pink and orange.

"You know, this is actually all okay. I didn't want to come to London to begin with," Madison said, breaking the silence. "I was perfectly content with staying in California."

"What made you come to London then?" Ryan asked.

"My mom. She was about to kick me out if I didn't get a job," Madison confessed. "She set me up with the interview and job at Forever London, and the rest was a blur. I wasn't ready to take the jump into a big job like this one, let alone moving across the globe."

"But you did it," Ryan chimed in.

"And I failed, so there's that," Madison said, leaning back onto her elbows, her legs stretching out in front of her. She closed her eyes, feeling the wind tickle her cheeks. *Magic.* Madison let herself relax next to Ryan as the air started to turn cold and the darkness set in.

"You know you are confusing, Ryan Eliot," Madison said, scooting closer to Ryan for warmth.

"How so?" Ryan asked, knowing fairly well what she meant. He felt her shiver a little next to him and pulled her in closer to him.

"Well for starters, this," she said, resting her head on this shoulder. "Some days you are kind, funny, and lighthearted, but then it's like you shift and become mean, guarded, and kind of a dick."

"The same could be said about you. Well, actually, I think I'm just confused when I'm with you," Ryan admitted.

Madison straightened up a bit so she could see Ryan's expression. His face was gentle and soft with the hints of twilight starting to fade. "What do you mean?"

"It sounds cliché and like a line, but when I'm with you, it's like the part of me that I've worked hard to lock away is unleashed. You make me want to be a better person by just being in your presence," Ryan explained, looking down at Madison who was still curled up next to him. She reached down tucking some hair behind her ear and softly tracing her chin. "I'm sad to see you go."

Madison let herself melt into Ryan. There would be no tomorrow where their actions here and now would be able to fill an office with regret. Surely, he was about to kiss her, she could feel the electricity between them pulsating through her body. His hand lingered at the bottom of her chin tilting her face up to his, his eyes locked on hers. She needed this, the perfect memory of London. She could feel her heart racing as his warm breath got closer to her face, their lips almost touching, the perfect kiss...interrupted by the ring of Ryan's phone. Ryan groaned, pulling away from Madison.

"I have to take this," he said, looking at his phone as he stood up. "Wait right here."

Madison sighed, her heart sinking low enough in her chest that her head finally had the space to sober up. She watched Ryan pace back and forth talking quietly on the phone along the edge of the lake. She closed her eyes, pulling her knees into her chest for warmth. As she reopened her eyes to see Ryan walking back up, she could also hear faint music playing in the distance.

"Do you hear music too? Where is it coming from?" she asked, looking around.

"I'm not sure, want to walk around and find it? The park is closing soon anyways, so we better get moving," Ryan replied, reaching out his hand to help Madison up.

Madison froze at the gesture, shaking her head. "You don't need to keep up the charade. Me leaving was part of your plan, you don't have to be nice to me now."

"That makes very little sense after what just almost happened between us," Ryan replied, as Madison stood up without his help. Madison shook her head, looking around the park for the source of the music. In the distance she could see a gazebo with string lights lighting up a small pavilion around it.

"Let's go over there," Madison replied, ignoring Ryan's latest comment and the almost kiss.

As they approached the area, Madison could see a giant open field near the edge of the park. The music was still playing at the gazebo, a man with his violin. "*Magic*," Madison thought, taking it all in. The sun was almost fully gone by now and the lamps along the tree lined path were starting to turn on. Madison spun around slowly letting the beginning of an idea start to grow in her head.

"That's it," she whispered, her eyes growing with excitement again.

"What is?" Ryan asked. Madison stopped facing away from Ryan, fully sobering up as her mind started to spin with possibility.

"Nothing, I'm sorry to do this but I've got to go," Madison replied hastily.

"At least let me walk you back," Ryan suggested. "I want to finish our conversation."

"Nah, I'm good. I think you've done and said enough this week. Thanks for the drinks and the walk. Umm, have a good weekend, see you Monday!" Madison replied, taking a few steps back from Ryan.

"Um, okay," Ryan replied confused, watching Madison quickly walk away from him.

Once Madison exited the park, she pulled out her phone dialing Allie. The call went straight to voicemail. "Allison, I know you fired me, but I have an idea, something way better than Altitude. I'm heading back to the house. Give me one more chance to make this right. See you soon."

Madison felt herself smile as she tucked her phone back into her pocket. "Just you wait London, we are about to throw the most beautiful party Hyde Park has ever seen," she whispered to herself.

Episode 10- Off to the Races

Myles rounded the corner of the park. It was beginning to get dark outside and cutting through Hyde Park was the fastest way to his flat. He felt his phone vibrate in his pocket. Pulling it out he saw Allie's name pop up. They hadn't spoken to one another since getting waffles almost a week ago. Clearing his throat, he answered the phone.

"Hello?"

"Hey Myles, its Allie, how are you?" she answered.

"I'm doing well. What can I do for you?" he replied, feeling nervous.

"Glad to hear it. I was hoping we could grab a coffee tomorrow morning," Allie said, her voice smooth and calming.

Myles felt his body heat up as his thoughts began to race. He continued walking down the path. "Is there any certain reason why?"

He heard Allie sigh on the other end of the phone. As she began to explain her reason for coffee tomorrow, he saw Madison and Ryan near the gazebo. He watched them from afar, stepping behind a tree so he wouldn't be spotted. Madison stood a little further ahead of Ryan, staring at the open field.

"So, what do think?" Allie asked. "I know it's a lot to ask, but…Myles? Are you there?"

"Did you know Ryan and your assistant are out in the park together tonight?" Myles asked, watching Madison walk away from Ryan, drawing out her phone.

"She's not my assistant anymore, so frankly I don't care who she is out with tonight. Interestingly enough, she's calling me now," Allie replied, clicking the ignore button to dismiss Madison's call.

"What do you mean she's not your assistant anymore?" Myles asked, continuing the path out of Hyde Park as Madison disappeared out of sight.

"Long story short, she screwed up big. I can explain more tomorrow if you want to grab coffee?" Allie asked.

"Yes, just text me where to meet at," Myles answered.

"Sounds like a plan!" Allie exclaimed.

****

"Allie!" Madison shouted walking into the townhouse. Madison could hear some music playing upstairs. Setting her bag and purse down she headed up the stairs to find Allie unpacking her suitcase with a glass of wine and some Nat Cole King. "Allie! I've been trying to call you."

"I know," Allie replied, swaying to the music as she put a dress on its hanger. "I've been ignoring you."

"I have an idea for the launch party," Madison said, stepping into the room. "An idea that if done right would be better than our plans at Altitude ever were."

"I don't really care," Allie said, grabbing the glass of wine. "The second you let Ryan in, you unraveled all the work we did regarding the launch party. I asked you to watch out for him. I told you to not leave the papers with him, but you couldn't help yourself. You fell victim to his charms and now we don't have a venue for the launch party and it's only a matter of time until there's an article or a hundred already calling us a flop. Whatever your idea is, I'm sure it's great, but it's not going to be enough to fix this."

"But what if it was?" Madison asked.

"I doubt it will be. Madison I really don't have time for this. You should get some sleep, you have an early flight," Allie answered, turning towards her closet to hang up a few sundresses starting to sway to the music.

"Allie, just listen. I'm talking about having it in a giant see-through tent on the edge of Hyde Park. Lanterns in the park along the paths, lanterns in the tree. Old Hollywood, but like really old and glamourous," Madison blurted out. Allie stopped swaying, sipping her wine again, and staring at the wall ahead of her.

Madison watched as Allie tilted her head, cradling her wine glass between her hands, processing the idea Madison blurted out. Allie spent all day trying to find a new place to hold the party and after hours of phone calls and brainstorming sessions with Clarissa she still didn't have anything, but this idea was good.

"Do you think you can pull it off?" Allison asked. "Permits, the tent, rentals, bartenders, caterers, decorations, a red carpet, invites, all of it?"

117

Madison let a deep exhale escape from her. "I think I could do it. Just give me another chance. Please, I promise to make this right."

Allie nodded slowly. "On one condition: no more lunches, side talks, bar meetups, cute notes, walks in the park, coffee dates, or dinners with Ryan. If I catch you two alone, I will fire you and there will not be another chance."

"Deal," Madison replied, her voice shaking.

"Then I guess you will need to cancel your flight. Don't let me down again Madison," Allie said, turning towards Madison. "There's more wine downstairs. It really makes the unpacking process move a lot quicker."

"Thanks, but I think I'm good. I have a lot of work ahead," Madison replied, heading back out of the room.

"Madison, you better pull this off. You ass isn't the only one on the line here," Allie imparted, before Madison got too far out of range.

"Understood."

****

"She just barged in and begged me for a second chance, saying she has all of these grand plans for the launch party taking place at Hyde Park," Allie continued to explain to Myles as she sat down with her latte.

"So, the party will be in Hyde Park then?" Myles asked. He sat uncomfortably straight in his chair. Allie text messaged him to meet her early this morning. Confused as to the importance or even the reason of this meeting. Allie was vibrant and chatty, as if she was talking to the old Myles, the one who hadn't broken her heart in years past.

"Apparently. I'm meeting with her later to discuss the details she's worked out. It was so frustrating to come back and find out that she lost the original venue because she fell victim to the charms of Ryan Eliot. I swear he's just out for my job," Allie continued, pulling her knees in towards her chest, getting comfy in the plush chair where she sat.

"I'm sure she will do fine," Myles replied, slowly sipping his coffee. "As long as she has you as a mentor, she'll be fine."

"We'll see. It's just so frustrating that I told her to be careful, to not let herself get tangled up with Ryan and the second she did, we lost the venue and if she doesn't pull this off, then we are going to lose our jobs. I leave for one week and it all goes to shit," Allie chuckled.

"That's right, where did you go again?' Myles asked.

"Back to California. I was," Allie paused taking a sip of her drink trying to decide carefully what to say next. "I was helping Mr. Garrison out with some items at the LA offices."

"And Nick? How is he?" Myles asked. Allie studied Myles's face before answering. He was searching for an answer about her love life.

"Nick is fine, he's been working really hard on a few scripts for my father lately, so we don't get to chat too often, just text messages and emails when we each get a second," Allie responded. Myles shifted uncomfortably in his chair again. "Anyways, the reason I wanted to grab coffee with you, was to ask you to do my headshots for my letter from the editor. Would you be interested? You can say no, I won't be offended," said as silence settled in between them.

"It's not that I want to say no, I just wonder if it would be a good idea for us to work so close together," Myles replied. "We still haven't discussed what happened between us."

"About the potential proposal? We really don't need to discuss it," Allie said hastily.

"You know I'm talking about Lorraine," Myles countered in a soft quiet voice. Allie straightened out her legs as the memory of seeing Lorraine in a sheet leaving Myles's room came flooding back in. Allie drew in a long deep breath, letting it out slowly, her chest trembling at her name.

"The photographs are just business Myles, there's no need to rehash the past in order to take some silly little headshots," Allie retorted, finishing off her coffee and standing up. "I need to head to an event. Let me know your answer by the end of Monday. If I don't hear from you then I'll find someone else."

"Allie," Myles said tenderly.

Allie forced a smile, shaking her head. "Let me know by the end of Monday," she said before grabbing her jean jacket and leaving.

****

Madison paced back and forth in her room, trying to get a hold of her third tent company. In just one weekend she secured some the verbal promises to use the park, rearranged the catering, and secured about a hundred LED lanterns. Getting a large clear tent, however, turned out to be more trouble than she thought. After about ten minutes on hold a voice came on the line stating that the company did not have any tents available that night.

She heard Allie call out from downstairs, it was time to head to the office. Madison straightened out her striped blazer and slid her feet into her black booties. Allie called out again.

"Here we go," Madison sighed. Sure, going into the office was a normal thing to do on a Monday, but now the stakes were higher. She felt a little sad going back, knowing she would have to ignore Ryan. Sure, she was mad at him, but the thought of having to ignore any sort of glance, any act of kindness, any comment from him, having to ignore him altogether after their almost kiss, made Madison feel sad and alone. Madison made her way downstairs, carrying a couple of binders in one arm.

"It's about time," Allie said, as Madison reached the bottom of the stairs. "You can give me an update on the party as we drive." Madison nodded before following Allie to the car. As the car made its way through the London streets Madison gave a thorough rundown of where she was at with the party plans.

****

Ryan hovered at the elevator doors. He had an idea, a way to save the launch party and get Allie to trust him. He paced back and forth, stopping as he heard the elevator moving.

"Ryan, I thought we talked about this," Allie said, stepping off the elevator.

"I wanted to catch you, to talk about the launch—" Ryan stopped as he saw Madison step out from behind Allie.

"I think you'll find that the launch party planning is back on track. "Now if you will excuse us, we have a lot of work ahead of us to fix the mess you made," Allie said, stepping around Ryan.

Madison kept her gaze on the back of Allie's head. She could feel Ryan's eyes piercing into her as she walked on by. Ryan stared at her, watching as she disappeared from the lobby. A smirk crossed his face. "Well, I'll be damned," he muttered buttoning his blazer.

****

Myles: I'll do it.
Allie: THANK YOU! :)

Allie smiled looking down at the words on the screen. After abruptly leaving coffee yesterday, thanks to the mention of she-who-must-not-be-named, Allie figured she would never see Myles again.

"He's in," Allie said as Madison entered her office.

"Did you think he would decline?" Madison asked.

"There's always the chance he could. Things are still odd between us to an extent," Allie replied. "Anyways, do you have the marketing plans?"

"Yes, Clarissa just sent them over to me. The creative team is going to do a virtual tour of the offices on Thursday. It looks like you are slated to be spotlighted and film some video content on Friday. Then after that each weekday leading up to the party a portion of the party will be posted until the end of the week when we then focus on the red carpet and the party," Madison reported.

"Can you believe we are about three weeks or so out from the first issue of the relaunch?" Allie asked. "It's very overwhelming and yet exciting at the same time."

Ryan appeared in the doorway. Allie nodded, waving him in. "Madison, please go check on how the book is coming along. Also, please work with Clarissa to get Brynn and Myles into the schedule for the social media spotlights."

Madison nodded, walking past Ryan, her head down as she passed.

"Wait," Ryan interjected before Madison was out of earshot. "No need to work with Clarissa on the social media schedule. Just stop by my office later and we can discuss it. I have more details than Clarissa on that."

"Well then, actually, just email the schedule over to me Ryan and I'll handle it," Allie interjected.

121

Ryan looked at Madison and then back at Allie. "Okay then," he said before walking away back towards his office. Madison looked up to see him leaving, shutting the door to his office behind him.

Madison sighed as she leaned back in her chair, pulling her hair up into a ponytail with only her hands and letting it fall back down to her shoulders. Her eyes flickered over towards Ryan's office. The door was still shut. It was 2PM now and he had yet to open it since she watched him shut it earlier today.

"Madison, I'm running out for a late lunch and then will finish working from home this afternoon. I expect to see you and the book around 7. Don't forget our deal," Allie said, leaving.

Madison nodded, her gaze returning to her computer screen. She stared at her browser as she heard Allie's footsteps disappear down the hall. After a minute, she let herself sink back into her chair, finally relaxing. She reached for her phone, dialing Charlie's number.

"What can I do for you Madison?" Charlie answered, loud music playing in the background.

"I need a favor," Madison said in a hushed voice, spinning around in her chair, her back to the office.

"Go on," Charlie replied.

"I need help finding a large clear tent for our launch party. Do you have any contacts? Do you know anyone who could help?" Madison asked.

"I'll ask around. Sorry again about the venue. If there was a way, I could bump this party for your event I would," Charlie apologized.

"It's okay, it's not your fault. Let me know if you get any leads on the tent," Madison replied before hanging up her phone.

"So that's how you did it. You came up with an alternative party plan and got Allison to give you one final chance," Ryan said, stepping up to Madison's desk.

"Ryan, not now," Madison replied.

"Let me guess, there's more to your deal with Allie. You are forbidden to talk to me," Ryan guessed.

"More like I have nothing to say to you after what you did," Madison replied coldly.

"How many times do I have to tell you that I didn't do anything to that paperwork?" Ryan asked, his voice low as he leaned in towards Madison's desk.

"Ryan, honestly, I don't think you can ever change my mind about it. Now leave me alone, before you do actually get me fired," Madison said, her eyes glued on the edge of her desk.

"So, she did threaten to fire you if she caught us speaking, but if she's gone for the day, then how will she find out? Can we please just finish what we started in the park?" Ryan asked cheekily.

"Ryan, go away!" Madison snapped, looking up to meet Ryan's gaze.

"Let me at least help. I can find someone with a tent like the one you need. I've attended many outdoor weddings, know people who have worked on the Great British Baking Show, dated a few Harry Potter extras and producers… I know people who know people. Let me help you," Ryan urged Madison.

"Go. Away. I don't want your help," Madison replied.

"Suit yourself," Ryan said, stepping back. Madison watched Ryan head back towards his office, summoning his assistant into his office. Madison felt her stomach churn as he shut the door.

A couple hours later, Madison shut down her computer, heading toward the breakroom to grab water while she waited for the book. Charlie didn't come through with any leads and Madison's internet searches were coming up short. She needed a miracle at this point to pull this off the way she told Allie it would go. Madison rubbed her eyes before opening her bottle of water. She was exhausted and lonelier than ever before.

Tired and ready to head home, she made her way back to her desk. She smiled seeing the book on the corner of it. "Thank goodness," she sighed, grabbing her bag and a coat before picking up the book to leave. As she picked up the book, she noticed a thin folder under it with a note on top:

Mads-

I know you'll never believe me when I say that I didn't mess with your paperwork, but this should help you with the launch party. No tricks, no games, just names and numbers of people who can help with the tent issue you are having. If you don't want to use them, then don't. Good luck. -Ryan

PS Shredding this is probably the best option.

Madison sat down in her chair, opening the folder. Inside she found a list of names and contact information for companies with tents, red carpets, tables, chandeliers, bars and more. She shook her head smirking a bit before tucking the folder into her bag. She read his note again before heading towards the shredder, to rid of this last piece of genuine correspondence between them.

"Please don't let me be wrong about this," she whispered as she slid the paper into the running shredder, demolishing Ryan's note.

Episode 11- Broken Heels

"Allie are you ready?" Clarissa called out from down the hall of the townhouse. "I think we should do a quick 'this is my morning routine' video for the social media post today."

"Do we have to?" Allie replied, calling out from her room.

"Yes," Clarissa replied walking into Allie's room. "After this, let's do a short tour of your closet. We can then head to the office and then we will need to do a couple of interviews for the press. Then we can do a short video about your workday for the website and call it quits."

"God this sounds horrible. Honestly, who wants to watch this?" Allie asked, rolling her eyes as she spread her make-up items on the counter for easy access.

"Well, my closet sneak peek video gave us an influx of about 500 followers and Ryan's tour of his favorite date spot gave us about 350 followers, so I think this will be helpful. People like to see into the lives of glamorous people," Clarissa said.

Allie laughed. "Yeah right."

"I think you have more power and influence than you might think. People want to know what it's like to have money and will do anything to reach the level of fame and success they see," Olivia, the Forever stylist, interjected finishing Allie's make-up.

"If people only actually knew what it was like to have money, they'd realize their lives aren't quite so bad," Allie retorted. "But fine, if it's going to help us become more and more relevant, I'll do it all."

"Now that's the spirit, however, on your live stream, I wouldn't talk about the woes of being rich or the daughter of a famous Hollywood director and all the misfortunes that come with it. People just want happy things on their social media feeds. They want to be inspired," Clarissa said, getting her phone out to log into Forever London's social media platforms.

"Typical," Allie muttered, leaving her bedroom to grab water from a table set-up in the hallway.

"What is?" Madison asked, scrunching her eyebrows at Allie as she approached.

"The fact that everyone just thinks my life is easy and glamorous and that it can never be anything less than that. You know it's not fun growing up in a fishbowl, where everyone watches you to see if you turn out pretty or ugly, fat or thin, talented or just a rich girl with dad's credit card. And I get it, there are people who can't afford to always put a meal on the table or a car to get to work, but for once I would like people to realize that we still all share one simple need at the end of the day: the need to feel loved and cared about. Not placed on a pedestal and forgotten, not given vacations and luxurious gifts in between movie shoots and premieres. Just simple love," Allie ranted. "But nevertheless, let's just get this make-up routine video filmed and posted."

Madison nodded in agreement. She sympathized with Allie. She also just wanted to feel loved, but a little money wouldn't hurt either.

****

"Thanks again for doing this Myles. It doesn't need to be fancy. Just a few pictures and we should be good to go," Allie rattled off, trying to calm her nerves.

"Alright," Myles replied, shrugging his shoulders. "How about we start with you at your desk. I want to take a few pictures of you working to give you some options. Just pretend to be writing something."

"Like this?" Allie asked, her hands trembling as she faked writing a to do list.

"Roll your shoulders back," Myles directed. Allie listened, rolling her shoulders back, immediately straightening her body up.

"Good, now look up at me," Myles said, as he started taking pictures. Allie could see the excitement in him as he moved around her taking photos. He was a natural behind the camera as he moved back and forth, capturing different angles of her sitting.

"I like the little smirk you have going on there," he laughed, pulling the camera away from his face to look at the recent pictures he took. "It's almost as if…"

"As if what?" Allie asked.

"Oh, it doesn't matter," Myles answered. "Shall we try some standing by the window?"

"As if what? You can tell me," Allie said, playfully grabbing Myles's arm as she headed over to the window.

"As if you were looking at someone you fancied," Myles confessed, his cheeks turning red. Allie let go of his arm, shrugging her shoulders in response as she continued towards the window.

"Do you want my standing or sitting?" she asked, ignoring his last statement.

"Standing first and then we can try sitting," Myles suggested. "Stand right about there."

"Here?" Allie asked, leaning against the edge of the window.

"Perfect, except…may I?" Myles asked approaching Allie to fix her hair.

"Um, sure," she replied, her heart racing as he reached up to tuck some hair behind her ear. She held her breath as his hand lightly brushed her cheek.

"There that's better," he said, taking a step back, bringing his camera up to his eye. "Try uncrossing your arms. Yeah, like that."

"Myles, I noticed you didn't RSVP for a plus one to the launch party. Are you not bringing a date?" Allie asked, as he moved around her taking pictures.

"Correct. Now try sitting in the green chair to your left," Myles said pointing to the chair near the window. "Actually, let's turn it slightly to get the shelves behind you in the background."

"Are you not seeing Lorraine then?" Allie asked, moving the chair.

"No. I haven't even spoken to her in a few years," he replied snapping a couple candid shots. "I take it Nick is flying out for the party?"

Allie took a seat in the chair. "He's flying out a few days before."

"That's great. He should support you in your big moments," Myles replied, feeling a shift in the energy of the room. "Relax your shoulders a bit, you look a little stiff." Allie rolled her shoulders back again, holding her breath a little with the suffocating tension building in the room.

"Okay, let's try a little bit of a smile. You look a little sad," Myles said snapping more pictures. Allie forced a professional smile.

"Hey Allie," Madison said appearing in the doorway of her office. "Brad Garrison is here. He's checking in with office staff right now, but he's requested that I clear your next hour or so to meet with him." Myles stopped snapping photos, taking a step back to look at the photos he recently took.

Allie nodded to Madison. "Just give us a moment," she said motioning to Madison to close the door. "Myles, you really should bring someone to the party. It's a big night for you. You deserve to have someone who loves and supports you by your side."

"Well, we don't all have someone like Nick in our lives, someone who is there to comfort us any time something goes wrong, any time someone wrongs us," Myles chuckled shaking his head as he returned his camera to its bag.

"Well, I'm sure Ryan can at least find you some eye-candy for the night. He seems to know a lot of models who are always looking to go to parties," Allie replied.

"Why are you so concerned that I'm going stag to this party?" Myles asked.

"I'm not. I'm just suggesting that you bring someone," Allie replied defensively.

"If you are worried that I'm going to ruin something between you and Nick, I think we both know I'm not trying to ruin your relationship. I'm happy with the way things are for each of us. The worst that will happen is that he will show up and give me a nice shiner like he threatened to do if we were ever in the same place at the same time," Myles replied cheekily. "But here's that thing, if you are going to marry him, then marry him. If you are in love with him, then be in love with him. I'm not going to get in the way of that. What we had was a long time ago, I think it is time we stop trying to understand each other, stop trying to interfere with each other's lives, and just let each other live the life they are destined to live. I don't tell you who to bring to a party, so please, don't tell me."

Allie opened her mouth to reply but closed it at the sound of Brad Garrison outside her door. Myles picked up his bag from the table and nodded to Allie. "I'll see you at the party. I'll be the one there without a date," he said, winking at her before turning to leave her office.

"Myles, wait," Allie said, but it was too late, he was already walking out of her office and shaking hands with Mr. Garrison. Allie stood up, straightening out her white dress before heading to greet her boss.

"Oh, I hope you don't mind me dropping in to check out how things are going," Mr. Garrison said, stepping into her office.

"Not at all, though I would have been more than happy to send you an email with all of the party plans and a mock-up of the first issue," Allie chirped, inviting Mr. Garrison in.

"I can't help but notice that the McGowan boy is hanging out in the office. Do you want to tell me anything?" Mr. Garrison asked, taking a seat across from Allie at her desk.

"He's our top photographer," she paused trying to pick her next words carefully. "I'm just as shocked as you are. It's a long story as to how he got here, but his photos are gorgeous. Here, take a look for yourself," Allie suggested, sliding the book over to Mr. Garrison.

"I will say, he's got a good eye," Mr. Garrison agreed, flipping through the pages of the book. "The issue looks to be shaping up well. I'd like to see the advertisements. Do you have those yet?"

"I'm afraid that Ryan and Mitch McGowan are still working those out. I'll send you an updated copy as soon as we have it," Allie responded.

"Seems like you are cutting it a little close," Mr. Garrison commented. "Please call Mitch and get the advertising this afternoon."

"I prefer to let Ryan handle relations with McGowan's advertising firm," Allie answered.

"Do I need to step in?" Mr. Garrison asked, closing the book as he leaned back in the chair.

"Why would you think that?" Allie asked.

"I remember a girl who came to me not so long ago, looking for a job, something to keep her busy because a boy had broken her heart not too long ago and she was on the verge of losing her will to live. She soon rose through the ranks to this very job, but the concern of the boy never dissipated. That boy being the McGowan boy. I warned you when I gave you this job that if it was too much at any point, I would pull you out of here. If working with Mitch McGowan or Myles creates too much drama, has any effect on my magazine, or causes you to relapse into the girl I met a few years back, then you know what I'll have to do," Mr. Garrison explained.

Allie nodded in return. "Understood."

"Good. Now tell me why we are no longer having the party at Altitude," Mr. Garrison requested.

****

Madison brought in the last of the salads and sandwiches, arranging them on the table so that all the names of the orders were easy to see. Allie, Clarissa, Ryan, and a few other key staff members were having lunch today to finalize the layout of the first issue. Madison grabbed her salad and set it on a chair in the corner. Allie needed her to take down any notes they may have, meaning Madison had to sit in a room with Ryan without looking at him or speaking a word that may come across as too friendly in Allie's mind.

She could see Allie heading over chatting away with Clarissa. Beyond Allie, Madison could see Ryan running his hands through his hair as he left his office heading toward the conference room. It had been over a week and a half since he left the folder with helpful items on her desk. She never got to properly thank him for helping her secure a tent for the party and she probably never would be able to with Allie's eyes constantly on the two of them in the office.

Allie grabbed her salad from the table without a word to Madison. Things were still pretty tense between them in the office and at home. Every now and then Allie would be friendly but usually it was business only between them.

"Now, everyone, the final mock-up of the issue is going to be displayed on the large screen for us to discuss and decide on any last-minute changes. We will start with the cover," Allie said, addressing the group now sitting around the table.

For the next two hours, the small group of staff members poured over every detail of each page of the first issue. Madison took notes in the corner, keeping her opinions to herself. Every now and then she would steal a quick glance at Ryan, who remained abnormally quiet as the group went through every single page, including the advertisements he helped secure. The only time he spoke up was on Allie's letter from the editor picture choice, stating that he "quite enjoyed the very obviously staged photo of her writing at her desk" and that he "didn't think she could look more human than in a picture like that."

Madison could have sworn she caught him looking in her direction a time or two, but every time she looked up from her notes, he was facing forward again. As the team finalized the back cover, Madison saved her notes, sending them in an email to Allie.

"Alright, I think that about does it," Allie said ending the meeting. "Thank you everyone for your hard work on this first issue. I think we are going to have a very successful launch."

"Speaking of launch, I'm curious, who is everyone bringing to the launch party? Anyone tabloid worthy?" Ryan asked brazenly to the room. "Clarissa, any chance you've wooed a young prince to come?"

Clarissa laughed. "Oh, stop it, you know I haven't been out with him in ages. I'm just bringing this cute guy I met at a pub recently. Which model are you bringing to this little soiree?"

"Oh, you know, I only decide which lucky lady it is going to be right before the party. I can't have her thinking I'm going to care about her beyond the party. If you tell a woman you are bringing her to a huge magazine launch party with celebrities and the like there more than 12 hours before the actual party, she starts thinking you care or she starts planning what celebrity to try and leave with at the end of the night. So, I guess we will just have to wait and see who I decide to bring," Ryan replied with a wink to Clarissa.

"You surely know how to make a woman feel special Ryan Eliot," Clarissa teased. Madison felt her stomach churn at the sight of Ryan and Clarissa flirting in front of everyone.

"How about you Allie? Are we finally going to meet this man of yours?" Clarissa asked, shifting everyone's attention to Allie. Madison looked at her closed laptop, avoiding the temptation to look up at Ryan. Her heart was slowly fracturing inside her chest imagining him kissing someone else in the glow of a lantern near the lake.

"If you must know, Nick is coming out for the party. He's flying in first thing tomorrow morning," Allie replied, shooting Clarissa a sharp look.

"Does your London boyfriend, Myles, know that your fiancé from California is coming here?" Ryan asked, shifting the energy of the room.

"On that note, I think it's time we all got to work on the items we just discussed. I expect to have the final edits in by tomorrow at noon. We need to send the first issue to the printers by 6PM tomorrow for it to be ready to send out to distributors in a couple of days," Allie replied attempting to diffuse the tension now filling the room.

"Clarissa and I are heading out early for drinks before her dress fitting if you want to tag along. I think you've earned a break this week," Allie offered as Madison began cleaning up the remaining condiments from the lunch spread.

"I have quite a few details to finish up on the party, so I'm going to pass this time," Madison replied graciously. She looked around the room for other items to clean up as everyone began to leave, seeing Ryan already heading back to his office.

"Glad to see you taking this seriously," Allie said, heading towards the door. "Oh, and Madison, we *all* can't wait to see how everything turns out."

"Whoa, let me help you with that," Ryan said, lunging for the papers starting to fall off the top of the boxes Madison carried into the lobby of Garrison Publishing.

"It's fine, I got it," Madison snapped as Ryan pushed the papers back in top of the boxes.

"Let me at least get the door for you," Ryan suggested.

"Ryan honestly, I don't need any more of your help. Thank you for the lists you gave me to get started, but I don't need any more help from you," Madison replied, setting the boxes down on a bench in the lobby. It was quiet around them. The lights were low, illuminating very little in the large lobby. "What are you doing here anyways? It's almost midnight."

"I could ask you the same," Ryan laughed. "I forgot something in my office, so I came back to retrieve it."

"Sure, in the middle of the night," Madison scoffed rolling her eyes. "What did you really come back here for Ryan?"

"Fine, you caught me. I had a feeling you were still here, and I wanted to see if you needed any help or I guess if you would let me help you with anything else. We are only a couple days from the party and Allie seems to be leaving earlier every day. I figured you were still here, and I was right," Ryan answered honestly. Madison stared at him shaking her head, a fury in her eyes. "By the look on your face, you really don't want my help it seems."

"What part of if you and I are caught speaking to each other I will lose my job do you not understand?" Madison replied angrily, stepping away from Ryan and her stack of boxes. "Also, what makes you think I would want your help anyways after the way you embarrassed Allie today? I just don't get it. You are condescending and rude to everyone else in the office, and then you are a totally different person to me. I don't get it. I don't want to get it. I just want you to leave me alone."

"But is that what you *really* want?" Ryan asked, pausing to sit down on the bench. "Because I think you want to see what could be between us. I think you know that I like you, that I've not seen a single model since the night we went to Platform 9 and ¾; that I've been doing everything I can to make sure you are successful and keep your job, while trying to still be close to you. The night you thought would be your last, when we were there in the park, I was trying to explain that I have feelings for you and that's why I treat you differently. And deep down I know you also feel the same for me."

"You're kidding right? You flirted with models in front of me every day since. You literally have a date to the party. Believe me we all heard you talking about it today. It's cruel to sit here and tell me you have feelings for me after all of that," Madison replied.

Ryan stood back up, walking over to Madison. "Madison, I'm bringing a date to the party because I can't be there with you, and it would tip Allie off if I showed up alone."

Madison took a step back from Ryan. "Tip her off to what? There's nothing between us."

Ryan grabbed her hand pulling her in closer to him. "Tell me you don't feel anything for me. Tell me you've never felt that spark between us and that I'm imagining it all and I'll leave you alone," he whispered in her ear.

Madison breathed him in. She could smell his signature cologne mixed with a tinge of sweat. She drew in a deep breath, slowly letting it out, trying to make her heart think rationally. Shaking her head, she pulled away from him. "Ryan, I can't do this with you," she whispered.

Ryan smirked at her, letting go of her hand. "That's not an answer. How about we do this. At the party, I'll give you a signal to meet me at our spot at the lake. I'll keep it discreet. If you show up, then I'll know you feel this spark between us. If you don't, then I'll leave you alone."

"Won't your date be upset if you just disappear?" Madison teased.

"I don't care what she thinks. Did you hear anything I said in that meeting?" Ryan asked, stepping closer to Madison again.

Madison felt goosebumps raise up on her arms at the closeness of Ryan to her. "Fine, the night of the party it is," she exhaled, stepping around him as her car pulled up outside. "I have to go."

Ryan nodded. "At least let me get the door for you," he suggested. Madison nodded picking up the stack of boxes before following him to the building door. Ryan stood back as the driver came around the car.

"I'll see you at the party," she said to Ryan, as the driver took the boxes from them both to load into the trunk of the car. Before he could answer, she disappeared into the backseat from the passenger side door.

"I'll see you then," he whispered in reply as the car pulled away. Madison couldn't hold in her smile any longer as she sat alone in the dark backseat of the car.

Episode 12- Mercy

"Well, it's not the beach house but this place is nice," Nick said rolling his luggage into Allie's townhouse.

"Right? Forever knows how to decorate a place," Allie laughed.

Madison could hear them from her bathroom upstairs. Allie began giving Nick a tour of the place, the two of them laughing as they wandered through the house. Madison smiled listening to them chatting away, as she finished brushing her teeth and headed downstairs.

"Good morning, Madison, this is Nick," Allie said as Madison entered into the kitchen. Nick and Allie were sitting at the table enjoying a cup of coffee and some pastries. "Nick this is Madison."

"Nice to meet you!" Madison exclaimed, grabbing a croissant off the table, sitting down to join them. "I've heard a lot about you, it's great to finally see you in person."

"I hope there hasn't been any trash talking though," Nick teased, pushing Allie's arm slightly.

"Nah, Allie's too nice for that," Madison replied, taking a bite of her croissant. Nick scoffed, taking a sip of his coffee as he rolled his eyes.

"That's not the Allie I know," Nick replied.

"Now, be nice. I'm a nice person. I wouldn't talk crap about you behind your back... I'd at least do it in front of your face," Allie laughed, leaning back in her chair, her legs stretching out over Nick's lap.

Madison liked how relaxed Allie looked next to Nick. All her walls seemed to be down in his presence. Nothing seemed calculated. Instead, she sat there, laughing, sipping her coffee, and enjoying pastries. There wasn't a care in the world in Allie's face, all rigidity, anger, tension, and anxiety of the past few weeks disappeared in his presence.

"Well, I'm going to head to the office to finalize a few more items before heading to the park to supervise the tent going up and the placement of items. I checked last night, and the edits made it into the first issue and was sent to the printer. Also, you have your final dress fitting for the party at two, and Nick, you have a tux fitting at noon," Madison instructed, getting up from the table.

"Thanks Madison. Wait, before you go, who are you bringing to the party?" Allie asked, turning to face Madison, without removing her legs from Nick's lap.

Madison scrunched her nose up, pursing her lips awkwardly, trying to think of a name of anyone she would bring to the party. "I'm not sure," she replied.

"Oh, come on, not you too. You need to have someone at the party. I mean, sure you'll be working a bit, but bring someone for when you aren't working. Once the party is going you'll want to have some fun. It's your first big party, you should enjoy it a bit," Allie encouraged Madison.

"If anyone knows anything about parties, it would be you," Nick teased. "Though it's been a while since you were actually invited to any big parties, hasn't it?"

"Shut up Nick!" Allie laughed, pushing Nick.

"You two are great together," Madison said, turning back towards the doorway out of the kitchen. "Don't forget your dress fitting Allie!" Madison called out as she grabbed her bag and opened the front door.

"Are you not working today?" Nick asked, getting up to refill his coffee.

"I have a couple of things I need to do that can be done from here, but otherwise no. I figured we would grab food after our fittings, and just hangout a bit. Madison is in charge of the party and if it flops that's on her," Allie answered, repositioning her chair to catch a bit of the sun coming through the window.

"Wait, you left your assistant in charge of your first big party?" Nick asked in disbelief.

"Well, it wasn't intentional at first. I was working on the party details with her and then she dropped the ball in a HUGE way. She lost our venue because she let Ryan, you'll meet him at the party, get involved. I fired her and then she came back with this new idea, I gave her another chance. If it flops then I'll fire her again," Allie responded, leaning back in the chair, closing her eyes.

"Wait, let me get this straight. Just to clarify, you are leaving the biggest party you've ever thrown up to your assistant, who by the looks of it is very young, naïve, and easily manipulated, so no wonder she let this Ryan guy do whatever he did. Do you remember how we acted at that age? Could you imagine not growing up in our world and having to throw a party for it?" Nick asked, sitting back down next to Allie.

"She'll be fine," Allie reassured Nick. "She has to learn that her actions have consequences. I told her not to get mixed up with Ryan, especially since he's after my job, and she didn't listen. Since I do know how we were at her age and she begged for a second chance, I'm giving her what she wanted."

"In my opinion, you're being reckless and a bit hard on a girl who simply fell for a guy with good looks and from what I've gathered, a sort of bad boy attitude. Remember what happened the last time you were in London and were caught up by the good looks of a guy?" Nick asked, leaning forward on the table, his hands around his coffee mug. Allie opened her eyes, straightening up a bit.

"Nick, this is different. Everything is different this time around. I'm not Madison and Madison isn't me. I was more mature at that age, and I wasn't just caught up by the good looks of a guy. Myles and I were more than that, so of course it hurt more when it ended. Madison is immature, and Ryan is manipulative. She needs to learn to stay away from people like that. I warned her, I did my part to protect her. She didn't listen and here we are," Allie defended herself.

"Don't you think as a boss, a role model, someone who has been in this world a lot longer than Madison, that you owe her more than a warning?" Nick replied, turning to look at Allie. "Don't you think you should protect her from the dangers of being in our world?"

"Nick, what dangers are you talking about? You act like we live in some sort of apocalyptic world where our lives are in constant danger. Our lives aren't a movie, there isn't danger lurking around every corner," Allie laughed. "You sound paranoid. She'll be fine and if she's not then maybe she doesn't belong in this world, as you put it." Nick sighed, as Allie leaned back in her chair, shutting her eyes again, the sun peering in on her face.

"Yeah, maybe you're right," Nick lied. "I think I'm going to go and unpack and go for a little walk to stretch out my legs."

"Sounds good. I'll catch up on some emails quickly and go with you," Allie replied, her eyes still closed.

"I'd prefer to take a walk alone to get some inspiration, if you don't mind," Nick replied.

"Inspiration for the secret project you are working on with my dad?" Allie asked.

"You know how he works. Nobody knows what we are working on until it's time to start filming and even then, only a select people know about it until it's ready to market," Nick answered.

"Alright, well just be back by eleven, so we can head out," Allie said, getting up to retrieve her laptop from her bag in the living room. "I figured we could grab some coffee before the fittings."

"Sounds like a plan!" Nick called out from the stairs.

****

"I'm not going to go," Myles said handing Patrick a tool. He volunteered to help Patrick with a new installation as a thank you for landing him the opportunity to work with the magazine. "What's the point? It'll just cause more drama if I'm there."

"Are you bloody mad?" Patrick replied. "You better go for my sake if anything. This could put the gallery on the radar."

"Why don't you go in my place then?" Myles asked. "I can't go and see Allie on Nick's arm. It's been hard enough seeing her at photo shoots. Everything between us is different now, and yet I still feel this pull to her. She's like a magnet pulling me in and she knows it. She pulls me in just to push me right back out if I get too close again. You know, I told her that I was going to propose to her before everything went to shit and she didn't react. She hasn't even brought it back up since I told her. Not a word."

"Sounds like you have some unfinished business with each other," Patrick replied stepping off a ladder to check the height of the new art piece. "What a better place to handle it then at a party?"

"I don't know. What's the point? From what I've heard, she's engaged now. I always knew Nick had a soft spot for her.

138

They've known each other since kindergarten. They grew up together. She brought him into her world, and he's been by her side ever since. They belong together, so there's no point in trying to reinsert myself into that story," Myles explained.

"Myles, go to the fucking party. You don't have to rekindle anything with Allison. All you need to do is go, show your face, help people associate you with the photos, drop the name of the gallery a few times and leave. It's that simple," Patrick said sternly. "That's it."

"We'll see," Myles replied.

****

Madison grabbed the last of her binders from her desk, getting ready to head over to Hyde Park to check on the tent which was scheduled to be put up by now. Everything seemed to be going smoothly, and yet she still felt stressed. She pulled out her phone to text Allie as she juggled the binders, walking towards the elevators typing.

Madison: Make sure you aren't late to Nick's fitting. It took some negotiating to get that time slot.

Allison: Just waiting on Nick to return from a quick walk.

As she looked up, she saw Ryan hand someone in the elevator an envelope before the doors closed. She backed away slowly, pretending to be engrossed in her phone, as Ryan turned around to walk back through the lobby doors into the office.

"Hey," he said, stepping through the doors. "How are the plans going?"

"Fine," Madison replied. "I'm just heading out to go and supervise the beginning of the set-up in the park."

"Let your boss know that the first set of issues are printing as we speak. They should all be ready to ship tomorrow, right on schedule," Ryan informed Madison. His tone was formal, a drastic change from the man who stopped her the night before.

"Will do," Madison answered, stepping around him.

"Thanks," he said walking away.

Madison paused, watching him walk away without even a wink or snide comment. Confused, she pressed the button calling the elevators back up, her phone vibrating in her hand.

"Hello?" she answered, not recognizing the number.

"Hey, its Charlie."

"Oh hey, where are you calling from? This isn't the number I have saved for you," Madison replied.

"It's the office phone. I was calling to see if you by chance needed a date for tomorrow night," Charlie explained. Madison furrowed her eyebrows in confusion.

"Don't you have a big event tomorrow night? An event that is taking place which caused me to not be able to properly book Altitude for my event?" Madison asked. "You know the party that ultimately got me fired at one point?"

"Yes, but I have more than enough coverage to get away for the night. I thought I would see if you wanted an ally in your corner at your first big industry party," Charlie said.

"I mean, I have to work a good portion of the party, so I was planning on just going solo," Madison answered, her mind racing at the idea of bringing Charlie mixed with her interaction with Ryan just now.

"Look, I've hosted many of these types of parties. The assistants usually work the door at the beginning and then just watch everyone have a good time. Why not at least have someone with you to have a good time with? Plus, to be honest, this party has a lot of buzz around it, and I don't want to miss the party of the year. You know people are talking about nothing else, right?" Charlie asked.

"Sure. Okay, yeah, you can come as my date," Madison said, feeling her anxiety rise. "You know you need to wear a tux right?"

"Don't worry I have one," Charlie replied.

****

"Allie, ready to go?" Nick called out as he entered the townhouse.

"Yeah! Just give me one second, I'm looking for my… ah found it! Let's go!" Allie said, running down the stairs in a pair of jeans with a white button down tucked in and a pair of white sneakers on her feet.

"You look nice," Nick said as she approached.

"Thanks! Ready for some coffee?" Allie asked, grabbing her purse.

"Yeah, let's go," Nick yawned. "I think more coffee would be a good idea right now."

"Uh oh, are we experiencing some jet lag? Did your walk not help?" Allie asked, leading Nick to the car.

"No, it was good. Got exactly what I needed from it. I'm just tired," Nick replied, getting in the car. "I take it we are headed to the coffee shop you used to work at when you were here last?"

Allie laughed. "How'd you guess?"

"You are one for nostalgia. It was a no-brainer," Nick teased as the car pulled away from the townhouse.

"I guess that's true. I can't help if this is the best coffee place in all of London!" Allie laughed. "Anyways, the tux you are being fitted for is on me. You aren't allowed to pay for it. You are doing me a huge favor by spending the weekend out here when I know you have a huge deadline coming up with my father. Plus, this tux will work perfectly for the wedding, so it'll be one more thing we can take off the planning list."

"You don't have to buy my tux. I can afford it. I'm not hurting for money these days," Nick replied.

"I know but I have more money than I know what to do with like normal. Let me treat you and then you can buy me a gift another time," Allie said, nudging Nick's arm playfully.

"Deal," Nick agreed as they pulled up to the coffeeshop.

****

Myles took a sip of his tea, taking a momentary break from his book. He always came to this coffee shop when he needed to mull over things. There was an indescribable comfort here that he couldn't find anywhere else in the city after Allie left years ago. This was the place he asked her to move in with him at, the place he would come and spend his evenings while she worked, and the only place he could still feel her presence regularly.

141

Myles set his cup back down, turning back to his book as a black car pulled up in his peripheral. He looked up to see Allie get out of the car. She looked beautiful, her hair glistening in the sun as it flowed freely down her back. He watched her push her sunglasses back into her hair. She always looked so put together these days, especially today in a pair of jeans and a while long sleeve shirt. Then Nick got out of the car.

Myles felt his hatred of Nick begin to rise in him. Nick looked as smug as usual, his hair parted to one side, a pair of sunglasses covering his eyes. Nick always dressed like he was heading into a casual business meeting with jeans, always a blue button-down shirt tucked in with a brown belt and brown dress shoes. Myles watched as Nick held the door open for Allie.

"After you Als." Myles heard him say. Not wanting to be seen, Myles switched seats, his back now facing the counter and front door. He listened as Allie ordered her coffee and started talking enthusiastically with the owner of the shop. She introduced Nick and let him order before the owner revealed that Myles was also in the shop.

"He's right over there." Myles heard him say, causing his levels of irritation to rise. Myles pretended to be deeply into his reading, not able to register that Allie and Nick were headed his way.

"Let's just get this awkward re-introduction over Nick," Allie whispered.

"No promises," Nick replied. Allie rolled her eyes, stepping around Nick over towards where Myles sat.

"Myles! Hey! Funny running into you here!" Allie exclaimed, approaching him as Nick trailed behind. Myles closed his book, turning around slowly to see Allie approaching. Setting his book on the small table in front of him, he stood up to greet them.

"Nick, you remember Myles," Allie said, attempting to break the ice between them.

"How can one forget the person who caused such a disruption to someone-you-care-about's life? Makes them a bit unforgettable," Nick replied frostily. Allie shot Nick a sharp look to play nice.

"Right. Well at least some of us aren't still pretending to come from wealth, like others," Myles retorted. Allie looked back at Myles, shaking her head.

"Alright gentleman let's remember we are in public and play nice," Allie interjected. "No need to rehash the past. We've all moved on."

"Some of us to better things," Nick replied, his eyes glued to Myles's face, as he pulled Allie in close. "What are you doing these days? Freelance photography?"

"At least I can have a hobby alongside a real job. What is it you do again? Oh, that's right, you work for Allie's father, writing the movies he makes millions off of and gives you the scraps of money left over," Myles said.

"Well, we can't all just have trust funds and live off our parent's wealth, now can we?" Nick snapped back, taking a step closer to Myles, his fist clenched at his side.

"At least we don't have to marry into our wealth or ride the coattails of the so-called people we care about. How does it feel to know that you only got where you are because Allie let you tag along?" Myles taunted.

"You're still the fucking snob you were all those years ago. I should have done this to that smug face of yours long ago," Nick said, lunging forward to hit Myles, only stopping as Allie jumped in between them.

"Ok, this was a mistake. Nick stop!" she yelled stepping in. "Go to the car. I'll grab our drinks and meet you there in a moment.

"Als-" Nick started.

"Go," Allie demanded pointing to the door. "I'll be out in a moment."

Myles watched Nick retreat to the car. "Good riddance."

"What the hell was that, Myles?" Allie said, turning around to face him after Nick left the shop.

"What? He came in here all hot and heavy. What did you expect to happen Allison?" Myles replied.

"But did you have to attack him like that? You know that money was and is still a sticking point with him," Allie lectured. "You didn't need to bring that up with him. Plus, I told you most of that in private and not so you could taunt him with it."

"Allie come on, you know he's not good enough to be with you," Myles replied.

"Don't start lecturing me about who is good enough to be with me and who isn't, unless you want to explain why you told me you were going to ask me to marry you, when we both know how things ended between us instead," Allie asserted, her voice shaking.

"Allie," Myles said softly, the anger wearing off, at the sight of upsetting her. "I'm sorry."

"You better not pull this shit tomorrow night. Nick's a great guy. Yes, he's angry with you still and has every right to be. Just try to get along with him for one night, for my sake, and for your own reputation," Allie concluded as her name was called from the counter. Myles nodded, sitting back down in his chair. Allie headed to the counter to grab their drinks.

"Allie don't marry him," Myles called out, looking over the back of the chair. Allie drew in a deep breath.

"Play nice with him tomorrow night," she replied, her eyes lingering on his for a few seconds more, before she turned to the door to leave. She set one of the cups on top of the car to open the door, handing Nick his drink, before retrieving her own. As she grabbed the drink from atop the car, her eyes met Myles's again through the window. Sadness replaced the fury she saw in his face only seconds before. She gave him a sad smirk before disappearing into the car. Myles sighed as he watched the car pull away.

"What in world were you going to do Nick? Punch him in the coffeeshop?" Allie asked, settling into the backseat.

"How did he know about my past?" Nick asked, taking his coffee from Allie.

"What do you mean how did he know? I was living with the man, of course I shared parts of my life with him," Allie explained.

"Yes, your life but not mine. Tell me how in the world that just came up for discussion. After all these years, I thought we were finally on a level playing field. And to bring Kara into this. What money does he think she has? God Allie, you can't seriously tell me that you are okay bringing that man back into your life," Nick continued. "He's nothing but a self-righteous daddy's boy, living off the wealth of his father."

"Nick, stop, you know I don't view you as lesser than because you didn't come from money. I didn't just bring you along to give you a better life or to give you a life different than the one you grew up with. You are the most important person in my life, the only person I want by my side at all my big life events," Allie tried to console. Nick stared out the window as the streets of London rushed past them.

"Hey, look at me," she said, grabbing his arm. "I'm still the same girl that you've spent the past 20 something years hanging out with on the beach. Sure, we've gone to parties, drank expensive drinks, rubbed elbows with some of the biggest names in the world, and we live in a huge house on the beach in Malibu."

"A house you own, and I live in for free," Nick interrupted.

"Nick, what is going on? Money has never been an issue between us before, what changed?" Allie asked.

"Allie it's always been an issue between us, just not one that I verbalize. I let you pay for things without an argument because I know it will upset you fi I don't. But to listen to him bring it up, now that felt like a betrayal," Nick confessed.

"Nick, you should have said something before. If it bothered you that I have a trust fund and that I come from a wealthy family, you should have said something before now," Allie scoffed.

"Allie let's just drop this and focus on your party tomorrow night. I'm over fighting about this," Nick replied, staring out the window.

"Fine," Allie whispered, turning to look out her window.

****

"Where's Nick?" Madison asked, seeing Allie alone in the living room, staring into empty the fireplace.

"He's upstairs," Allie replied, looking up from her drink. "How's the party planning going?"

Madison looked at Allie confused. The carefree Allie of this morning was replaced by a melancholy version of her. "It's going well. The tent is up, the temporary floor is in and when I

145

left, they were putting in the lights and tables and setting up the bar area sans the alcohol of course. Oh, and I was told to tell you that the first issue is in the process of being printed and packaged to be distributed tomorrow, right on schedule.”

“Sounds like you have it all under control,” Allie chuckled. “See you don’t need me to protect you from this world. You are navigating it perfectly fine without my help.”

“Ummm… sure?” Madison replied.

“Never mind. Anyways, thank you for setting up the fitting for Nick. He looks great in the tux, like I figured he would,” Allie said changing the subject.

“No problem,” Madison replied. “No need to worry about anything tomorrow. Your hair and make-up teams are scheduled to arrive at about 3pm. I’ve also had food ordered for everyone to be delivered here at the house. I believe Clarissa will be over around 2:30pm so you can both get ready.”

“Thanks Madison,” Allie answered sincerely, getting up from the couch. “I think it’s time to call it a night. Make sure to get some sleep tonight.”

“Will do,” Madison replied, watching Allie head out of the living room and upstairs.

Allie entered her room quietly, seeing Nick asleep in her bed. He left the lamp on by her side of the bed. Gently she slid under the comforter so as not to wake him. They had barely spoken to one another the rest of the day after the coffeeshop debacle. Allie rolled over, facing the nightstand on her side of the bed, reaching to turn out the light. As she settled in to get some sleep, she felt Nick’s arm wrap around her and pull her in.

“I still love and care about you,” he whispered. Allie felt her body melt in relief.

“I didn’t mean to hurt you,” she whispered back.

“I know,” he reassured her. “I know.”

Episode 13- Enchanted

"I brought champagne and a copy of our first issue, fresh off the presses!" Clarissa announced walking into Allie's living room which was now a makeshift salon. There were three chairs set up each with a matching vanity in the center of the room. The couches were now moved to sit along the large windows at one end and a buffet table sat with an array of light snacks on the other side of the room.

"Ohhhhh let me see!" Allie exclaimed, coming around the corner from the kitchen with champagne glasses in her hand.

"Here you are!" Clarissa squealed handing over the magazine.

"It looks so good!" Allie trilled, scrunching her nose.

"Who else is joining us?" Clarissa asked, pouring three glasses of champagne.

"Brynn and Olivia. They should be here any second," Allie replied distractedly, her voice trailing off as she flipped through the pictures of the magazine.

"Ladies," said Nick, coming from upstairs. "What are we toasting to so early?"

"This!" Allie beamed, handing him the magazine. "It's done! I mean we still have copies printing and it's not out just yet, but it's done!" Nick smiled at her, pulling her in for a hug and kiss on the cheek.

"I'm so proud of you," he whispered.

"Awwww you two are so cute," Clarissa commented, handing them each a glass of champagne.

"You better have two more," Brynn said, entering the room with Olivia.

"Oh, let me grab a couple glasses from the kitchen," Allie replied, disappearing into the kitchen.

"Where's Madison?" Nick asked Allie quietly watching Clarissa pour two additional glasses.

"Probably at the park, finalizing party details," Allie replied, watching the girls laugh as Clarissa spilled a little.

"You didn't invite her to get her hair and make-up done for the party?" Nick whispered.

"Nick don't worry about it, she's fine," Allie replied quickly as Clarissa walked back over her glass raised for a toast.

"Cheers to finishing our first issue and for a successful relaunch party!" Clarissa exclaimed.

"Cheers to that!" Allie echoed, clinking her glass against the other two girls. Nick set his glass down on the table next to him, walking away from the group and back upstairs.

****

Madison slid her dress bag onto a rail in the coat check room, setting her backpack with her makeup and a curling iron on the ground in the corner before heading back into the main portion of the tent to finish putting the battery powered candles into about a hundred lanterns that were to be scattered along the path way of the park and the various tables in and out of the tent.

"Do you need any help?" Nick asked, approaching Madison who was now seated on the ground surrounded by candles and lanterns.

"Oh no, I'm fine. You should be with Allie right now, not here," Madison told Nick.

"Oh please, I'd much rather escape the chaos of those girls carrying on and help you put candles into these lanterns," Nick confessed, grabbing some of the lanterns and candles and sitting down near Madison.

"Honestly, you don't need to do that. I've got it under control," Madison replied.

"She doesn't have to know. Quite honestly, between you and me, she should be here helping. She's different in London though. Every time she comes out here something changes in her. I swear she's a great person, she's funny and so lighthearted in L.A., but out here it's like something clouds her judgment," Nick shared.

"It's probably just the stress of this job and wedding planning," Madison replied. "I've actually met you both in L.A. before."

"Oh yeah?" Nick asked, closing another lantern.

"Yeah, you wouldn't remember. I waited on you both at a restaurant a couple of months before getting this job. You tipped very well, and both seemed so nice," Madison explained.

148

"Did you grow up in California then?" Nick asked, snapping a few more batteries in place.

"Yep," Madison answered, getting up to grab more lanterns and candles.

"Interesting. So how are you liking London?" Nick continued the conversation.

"It's a bit cold, a little dreary, but overall, not bad," Madison said sitting back down.

"Understandable. Question. Who is going to turn all of these on when it gets dark?" Nick asked, pushing aside some filled lanterns.

"The catering staff," Madison nodded.

"Got it. So, are you bringing anyone to the party tonight?" Nick inquired.

"I have a friend coming. It's nowhere near as glamourous to come to a party like this with me, someone who has to work at the start of the party, as it would be to be on the arm of someone like Allison Davis, but he wanted to tag along. Probably to just rub elbows with some of London's elite and that's okay with me," Madison replied honestly.

"It's not that glamourous to be on Allie's arm at these parties, but I'm happy to see her shine in her own right, out from behind her dad's shadow," Nick shared. "A piece of advice: don't get sucked into this world. It can get pretty dark really fast and once you are sucked in there's not an easy way out."

"Yeah, but when you are engaged to Allison Davis, it must be pretty easy to navigate. The world of movie premieres, VIP tables at clubs, the best tables at restaurants and more can't be all that bad," Madison asserted.

"Who is Allie engaged to?" Nick questioned puzzled.

"You. Right? That's why she's planning a wedding with you?" Madison said with a nervous giggle. "Right?"

Nick scoffed, shaking his head. "Sounds like I need to have a conversation with Allie. Let's just keep this all between the two of us, okay? I'm going to head back to the house, I was never here," Nick said getting up.

"Sure," Madison replied, watching him get up and head towards the exit of the tent.

"Hey Madison, remember what I said though, don't get wrapped up in all of this. It's not all it appears to be and can turn on you quickly," Nick warned before leaving. Madison nodded slowly, watching him leave.

"So much for helping with these lanterns," Madison muttered.

****

Nick wandered back to the house. He could see Allie's friends in their dresses, one in a very tight gold glittery dress and the other in cream colored flowy dress with a form fitting bodice. Allie was nowhere in sight through the windows. Nick shook his head as he approached the front door.

Allie headed down the stairs in her shimmery emerald green, off the shoulder, gown. The gown pulled in at the waist before cascading from the hip. Her hair was pulled into a gorgeous low bun at the nape of her neck. A set of hanging diamond earrings set in gold dangled from her ears. Nick entered as she reached the bottom of the stairs.

"Where did you go?" she asked with a smile.

"Just went for a walk. You look beautiful like always," Nick said, grabbing her hand and twirling her around.

"Do you think it's too much?" she asked.

"Never! You look awesome!" Brynn called out from the living room. Allie studied Nick's face. He looked unhappy at the sight of her, but before she could ask why, Clarissa stepped in between them, pulling Allie over for a selfie and Nick disappeared upstairs to change.

****

Ryan stepped out of the car, buttoning his jacket, his date trailing behind him. She was boring him already, as she spent the entire ride over oohing and awing over the potential celebrities she could meet at the party. His eyes scanned over the crowd, hoping to see Madison working somewhere along the red carpet and flashing lights of cameras.

"Ryan? Are we going in this way?" his date asked. Not seeing Madison, he nodded and gestured towards the red-carpet

150

entrance, stopping to take photos with her as they made their way down the red carpet.

Madison spotted him on the red carpet. Her heart dropped at the sight of the tall leggy red head on his arm. Madison couldn't keep herself from staring. Ryan's date was gorgeous. She had to be a model, or at least an aspiring model, in her long black slinky backless dress. Madison felt her heart in her stomach. Why did his date have to be so pretty? Did they have to look so good together on the red carpet?

Madison headed back into the large clear tent. Distracting herself with work would help. Allie was due in 10 minutes and Madison's date for the night would be arriving any minute. While she was alone, unguarded from Ryan, she needed to look busy, to look distracted before Ryan came walking in here with his date. The anxiety started to take over, as she felt a flutter of emotions pulsing through her. Her eyes quickly scanned the people in the tent looking for someone she could talk to before Ryan entered.

Ryan spotted her over in the corner of the tent talking to the caterer coordinator. He could only see her back, but he knew it had to be her in a last season short cream sparkly dress that tied up around her neck with a black ribbon. He watched her interact a bit, her head shaking in disapproval of something. A smile crossed Ryan's face imagining the ear full she was giving this poor caterer, and in that moment, Madison turned around, her eyes meeting his. She forced a smile as he nodded to her. Madison looked gorgeous, then again to Ryan she always looked gorgeous, even in a hoodie and sneakers she looked better than any other woman in the room.

"I'm bored, can we get a drink?" Ryan's date interjected.

Madison looked away as Ryan's date grabbed his arm, pulling Ryan back into the realities of the night. He turned around reluctantly nodding to his date and heading to the bar.

Madison watched Ryan turn back to his date. Madison felt self-conscious in her hand- me down dress given to her by Allison at the last minute. Madison hadn't planned on wearing a dress to the party. She planned on wearing all black and working in the back, directing the catering teams, the bartenders, and the like and yet here she was in a dress that made her look like a giant cream tent. She felt embarrassed with a tinge of sadness watching Ryan's date led him to the bar. There was no way he would ever date someone like her. She would never look like the way a girl like Ryan would or even should date. She would never be the girl on his arm to a party like this, even if he said otherwise.

"So stupid," she whispered to herself.

"Who is?" Charlie asked, startling Madison. Madison jumped a bit at his touch.

"Shit! You scared me," Madison replied spinning around.

"Who are you talking to?" Charlie asked laughing at Madison's reaction.

"No one," she replied, her eyes scanning back over the tent for Ryan again.

"You know, this place looks amazing! You really pulled this all together at the last minute," Charlie said, stepping in front of Madison, into her line of vision. "Although, my venue would have been more charming had you booked it properly."

"Maybe. Speaking of your venue, it's still interesting to me that when I tried to fix my mistake and book your place tonight, it was most definitely already booked with a huge event that would pay more than this one, and yet, you were able to take tonight off to join me here on the exact same night," Madison joked, her eyes still scanning the crowd. *Where did he go?*

"Like I said before, that's what I have a staff for. Now let's get a drink, or are you not allowed to while working?" Charlie asked, stepping back into Madison's line of sight, waving his hand in front of her face. "Who are you looking for?"

Madison stopped looking around, focusing in on Charlie. He looked so different all cleaned up and sophisticated in a tux.

"I'm just looking for Allie. Also, you look very nice," she said, lying in part. Madison grabbed Charlie's arm and gave it a squeeze. "Thank you for being here tonight. It means a lot to me. And yes, let's get a drink." Charlie smiled and offered Madison his arm to escort her to the bar.

Ryan caught Madison taking Charlie's arm as the two of them headed to a bar on the other side of the tent.

"You really sure I have to go to this? I already got in a fight with Allie's fiancé," Myles asked over the phone, struggling to button his shirt.

"Come on mate, it's literally across the street from your flat. You will go in, have your photo taken, get some accolades, since you are the main photographer for the relaunch issue, and then you can head right back to your flat. You will wake up tomorrow with a bigger name than you are today. Just go," Patrick replied.

"But what-" Myles stopped his mind picturing Allie's face.

"What about Allie? She gave you this opportunity. The least you could do is show up, support her and then of home knowing you both owe each other nothing more," Patrick replied. "She's nothing more than the person putting your name into print and launching what is certain to be a fantastic career." Myles thought for a second, letting a heavy silence fall between him and the phone.

"The two of you will be even now," Patrick continued. "Whatever happened between the two of you in the past, however bad you feel about it, she has clearly moved on and you deserve to go and celebrate this achievement. If not for you, do it for my gallery, which is getting a lot of publicity from this already."

"Fine. I'll go for an hour. You better have more opportunities lined to by tomorrow evening for me or else this is a waste of time…for both of us," Myles replied.

"Let's just wait and see how great these photos are for the magazine are first," Patrick laughed before hanging up.

Myles tossed his phone on the bed and turned back to the mirror attempting to tie his bowtie. He could see the huge white tent set up in Hyde Park for his window. Cars cluttered the streets letting people in gowns and tuxedos out in sets. He could see the camera flashes going off along what he presumed to be the red carpet.

He always imagined this life for Allie, her dad being a famous American film director and all. Myles loved to picture Allie in a gown, smiling with her father at a movie premiere. At one point in life, he imagined himself standing there with her, part of the family, part of her support system. Those dreams disappeared when Allie left London and left him. In 10 minutes, he would be walking down a red carpet, fulfilling the dream, except this would be for Allie, not with her.

"Thank you for flying out for this Nick," Allie said as their black limo pulled up to the entrance of tonight's event. Nick could feel the excitement buzzing off Allie. Clarissa and Brynn rode together in a separate limo giving Allie and Nick a chance to be alone together.

"I wouldn't miss it for the world. Plus, when's the last time we got to walk a red carpet together?" Nick laughed half-heartedly.

"It's been a while, hasn't it? I used to love it when we would go to my dad's movie premieres and watch all of the big names of Hollywood show up on the red carpet," Allie said. Her nerves were starting to build up inside, her mind starting to race, starting to worry about every detail of tonight, this week, and this year. "Maybe we should walk separately. I don't want anyone's feelings to get hurt."

"Allie, just get out of the car. Who cares what he thinks." Nick nudged Allie towards the car door. Allie sighed, her hand resting on the car handle.

"I just don't want you two to fight tonight," Allie exhaled.

"I promise I'll be on my best behavior," Nick reassured.

"Nick are you okay? You seemed a little off this afternoon, especially after that walk you took. What's wrong?" Allie asked, partially stalling for time but partially out of concern.

"It's nothing you need to be bothered with right now. Let's just go into the party and we can talk about whatever else you want to after the party," Nick reassured Allie.

"You promise you'll tell me what's wrong afterwards?" Allie asked, searching Nick's face for an honest answer.

"I promise, now let's go. This is your night and I'm going to make sure you enjoy every moment. Now get out of the car," Nick said, reaching around her to pull the door handle.

Allie nodded, grabbing his other hand as she exited the car into the flurry of flashing lights. Nick let himself be pulled with her like old times. She shined in the spotlight, a place she always desired to be, but rarely managed to do so on her own.

Nick smiled at Madison as she greeted them at the beginning of the red carpet.

Madison motioned Allie and Nick towards the start of the red carpet. Charlie was inside, talking to a small group of important people, just like Madison expected him to do. Ryan was nowhere in sight and Myles was expected to show up any minute now. Madison watched Nick and Allie pause every few feet for a picture. They looked comfortable together, professional party goers not distracted or overwhelmed by the cameras flashing in front of them.

"She always looks beautiful at these things," a voice behind Madison whispered, causing Madison to jump. As she turned around, she saw Brad Garrison standing close to her.

"Why do people keep sneaking up on me like that tonight?" she laughed.

"I'm sorry, I thought you saw me walk up," he replied.

"It's okay, but yes, she looks amazing, doesn't she?" Madison asked, turning back to see Allie take her final pictures before disappearing inside.

"You've done a great job here tonight Madison," Mr. Garrison said, taking a step forward to now stand beside her.

"Thank you, it was truly a team effort, Allie did a wonderful job leading this project," Madison replied.

"Don't be so modest. I know that Allie threw this all on you. I sort of expected it, knowing Allie's work ethics and temperament. *You* did a great job and I look forward to seeing what else you can do at the magazine. Who knows, maybe one day there will be a creative director spot open for you to fill," Mr. Garrison said, before stepping onto the red carpet.

Madison smiled, letting the praise sink in. "Hey!" a voice said loudly, startling her yet again.

"Why?!" she exclaimed, turning to see Myles next to her.

"Sorry, maybe if you didn't daydream so much," Myles teased shoving his hands into his pant pockets. "God, I don't want to walk down that red carpet. Is my father here?"

"Yes, he's inside already," Madison answered, looking down at her clipboard. "You are essentially that last important person to show up."

"So those photographers won't even mind if I don't walk down the red carpet then? They'd probably love to call it a night and head home," he suggested.

"You better just suck it up and walk down that red carpet and get it over with," Madison replied, motioning towards the carpet in front of them. "Clarissa might have a cow if you don't get press photos for her to put on the website."

"Oh, they don't even know who I am, no one will care if I walk down that carpet or not," Myles said, rocking back and forth on his heels.

"Allie will care," Madison said with a stern face. "Plus, after tonight, they will all know your name, and this will be the least of your worries. So just get out there, stop every three feet for a picture and get it over with."

Myles thought a moment longer. "Fine."

"Good," Madison noted, crossing his name off her checklist before disappearing into the tent through a side entrance.

Madison searched the tent for Ryan as a waiter approached her with a drink. "No thanks," she said politely.

"I was told to not take no for an answer," the waiter replied, gesturing the drink to her again.

"Honestly, I can't I'm working," she replied.

"I can't leave until you take the drink," the waiter whispered pushing the tray towards her.

"Says who?" Madison whispered back.

"Him," he said, pointing to Ryan who nodded to the two of them. "He said you had to take it."

Madison shook her head, grabbing the drink. Ryan raised his glass to her from across the tent. Matching his cheers, Madison scrunched her nose at him, flashing a quick smile before taking a sip of the old fashioned he ordered for her and turning away. Allie was headed straight for her.

"You did it. This looks great, probably better than Altitude 360 would have looked to be honest," Allie said. "Continue to stay away from Ryan and your job is safe."

Madison smiled, nodding as Brad Garrison approached.

"What a lovely party Allison. Your team did a fantastic job," he said shaking her hand.

"Thank you. It was quite a struggle having to change venues at the last moment, but we managed to pull it off," Allie replied. "Have you had the chance to say hi to Nick yet?"

"No, I didn't realize he flew out for the party. Where is he?" Mr. Garrison asked.

"I'll show you," Allie said, leading Mr. Garrison away from Madison. Madison threw back her drink as they walked away. Setting her glass of ice down on the bar, she made her way around the tent spotting Charlie in the corner chatting animatedly to a group of people. Allie, Nick, and Mr. Garrison stood near entrance chatting, a few people were dancing in the center of the tent under a giant chandelier as the DJ played party jams, Myles was brooding alone in the corner eyeing Allie and Nick, but Ryan was missing from the action. The party looked magical under the warm lights of the tent, juxtaposed against the vast dark night sky.

Madison smiled. "Magic," she whispered.

****

"Ready?" Madison asked Allie, an hour into the party. "It's time for your speech."

"Oh, yes, I guess we should get that done so we can continue to enjoy ourselves," Allie replied before excusing herself from Clarissa and Brynn. "Do you have my speech?"

"Yes, here you go. I'll grab the microphone from the DJ and turn the lights up a bit until you start and then we will dim the lights on the crowd and put a spotlight on you," Madison said leading Allie to the DJ booth. Allie nodded.

"Alright ladies and gentlemen, we are going to pause the music for a moment so that Forever London's editor-n-chief Allison Davis can say a few words," the DJ announced, cutting off the music.

"Thank you," Allie said taking the mic from Madison. "And thank you all for coming out to celebrate the relaunch of this amazing magazine. I am so honored that Brad Garrison trusted me to lead this group of fantastic minds on the Forever London staff. Each person on my staff has worked extremely hard to ensure that this launch is Garrison Publishing's best launch yet."

The crowd erupted into applause. Ryan rolled his eyes as Allie continued her speech, inviting Mr. Garrison up to say a few

157

words. Ryan made his way through the crowd avoiding his date as he approached Charlie. "What's the game here?" he asked, standing next to Charlie.

"Nice to see you again Ryan," Charlie said keeping his eyes glued on Madison who stood next to the DJ booth, out of Allie's spotlight.

"Cut the shit. How'd you manage to get away from the club tonight?" Ryan asked. "I thought you had a big event booked tonight."

"It helps to be the manager and owner of a club. You can pay people to cover for you," Charlie answered.

"Or it helps if there's no one in your club at all," Ryan suggested.

"I'm not sure what you are getting at Ryan," Charlie answered, faking a smile, and clapping as Mr. Garrison handed the mic back over to Allie.

"I think you know exactly what I mean. Just like I think you know exactly what will happen if you don't stay away from Madison after tonight," Ryan warned.

"Is that a threat?" Charlie asked, clapping again as Allie introduced Myles and playfully searched the crowd for him.

"Could be, but it's your choice to test that theory."

"You know he won't be happy to hear you've threatened me," Charlie replied.

"It's not a threat if you leave her alone, that's all I'm going to say," Ryan answered, smiling as the spotlight briefly shined on the two of them, still searching for Myles in the crowd. Ryan looked at Madison, who appeared concerned at the sight of Charlie and Ryan next to each other.

"Have a good night, Charlie," Ryan said before making his way to the bar.

Nick stood at the bar, listening to Allie speak and search the crowd for Myles. He sipped his drink in peace listening to her praise Myles and his photography skills. As Allie and Myles unveiled the cover of the first issue together, Nick found his view suddenly blocked by Brynn and Clarissa.

"Question," Clarissa started, her words slurring slightly.

"Yes?" Nick replied, trying to see around the two women in front of him.

"Where is Allie's ring? She said you were still working on getting her one. What's the hold up?" Brynn asked.

"What do you mean?" Nick asked, confused at the question. "What ring?"

"Her engagement ring dummy. Geez, what other ring would be asking about?" Clarissa asked, swaying to the music as it began again.

"Oh, I'm not engaged to Allie," Nick replied. "She's helping me plan my wedding to my fiancé Kara who is out of the country doing Doctors without Borders currently."

"What? Wait, I'm confused," Brynn said.

"Well, that makes two of us. If you'll excuse me," Nick said politely, heading towards Allie who was standing next to Myles near the DJ booth still, surrounded by people congratulating and praising Myles.

"Allie, I need to talk to you in private for a moment," Nick whispered in her ear.

"Can't it wait? I'm in the middle of something," Allie asked, her voice low as she faked a smile for those around her.

"I'm afraid not," Nick replied.

"Okay," she said to Nick before turning to the group and Myles. "If you'll excuse me. I think I've been neglecting my date a bit."

She followed Nick to the corner of the tent. "What is it?" she hissed. "What couldn't wait until I was done over there."

"Why do people keep asking me about what it's like to be engaged to Allison Davis, or why I still haven't given you an actual engagement ring?" Nick asked.

"Can we talk about this later?" Allie whispered. "I really need to be out there tending to my guests."

"You mean Madison's guests since you left her to do all the work," Nick snapped. "Answer me please."

"Okay I fibbed a little and told people we were engaged, what's the big deal?" Allie answered. "No one is hurt by it."

"Why?" Nick said. "I want to know why you lied and told people we were engaged when we aren't Allison."

"Wait, so you two aren't engaged?" Myles asked, approaching them.

"Great, just what we needed in a private conversation, an inconsiderate prick," Nick snapped, rolling his eyes.

"Hey, you are mad at me, don't take it out on him," Allie said pulling Nick back around to face her. "We can discuss this later. What do you need Myles?"

"I was going to ask you to dance," Myles replied.

"I would love to. Just give me a second," Allie said, turning back to Nick. "Let's discuss this later, okay? It isn't a big deal, I promise."

Nick nodded, letting out a deep sigh. "Fine."

"Okay," Allie said squeezing Nick's arm before walking away with Myles.

Madison watched Allie walk away from Nick, her hand in Myles's hand leading her to the dance floor. Madison watched Nick head to the bar. Slowly she made her way to meet him and see what was going on, only to be stopped by a waiter holding another old-fashioned.

"Let me guess, Ryan Eliot says I have to take the drink and then you'll leave," she whined, taking the drink from the tray expecting the waiter to nod and leave.

"What?" she asked as the waiter lingered in front of her.

"He also said you had to take the note right there," the waiter replied nodding to a small, folded piece of paper on the tray. Madison rolled her eyes, retrieving the piece of paper.

Signal.

Madison smiled, turning to leave the tent. Slowly she grabbed a lantern off the table at the entrance, heading down the lantern lit path passing people talking or kissing against the trees. Madison continued as the party grew distant behind her, continuing down the path even as the lanterns ended until she stopped at the edge of the lake.

"You look amazing tonight," he said, turning on his lantern behind her. Madison turned around, the warmth of the candle lighting up her face a bit.

"Thank you," Madison replied.

"You threw one hell of a party tonight," Ryan said, standing only a few feet from Madison now.

"Thank you. You and your date seem to be having a good time," Madison said. She could feel her heart racing as Ryan took a step closer to her.

"Oh, I don't even know where she disappeared to. She's quite boring to be honest," Ryan said, taking another step towards Madison.

"She gorgeous though," Madison chuckled. "You couldn't have brought an uglier date?"

"I don't care what she looks like," Ryan said, setting down his lantern at his feet. "Did you think about what I said the other night?"

"About finishing our conversation?" Madison asked, as Ryan reached out, taking her lantern from her hand, and setting it down next to his.

"Yeah," he said, brushing a few loose strands away from her cheek. He could feel her shiver at his touch. He traced her bare arm, feeling goosebumps form.

"Ryan, whatever happens here between us, you should know I'm not going to sleep with you tonight," Madison exhaled.

"I don't care if you sleep with me, I just want to do this," he said wrapping his arm around the small of her back and pulling her in for a kiss. Madison dropped the drink in her hand, as she let herself melt into his arms, feeling his warm lips on hers. Slowly she drew him in tighter, her hand reaching up to feel his hair on the back of his head, pulling him in deeper. A few seconds later she pulled away, laughing as she tried to catch her breath.

"We can't do this, it's crazy. I'll lose my job!" Madison exclaimed, turning to the face the water in front of them. The moonlight danced on top of the small waves as if it was trying to enchant someone to jump into the cold waters.

"Madison, I'd love to see her try to fire you after throwing this party. Brad Garrison would never let it happen," Ryan said walking up behind her, his hands running down the side of her arms. They could hear an eruption of applause back at the tent behind them.

"She doesn't have to know," he whispered. Madison turned around to face Ryan again, looking into his deep blue eyes.

"She doesn't have to know," Madison repeated running her finger along Ryan's jawline, before pulling him for another kiss.

After a while, Madison reemerged into the party which was in full swing with people drinking and dancing. She made her way over to Charlie, who was leaning up against the bar people watching.

"What did I miss?" she asked, leaning against the bar next to him.

"Allie and Myles ended their amazing waltz of a dance in a kiss, which seemed to shock a lot of people while pleasing them at the same time," Charlie answered. "Where'd you wander off to anyways?"

"I needed a moment to myself with everything going on," Madison lied, eyeing Ryan re-entering the tent. "So, they kissed? Did you see where Nick went?"

"I didn't," Charlie replied. He saw Ryan eyeing him from the other end of the bar. "But I'm glad you found me. I'm going to head out. I think I've spoken to everyone I needed to tonight, including Brad Garrison, what a guy! Thank you for letting me be your plus one. I owe one."

"No problem, thanks for keeping me company a bit," Madison replied, giving Charlie a hug before he took off.

"Wait, so they aren't engaged?" Olivia asked Brynn as they ordered another round of drinks. "No wonder that Nick guy was so confused by my question."

"I guess. Did you see him leave in a huff when Myles kissed Allie," Brynn asked, propping herself up against the bar, resting her head on her hand.

"Yeah, I wonder what that was about. I don't like him very much," Clarissa replied.

Madison sighed, searching the crowd for Allie, seeing her still dancing with Myles as they swayed back and forth to a slow song. Nick was nowhere to be found.

Episode 14- When We Were Young

A Few Minutes Earlier...

Allie smiled, as Myles led her to the dance floor. The music changed to a slower song as they approached the dance floor. Myles placed his hand on the small of her back, her hand in his other one. Slowly he started leading her in a waltz. Surprised, she looked at him with an amused smile.

"So, you aren't engaged?" he asked as they started moving around the dance floor.

"No, I'm not engaged," Allie replied.

"Dating Nick?" Myles asked.

"No and I'm sure after the conversation we are going to have later, we won't even be friends," Allie replied, as Myles effortlessly led her around the dance floor.

"I'm sure that's not true, though he did sound a little harsh earlier, but why did you lie?" Myles asked before giving her a spin.

"I guess I just wanted everyone to leave our past alone and if I was engaged to someone else, then they wouldn't be able to ask questions about you and me," Allie replied.

"Hopefully Nick doesn't get too upset that he was your cover," Myles teased. "He didn't seem too keen on having to share his spot next to you with me tonight."

"It'll be okay. I'll go home, and we will do our traditional after party ritual of eating cookie dough and laughing about the ridiculous things we saw at the party and everything will be fine," Allie said.

"Or you can come home with me tonight."

"Myles."

"I don't know Allie, maybe it's the drinks, or maybe it's sharing the spotlight with you and this party, but I want you to come home with me tonight. I want to stop pretending like we don't feel drawn to each other. I want to forget the past and start over tonight. And I think you want to too, why else would you lie to everyone about being engaged," Myles whispered, pulling her in. Allie looked around them, no one was dancing around them.

Instead, every eye was glued on them as they floated around the dance floor.

"What do you say Allie? Let's bury the past and start over," Myles said. Allie felt her heart racing, her eyes catching Nick's as Myles spun her around. He still looked upset with her, taking a drink of a beer. Allie felt Myles slow down as the music began to wind down, softening all around them. She felt torn between the easiness of being in Myles's arms again and wanting to repair whatever was fracturing her relationship with Nick.

"Nick will be here all weekend, so I'm sure it will be okay to spend one night apart," Allie said, following her heart.

"One night is all I ask," Myles said, pulling her in for a kiss as the music ended.

****

The party was over, only catering and bar staff left, gathering the remains of their equipment and dishes. Madison slid her feet out of her shoes, taking one final walk around the tent, taking in the magic of the night. She spun around on the empty dance floor one final time, letting herself smile as big as she could and soak in as much magic as she could before heading to Ryan's place across town.

Madison slid her feet back in her shoes as she left the tent, heading to the car Ryan sent to pick her up. After a fifteen-minute ride, the car stopped in front of a huge ivy-covered gate. Ryan stood outside it leaning against the wall. He looked just as good in a pair of sweats and a T-shirt as she imagined. Madison got out of the car and slowly walked up to him. He smiled, pushing up from the wall, waving a thank you to the driver as he opened the gate motioning Madison to step through. She smiled at him walking through, waiting for him on the other side. Silently, he led her up to his flat.

"I'm glad you came over," he said, opening the door before stealing another kiss. "Make yourself at home. I'm going to grab some drinks."

"This place is amazing," Madison said, walking around the large living room. The walls were painted a cream color with a dark wood trim. In the middle of the room sat a large dark gray sectional, facing the wall with an abnormally large television. The other side of the room had large windows spaced out just enough to fit a series of shelves covered in books and various plants between them. A large green fiddle fig leaf plant sat quietly in the corner near the windows next to a desk with a large abstract painting hanging above it. There were three doors along the remaining portion of the wall.

"The middle door is the bathroom. The door on the right, my room and the one on the left, my roommate's room. Don't worry, he's never home. He travels for work, and I believe he's currently in South America somewhere," Ryan said, setting a bottle of sparkling water and a bottle of wine on the round coffee table near the sectional.

"This place looks amazing," Madison repeated, sitting down on the couch.

"You look amazing," Ryan said, sitting down next to her, pulling her in for a kiss. Madison readjusted herself, leaning into Ryan's inviting lips.

"This is crazy," she said pulling away.

"A good crazy, I hope," Ryan said, pulling her back in.

"I don't even know much about you," she said, pulling back again. Ryan groaned as she settled onto the couch.

"Well, what do you want to know?" he asked, straightening up on the couch, popping a lid off the bottle of water and pouring a glass, handing it to Madison.

"Well, what's your middle name?" Madison asked, accepting the bottle of water.

"Liam," Ryan answered, grabbing another bottle of water.

"Okay, why did you move to England when you turned 16?" Madison asked.

"Wow, I'm impressed you remembered that. Anyways, I moved here when my mom married my stepdad. He lived out here, so we moved," Ryan replied.

"Where's your biological father?" Madison asked, taking a sip of water, and smoothing out her dress.

"I don't know actually. I've never met him," Ryan replied, his tone riddled with hints of sadness.

"Same," Madison said. "I've never met my father either. I don't even know how my mother met him. She refuses to talk about him with me."

"I'm sorry to hear that. I at least know that my father just wasn't who my mother thought he would be, so she left him when I was young and never looked back," Ryan continued. Madison shifted a bit on the couch, trying to get comfortable in her dress which kept riding up her legs.

"Do you want a pair of sweatpants?" Ryan asked, getting up from the couch, heading towards his room.

"I'm good. I'm not sure how long I'm going to stay," she replied, as Ryan disappeared into his room. "Plus, I doubt I'll fit into your sweatpants," she muttered to herself.

"Here," Ryan said tossing her a shirt and pair of sweats. "You'll be so much more comfortable in these than in that dress. You can change in the bathroom."

"Thanks," Madison said, hesitantly getting up from the couch, clothes in hand. "I'll be one second."

"Take all the time you want," Ryan replied, settling back on the couch, pouring the wine.

****

"Well, I wasn't expecting that as our restart. I thought we would at least talk about things first," Allie said, rolling off of Myles and covering her bare skin with the bed sheet. Myles rolled onto his side to kiss Allie again, as she settled back in.

"You're just as beautiful as imagined you to be after all this time," Myles whispered. Allie reached up, running her fingers through his hair, breathing him in.

"God, I missed this. I missed you, this apartment, this life," she said, snuggling up next to him. He wrapped his arms around her pulling her in.

"I missed you too Allison Marie Davis," he said, kissing her temple as she began to drift off to sleep.

****

Nick paced back in forth, calling Allie's phone again. "God dammit, Allie, pick up your fucking phone," he mumbled as her phone went straight to voicemail again. She was supposed to meet him back at her house over an hour ago. Angry, Nick began packing, aggressively tossing his clothes unfolded into his bag, only pausing to pick up a folded-up envelope that fell out of a

166

worn pair of jeans. He slid the envelope securely into the front of his carry-on bag and turned back to pack his remaining items.

****

"Well look at you," Ryan teased Madison as she exited the bathroom in his clothes. "You have some great taste in loungewear."

"Shut up," Madison giggled. "I'm surprised they fit."

"Of course, they fit. Madison, you are not as big as you may think," Ryan replied. "And again, I'm sorry for ever insinuating you were fat."

"It's fine. It's in the past," Madison replied, returning to the couch after draping her dress over the back of it. "Though, I'm still confused about you. Why are you only nice to me and such an ass with other people? I mean you are like two different people. It's mind boggling."

"What if I told you I was a Gemini? Would that help?" Ryan laughed.

"Not to me. I have no clue why that has anything to do with this situation."

"Interesting. That usually works with most women."

"I'm not like most women," Madison bragged mockingly tossing her hair back.

"I'd say," Ryan agreed handing her a glass of wine. "Okay, my turn for a question. Why'd you leave school?"

Madison drew in a long deep breath, letting it out slowly as she prepared to tell Ryan her story. She hadn't told anyone the reason why she left school, not even her own mother. Madison took a sip of wine trying to buy her time before having to tell Ryan her story.

"Alright, I'll tell you if you promise not to judge me," Madison began, picking at the hem on his sweatpants. "No matter what I tell you, please don't judge me."

"Now I'm intrigued," he said.

"Do you promise?" Madison nudged.

"Yes, I promise. Answer the question," he replied.

"Okay, so it all boils down to my first semester English class," Madison explained. "You see, I grew up in a sort of bubble on the outskirts of L.A. and then decided to go to UCLA on my

167

own, not knowing anyone in the actual city. I lived on campus in the dorms with a roommate. I had this amazing professor, Professor Timothy Hampton. He was young, unlike my other professors who were all clearly middle aged or older. One day I went to talk to him about an assignment during his office hours. He came around his desk to talk to me and he was a little flirty, which didn't really bother me. I didn't even think anything of it at first, but probably should have but let's be honest, I was very naïve and a bit lonely.

"He was so easy to talk to about things, so I went back for every set of office hours and then he asked me to dinner. Still, not thinking anything of it, I agreed. Well one thing led to another, and we started to see each other in secret. I would spend nights at his apartment near campus. We slept together regularly. I didn't think of it as being wrong, he said he wasn't married and wasn't seeing anyone else. And even though I knew getting involved with my professor wouldn't be a good idea, I figured this would be fine. And boy did I learn that lesson the hard way.

"One day his wife came to class, she was in town visiting from Northern California, where she taught writing courses. Devastated that he lied to me I went to his office hours to break it off, but when I got there, he begged me to understand, explaining that his relationship with his wife was on the rocks. Stupid me, believed him and the relationship continued for a couple more weeks, until I got an email from his wife calling me a 'whore' and a 'slut.' She threatened to go to the Dean about it if I didn't break things off. When I approached him about it, he denied ever telling her and threatened to fail me if I broke things off," Madison paused, feeling her voice tremble.

"So, I kept sleeping with him until after finals. Over winter break he stopped reaching out to me, presumably going home to his wife for the break. Feeling relief that it was over, I headed back to campus for the spring semester. About halfway through the semester I was called into the Dean's office to discuss how I had earned my A in English. Ashamed and embarrassed, I agreed to finish out the semester and not return the following year. Not wanting to explain it all to my mom, I pretended that school was just too much for me and I didn't go back," Madison explained.

Ryan watched her re-tuck her loose strands of hair behind her ear and take a sip of wine, fighting back tears. He rubbed her leg trying to let her know she was safe here in this room with him.

"What a prick," Ryan said. "I hope you know what he did was not okay and not your fault."

"You don't have to try to make me feel better about it. It happened, and I should have known better not to get involved with my professor," Madison replied, taking another sip of wine. "Damn, my life sounds like a sad Lifetime movie, doesn't it?"

"Come here," Ryan said, straightening up on the couch. Madison scooted across the couch over next to Ryan. Ryan propped his legs up on the coffee table as Madison snuggled up next to him. "None of that was your fault, but it makes sense now why you have been so resistant to my charms."

Madison laughed, leaning in closer to Ryan, who put his arm around her and kissed her forehead.

"This secret, me and you, if it's too much, I'll understand," Ryan said tracing circles on Madison's arm. "I won't make you feel bad about it. I meant what I said when I said I like you, Madison. We can take this as slow as you want. I just want to see you happy, and even more now that I know you've been hurt so deeply."

Madison looked up at Ryan nodding. "Deal," she said, before he kissed her softly.

****

"Hey," Allie said, stepping inside her townhouse the next morning in her gown from the night before. Sunglasses covered her eyes shielding their hangover state from the bright light of morning. Nick was standing at the bottom of the stairs. "Sorry to ditch you last night, things just took an unforeseen turn, and I was going to text you, but my phone died."

"I noticed. I left probably five voicemails for you before giving up," Nick replied, sliding his suitcase behind him.

"What is that? Wait, are you packed? Where are you going?" Allie asked.

"I'm going to go home," Nick answered, his voice monotone.

"Wait, we had a whole weekend planned. What changed? Don't leave," Allie demanded, removing her sunglasses to look Nick in the eye.

"Allie, you've been lying to me and well it appears everyone since you returned to this place. Answer me honestly, why did everyone think we were engaged? You started to tell me last night, until he interrupted us," Nick said, taking a seat on the stairs.

"Nick, it's not what you think. Ryan insinuated that I was engaged, and for the sake of keeping my personal life private, I didn't correct him," Allie said. Nick shook his head giving her an incredulous look. "Don't look at me like that. I was trying to protect myself from the games Ryan was clearly already playing bringing Myles in for an interview and dangling the advertising contract we have with Mitch in my face the second I got here."

"So, you did hear from the McGowans on your first day here? When you explicitly told me you hadn't heard from them," Nick responded.

"So what? I fibbed a little. I didn't want you to worry about me, which you started to do the second you found out we hired Myles."

"And rightfully so. Allison, do you know what it was like to find you passed out on the bathroom floor, skin, and bones, exhausted from dehydration, and not eating, near death? Do you know how terrifying it is to find the person you love more than anything else in this world hurting because someone made her feel unlovable? What was even harder than that was knowing that you were finally better and putting yourself right back into the fire that burned you in the first place. Well, actually, watching you kiss him last night was the worst part of it all," Nick explained. Allie could see hurt and rage swirl together in his face as they also met together in her chest, rising to her mouth.

"You mean Kara is the love of your life. Don't say otherwise because that's not fair to her. You are marrying her. Do not sit here and say that you love me more than anything or anyone else in this world when you are promised to someone else," Allie blurted out in anger.

"You're lying to yourself if that's what you truly believe," Nick confessed.

"Nick, that's not fair. You've never said anything in the past, and now, I'm hungover, exhausted from work this week and finally on a track that makes sense. I finally have the career I deserve and the love I've craved for so long. Don't ruin our friendship over this," Allie said, her voice trembling.

"Save the sob story for someone else Allie. You've barely worked for anything all these years. You've been handed everything you have around you and instead of actually working for it, you pawn it off on people like Madison. And don't try to convince yourself that you are in love with him again. Did you tell him that he almost killed you when he broke up with you? Did you tell him any of it?" Nick asked, getting up from his perch on the stairs and walking towards Allie. Allie drew in a deep breath as he reached out to touch her arms.

"Nick," she whispered, as he pulled her in, his mouth meeting hers. Allie felt a tear roll down her cheek, as she kissed him back for only a second before pulling away. "You are engaged to Kara and I am with Myles. Don't."

"There it is. The truth. I'm moving out of the beach house," Nick said, turning back to grab his bags. "We won't need your help with the wedding any longer."

Allie tried to choke down her tears as she watched Nick grab his stuff. "Stop, please," she cried.

"Allie, it's best if we just cut ties here and now. You've made your choice again and chose someone who, mark my words, will hurt you again but this time you know that and you went into it willingly," Nick replied coldly. Allie felt her chest begin to collapse giving way to the beginning of a sob.

"Nick, it's not fair. You can't just randomly kiss me, tell me you're in love with me," Allie paused trying to catch her breath. "And- And- And just- just- leave like this."

"Tell me you won't see him again. Tell me you won't date him, that you don't want him, and I'll stay," Nick replied, his hand on the doorknob to the front door, his back to Allie.

"Nick, please," Allie begged.

"Good luck Allie," Nick said, opening the door and leaving without looking back.

Allie collapsed to the floor in tears as the door shut, closing the book on a lifetime friendship. Allie laid her head on the cold tile floor, letting reality sink in. This morning started out as a daydream and ended in a nightmare.

****

"Breakfast is served," Ryan said, entering his bedroom, carrying a tray of food into the room. Madison was shimmying on her jeans as he entered, her hair up in a messy bun at the top of her head. Her hair sparkling a bit in the sunlight peering through the curtains.

"You didn't have to make me breakfast," she said, eyeing the waffles on a plate with two cups of coffee on the tray.

"I only give first class treatment when someone sleeps over," Ryan teased.

"So, you do this for every woman that comes over?" Madison replied.

"Oh, they don't usually spend the night. You might actually be the first." Ryan shrugged, as he set the tray down at the edge of the bed. Madison's eyes narrowed in on him.

"Surrrrrrrrrrre," Madison laughed, rolling her eyes. "You don't have to lie."

"I'm not lying. Honestly, I usually kick them out about one in the morning and get some sleep alone in my bed. You're the first to stay the night. Now please stop getting ready to leave and let's eat these waffles that I just made," Ryan said, motioning toward the bed.

"I don't get you still," Madison said taking a waffle and ripping a piece off and popping it into her mouth.

"And I don't get you. Don't you want syrup?" Ryan asked, feigning to be appalled by Madison's behavior.

"I prefer them without syrup," Madison replied, shrugging as she popped another a torn corner into her mouth.

"That's barbaric," Ryan laughed, offering Madison a cup of coffee. "I don't know how you like your coffee, but I made it with cream and cinnamon."

Madison took the cup. "Sounds good to me," she replied, her eyes glued on him as he removed an extra plate from under the plate of waffles.

"Okay but honestly, why me?" Madison asked. "I still don't get it. You could have any supermodel, above average beautiful woman, and yet you brought me home, we didn't have sex but had a heart to heart instead. And now you are telling you let me sleep over and made me breakfast, which you never do with anyone else. Why? What's the catch?"

"I don't know how many times I have to tell you that I think you are beautiful, intelligent, funny, and the only person I have ever felt this comfortable with in my life. There's no catch. I can't explain it, but the moment you stepped off that elevator behind Allie on your first day I've been drawn to you," Ryan explained, leaning over and kissing Madison on the cheek. "It's not a game. There's no catch."

"Okay," Madison exhaled. "Don't make me regret taking this chance with you Ryan."

"You won't regret it. I promise," he said, pulling her back down to the bed for a slow deep kiss.

****

Nick stepped out of the car and into the airport. His phone rang in his pocket. Ignoring it, he retrieved his plane tickets from the folded envelope in the front pocket of his carry on, leaving a check inside it as he put it back in this luggage. He handed the ticket to the lady at security, with his passport. After she scanned it, handing it back and waving him through, he slid his shoes off his feet, placed his items on the baggage security check belt and headed through security and then to his gate, luggage in tow.

Sitting at the gate, he pulled out a book to help pass the time waiting for his plane to arrive, but his mind felt too muddled to read. He set the book aside, retrieving the envelope from his bag again, pulling out the check and a small note. He studied the check written for two million dollars, letting out a deep exhale through his nose before sliding it back into place. He unfolded the note again looking at the handwritten words on Forever letterhead:

Nick-
Like always I can count on you to make a great story.
Here's a little something to make this all sting a little less.
Thank you for your help.
        -K.D.

Episode 15- Next to Me

"So, he just left?" Madison asked, bringing Allie a cup of tea in her room.

"Yep, said he was in love with me, said he didn't want me to be with Myles, kissed me and then left. Oh, and he's moving out of the beach house, which means I need to call my mom to go and take care of it while I'm gone," Allie said, holding her cup of tea close to her face letting the steam rise up against her face. She pulled her knees in close to her chest, closing her eyes as she leaned her head up against the headboard of her bed.

"I'm sorry to hear that," Madison said. "But I think I have something that will cheer you up, if you are ready?"

"Don't know how cheery I can be, but I'll try. What is it?" Allie asked, opening her eyes as she dragged her head forward again.

Madison disappeared out of the room, reappearing a few seconds later with a couple of newspapers. "I've circled the bits about the party last night. Also, if you check your email there are a few online reviews too. It was a hit!" Madison exclaimed. "Everyone is buzzing about the reveal of the cover and that kiss between you and Myles. We are going to sell so many issues!"

Allie forced a smile, taking a newspaper from the stack and letting Madison celebrate the news while she flipped to the marked page. There it was, in black and white, a photo of Myles and Allie kissing on the dance floor.

"That's a gorgeous photo," admitted Madison as she sat back down on the edge of the bed. "You looked magnificent last night."

"Thanks," Allie replied softly.

"Well, I'll leave you to look over all of this. Everything is taken care of at the park and the office," Madison said leaving Allie's room. As she left, she took one more look at Allie. Her eyes were glossed over as she stared at the newspaper. Her typical peppy persona was replaced with a deep sadness. Madison felt guilty getting ready to secretly head over to Ryan's for dinner. She headed down the stairs, setting her guilt aside. From the kitchen she heard Allie's phone ring and Allie's peppy persona come snapping back.

"Hey, would you like to go to dinner tonight?" Myles asked as Allie picked up her phone.

"Um, how about we stay in? I can order us some takeout," Allie suggested, putting Myles on speakerphone so she could scroll through social media while they made plans.

"Are you okay?" Myles asked.

"Yeah, why?" Allie answered distractedly.

"You just don't seem like yourself. Allison Davis always wants to go out for dinner if it's offered. Why not tonight?"

Allie sighed, her eyes landing on a picture of the two of them kissing from the night before on the Forever London feed. They looked so happy in the photo and now she felt so sad about the whole thing.

She looked closer at the caption on the photo: "Allison Davis and Myles McGowan, Editor'n'Chief and star photographer rekindle a past relationship during hot new launch of Forever London, hitting the shelves near you in two days."

"Allie? You there?" Myles asked. Allie snapped out of it, closing the app on her phone.

"Yes, yes, sorry. What was the question?" Allie asked, getting out of bed.

"Are you okay?" Myles asked again.

"Yes, I'm fine. I would just rather stay in tonight, still nursing a slight hangover," Allie replied, grabbing a pair of leggings and a t-shirt from her closet.

"Alright, how about you come over and I'll cook for you instead?" Myles replied.

"Sounds good. I'll be over in about two hours," Allie said, struggling to get her leggings on while holding her phone.

"I will see you then," Myles said before hanging up.

"Where are my running shoes?" Allie whispered to herself, searching her room before finding them still in her suitcase from her trip to California.

****

"And you are meeting me out in the hallway why?" Madison asked, seeing Ryan standing outside his flat.

"I have a surprise for you," Ryan said his face lighting up at the sight of her. As Madison got close, he pulled her in kissing her tenderly.

"Is that the surprise?" Madison laughed.

"Not even close," Ryan replied, reaching behind him to open the door. Madison gasped at the sight behind him. The couch was turned around, facing a large movie screen, with a projector on a small table slightly in front of it. There was a table behind the couch filled with boxes of candies and a small popcorn maker.

"This is amazing!" Madison said, stepping around him. "You didn't have to do all this!"

"Oh, that's not even the best part. We are having dinner prepared by one of the best chefs in London, my dear friend Chef Collins. He's in the kitchen right now preparing it," Ryan said, leading Madison to the kitchen to see the food preparation in action.

"Honestly, you didn't have to do this. I would have been fine with just takeout and the TV, but this is amazing," Madison said, turning around to give Ryan a kiss on the cheek.

"Shall we?" Ryan asked, motioning towards the living room. Madison nodded, a smile plastered to her face as she followed him to the couch. "How does red wine sound?"

"Sounds great," Madison replied, settling in on the couch as Ryan poured some glasses on a cart in the corner of the room. He looked handsome, relaxed in a pair of dark jeans and a gray V-neck shirt. Madison felt butterflies in her stomach at the sight of him. No one would ever believe that this was the same man who came into the Forever offices everyday or went out with supermodels every night. This was her very own version of Ryan.

"Alright, on the menu tonight we have salad," Ryan said, handing Madison a glass.

"Only salad or is there more?" Madison replied, sipping the wine.

"Nah, just salad. I thought that was your favorite meal," Ryan said coolly, not making eye contact. Madison set down her glass of wine on the edge of the table in front of her as she straightened up on the edge of the couch.

"You're kidding right?" Madison asked, nervously giggling.

"No, I honestly thought that was what you would have wanted to eat," Ryan replied, still avoiding eye contact with Madison.

"Look me in the eye and tell me you aren't serious," Madison replied, scooting closer to Ryan. Ryan looked away, a smile forming on his face.

"Ryyyyyyan," Madison said playfully, scooting closer.

"Yes?" Ryan asked, setting his glass down.

"Tell me you're lying."

"But what if I'm not?" Ryan teased.

"Ryyyyyyan," Madison replied, now sitting right next to him. She nudged his arm.

"We are having salad for dinner," Ryan replied with a sly grin on his face. He finally turned to face Madison. "Are you excited?"

"Shut up," she replied, pushing him playfully.

"You don't believe me?" Ryan said, inching his face closer to hers.

"There's no way you are being honest." Madison pursed her lips, shaking her head slightly at Ryan as she spoke.

Ryan leaned in, his lips barely grazing hers. "I may be only slightly kidding," he whispered. Before he could press his lips against hers, she laughed and pushed him away.

"I hate you," she said, getting up to head back to where she sat before. Ryan grabbed her arm, pulling her back down onto the couch.

"No, you don't. I think you actually like me a lot," Ryan said, moving her hair out her face. He gently stroked her cheek, before pulling her in for a kiss.

"I would say, I like you only a little and a lot less if all we are eating is salad," Madison whispered as she pulled away giving Ryan a wink, before scooting back over to her spot on the couch.

****

Allie set her bag down as she entered Myles's Hyde Park flat. Only 12 hours ago she left this flat feeling hopeful and full of life again and now here she was feeling uncertain and sad. Everything was different than the night before. Myles was in the kitchen whistling to himself as he prepared dinner. She smiled

177

listening to his joyous tune. She could see the table all set with candles and white plates. He was pulling out all the stops for her tonight.

For a moment Allie let herself feel a little happy and certain in her choice between Myles and Nick. She felt her shoulders relax and the knot in her stomach loosen a bit as her mind wandered down memory lane. They had spent so many nights curled up on his couch watching old movies together eating takeout from their favorite restaurants. She enjoyed their alone time together, a stark difference from her life back in California full of movie premieres and mandatory public appearances staged by her father. She was her happiest self here in this old apartment with Myles by her side.

The trip down memory lane was cut short by her phone dinging from her back pocket. Allie grabbed her phone to see a text from her mom regarding the beach house and the sadness of this morning hit her like a tidal wave once again.

"Hey, I didn't hear you come in," Myles said emerging from the kitchen. Allie smiled, sliding her phone back into her pocket.

"I just got here, no worries," Allie said.

Myles walked over, leaning in to kiss her. "I'm glad you are here," he whispered before giving her another kiss.

"Me too," Allie replied, pulling him in for a hug. She rested her face on his chest breathing in the familiar scent of his cologne mixing with his laundry detergent. Myles rubbed her back, holding her tight.

Allie drew in another deep breath before letting Myles go. "What's for dinner?"

"Your favorite: pork chops with mashed sweet potatoes, and brussels sprouts," Myles said, leading her to the kitchen.

"It smells delicious. Is there anything I can help with?" Allie asked leaning against the counter, near the stove.

"You can get the charcuterie board out of the fridge and unwrap it," Myles replied as he poured the pot of potatoes and water into the colander in the sink.

"You made a charcuterie board? When did you get so fancy?" Allie teased, retrieving the nicely laid out board of meat and cheese covered in plastic wrap from the fridge.

"I have always been quote-unquote fancy. I just thought I would try to make tonight a little more special," Myles replied.

"You're sweet," Allie replied. "But real question, do you have any wine?"

"In the living room on the bar cart," Myles replied. "But first, come here." Allie took a step over, and Myles kissed her on the cheek. She smiled, squeezing his arm before heading into the living room. Things were starting to feel like they used to.

****

"Okay, now this looks amazing," Madison said as Chef Collins set down a dish in front of her on the dining room table.

"What we have here is a filet mignon on top of creamy whipped mashed potatoes with gruyere cheese and some heirloom carrots sautéed in a butter cream sauce. I have also placed some freshly made rolls with a dill butter spread here on the table. For dessert we have a few small pastries including eclairs and fruit pastries, as well as the spread Ryan set up in the living room. Let me know if you need anything else," Chef Collins explained.

"Thank you," Ryan said, nodding to Collins.

"Ryan, honestly, you didn't have to do this," Madison repeated.

"I wanted to make tonight special. I know we are not going to have many chances to go out to nice dinners together and so I thought I would bring the nice dinner to you," Ryan said.

"No one has ever done something this sweet for me before. Thank you," Madison said.

"You don't have to thank me. It's what someone should do for somebody special to them," Ryan replied. "Now dig in before it gets cold!"

****

"Alright, let's eat!" Myles announced, bringing two plates from the kitchen. Allie was in the corner, putting a record on an old record player Myles had on a dark wood table.

"That looks great," Allie said, sitting down at the table.

"Thank you." Myles sat Allie's plate down in front of her before sitting down across the table from her. "I hope you like it. It's been a long time since I made a meal like this."

"I'm sure it will be great. You were always great at cooking dinners, though we did tend to eat out a lot, so maybe I'm remembering it wrong," Allie teased, cutting her pork chop. Her stomach was still in a knot and the thought of eating a full meal made her feel sick.

"So, I guess we should probably talk about some things," Myles said setting down his fork after taking a bite of food.

"Yeah," Allie sighed. "Last night was a bit of a whirlwind."

"A good one I hope," Myles replied, reaching his hand out for hers. Allie smiled, giving his hand a squeeze.

"Last night was perfect. This morning not so much. Nick was sort of upset about the whole thing and left this morning," Allie admitted.

"Upset about what?" Myles asked, shifting in his chair.

"About us, the kiss, me being here and not there," Allie replied.

"Well, it's about time he was honest with himself and you about his feelings," Myles scoffed. Allie looked at him confused, wrapping her fingers around the stem of her wine glass.

"What do you mean by that?" she asked.

"Allie, he's been in love with you for years. Everyone knows it and he was probably happy to have you back in his life without having to share you with another man. Then last night happened and he acted like a child instead of being an adult," Myles explained.

"I just don't get it. He's engaged to someone else. Someone amazingly gorgeous with a heart of gold. It doesn't add up," Allie replied. "But he was so upset in a way that I've never seen before. It broke my heart to see him that way this morning."

"Give it time Als, he always comes back," Myles consoled her. "I mean he wasn't so happy about you moving out here the first time, but he eventually got on board with it."

"This time feels different though," Allie said.

"Everything feels different these days because we are all older and wiser," Myles retorted as he continued to cut his pork chop and eat.

"I guess so," Allie said, picking at her food. "So, tell me then, how are you different now?"

"Good question," Myles replied, taking a sip of water. "Let's see for starters, I work for my father now. I no longer run around with the hooligans I used to run around with before. I've finally started to get my life together, I guess."

"How did you start working for Mitch anyways? You used to be so against it. What changed?" Allie asked.

"It just suddenly became time to grow up when you left."

"You mean when you sent me home," Allie retorted, taking another sip of her wine.

"I'm really sorry about how all of that unraveled," Myles said. "I promise you though, what you saw with Lorraine wasn't what you think."

"She left your room in only a sheet, her perfectly tan and shaped ass out in the open. You can't tell me that something didn't happen between the two of you," Allie replied.

"Allie, I've explained it so many times that all I can do is say that I'm so sorry," Myles said sincerely. "I never wanted things to unravel between us the way they did."

Allie sighed, looking down at her food thinking that maybe Nick was right about all of this.

****

"Okay, what is the name of the last woman you had a serious relationship with?" Madison asked, digging into a chocolate éclair.

"Samantha," Ryan answered quickly.

"Wait, Mr. I-only-date-supermodels-and-never-let-them-spend-the-night really has had a serious relationship?"

"Only one and she broke my heart. She left me alone in Paris after I took her there for a romantic getaway. Under the lights of the Eiffel Tower, she told me she was in love with someone else, who was waiting for her, in Paris, because she invited him to meet her there. It was horrible and honestly the biggest turning point in my life. I swore I wouldn't get entangled in a relationship with another, until you," Ryan said.

"Why me? I'm not looking for compliments or anything. I'm just curious," Madison asked, setting down her fork and leaning in closer to Ryan over the corner of the table.

181

"This again, I hope I can one day give an answer that makes you stop questioning all of this. But here goes nothing," Ryan said, taking a deep breath. "Madison Stevens, you are intoxicating. You are so deeply beautiful in a quiet way but at the same time there's this fire in your eyes that I've never seen anywhere else before. You light up every room you walk into, even though you prefer to be off in the corner. People notice you. They want to be around you and they don't know why. You draw people in even if you don't realize it yet," Ryan answered, reaching for her hand under the table.

"Wow, I don't even know what to say," Madison replied.

"I mean every word. Just wait, you'll see what I mean one day, I promise," Ryan said, leaning in to give her a kiss.

****

"Was dinner bad?" Myles asked, clearing the plates from the table.

"No, I just wasn't so hungry. Save it for me and I'll take it with me for tomorrow," Allie said, scrolling through her social media feed.

"Are you sure? You don't have to eat it if you don't want to. My feelings will not be hurt," Myles replied cheerfully.

"No, I want to. Sorry, today has just been a whirlwind day. Let's put the food away, watch a movie and cuddle a bit before I go back home," Allie replied.

"So, you don't plan on a repeat of last night then?" Myles asked, grabbing the empty bottle of wine.

"Let's ease back into this," Allie suggested.

"Okay," Myles agreed, heading into the kitchen. Allie sat at the table for a moment longer continuing to scroll through the pictures of people from the night before. Picture after picture were of the two of them, kissing, laughing together and Allie presenting Myles's cover photo. Some people posted that it was quite the publicity stunt between them, while others cheered them on in the rekindling of their romance.

Allie got up from the table, joining Myles in the kitchen. She stood at the edge of the kitchen, watching him hum as she rinsed off the plates. He was physically right there in front of her but she felt like she was watching a ghost of her past. For the past few months, they danced around the pain they both still held deep inside, never knowing if they would get a chance to redo the past. Now the chance stood in front of her, and she couldn't decide whether to stay or to run as far as she could.

"Hey, if we are going to do this, let's just promise to not hurt each other this time around. If the time comes when this runs its course, let's just be honest, no women in sheets, no games, just honesty. Can we promise that?" she finally asked.

Myles paused for a moment, turning to look at Allie. She looked scared and tired. "Is this what you really want? Do you truly want to give this another chance?"

"I just want to be in your arms and feel safe again like before. Just you and me against the world again," Allie replied. Myles nodded, pulling her into him. "Well, you, me, and the internet at this point."

Myles laughed. "So, I noticed and deal."

Episode 16- Paris (Oh La La)

"We should probably head into the office," Madison said, untangling herself from Ryan on the couch.

"Do we have to? I don't get to do this once we leave here," Ryan replied, pulling her back into him.

"Ryan, come on. I have to make it in before Allie does," Madison groaned as he started kissing her neck.

"Five more minutes," he requested.

"Fine, but then I'm leaving and you're getting dressed and heading to the office twenty minutes later," Madison insisted.

"Yes ma'am," Ryan whispered.

Fifteen minutes later couldn't help but smile as she stepped off the elevator heading into the bright Forever London lobby. The launch party was five weeks ago today and without question from anyone, Madison and Ryan remained inseparable ever since. Well at least as inseparable as two people can be keeping their relationship a secret. Madison's smile started to quickly dissipate as she stepped through the glass doors of the lobby and into the office.

The whole office was buzzing with weird energy as she made her way to her desk. She watched Ryan enter in a few minutes after her making his way to his office. His assistant stopped him before he could enter in. Madison watched as he looked over at Allie's closed door. He exchanged a few words with his assistant before heading into his office and shutting the door.

Madison sat down turning her computer on. She looked up at Allie's door as her emails loaded. The second issue came out a week ago and wasn't doing so well. The traction of the launch party beginning of Allie's relationship with Myles wore off quicker than expected. Ryan was trying to keep everyone interested through constant social media updates and livestreams, but people just didn't seem to be biting any longer.

"Hello?" Madison answered her office phone.

"Do you know who is in Allie's office?" Ryan asked, his voice low and soft.

"No, do you?" Madison replied.

"Brad Garrison and her father are in there," Ryan said.

"Wait? Why?" Madison asked, searching her emails for something from Allie about it. "Shit, I've gotta go" she said seeing an email from Allie this morning with the subject line 'Visitors Today.'

"Let me know if you find out anything," Ryan said before hanging up. Madison got up from her desk to go and grab some coffee to bring into Allie's meeting.

"All I'm saying is that the first issue was amazing. Every picture in the cover story was a dream. The second issue lacked a lot of the same passion and desire. The readers must agree since our readership between the two issues declined drastically," Brad Garrison explained.

"I mean, we used a different photographer for the cover story, so the style of the photography is different. I think it's just a sophomore slump type of situation and the readers will come back with the next issue," Allie replied defending the issue. Madison knocked politely on the door, entering with a tray of coffee, milk, and sugar for Allie's guests. As she set down the tray, she mouthed sorry to Allie.

"I think the problem is that the two issues are not cohesive. There isn't something that connects the two, even the fashion stories are all strikingly different between the two issues. The first issue looks like it's straight out of a fairytale woodland and the second one smacks you in the face with vibrant cityscapes. You need to solidify the voice and vision of the magazine," Garrison replied pouring a little milk into his coffee.

"I think that's a fair statement," Ken chimed in. Allie looked at him, a confused expression on her face.

"I stand by these two issues. Life isn't all fairytales and love stories. Sometimes we must stop and face the hard truths. But also, I'm sorry, can you explain to me why my boss and my father had to come to tell me this?" Allie asked, nodding to Madison to leave her office. Madison smiled and disappeared out of sight.

"Yes, right. I'm sure it seems a little odd having both your father and me here," Garrison began to explain. "As I'm sure you know, your father has a movie premiere here this weekend and I think it would be a great opportunity to get the Forever London magazine on people's radar if you and Myles attended the premiere together and if you sent a writer and photographer to cover the event."

Allie scrunched her eyebrows and pursed her lips as she thought about it. She wasn't sure they were ready to be on a red carpet together, but then again it could be something to maybe bring them a tad closer without it feeling forced. During the last five weeks Ryan pushed them to be captured on every social media platform possible which seemed to be pushing them apart a bit.

From the shooting of the third issue's cover story to dinners out to planning meetings for the magazine, every second they spent together was strategically curated to help boost the magazine's social feed. Most of the time they were having fun, enjoying each other's company, and laughing harder than they ever had before, but Allie knew that it was starting to wear on Myles already. They agreed to take things slow, and so far, putting their relationship all over social media felt like throwing gasoline on their love flame. And now, throwing Myles into the deep end of her world felt unfair.

"What do you say Allison? It's been a while since you were at one of my movie premieres," Ken said calmly. "It would mean the world to me to have you there."

"Is mom flying in for it?" Allie asked.

"No, she's busy putting together a charity event in Malibu, but she does send her love," he replied before finishing off his coffee. "So, what do you say? Bring your boyfriend, who mind you I never got to meet the last time you were together and come to the movie premiere. I'll even throw in a few passes for the staff here to get exclusive interviews for online content."

Allie thought about it a moment longer looking over at Brad Garrison who nodded to her. "Fine, but I'll need a dress," Allie agreed reluctantly.

"Oh, that's not a problem. I'll get Sophie to send dresses to your house tomorrow afternoon. She can coordinate everything for the two of you. Also, there will be an after party at this extraordinary club in town, which you must attend," Ken said.

"Well then, it's all set. Allie, please have Madison send over a copy of the latest mock-up of the third issue. I would like to see about four pages reserved for the movie premiere coverage," Garrison requested. "Now if you don't mind, I will leave the father and daughter duo some time to bond as I have to rush off to another meeting."

"Will do," Allie said, standing up to shake Brad Garrison's hand before he left her office.

"How about lunch today? I have a few errands to run but I can meet you afterwards and we can catch up. How does that sound?" Ken asked as Brad Garrison shut the door. Allie nodded as the pit in her stomach grew.

"Sophie will text you with the address of the restaurant," Ken said getting up from his chair, heading to the door. "See you in a few hours."

As Ken left her office, Allie got up from behind her desk to address Madison's tardiness. Standing in the doorway of her office, she watched her father head out the frosted glass doors into the lobby. Madison was sitting behind her desk, her eyes flickering up from the screen every few seconds to check on Allie who stood there silently.

"What happened this morning?" Allie asked finally.

"I am sooooo sorry about that. I spent the night at Charlie's again and woke up late forgetting to check my emails in a rush to get here," Madison lied. For the past five weeks she told Allie she was seeing Charlie and spending quite a bit of time at his place or out at dinner with him.

"How did the meeting go?" Madison asked.

"It went okay. Garrison isn't happy with the numbers on the latest issue, but I really don't think it's a big deal. The thing I'm worried about is the fact that my father is now involved in all of this. That's never a good sign," Allie said, looking back towards the doors to the lobby.

"Did he say why he was here?" Madison asked.

"It doesn't matter, I came out here to address you being late today. Don't let it happen again. Understood?" Allie asked, her voice turning stern and unwelcoming.

"Yes," Madison replied.

"Good. Now then, please email Garrison a copy of the latest mock-up for issue three this evening and then make sure I have the actual book this evening on the kitchen table like normal," Allie requested. She lingered a moment longer to see Madison nod her head and then she disappeared back into her office, shutting the door.

****

"So did you hear the news?" Ken asked sitting down across from Allie.

"What news?" Allie asked, thanking the hostess who guided them to their table.

"Nick and Kara called off the wedding," Ken said nonchalantly as he opened the menu.

"When? Why? Do you know details?" Allie asked as a mixture of panic and sadness came over her like a tidal wave.

"A few days ago. He was going to fly out for the premiere here in London, but when the news broke, he decided to stay back and deal with that. He's also tightening up some writing on the latest script we've been working on, so he's a bit of a mess right now with work and his personal life in shambles," Ken said. "I think I'm going to get a good old-fashioned hamburger, how about you?"

"Umm, I'm not feeling too hungry actually, so probably a light soup or salad," Allie said, trying to digest all the information her father causally spilled out without knowing the last thing Nick said to her before leaving London.

"Make sure to get a cream-based dressing and some chicken in it please. You are looking thin again," Ken said setting down his menu. "So, tell me about Myles this go around. How are things going so far?"

"They're fine. I mean we haven't really discussed the past in great detail which feels like it's lurking behind every corner, but we are having fun, going out to dinners and now I guess movie premieres. It's different this time, which is expected. We're older now, so I think a bit of that romantic notion of living together poor and struggling to make it on our own has worn off a bit. All that to say, we are just having fun," Allie replied, sipping her water.

"Well, I brought you these to help you remember the romance of the past and maybe to help you find some inspiration for the magazine's future issues," Ken said handing Allie a decorative wooden box. Allie took the box, her hands trembling a bit as she opened the lid to see about a hundred letters addressed to her, relics of her past with Myles.

"My letters from London," Allie said smiling as she took the first one out of the box, examining Myles's handwriting on the envelope.

"I remember when you first wrote that boy a letter. We all thought it was harmless until the letters never stopped. Years and years of letters and emails between the two of you. No one was surprised when you decided to come out here for your last year of school. I mean we were disappointed a bit when you announced you were willing to step away from the family forever to chase after the fairytale romance, but none of us were ultimately surprised," Ken explained. "But Allie, please remember what it was like when you returned from that fairytale. You were a shell of a human. Not the vibrant young woman who enjoyed her life. Guard yourself. Be honest with yourself about what's going on between the two of you and make sure he's honest with you."

"You don't need to worry about me dad. I can handle this," Allie said.

"It's definitely my job to worry about what happens to you and this family. You know how dangerous it is when things get twisted in the media and reputations are ruined," Ken said as the waiter approached the table to take their orders.

"Yeah," Allie mumbled under her breath.

****

Madison sat on Ryan's couch thumbing through the second issue of Forever London after leaving the book for their third issue at home on the table for Allie per her request. Madison was relaxed in a pair of Ryan's sweatpants and her tank top, her hair gathered at the top of her head in a messy bun, and a pair of reading glasses.

"Maybe they were on to something today," she called out to Ryan who was in the kitchen making popcorn for the two of them.

"Who?" he said, his head poking out around the corner.

"Brad Garrison and Allie's dad. This issue does seem to lack some passion and desire that the first issue had," Madison answered loudly back to Ryan. She could hear the popcorn popping on the stove. "I mean the pictures feel so stuffy compared to the magic of the last issue and our article choices just seem so blah. Where is the va-va-voom? The stuff that makes you go oh-la-la?"

Ryan emerged from the kitchen holding a bottle of wine and two wine glasses by the stem in one hand and a bowl of popcorn in the other. "Maybe it's because Allie and Myles spent the whole time, we worked on the first issue pining for one another and now they are together, and the passion is gone and it's showing in Allie's judgment. Didn't take too long, did it?"

"I doubt the passion is gone. And Brynn took these pictures back when we were working on the first issue," Madison replied as Ryan set everything down on the table.

"You know what I mean though. Allie is a creature of her emotions. Every choice in this issue shows it. We just need to come up with something even better for the next issue. Maybe you should book them a vacation together of some sort," Ryan suggested, pouring Madison a glass of red wine, and handing it over to her.

"Funny you should say that. I was actually thinking you and I should go away for a weekend. Go somewhere we could be out in public together," Madison said, accepting the glass of wine and leaning back against the couch cushion.

"I'm game. Where are you thinking? We could go to the Lake District. I think you would love it up there. It's quiet and romantic," Ryan suggested, pouring himself a glass of wine.

"Hear me out, what if we went to Paris for the weekend?" Madison asked, getting comfortable next to Ryan as he sat down on the couch looking for a movie to watch.

"Madison, I don't know. I don't like Paris much and you know why," Ryan said setting down the remote and turning to face Madison whose legs were draped over his lap.

"I know, but what if we went together. Wouldn't that replace those bad memories with good ones? I don't know any really hot male models that I could run off with in Paris. It would just be you and me and the most romantic city in the world," Madison explained, scooting closer to Ryan to smooth out a fly away hair.

"Madison," Ryan started, pausing to collect his thoughts.

"Please? Pretty please?" Madison asked, batting her eyes playfully at Ryan.

"Did you already plan an itenary?" Ryan asked.

"Mayyyyyyyyyyybe," Madison laughed.

"Fine, but you better not make me regret this," Ryan agreed. Madison scooted even closer, now sitting on his lap, to give him a kiss.

"I promise, you won't regret a single moment of it."

****

"Hello?" Allie called out from the living room as Madison entered the house.

"Hey!" Madison said setting down her bag on one of the couches now shoved up against a wall, away from its normal spot in the room where a few racks of couture dresses now sat. "What's going on here?" she asked.

"My father's assistant sent over a ton of dresses for me to try on for his big movie premiere this weekend," Allie said, putting a dress back on one of the racks. "Myles and I are apparently attending and walking down the red carpet."

"Sounds fun," Madison said, perusing the beautiful dresses in front of her.

"We will see. I've never walked down the red carpet with someone other than my father or Nick," Allie said shrugging her shoulders. Madison stopped looking at the dresses to look at Allie.

"Are you okay Allie? You don't seem as chipper lately," Madison asked, her voice soft and low. Allie nodded slowly.

"Are you sure?" Madison asked again.

"Yeah, don't worry about me. It still stings to think about the Nick situation. Then my father and Brad Garrison threw this whole going to the movie premiere onto my lap. It's just a lot to handle while trying to wade through making the third issue even better than the second one," Allie paused for a moment, sitting down on one of the couches. "That reminds me, Garrison sent over a ton of comments on the third issue's mock-up. He pretty much wants to scrap the whole issue. Can you divide up his comments by department and send them out tomorrow morning?"

"Of course. He's not really giving us a whole lot of time to redo the entire issue," Madison replied.

"At least he did like a lot of Myles's photos for the cover shoot, he just wants them laid out a little differently with the article. As for the rest of the issue he has requested for us to cut quite a few items and replace them with something a little more 'va-va-voom' as he put it," Allie said. Madison chuckled a little remembering her earlier conversation.

"Got it. Speaking of 'va-va-voom' Charlie and I are thinking of going on a little weekend getaway to Paris this weekend, unless you need me of course," Madison said as she resumed going through the dresses in front of her.

"That should be fine. Sophie, my father's assistant, can handle my schedule this weekend. She's used to doing it anyways. Go and have fun with Charlie. You guys seem to be doing well," Allie commented, standing back up to go through the dresses.

"He's a lot of fun to be around," Madison replied.

"We should double one night. I'd love to get to know him more," Allie said.

Madison grabbed a long gold mermaid gown with a sweetheart neck off the rack. "You should wear this one. It'll look gorgeous on you, though you may need it taken in a bit. You look like you've lost some weight," Madison said, handing it to Allie.

****

"Off we go!" Ryan exclaimed, leading Madison out of the car, into the private airport in front of them.

"Why aren't we at the bigger airport? We didn't have to take a private jet," Madison said following Ryan into the small building in front of them.

"It's faster this way and easier to get a car straight to our hotel once we land. We only have a couple days in Paris and I'm sure you have a lot on your list to get done. Let me spoil you a little as we go, okay?" Ryan suggested, stopping to kiss Madison on the forehead.

"Fine," Madison groaned.

"Thank you," Ryan said giving Madison a wink. "Now get your cute butt out those doors over there and onto that plane."

*****

"You look stunning tonight," Myles said, sitting next to Allie in the back of the limo.

"Thank you, you look great as always. I like you in a tux," Allie replied, kissing Myles on the cheek. "Ugh, I really don't want to do this though."

"It's just one night, you can do this," Myles said, giving Allie's hand a squeeze. "Plus, I've always wondered what it would be like to attend one of these events with you. Dream come true."

"Don't call it a dream until you've lived it," Allie laughed. "I'm sure it will be the same old same old with my dad. He'll want a few photos with me at the start and then he will head off to make sure the press gets pictures of him with his lead actress and actor."

"So, we will get some time to ourselves then?" Myles asked, a sly grin crossing his face.

"Maybe," Allie chuckled, leaning over to kiss Myles on the cheek. "Thank you for coming with me tonight."

"Always," Myles replied as the limo pulled up to the edge of the red carpet. Allie could see her father standing at the end of the carpet waiting for her.

"Here we go," Allie whispered as the car door opened letting Myles out first.

****

Madison looked out the window of the town car as Paris whizzed by her. She could feel her face getting tired from the giant grin on her face. Paris at night was just as beautiful as she imagined. She could feel Ryan rubbing her back enjoying her excitement. She could see the Eiffel Tower in the distance all lit up as the car zoomed through the streets. As the car slowed down, Madison turned to Ryan, kissing him on the cheek.

"Thank you for coming on this trip," Madison said.

"Just you wait until you see the view from our room," Ryan replied. "Then you'll really want to thank me."

Madison shook her head chuckling. "We'll see about that."

****

Allie and Myles made their way down the red carpet, following behind Ken Davis and his all-star cast stopping here and there to take pictures. Myles never let go of Allie's hand as she guided him through the wave of flashing lights. Once inside, Allie found her father.

"Dad, this is Myles, Myles this is my father, Ken Davis," Allie said introducing them to each other.

"Well, it's about time we meet," Ken said, shaking Myles's hand.

"That it is. You have a wonderful daughter sir," Myles replied. He felt nervous, unsure what Ken thought of him after all these years.

"I know. I just hope that she's not in the wrong hands again," Ken said. "Now, I'm sorry to cut this short right now, but I've got to get ready for my speech before the movie. I'll see you at our seats."

"Well, he doesn't like me much, does he?" Myles said, turning to Allie as Ken disappeared into the crowd.

"Don't take it personally. He doesn't like anyone in my life," Allie said, giving Myles's arm a squeeze. "Should we get a drink before the movie starts?"

"Let's do it," Myles replied, kissing Allie on the cheek.

****

"Are you fucking kidding me?" Madison exclaimed, stepping out onto the balcony of their hotel room. She could see the Eiffel Tower in the distance. They were on the top floor of the hotel a few blocks from the center of town. The room was huge with a large bed, complete with a couch and set of armchairs in a small seating area before two French doors leading to a huge bathroom complete with a clawfoot tub in front of a large window with a wonderful view of the city.

"I told you it was spectacular," Ryan said appearing behind her with a bottle of champagne and two glasses.

Madison squealed in excitement turning towards Ryan embracing him in a hug. "You did not have to do this."

"It was not a big deal. A family friend owns the hotel, I simply requested the room," Ryan replied. He set down the bottle and the glasses on a small table near the door before pulling Madison in closer. "Thank you for convincing me to do this trip."

"Don't even mention it," Madison said, inching up on her tip toes to kiss Ryan tenderly. "This is going to be the best weekend ever."

"Just you wait," Ryan said, spinning Madison around and pulling her in again, holding her as they took in the city all around them.

Episode 17- Wonderland

"That wasn't so bad," Myles said getting into the limo behind Allie at the end of the movie premiere.

"Are you kidding me? My dad's speech and bringing me up there? It's all just a publicity stunt, surely at the request of Brad Garrison to plug the magazine" Allie explained, straightening out her dress.

"I think he legitimately brought you up there because he's so proud of you," Myles replied, grabbing her hand. "Let's just have some fun tonight. Where are we headed for this after party anyways?"

"I'm not sure actually. Hold on I'll text Sophie," Allie replied. Within seconds of sending the message, Sophie replied.

"It looks like we are going to Altitude 360," Allie said slowly, giving Myles an inquisitive look.

"Interesting. I thought Charlie went to Paris with Madison," Myles commented.

"That's what she told me," Allie replied.

"Maybe he has someone else running the party tonight," Myles shrugged.

"Maybe, but I can't imagine that he would not be at the club for an after party this big," Allie said as the car came to a stop in front of the club.

After another series of poses for photographers, Allie and Myles headed up into the party. Allie looked around for familiar faces. The who's who of London filled the room. Everyone was there except her father. Slowly she led Myles to the bar wading through the crowd. The bar was packed with people ordering drinks. Allie and Myles waited behind another couple as the bartender poured a few cocktails.

"Well, I'll be damned. Myles McGowan out and about at event such as this," Patrick said walking up behind them.

"Hello Patrick, nice to see you here!" Myles exclaimed, shaking his hand. "What are you doing here?"

"I'm sort of on a date," Patrick replied.

"With whom?" Allie asked, greeting Patrick with a kiss on each cheek. "Who's the lucky guy?"

"He's around here somewhere. I'll introduce you," Patrick said looking around. "Oh! There he is." Patrick was pointing to a man emerging from a door at the side of the club. Allie stood up higher on her tip toes, trying to get a good look at him. *And there it is.*

"This is Charlie," Patrick said introducing Charlie to Myles and Allie.

"Nice to meet you Charlie," Myles replied, shaking his hand shooting a look of surprise to Allie.

"So, you're dating Patrick? How long as this been going on?" Allie asked, taking a step back. Before Charlie or Patrick could reply, Ken tapped on a microphone and began to thank everyone for coming to the party. Allie and Charlie locked eyes before Charlie whispered into Patrick's ear and disappeared back into the crowd.

"I'll be right back," she said to Myles and Patrick before following Charlie.

"Charlie, wait I have a question for you," Allie said, following him into the stockroom.

"You really shouldn't be back here," Charlie replied.

"Why aren't you in Paris with Madison?" Allie asked, ignoring Charlie's comment.

"Where?" Charlie asked, grabbing a few bottles of champagne off a shelf.

"In Paris. I thought you two were going away for a weekend in Paris… a romantic weekend…" Allie stated.

"Well, it wasn't a romantic weekend clearly, more like a platonic friend weekend. Not sure why you would think it was a romantic one," Charlie chuckled.

"But you were supposed to go?" Allie asked.

Charlie drew in a deep breath. "Yes, but at the last minute I couldn't make it due to this enormous party thrown together by your father with a week's notice," he exhaled.

"Wait, what? There's no way he decided to throw a party a week out," Allie replied.

"What can I say, I got a call last week scheduling this party. Luckily, we had an open date. I told Madison I would play this weekend by ear, and then couldn't go at the last minute. I think she went with a girlfriend or something," Charlie explained. "Now, if you don't mind, I need to get these bottles out to the bar."

Allie stepped out of the way, letting Charlie leave. She could hear the crowd applauding her dad's speech. Her mind was racing between who Madison was in Paris with and why her dad would wait to set up his after party for his movie premiere a week out. Growing up her father would have a team of people in and out of the house putting together his parties months before. Allie and her mother would have dress fittings over a month out. Everything was meticulously planned. Someone was lying and Allie knew it couldn't be her father. Slowly, she stepped back through the door and into the party again.

She saw Myles across the room at the bar. His hair was still perfectly parted, his eyes sparkling under the dimmed lights as he spoke passionately to Patrick while holding two glasses in his hands. He looked happier than ever before. Allie smiled, making her way back over to him.

Being with him made her happy, yet there was still the tinge of guilt and sadness over Nick leaving the way he did. She wanted to be present here with Myles, the man of her dreams, the man she spent years chasing, the man she lost and finally had back in her life but knowing that having him back while losing the other most precious person in her life cut her deep on the inside. This was one of the first big movie premieres where Nick was absent, and her heart ached to see his face in the crowd.

"There you are. Is everything okay?" Myles asked as Allie approached. She nodded as she took one of the drinks out of his hand.

"Everything's perfect," Allie whispered, pulling him onto the dance floor with her.

****

Madison opened her eyes blinking a few times to take in the sun filled hotel room. She could see the Eiffel Tower in the distance through the windows of the balcony doors. Ryan had his arm wrapped around her waist as he slept cuddled up next to her. Trying not to move too much she reached for her phone on the nightstand. She unlocked it, opening the Forever London social media pages to see glamourous photos from last night's movie premiere. Allie, of course, without any help looked stunning in a crimson and gold gown cut short in the front showing off her legs and long in the back. Myles cleaned up well too, looking a tad uncomfortable around Allie and her dad.

Madison smiled a bit, scrolling through all of the photos from the premiere when she heard a knock at the door. Confused, she set her phone down shifting a bit in the bed.

"It's just room service," Ryan muttered, rolling over. "I ordered breakfast last night. Thought we might need some sustenance after what we did. Hope that's alright."

"Oh yeah, of course," Madison sighed trying to play it cool. Never in her life had she been in the position to order room service when staying at a hotel. She smiled as she watched Ryan get out of the bed without a shirt and only a pair of sweatpants on. He opened the door and rolled in the room service cart.

"I figured crepes, eggs, and sausage would do the trick," Ryan yawned, still groggy with sleep.

"You're the best," Madison giggled in delight, unable to be cool any longer as she slid her bare legs over the side of the bed.

"Dig in, I'm going to shower and try to wake up," Ryan said, kissing her on the forehead before stumbling toward the shower. Madison watched him leave, before taking the lids from the plates to uncover the food. Everything smelled amazing as she unloaded the plates from the cart onto a table outside on the balcony. She felt giddy for a moment as she poured herself a cup of coffee and sat down to take a bite of the delicious breakfast in front of her. She was in Paris.

****

"Looks like another successful night of free publicity for the magazine," Myles said gently tossing a newspaper on the side table as he entered his apartment coming back from a run. He slid his shoes off while juggling a box of croissants in his other arm.

"I saw that we made the front cover with my dad on a few papers. We looked great last night, but I'm not in love with those photos. I'm waiting for Clarissa to send over the other photos and the article we had a staff writer prepare for the next issue. I'm

199

hoping there will be some better ones," Allie said, sitting on the couch with her laptop on her lap.

"I think we great in all of the photos," Myles replied, grabbing a couple of plates from the kitchen, and walking into the living room with the croissants.

"We look okay. I'm just hoping for some really amazing photos for the magazine. We need something to wow Brad Garrison or I'm almost certain he's going to fire me. This issue has to be amazing," Allie replied distractedly.

"Here, take this croissant," Myles said, waving a plated croissant in front of her face. "I know how much you love them."

"I'm not hungry," Allie said, her eyes glued on the computer screen.

"Come on Allie, I made a special trip to get these just for you," he said, waving the croissant around again.

"I said I'm not hungry," Allie replied. "Plus, that's nothing but butter and carbs. You have to start eating better, we are in the public spotlight now."

"Screw what people think about what I do and don't eat. I didn't ask for their opinions," Myles commented, taking a bite out of the croissant Allie turned down.

"Even if you didn't ask, they are going to comment on it. You have to start eating better, fruits, veggies, lean protein. You also should probably start lifting weights, you look a little wimpy in these photos," Allie said, her eyes glued on her laptop screen.

"Allie, look at me for a second. Shut the laptop," Myles said, his voice now low and annoyed. Allie looked up as Myles started to push the laptop shut.

"What?" she asked.

"Where is this coming from? I've let it go that you keep turning down meals close to events or photo shoots. I figured it was part of your preparations for those events, but you've never turned down a croissant on Saturday morning. Now you are attacking my body, which mind you, you quite liked after the party last night," Myles said with a wink.

"Look, you don't know much about my world. You can't just show up to an event, rub elbows with some of the most powerful and influential people in the world and not look good. The press will ridicule you and mind you they already have. Every day we get comments from people saying we look too posed, too fake, not in love, frumpy, etc. I'm just trying to protect you from the shitstorm that is the fallout from one of my father's events. Believe me, you have to appear to be the fittest people at an event like this," Allie replied. "I don't want a croissant because I'm actually not hungry, but also because it's not going to do me any favors later."

"Get up and get dressed, we are going out," Myles said.

"Myles, I have a lot of work to get done today. I can't just go out," Allie replied, reopening the laptop.

"Screw your work. We are going to go and have some fun," Myles said.

"It's not that easy to just blow off work. I'm working with Sophie to do some damage control about last night. I'm waiting on Clarissa-"

"If you don't shut the laptop and get off the couch to get ready, I swear," Myles interrupted.

"You swear what?" Allie asked, getting irritated.

"I swear I will pour coffee on that bloody laptop and carry you out of this flat," Myles retorted. He was now standing close to the kitchen again, finishing off another croissant.

"Myles, I have to get this work done or I might lose my job. Also, my dad is not happy with how stuffy we looked last night, and I am trying to help do damage control. People are really starting to question us as a couple," Allie admitted.

"In this moment I am too," Myles said, walking into the kitchen away from Allie.

"What does that mean?" Allie asked getting up to follow him, leaving the laptop behind.

"Als, maybe people are on to something. Everything we do is documented in pictures and interviews. We either go out for a photo op or social media post for the magazine or we sit here, and you work on the magazine. What sort of relationship is that? I want to do something that doesn't require us to discuss the bloody magazine," Myles said.

"I'm sorry that the magazine that gave you your biggest break as a photographer is causing you so much grief. You wanted into this world and here you are now babe. This is the world I grew up in, the one you wanted to be part of for so long. Well, welcome this is it!" Allie snapped.

"What happened to the girl who was content with eating croissants on the weekend and reading together? What happened to the girl who wanted to have picnics in the park and not take a hundred photos of it? What happened to the Allie of the past?" Myles yelled.

"You lost her the second Lorraine walked from that room to the bathroom in a fucking sheet!" Allie yelled back, getting up from the couch angrily grabbing her items around the living room. "You sent her packing. You don't get to now question where she went, because you are the reason she is gone."

"God you are so fucking dramatic all the damn time. I told you nothing happened between Lorraine and me. She crashed here that night and I slept on the couch. Colin and Lorraine got into a fight, and she needed a place to stay," Myles explained loudly as Allie disappeared into his bedroom.

"Naked? She needed a place to stay with no clothes on?" Allie asked.

"I stepped out to grab some coffee and give her a chance to gather her things and go. I don't know why the hell she was naked in my flat, and quite frankly I'm tired of explaining it to you over and over again Allison!"

"Then don't. I'm going home for the weekend. I need to get this work done," Allie replied calmly, shoving her laptop into her workbag. "I'll see you Monday at the magazine you hate so much." She shoved past him towards the front door.

"Allie, wait a second, let's cool down and talk about this," Myles called out as Allie opened the front door. Without a word she slammed the door behind her, and Myles perched himself on the back corner of the couch, staring at the closed door.

****

"What's on the agenda today?" Ryan asked, finishing the last bite of eggs on his plate. His hair was still a bit wet from his shower and his shirt still missing. Madison smiled at the sight of him. "What?" he asked.

Madison gave him a wink. "Do you just try to always be hot like this or does it come naturally?"

202

"That's Paris talking. Also, my eyes are up here," Ryan chuckled raising his eyebrows at Madison.

"Shut up," Madison muttered, turning her head away from him and taking an exaggerated side glance at him.

"You started it," Ryan teased, stretching back a bit, flexing his arms a bit.

"Now you're doing it on purpose," Madison giggled.

"And you like it," Ryan laughed.

"Maybe," Madison replied. "Anyways, I was thinking we could picnic under the Tower this afternoon, go to the Luxembourg Gardens, maybe check out the Pere-Lachaise Cemetery, eat some croissants and walk along the Champs-Elysees?"

"You want to go to a cemetery?" Ryan asked looking confused. "Why?"

"Because it's old and beautiful and not something every other American wants to go and see. It's not like I requested we go to the Louvre," Madison said defending her choice.

"But the Louvre is quintessential," Ryan moaned. "And I hope you aren't serious about skipping the Louvre since I already arranged a private tour of it tonight."

"You did what?" Madison replied. "Ryan, you didn't have to. I told you I had the itinerary covered."

"Well, it's already done. So, let's do this. Get dressed and we will go get croissants and walk along the Seine to the Champs-Elysees. Once we are done there, we can visit the Jardin du Luxembourg and then we can grab the makings of a great lunch and picnic under the Tower. After that we will come back, get dressed up and go to the dinner reservations and private tour I have set-up for us. How does that sound?" Ryan proposed.

Madison crossed her arms and pursed her lips. "For someone who didn't want to come to Paris, you sure have a lot planned out already."

"Let's just say being here with you is worth it all," Ryan said, leaning up and over the table to kiss her on the cheek. "Now does that plan work for you or should we just stay here the rest of the day and make out some more?"

"Tempting but yes, the plans work. Except one potential problem, how fancy are these dinner reservations? I didn't plan on a fancy evening out, so I didn't pack for one," Madison replied.

"Don't worry, I have you covered," Ryan said, getting up from the table and dropping his towel to the ground as he disappeared around the corner.

A few hours later, they sat on a blanket with an array of meats, cheeses, bread, and champagne in a grassy area near the Eiffel Tower. Madison leaned back on her elbows, her legs stretched out in front of her, her face basking in the sunlight. Ryan smiled looking at her in her black shorts, a pair of maroon sneakers on her feet and a flower print button down shirt tied at the bottom pulling up a bit showing off a sliver of her midriff.

"God this place is magical," Madison said adjusting her sunglasses as she sat up.

"It's not too bad with the right company," Ryan replied, popping the bottle of champagne open.

"So, you agree then? It's pretty magical, eh?" Madison asked.

"With you, any place is probably magical," Ryan replied.

"What makes you say that?" Madison questioned Ryan, feeling a little embarrassed by his comment and the way he was looking at her.

"You have this indescribable way of making everything seem more alive, more enchanting. It's like when I'm with you, I see the world through new eyes. It seems less tainted. I don't know how you do it, but you add a little sparkle, a little positivity, a little hope to things that once seemed hopeless and mundane," Ryan explained. Madison blushed.

"I wish we didn't have to hide our relationship," Madison sighed.

"Same, but we also don't want you to lose your job," Ryan replied. "Give it time. Make yourself indispensable in the eyes of Brad Garrison. That way Allie can't fire you for something like a relationship. You've already caught his attention with the launch party. Just keep it up."

"Speaking of that, did you tell him I put the party together?" Madison asked, grabbing a piece of bread and cheese.

"I may have mentioned it to him," Ryan admitted. "I don't think you understand how amazing that party was. It was impressive. If you aren't looking into working in publishing full time one day, you should consider event planning. You are a natural at it."

"Thanks, I'll keep that in mind," Madison said blushing. Ryan took a sip of champagne. Madison watched him look at the people wandering all around them. He looked so relaxed in the sunlight, his legs stretched out on the blanket, his hair slightly tussled. Vacation Ryan was quickly becoming her favorite.

"If you didn't work for the magazine, what do you think you would do?" Madison asked, grabbing another piece of cheese.

"I would write and illustrate books, as odd as that sounds," Ryan answered without hesitation.

"Like children's books?" Madison asked puzzled.

"Children or young adult would work too. I'm actually a pretty good artist. I like to draw real life people and I think I could draw some amazing characters. It's always been a dream of mine to write books," Ryan replied.

"Can you show me these artist skills you have?" Madison asked.

"When we get back to the room," Ryan laughed. "For now, come here and sit with me." He moved their various food items and basket to the edge of the blanket, making room for Madison to sit next to him. There they sat basking in open air and sun, staring up at the tower.

****

"Allie, just text or call me back? You're being childish ignoring me," Myles said in his third voicemail to Allie. Upon hearing it she immediately deleted it. She had nothing to say to him. Sitting at her kitchen table she spotted the decorative box of letters her father gave to her at lunch the other day. Ken Davis was already heading back to California to work on his next project and had left without saying goodbye. Allie stood up from the table, retrieving the box from the counter.

She ran her fingers over the lid of the box where she had gently etched into the wood three words "Letters from London."

205

Maybe she was being too hard on Myles. It wasn't his fault she was feeling uneasy lately. Slowly, she unlatched the box and opened it. Letters started to spill out. She ran her fingers over them, feeling the past creeping back. She sighed as she unfolded one.

Future Allie,

DO NOT READ THESE LETTERS EVER AGAIN.

Love,
Past Allie

Allie chuckled, refolding the paper. "Maybe I am a bit dramatic," she whispered collecting the letters and putting them back into the box.

****

"Alright, close your eyes," Ryan said as they approached the door of their room.

"Why?" Madison replied.

"Just trust me," Ryan whispered in her ear before kissing her on the cheek.

"Fine," Madison groaned closing her eyes. She listened as Ryan unlocked their hotel door and opened it. He placed his hand on the small of her back leading her inside a bit before stopping. "Can I open my eyes?"

"One second," he said, turning on the lights. "Alright, open them."

Madison gasped, shaking her head at the sight of a gorgeous black and white dress and a pair of red bottom black heels worth more than anything she could ever afford gently laid out on the bed. The black bodice of the dress was fitted, filling out at the bottom into a white scalloped skirt with gold plates in shapes of petals filling in the rounded edges. Madison ran her fingers along the edge of the skirt amazed.

"Ryan, there's no way I can accept this, it's too much!" she exclaimed, bouncing over to him pulling him in for a kiss. He smiled kissing her back.

206

"It's a gift and you deserve nothing but the best," he whispered. "Now get dressed and let's go have some fun."

As Madison scurried off into the bathroom to do her hair and make-up, Ryan pulled out his phone. He had ten missed calls and numerous text messages from Mitch McGowan wondering where he was. Ignoring them would get him into trouble but seeing the excitement in Madison's face was worth whatever consequences lay ahead. He turned off his phone and put it in the drawer next to the bed, turning to get ready for the night ahead.

****

"Hello?" Madison called out as she entered the townhouse returning from the airport the next evening.

"We're in here!" Clarissa called out from the living room. Madison abandoned her luggage at the foot of the stairs entering the living room to see Allie pouring martinis.

"You are just in time, want one?" Allie asked.

"Sure," Madison replied nodding her head and slipping off her shoes. "What's the occasion?"

"Allie's had a rough weekend, so we are drinking to forget the weekend," Clarissa replied, taking a full glass from Allie.

"Sorry to hear it. Do we have any snacks? These smell like pretty strong drinks," Madison inquired, setting her glass down on the coffee table in front of her.

"Who needs snacks?" Allie scoffed.

"Oh wait! I have something we can indulge on," Madison said, leaving the living room to fetch some treats from her luggage.

"I just don't know. He doesn't seem to understand how important this job is. It's like every five seconds he needs new attention, or he lashes out like a child," Allie continued explaining to Clarissa, taking a sip of her martini.

"I thought things were going well between the two of you," Clarissa said, tucking her feet under her as she settled on the edge of the couch in front of Allie.

"They were until this weekend. I knew better than to invite him to my dad's movie premiere," Allie replied.

"You both looked gorgeous on the red carpet," Madison said reentering the room with a tray of macarons.

207

"Ohhh, those look delightful," Clarissa squealed grabbing a purple one from the tray.

"I got them in Paris earlier today," Madison gloated. "Though I am sad to have missed the big movie premiere. I would have loved to be there to see the film before anyone else."

"Believe me, movie premieres are extremely dull, I'm sure Paris was way better," Allie retorted rolling her eyes at the thought of the movie premiere.

"Oh, shut it Allie, you are just bitter because you and Myles got in a fight over the premiere press," Clarissa teased. "At least I think that's what you got in a fight over right?"

"I'm not even sure now. I think it was actually over a croissant. He kept waving this pastry in front of my face as I was trying to write a message to Sophie lying and saying that Myles had the remnants of a stomachache from food poisoning the night before and that's why he looked so stuffy in all the pictures. I kept telling him that I didn't want a croissant and then everything blew up. We ended up fighting over the whole Lorraine issue again," Allie explained, popping a red colored macaron in her mouth.

"And who is Lorraine?" Clarissa asked, finishing off her martini and shaking the glass in front of Allie for a refill.

"Lorraine is the woman that Myles cheated on me with. Though he says he slept on the couch that night and doesn't know why she left his room in only a sheet when I came in that morning fresh from a trip back to California where I had just told my father to go ahead and cut me off from the family's money because I was going to stay in London with Myles and build a life together with him." Allie laughed. "Joke was on me."

"Wait, he cheated on you!?" Madison interjected.

"Yeah, and honestly, I don't want to keep reliving it, I just want him to admit it so we can move on," Allie replied. "Instead, he just denies it over and over. But I know what I saw, and I can't unsee it. Until he admits it, I feel like we will just keep having this fight over and over again. Well, this fight and the one about the magazine. I should have never hired him and let this whole situation turn into what it's turned into- a mess."

"But you love him, right?" Clarissa asked. "Outside of this fight, he treats you right?"

"I do love him, and I think that's why I keep trying," Allie sighed. She took a sip of her drink. "Anyways, enough about me. Madison how was your trip?"

"Magical. It really is the most romantic city in the world. I just felt enchanted everywhere I went," Madison answered.

"Who did you go with? We saw Charlie at the movie after party," Allie asked. Madison could feel her cheeks turning red. She found out Saturday morning that the after party for the movie premiere was held at Altitude, meaning Allie would see Charlie and know that he didn't go to Paris. After a couple days of thinking about it, she knew she would have to come up with the perfect lie in order to cover up her weekend with Ryan.

"I went on my own. I already had the plane ticket, so I figured I shouldn't waste the money," Madison lied. "Charlie got his ticket refunded. He was bummed that he couldn't make it."

"You went to Paris alone?" Clarissa asked. "Brave."

"Yep. It's pretty cool to travel a bit on my own. I stayed at a hostel and wandered the city streets during the day. I even had a solo picnic below the Eiffel Tower. I can only imagine how much more romantic the city is when you go with someone you love," Madison said. Allie was staring at Madison, watching her every move. Madison made eye contact smiling at her as she took a nervous sip of her drink and reached for another macaron.

"You know who else went to Paris this weekend?" Clarissa asked.

"Who?" Allie asked, diverting her eyes to Clarissa.

"Ryan. Did you bump into him at all Madison? He was probably there for some private event at the Louvre by the looks of his social media feed," Clarissa said. "He posted some pictures of the Louvre at night. I think he was there with some model most likely. He only posted the back of her, not her face. Probably to make sure none of his other girls get jealous. Though she had a gorgeous little dress on."

Madison could feel Allie's eyes back on her face. Her heart was racing. "Nope. No sight of him," she replied, trying to play it cool.

"Maybe we should take a girl's trip to France, Allie! That would get your mind off the whole Myles thing for sure. We can drink champagne, head to southern France for a little topless beach action and just relax a bit. What do you think?" Clarissa proposed shimmying her shoulders a bit.

"I think that sounds like a great idea," Allie replied, her eyes still locked in on Madison's face.

"Give me some dates and I'll book it for you both," Madison offered, nervously taking another bite of a macaron.

A couple hours later, Clarissa left, and Allie wandered into the kitchen where Madison was cleaning up the glasses from their happy hour.

"I better not find out you went to Paris with Ryan. You remember what happens if I find out you did," Allie warned as she filled a glass with water.

"I have nothing to hide about my trip Allie," Madison lied. "I think the only issue we have here is the email we just got from Brad Garrison about the third issue."

"What email?" Allie asked, reaching into her back pocket to retrieve her cellphone. "Oh great, he hates it all still. I hope you are ready to pull a late night. I'm going to call Ryan and have him get a few staffers ready to polish up some of the back-up articles. Hopefully Clarissa isn't back home yet."

"Do you want me to order food?" Madison asked.

"Only if you want some, I'm not hungry," Allie replied, dialing Ryan's number, and stepping out of the kitchen, back into the living room.

"Crisis averted," Madison whispered to herself leaning up against the counter.

Episode 18- Cruel Summer

"Ryan, what the hell?" Madison whispered over the phone. "You posted a photo from our trip on your social media? Have you learned anything about posting pictures of me anywhere on the internet? Someone always sees them."

"What's the big deal? Your back was turned to the camera. It wasn't a big deal. No one will know it's you," Ryan replied.

"Allie knows. I swear she knows. She ran into Charlie this weekend. I told her I was going to Paris with him and then Clarissa brought up the photo. She's going to put it together," Madison whispered.

"Why are you whispering?" Ryan laughed.

"Because she's downstairs. I don't want her to hear this conversation," Madison replied.

"Well maybe I should whisper then too, since I'm outside your house," Ryan teased. Madison walked over to her window to see Ryan down below. He looked up and smiled.

"Why are you here?" Madison asked, stepping back from the window.

"I was asking myself the same question when summoned by your boss. Seems like we have some work to do that can't wait eight hours. I think a few of us are coming over, including Clarissa who is walking up behind me," Ryan muttered.

"Well, well, well, if it isn't the smug Ryan Eliot back from his little romantic vacation," Clarissa taunted as she approached him. Madison hung up her phone. She hated Clarissa's flirty tone. Madison smoothed out her top and fixed her messy bun a bit. She hadn't washed her hair from last night's date with Ryan, so it still held the bouncy curled ends from the picture Ryan took and posted. She quietly pulled the dress bag holding the dress Ryan bought her from her luggage and hung it up in the back of her closet. Luckily Allie respected her privacy, so she wouldn't go rummaging through her closet. Madison stashed the Louboutin heels under her bed. She could hear people coming inside downstairs.

"Here goes nothing," Madison whispered to herself as she exited her room and headed downstairs. Ryan, Clarissa, Allie, and a couple of other staff members were sitting in the living room chatting away already. Madison stepped in quietly, taking a seat in an armchair without anyone noticing.

"Shall we order food?" Ryan asked. "I'm starved."

"We don't have time to eat Ryan, we need to get this issue fixed and start figuring out how we are going to wow Brad Garrison in the next few issues, or we all won't be able to afford food any longer," Allie snipped.

"Speak for yourself on the money end," Ryan replied rolling his eyes. "Anyways, I think we can at least order a pizza while we discuss these issues."

"You just got back from one of the culinary capitals of the world and you want to order a pizza?" Clarissa asked.

"Your point?" Ryan asked. "Maybe I want pizza after suffering through French food all weekend."

"Oh, did the girl you take make you eat only stuffy French food while there? Let me guess she was overly excited to eat bread and croissants and cheese… but then she never ate any of it because she has to keep her figure," Clarissa teased. Madison could see Allie staring at her again, finally noticing she was in the room. Madison kept a straight face void of any telling expression, looking at Clarissa as she spoke.

"Do you think I would want to order pizza which is bread and cheese if all I ate was bread and cheese when I was in France?" Ryan scoffed.

"Touché," Clarissa laughed patting Ryan's arm.

"How about I just order some pizzas and Allie can get along with telling us why you are all here?" Madison interjected getting up from her chair to go and call for pizza. Ryan watched Madison exit the room.

"So, tell me, who was the girl?" Clarissa asked playfully.

"No one you know," Ryan replied.

"So where did you meet her?" Clarissa questioned.

"Let it go," Ryan said sternly.

"Geez, it's almost as if you have something to hide," Clarissa replied rolling her eyes.

"I have nothing to hide, I just don't need your jealous line of questioning to continue," Ryan replied coolly.

"Jealous? Oh please," Clarissa said getting up from her seat next to Ryan and repositioning herself on the chair Madison was sitting on.

"Anyways," Allie started, breaking the tension. "I called you all here tonight because Mr. Garrison is not happy with the third issue. As it's supposed to go to print in a few days, I need you all to pitch your best article ideas and go through the layout with a fine-tooth comb. We will start with article pitches and then we will address Mr. Garrison's suggestions."

"And this couldn't have waited until tomorrow morning in the office because?" Ryan asked.

"Because it's a lot of work and we have less than two days to finalize this issue and get it to the printers," Allie replied. "Clarissa, while we pitch article ideas, can you get us set-up to view the layout on the tv screen over there?"

Clarissa nodded, getting up from her chair and Madison strolled back in.

"Pizza is on its way," Madison said.

"Good. Now grab your notepad and let's take some notes," Allie directed.

****

Madison got up early, tired from the night before. Their brainstorming and comment addressing night with the Forever staff went until the early morning hours. Knowing they had a lot of work to do Madison made herself get out of bed, make some coffee, and review her notes from the night before. As she sat down at the kitchen table, she noticed a decorative box with the words 'Letters from London' etched into the top. Intrigued as she sipped her coffee, she slowly opened the lid to see a bunch of folded letters spilling out from the top.

Madison grabbed one from the top unfolding it. The handwriting was very clean and straight. The letter was addressed to Allie. Madison flipped it over to see who sent it, seeing it signed by Myles. Intrigued Madison started to read the letter:

My Dearest Allie,

I am so excited for you to come and stay in England for a while. I cannot wait to show you around London, even if that means riding around on one of those god-awful buses and take the ridiculous photos in front of one of those phone booths. I know things are tough with your dad right now, families are hard, but Allie, you are one of the strongest women I've ever had the pleasure of knowing. Getting out of America for a while might do you some good. Plus, then I'll finally get to kiss you like I've waited to do for so many years.

I cannot wait to finally have you all to myself in person and not just through these letters. While I've enjoyed writing to you and talking on the phone occasionally, I really want to know what it's like to feel your skin against mine and to hear a genuine laugh escape from you. I want to know how your eyes glisten in the morning when they first see the sunshine. I want to hear you breathing next to me as I fall asleep...

"Morning," Allie said as she stumbled into the kitchen wearing a pair of loose sweatpants and a tight tank top without a bra. "Is there coffee?"

"Yes," Madison answered. Allie groaned a 'thank you' and began pouring herself a cup. Madison folded a piece of paper and put it back in the decorative box on the table. Before Allie could notice the box in front of Madison, Madison pushed it back to the center of the table, pulling her notepad back in front of her.

"Geez, that was a productive but a very late night," Allie said, sliding into the chair next to Madison.

"Yeah, it was. Are you hungry? There's some leftover pizza, but we can also stop for some pastries on the way into the office," Madison suggested. Allie took a sip of her coffee, resting her elbows on the table.

"I'm good, but if you want to stop, we can," Allie replied. "We do have a lot of work to get done, so I guess I should get ready."

Madison nodded as Allie got up from the table and headed back upstairs with her coffee mug in hand. Madison waited until she was soundly upstairs before sliding the box back over towards her to finish the letter.

...You've done so much for me over the years from so far away and I can't wait to show you how much that's meant to me. To be honest though, my biggest fear is that you will come here, and we will finally be in the same area together and you will realize that I have so many more faults than you imagined, or that I will no longer see me as someone you love. I hope that it won't be true, but I'm so nervous for you to get out here.

Alas, I hope that you write back soon. Only three months until you are out here. Until then, your letters will suffice.

Love you always,
Myles

Madison smiled as she folded the letter back up. Myles was so cute to be so nervous for Allie to come to England for a while. She loved that Allie kept his letters tucked into this box. There had to be hundreds of tiny, folded letters in the box. Wanting to read more, Madison stole a few letters, tucking them into her notepad before heading back upstairs.

****

"Today has been a living hell," Allie said as she entered the restaurant with Myles.

"How so?" he asked.

"Well as you know we've been working on fixing issue three for the past few days and today was the final push before sending it to the printers. I spent at least twelve hours there today and twelve hours yesterday and we just barely met our deadline," Allie explained as they were escorted to their table.

"Are you happy with the end product?" Myles asked, unbuttoning his suit jacket to sit down. Allie settled in the chair across from him.

"I think it's alright. I'm a little nervous that if this one doesn't do well that Garrison is going to put me on probation. If I can just get a little bump in the numbers off this issue, then maybe

215

I have a chance to turn this all around. I'm just going to need a new approach for the next issue," Allie replied as the waiter approached. Allie ordered water and salad, checking her phone to see whether or not she had any new emails from Brad Garrison.

"I'm sure it will be fine. You've always managed to make something amazing from something less than ideal," Myles assured her after ordering.

"Thanks Myles. Anyways, enough about the magazine. Have you had any more photography jobs this week?" Allie asked.

"I have one tomorrow night, but that's about it at this point," Myles answered.

"Well, I'm sure…." Allie started to say before she felt a pit grow instantly in her stomach. She turned her gaze down to her lap, trying to avoid making eye contact with a tall leggy tan brunette walking towards their table.

"You're sure what?" Myles asked, confused by Allie's sudden change in behavior.

"Lorraine," Allie whispered.

"Allie, not this again," Myles groaned before looking around the restaurant to see Lorraine give him a little wave as she approached the table. "Oh," he whispered getting up from the table to greet her.

"I saw this gorgeous woman from across the restaurant and I just wanted to come over and say hello," Lorraine said approaching the table. She kissed Myles on each cheek before turning to Allie. Allie forced a smile, stood up and exchanged pleasantries with her.

"I didn't know you were back in town Allison. And wow you look so good!" Lorraine screeched, looking Allie up and down.

"Thank you, Lorraine. You look about the same as when I last saw you in a sheet, except you are more clothed now," Allie replied, immediately regretting the words as they left her mouth.

Lorraine sighed, nodding her head. "I guess that's fair for you to say."

"Yeah, now if you are done saying hello, we are going to get back to our conversation," Allie responded, sitting back down.

"I'll leave you two to it then. Myles, I hope you are still available to take photos at our event tomorrow night," Lorraine said turning to Myles.

"Yes, please let Colin know I will be there," Myles responded. Lorraine nodded and walked away back to her table with a group of friends.

"Wait, what is this event?" Allie asked.

"Colin is hosting a charity event and asked if I could help take some photos of the performances and speeches for him," Myles replied shrugging it off.

"So, who have you been talking about this event with? You've been talking to Lorraine? Were you going to tell me about this?" Allie asked, feeling the panic and hurt of the past rising inside of her.

"Allie, stop. Colin emailed me about it. I was going to tell you about it, I swear."

"When? Tonight? After it happened?" Allie asked, feeling her emotions starting to run high. She could hear Lorraine laughing with her friends. The waiter appeared with food at the table, setting her salad down in front of her. Myles thanked the waiter.

"Allie, please don't make this a big deal," Myles requested. "I don't know how many times I have to explain to you that there has never been something between Lorraine and me. I swear."

"You know what, I'm not too hungry. Do you think we could take the food to go?" Allie asked, looking for any way to escape.

"Okay," Myles said, setting down his fork.

"Thanks. I'm also not feeling great so I'm going to head home tonight," Allie said. Myles sighed, rolling his eyes as he nodded his head.

****

Madison barged into Allie's office where Ryan and Allie were meeting about the next few issues holding a tray with food on it and Allie's box of letters under it. Allie looked at Madison with alarming concern as Madison not only startled her coming in so quickly but was also holding her private box of letters.

217

"Is everything okay?" Allie asked.

"Yeah, sorry. I know you two are meeting about the next issue, and I wanted to pitch something to you both. I didn't mean to come in so abruptly," Madison replied. Her heart was racing with excitement. "Oh, and here's lunch. I know you said you weren't hungry, but you skipped breakfast this morning and I saw your dinner still in the fridge from the restaurant, so I thought you had to be starving by now. I brought you something too, Ryan."

"Thanks. What else do you have there?" Ryan asked, taking a sandwich from the tray of food Madison set down on the table. Allie shot Madison a tense look.

"Where did you get that?" Allie asked.

"From the kitchen. Before you get angry, hear me out. I think I have an idea that might help us plan the next three issues," Madison said, pausing to see if Allie would let her continue. Ryan sat back, eating his sandwich watching the two of them interact.

"Okay…" Allie replied terrified of what Madison was going to do with her personal letters from Myles.

"Alright. The first issue really took off because of this rekindled love between Allie and Myles, right?" Ryan and Allie nodded their heads. "Okay, ever since then we've been trying to build momentum off of that moment on social media while putting out magazine issues that don't really capture the reason everyone fell in love with the first issue. I mean hell, even Taylor spoke about love in the first issue. Every issue since then has fallen flat. The third issue had a small bump in readers, probably due to Allie and Myles attending the movie premiere, but we haven't seen much more engagement beyond that. People love what seem like unattainable love stories. They eat those types of stories up, and we gave them one and then sort of stopped showing them the story."

"I don't think that's exactly what happened," Allie interjected. "Also, we can't build a whole magazine on my love story."

"Or could we? I say for the next few issues we do a featured series called 'Letters from London.' In the first issue we can spotlight a few of your early letters with Myles and ask people to send their love letters to us. The next two issues we can publish a few of our favorite letters as well as other amazing celebrity lover stories. Think of it as a feature of summer love, ending in the third issue as summer comes to an end. I've read almost every letter in this box, and I can only imagine how amazing it would be to read the letters you wrote in response. The world will fall in love with you and Myles more and then by having people send in their letters they will feel even more connected to the magazine," Madison pitched.

Allie shifted in her seat. "I don't know. It's supposed to be a fashion magazine, not a romance novel," she said.

"I think it's brilliant, we can add the fashion in as part of the story," Ryan said. "Are you going to eat that sandwich?"

Allie shook her head. "I'm really not hungry." Ryan gave her a concerned look that only Madison caught as he reached for the sandwich.

"Here's the best part. We can throw a romantic end of the summer party to coincide with the sixth issue, the last featured issue," Madison said. "I was thinking we could do it in the gardens at St. Dunstan In the East."

"Oh, now that's a good party spot," Ryan chimed in.

"I don't know. Let me think about it and let me talk to Myles about it. I'm not sure he'll go for it," Allie said letting out a deep breath. "Leave the box on my desk please."

"Okay," Madison said feeling defeated. She smiled and turned to leave the office. "Let me know if you want me to order you some food later."

"I'm sure I'll be good. Thank you, Madison," Allie said. Madison nodded and shut the door.

"Allie, I'm curious, beyond you being uncomfortable with the idea of your personal life being on display, what was wrong with her pitch?" Ryan asked.

"I just think it's a little childish, don't you?" Allie replied.

"Not at all. I think if done right it will cause a lot of stir and publicity for the magazine. And I think people will devour your letters with Myles," Ryan said. "My vote is to have her pitch that idea to Brad and see if he goes for it. I can work on a social media campaign to present along with it."

"I don't know. I'll think about it," Allie responded.

"Alright. Should I schedule a lunch meeting with some of our investors tomorrow?" Ryan asked, getting up and rebuttoning his suit jacket.

"Can we do drinks instead of a meal? I honestly don't want to eat in front of our investors. It's always so awkward," Allie replied.

"Sure," Ryan said, walking to the door. "And honestly, think about it. Madison's idea is exactly what we need."

Ryan left Allie's office stopping by Madison's desk first. "Don't worry this is a business question. When's the last time you saw her eat a meal?"

"I'm not sure. She's usually at Myles's place at night and I meet her at the office in the morning. I mean I haven't seen her eat at home lately and we haven't had any new groceries lately. Why do you ask?" Madison whispered.

"She declines a lot of lunch meetings lately and is looking rather tired and extra thin these days. It's a little worrisome," Ryan said.

"I mean she does go for a run every day and they seem to be getting longer. Maybe that's why she's leaned out a bit?" Madison speculated.

"Maybe," Ryan shrugged. "Anyways, I think you are brilliant. Just give Allie time, she'll come around to the idea. She has to, it's too good to pass up on."

Allie dialed Myles's cell after Ryan left her office. She had avoided him since last night's awkward interaction with Lorraine. She didn't want to immediately validate that Madison's pitch was a fantastic idea without consulting Myles first. Even though putting their relationship out there through their personal letters, she had to admit Brad Garrison would love this idea as would many of their readers, but first, she needed to get Myles on board.

"Hello?" Myles answered.

"It's me. Look I'm sorry for freaking out last night. I just hate seeing her," Allie explained pacing in her office.

"I understand, I just wish you could remember how much I love you and believe me when I say that I didn't sleep with her. I wish you could just finally trust me," Myles said.

"I'm working on it, but it doesn't help when you don't tell me that you are doing work for her" Allie sighed. "It's just hard because it's an image seared into my mind, but I'm working through it and part of that process is reading your old letters that my dad brought with him on his trip to London."

"Oh yeah?" Myles asked, his voice lighting up with excitement and intrigue. "All of them, including the rather spicy ones?"

"Of course." Allie chuckled. "Anyways I was reading them until they sort of disappeared into Madison's hands apparently," Allie continued.

"Odd. Not sure why she would want to read them. Did she have much to say about them?" Myles asked.

"Well, she sort of pitched the idea that we do a three issue series based off of them. We would kick it off with the feature of a few of our letters, if you still have mine, and then get others to send in their love letters. I'm sure we could even get a few big celebrity names to let us publish some love letters too or at least their love stories," Allie explained.

"Of course, I still have your letters Als. I could never part with those," Myles replied. "How do you feel about Madison's pitch? Do you like the idea?"

"I think it could be good. It would also be fun to go through all of our old letters together and walk down memory lane, don't you think? We could turn it into something more than just a feature. It could be good for us to do together," Allie replied.

"Allie, my only desire here is to make you happy and if this could bring us closer and help you at work, then I'm willing to do it," Myles said.

"Are you sure? It's pretty personal," Allie asked.

"Well, we will just have to leave the racy ones out of it. Don't need anyone ridiculing me over those," Myles teased.

"Oh, we definitely will not be publishing any of those letters. I promise," Allie laughed.

Madison returned to her desk from dropping off something to layout. She sat down to open her email back up to see an email from Allie to Madison and Ryan with three words: "Let's Do It." Madison felt herself smile.

****

"Ryan, I noticed that Allison is looking sickly again. You've all been working closely lately for your pitch to Brad Garrison, have you seen her eat anything?" Mitch McGowan asked on the phone.

"I can't say I have," Ryan replied thinking back to the past few days spent with Madison, Allie, and Myles in the conference room rummaging through hundreds of letters and emails between the two of them. "She tends to no be hungry when we break for food."

"You know she has a history of anorexia, and you need to address it before something bad happens again. People are commenting on it online and in the media. You better find a way to fix it," Mitch explained tensely. "Everything is on the line if she ends up back in rehab."

"Understood," Ryan said before hanging up and heading back to the conference room. Everyone was laughing as he entered.

"What did I miss?" he asked reentering the room. For the past three days, Allie, Myles, Madison, Ryan, and Clarissa spent hours each evening scouring through hundreds of letters written between Myles and Allie of the years, trying to find the perfect letters to include in their pitch to Brad Garrison. After the third issue of the magazine did worse in sales than the second and quarterly reports on website traffic showed a drop off in visits, every move they made had to be approved by Brad.

"There are a series of letters where Allie just wrote jokes instead of anything of substance," Myles explained. "They were quite funny actually."

"How about we order in some Thai food? Thoughts?" Ryan asked. "It's been a while since lunch and Allie you have to be starving since you didn't eat with us."

222

"I'm good, but the rest of you feel free! I really want to finish up here and see if these letters we chose will scan properly," Allie explained. "I'll eat a protein bar later."

"Are you sure? You love Thai food," Myles asked.

"I do normally, but I'm honestly not hungry and don't want to waste any," Allie said, getting a little annoyed.

"Just a protein bar today? You didn't eat breakfast," Madison blurted out.

"Geez, who made you all the food police?" Allie asked, clearly getting upset about it.

"No need to get upset. I just wanted to know if you wanted Thai food, if you're good then I'm good," Ryan said with a smile, trying to diffuse the tension.

"I'm going to go scan these." Allie got up, leaving the room and everyone in it behind.

"Is everything okay with Allie? You all seem concerned about her eating habits," Myles asked.

"Shouldn't you know the answer to that question?" Ryan snapped at Myles.

Myles shrugged, folding up letters and putting them back into their respective boxes. "I don't know what's going on here, but you've clearly upset her. Watch your back mate."

"Whatever," Ryan replied as Myles left the conference room, letters in tow.

****

Ryan could see Allie's office light still on from across the office. Wanting to address her outburst earlier and Mitch's worries, he headed over to her office. He knew she had an issue long before it was brought to his attention. He remembered her mother going away for a while when he was young because she became so ill from not eating. If Myles and Madison weren't going to address Allie's issue, he would.

"Allie, if we are going to call a long-term truce and go to Brad with this pitch, I need you to be honest with me," Ryan said, closing the door to her office. It was late, and Madison was gone for the day, but Ryan still felt the need to close Allie's door as he approached a sensitive subject.

223

"Honest about what?" Allie asked, staring at her computer screen, trying to see which of her letters scanned the best for their pitch.

"Stop looking at the computer for just one second," Ryan said. Allie looked up and sat back in her chair.

"You look serious but not in the normal 'I'm Ryan Eliot, here to destroy your life' serious. What's going on?" Allie asked nervously.

"Tell me the truth. Why did you get so upset earlier when we brought up the fact that no one has seen you eat in a while? Are you struggling with an eating disorder again?" Ryan asked sitting down in one of the chairs across from Allie.

"What makes you think you have the right to come in here and ask me something like that?" Allie snapped.

"Allie, there's no need to get upset. I want to make sure you are okay. For once, there's no ill intent here," Ryan explained.

"Why the sudden change? You've never been nice to me before, no need to start now," Allie replied.

"You know that's not true," Ryan said.

"The fuck? It's the only true thing," Allie said.

"Allie, look I just want to help. Don't fight me right now, you are clearly unwell and it's showing. Now are you relapsing into your eating disorder or not?" Ryan asked again sternly.

Allie drew in a deep breath, a tear rolling down her face. Slowly she nodded her head, finally letting herself acknowledge the truth she was trying to hide from herself. "How did you figure it out?" she asked.

"You've lost quite a bit of weight since starting here and you've declined food every single time that Madison has asked. I haven't seen you eat in a while and I know Madison hasn't seen you eat either," Ryan replied, scratching his neck, leaning forward in his chair as Allie let more tears fall from her eyes.

"How do you know Madison hasn't seen me eat. I swear I will fire her if I find out the two of you...."

"Stop. I asked her today after I met with you. She didn't want to answer, but we are all worried about you Allison."

"I've just been stressed out with things not working the way they are supposed to." Allie started to cry. "And things with Myles... well you don't need to know about that...."

"It's okay that you've been stressed out, but you have to eat Allie. As much as you don't want to, you have to eat, and I want to help you," Ryan said comforting her.

"Why?" Allie asked, wiping her eyes.

"Because I know how this goes. My mother has struggled with an eating disorder most of her life. I know how this all works, and I can help you steer away from this path before it becomes damaging. Plus, we have a magazine to run, as a team." Ryan winked at Allie who finally smiled.

"You don't have to be nice to me or pity me Ryan," Allie said, straightening up in her seat.

"Believe me the last thing I want to do is start a friendship with you, but if the magazine fails because you can't get yourself together, we all get fired. Not worth it," Ryan said.

"Fine," Allie said, wiping the tears away from her eyes.

"Good," Ryan replied. He slowly got up and headed to the door. "Make sure to get some sleep tonight for tomorrow's pitch or Brad will never go through with it."

Allie watched Ryan leave before pulling out her phone and typing in his Instagram handle to find the photo he posted from Paris. "That's what I thought, not a model at all," she whispered to herself.

Episode 19- Cruel Summer pt 2

The next day Madison woke up excited to head out with Ryan and Allie this afternoon for a lunch pitch to Brad Garrison. After pouring over the love story of Allie and Myles to curate a perfect set of letters for the first of their new three issue summer series, it was finally time to get Mr. Garrison on board with the project. Madison turned on some music to help her get ready for today's meeting. Slowly, she slid clothes back and forth in the closet, looking through a now overwhelming amount of clothing to find the perfect outfit.

Madison smiled at the thought of everyone getting along. Allie and Ryan were working together without bickering or making snide remarks for once. Things were going perfectly. She settled on a pair of black straight leg trousers, a tan sweater to go over a white button-down shirt and a pair of black pointy heels. She swayed to the music as she pulled a brush through her hair.

After getting ready she headed downstairs expecting to see Allie in the kitchen with a coffee cup in her hands. The kitchen was empty and the rest of the house quiet. Madison touched the side of the coffee pot to see if it was warm, a signal Allie was just here. The coffee pot was cold with yesterday's coffee. Confused, Madison headed back upstairs to Allie's room. The door was open and the room empty.

"Maybe she went on a run," Madison thought heading back downstairs. As she entered the foyer, she saw Allie's running shoes near the front door. Madison shrugged her shoulders, heading back to the kitchen to make herself some coffee. As the coffee pit started brewing, she slid her phone from her pocket and dialed Allie's number.

****

Allie pulled her phone out from her coat hung on the back of her chair. "One second," she said, ignoring the call and putting her phone on silent. "Sorry about that, where were we?"

"You were going over the letters," Brad Garrison replied, sitting back in his chair a bit, intrigued by the pitch Ryan and Allie were making to him.

"Right," Allie said, regathering her thoughts. Instead of lunch, Allie had proposed going to her favorite coffee shop for a cup of coffee and a pastry. Lunch felt stuffy to her, too formal when trying to pitch a romantic idea such as this. "We've spent a good portion of the last few weeks pouring through hundreds of letters between Myles and I from the start of our relationship as pen pals until I ultimately moved out to England. I think we've chosen the best ones for print. The goal is to enchant our readers into sending us their best love letters for the second and third issues of the summer magazines. We start by publishing our love story through love letters and ask people to send in their love letters and love stories, and then we publish the best ones.

Since we are a fashion magazine, I've also reached out to some of my favorite designers to put together some outfits or even sketches to go along with the letters we receive. Then with the last issue we will announce a big end of summer romance party and the issue will include some updated letters between Myles and I to end the series."

Brad Garrison leaned forward grabbing his coffee to sip. His face was expressionless as he mulled over the idea. Ryan watched intently, waiting to answer any questions that Brad could come up with. Allie nervously uncrossed her legs and re-crossed them, feeling her coat vibrating behind her. After a few more seconds, Mr. Garrison reached for the folder of letters between Allie and Myles, setting his coffee cup back on the table. He skimmed through a few of them, chuckling at a few parts before closing the folder.

"What's the social media plan here?" he asked.

"I'm glad you asked," Ryan started. "With the letters we've also been curating a series of old photographs of Allie and Myles. We will announce the issue with a short video montage of their photos and some interview material we will capture soon. We will also have some live streams and do interviews with other staff members and celebrities about summer romances they've had in the past."

"I thought the point of a summer romance was for it to only last a summer. That doesn't quite seem to go with the love story of Allie and Myles, now does it?" Mr. Garrison interjected.

"We thought you might have a problem with that. Now sure, Allie and Myles didn't have just a summer fling and that's the point. What if we could take the idea of a summer romance, a supposedly short-lived romantic encounter and turn it into a longer love story? What if summer romances could turn into the next lifelong fairytale? What if we could make a summer romance last 'forever'?" Ryan said, emphasizing the last word.

"Interesting," Mr. Garrison replied, nodding his head. Silence fell between the three of them again as Mr. Garrison took another drink of his coffee. Allie nervously pulled apart a croissant, never eating a piece.

"So, what do you say?" Ryan asked.

"I think it's a genius idea. I knew if the two of you could just work together that something like this could come out of it," Mr. Garrison said.

"Well actually we couldn't have done it without-" Ryan started.

"Without your support and push to be better," Allie interjected, cutting Ryan off before he could admit that this was the brainchild of Madison. Ryan looked over at her surprised.

"Well, whatever it is that pushed the two of you to finally set your differences aside and come up with this creative idea, please continue to do that. I look forward to seeing the mock-ups on these issues and will be intrigued to see how many letters we eventually get from our readers," Mr. Garrison said getting up from his chair. "Now if you'll excuse me, I need to head out for another meeting."

"Of course," Allie said, standing up to shake his hand. Ryan and Allie watched Mr. Garrison leave the coffee shop before high fiving at the success of their pitch.

"Well, we have a lot of work to do, but he seems to be very interested in this idea!" Allie exclaimed. "These issues might be just what we need to get our numbers up. We should celebrate!"

"How about you start with actually eating that croissant instead of just picking at it?" Ryan replied.

"Fine," Allie said with a playful pout as she took a bite. "I'm so happy that all of the hard work and emotional rollercoaster of reliving the past through reading all of these letters these past couple of weeks has really paid off today."

"I bet," Ryan said, looking out the window of the coffeeshop as people walked past. "Question though, why did you cut me off when I was going to give Madison some credit for this idea? She did come up with it."

"Well, I found out from my dad's assistant that our dear Madison took credit for the launch party already instead of calling it a team effort. Seems a little desperate to climb the ladder if you ask me, and that's not someone I want pitching the owner of the company," Allie replied. Ryan sneered shaking his head.

"Sure, she came up with the initial idea, but I'm the one who put it all into action and I didn't need him thinking that she was doing all the work and planning here. She's just an assistant and one day when she's ready she can step into the spotlight and take the credit, until then she can wait her turn," Allie explained. "Plus, she couldn't even make it to the meeting this morning, what makes you think she should get credit for any of this?"

****

Madison sat down at her desk, turning on her computer. Allie was still missing in action and not answering her phone. Madison felt uneasy about the whole thing, as if she was missing out on something big, as if something was being kept from her. She opened her calendar which also showed Allie's calendar alongside hers. Intrigued to find out where Allie was this morning, she scanned her morning appointments and there in black and white laid a meeting with Brad Garrison this morning. Feeling her anxiety rise, she scrolled down a bit to see that the lunch meeting with Mr. Garrison was cancelled and removed from both of their calendars.

Feeling betrayed and upset, Madison got up from her desk and calmly walked to the bathroom. She could see Ryan's office door open, and the light turned off. Clearly, he knew the meeting was moved to this morning. Madison could feel her coffee and cereal churning in her stomach. She quickly headed into the bathroom, locking the door behind her. She could feel a cold sweat on her back. It was one thing to be betrayed by Allie but another to be betrayed by Ryan. She looked at herself in the mirror as she hunched over the sink, trying to suppress the urge to throw up and relieve herself of the pit in her stomach.

After a few moments and without throwing up, Madison emerged from the bathroom, her head held high. At any moment Ryan and Allie would be returning to the office for today's work. If the pitch went well, they needed to start moving towards putting together the layout for the feature in the next issue. If it didn't go well, then they would need to scramble and put together a new concept. Madison sat back down at her desk. Allie was already in her office, the door shut. Madison could hear her on the phone, talking excitedly. *Things must have gone well then,* she thought to herself as she scanned through her emails, looking to see if Allie sent any assignments along for today.

As she cleared her inbox a small message popped up on the interoffice chat platform. "Dinner tonight?" Ryan asked in the message box.

Still feeling upset over being cut out of the meeting, she typed back a hasty "No."

"I'll make your favorite…" he replied.

"I'm good, but thanks. Lots of work today. Talk to you later…" she replied before signing out of the chat. She could see Ryan now standing in his office doorway looking at her across the large room. Allie emerged from her office carrying a couple of folders. "Come with me," she said heading towards the conference room. Madison stood up from her desk and followed, watching Ryan disappear back into his office and close the door.

"Mr. Garrison moved the meeting up late last night, so I'm sorry I didn't have time to give you a heads up about it. It would have probably been extremely boring to you anyways," Allie said, laying out the letters and some mock-up sketches of potential photo ideas on the large table. Madison took a seat at the table, afraid to say anything at this point and risk losing control of her emotions.

"Anyways, he loved the idea of these three issues and the party at the end of summer to wrap it all up. Mr. Garrison started to question the whole 'summer love' concept, as we knew he would, and Ryan did a fantastic job at spinning it into the whole reframed idea of making summer love last forever," Allie gushed. Madison watched her smiling and laughing as she spoke about the meeting, describing how amazing Ryan was and how excited Mr. Garrison seemed to be about the new concept.

"Now, I need you to order lunch for the layout department, myself, and Ryan. I'm thinking Chinese food today. I'm feeling rather hungry, so get some extra crab rangoons. Then I will need you to run some errands during the meeting. I printed off this list of items I need you to retrieve for the other photoshoots for the next issue. Ryan and I are going to meet with layout team to talk logistics for the issue over lunch, and then we will meet with his team to talk about the social media strategies."

Madison nodded. "You don't need me at any of these meetings?"

"Not today. I'll get Ryan's assistant to take notes and type them up to circulate for everyone. I need you to go and grab my dry cleaning and run some other errands for me," Allie replied.

"Okay then," Madison said, taking the list of errands Allie needed done from the table before quickly exiting the room.

She headed back to her desk to see a sticky note on her monitor with the words, "I didn't know. Come over tonight please" scribbled on them in Ryan's handwriting. Upset Madison crumbled up the sticky note and tossed it in the bin before grabbing her jacket and bag to start on the list Allie gave her.

****

Madison groaned at her phone which was ringing for the fourth time in a row. Ryan was relentless with text messages and phone calls all evening about coming over for dinner, so he could explain what happened. Upset and annoyed, she finally answered the phone.

"You both literally cut me out of the whole project. You went with Allie to discuss the idea I pitched to the two of you for the next three issues and left me out of it," Madison said, her voice piercing with anger as she answered the phone.

"I don't know why you are mad at me about this. Allie is the one who took the credit. Not me, which I could explain to you if you just came over," Ryan replied calmly.

"Why didn't you say anything? Why didn't you tell me the meeting time changed?" Madison snapped back.

"Madison, how was I supposed to know you didn't know? I tried to give you credit, which you would know if you let me explain to you. But also, what did you want me to say? Did you want me to call Allie a liar in front of the owner of the company? Did you want me to call her out and tarnish her reputation?" Ryan asked, becoming annoyed.

"You could have stood up for me. You could have found a way," Madison said.

"And what? Risk Allie knowing about us? You really wanted me to get you fired today and risk never seeing you again? Do you think she wouldn't know that we are together if I continuously go up to bat for you when she lies to her boss about it all? Dammit Madison, stop and think about what you would do in that situation," Ryan replied. Silence fell between them for a moment. "Just come over for dinner, please. I'd like to see you tonight."

"I hate that we have to keep this all a secret," Madison whispered, her voice trembling. "I hate that to have you in my life this way, I have to keep it a secret."

"I know, but our alternative is you going back to California for good. Please come over for dinner and we can talk some more," Ryan begged.

"Fine, but dinner better be good," Madison said hanging up immediately.

****

"Looks like we have the top selling magazine in the company today!" Allie announced to everyone gathered into the large open space of the office. "We could not have done it without all your hard work over the past month. Let's have a round of applause for everyone."

Madison begrudgingly clapped her hands, still annoyed by Allie taking credit for the idea of this issue. Madison overheard Brad Garrison calling to congratulate Allie this morning while going over Allie's schedule this week with her. Allie, of course, thanked him and made sure to thank her entire team for their efforts. She made no mention of Madison's initial suggestion of the summer romance idea as Mr. Garrison praised Allie and Ryan over and over for their genius concept. Now Allie stood beaming as she toasted her staff with mid-morning mimosas.

For weeks now, Allie sent Madison off on errand runs while key meetings for the issue were happening. Madison was shut out of any planning, including the plans for the end of summer party. Ryan's assistant was brought in for meetings to take notes and coordinate the venue and party planners. Even at home Allie would simply go straight to bed or stay over at Myles' flat to avoid talking to Madison.

Madison scanned the room for Ryan who once again was nowhere to be found. They kept missing each other lately. He was hard to reach by phone and when they would make plans, he would be stuck at the office late, working with Allie on the next set of issues. She would head over to his flat and wait for him to come home. Out of the last three weeks she had seen him a total of two times outside of work and even then, he was too tired to even hold a full conversation with her. At work, Allie would call him into her office for private meetings or they would go to lunch leaving Madison behind.

Suddenly, he emerged from the lobby, yawning as he made his way through the crowd of people chatting away. He looked exhausted. Madison watched as he escaped the crowd heading straight into his office shutting the door behind him.

****

After another long day of running useless errands for Allie, Madison headed back to the townhouse alone for the night. The garden was now fully bloomed with bright flowers in hues of yellows, blues, pinks, and purples. Every time she entered the garden gates here or even at Ryan's place, she was met with a beautiful summertime fragrance.

Madison pulled out her phone to check for messages from Ryan, but once again, there was nothing. Feeling defeated, Madison made her way into the townhouse and upstairs, pulling her shoes off at the top of the staircase. Wobbling a little, she noticed her room door was open.

"I swear I shut this door this morning," she whispered, slowly peeking inside. A cold sweat started to build at the nape of

233

her neck, at the sight of a dress bag on her bed with a note in Allie's handwriting:

The truth always eventually has a way of coming out.

****

"What's on the menu for tonight?" Ryan asked as he entered the conference room.

"Indian food," Allie replied motioning to the containers of curry on the table. Ryan nodded, taking a seat next to her.

"How many letters did we get today?" he asked, reaching for the curry to pour over some rice on a plate in front of him.

"I think we received about a hundred," Allie replied taking a bite of food.

"Remind me again why we can't have at least Myles or even god forbid Clarissa, Olivia, or even her assistant who goes around kissing everyone's ass, here to help us go through these?" Ryan sighed.

"Because I don't want anyone to know how hard it is for me to sit here and eat dinner. Myles is always watching me when we are together. When it's just you here with me it feels more natural, like I can be myself and not under constant scrutiny," Allie replied. "Plus, Myles finds all of this letter stuff extremely boring. And be nice. I thought you and Clarissa would be good together at the start. You two were extremely flirty."

"She's really not my taste," Ryan replied taking a bite of food before rummaging through some of the letters in front of them.

"Let me guess, you prefer the forbidden fruit, like assistants told to stay away?" Allie asked, looking over at him for a reaction. Ryan stared forward ignoring her pointed question.

"I know you've been seeing her despite my threat to fire her," Allie said. "It's very evident by the way you've softened up over the past month or so. Well, that and I found the dress she wore in Paris when the two of you went on your little romantic getaway. Never hang things in the closet that you don't want to be found."

"Don't be petty and fire her," Ryan said, setting down his spoon. "I pushed her to do it and quite frankly I don't understand why you felt like you had the right to tell her what to do in her personal life to being with.”

“Well, that was before I knew I could trust you,” Allie replied, pushing a piece of chicken back and forth on her plate. “You’ve changed though. Dare I say, I kind of like this version of Ryan Eliot.”

“How long have you known? Is this why she’s never in the meetings lately or hell even the office?” Ryan asked.

“I had a feeling that she went to Paris with you since I met Charlie and his partner, Patrick, at Altitude the weekend she was supposed to be in Paris with him. I let it go and put business first, until your compelling speech about needing to eat. That’s when I finally saw the picture you posted from that weekend. Clarissa thought you went with some model, but we both know Madison doesn’t have the shoulders of a model. Then I went looking for the dress you more than likely bought here and voila, the rest is history,” Allie answered, taking a bite of rice.

“So, what’s your next move then?” Ryan asked.

“Oh, I don’t have a next move. I’m sure she found the dress on her bed with my note this evening and that buzzing noise coming from your pocket is her freaking out. I’ll let her spin out a little, before saying anything,” Allie replied.

“That’s fucked up, even for me Allie,” Ryan replied. “She did nothing wrong here. If you fire anyone it needs to be me.”

“So, she could what, take your role here at the magazine? I think not. The two of you won’t last now that your relationship is no longer a secret,” Allie replied snickering. “If it doesn’t fall apart because the two of you actually do like each other, it’ll fall apart once the media and all your past flings start to tear her apart.”

“I think we’re done here Allie,” Ryan replied, getting up from the table. “Enjoy the rest of your dinner alone.”

****

Myles entered the office to surprise Allie with dinner after she cancelled their plans again at the last minute due to a large number of letters to go through and no time to do it during the time that the office was open. The lobby was dim and quiet as he stepped off the elevator carrying a picnic basket with chicken,

235

vegetables, and mashed potatoes he whipped up before heading to see her.

He made his way to her office to see it dark and empty. He checked her desk to see if her bag was still there or if maybe she had left for the evening. There it sat on her chair with her coat neatly folded below it. He made his way out stopping to check Madison's desk for any sign of her being here with Allie, before heading to the conference room. Without a sign of Madison, he headed down the hall.

He could hear Allie talking to someone as he rounded the corner of the room. A familiar male voice replying. Myles watched Ryan leave the conference room. Curious, Myles peered into the room seeing two half eaten dinners in front of stacks of unopened letters. Myles felt anger rising in him. Allie said she would be here with Clarissa or Madison, not Ryan. Upset, he stormed into the room tossing the basket on the floor as Allie looked up at him, her eyes filled with shock.

"Just reading letters with the girls," Myles mocked. "I guess this is your way of trying to make us even for the Lorraine incident. "Myles turned to leave shaking his head. Allie got up from the table chasing after Myles.

"Myles! Wait!" she yelled as he headed through the lobby doors. Allie caught up with him as he waited for the elevator.

"You lied Allie. I saw Ryan leave the conference room, His face all red and sweaty. What the hell were you two doing? When did you start seeing him?" Myles asked, angrily pushing the elevator call button.

"Oh, come on Myles. It's not like that and you know it," Allie snickered.

"Looked like a nice little date to me," Myles snapped.

"We were working," Allie replied. "It's work. We have about three hundred letters to go through as a reply to our love story. You know the one where you and I were, I mean, are happy?"

"I think 'were' was the right choice of words. I haven't seen you in a couple of days because of your little project and then we finally make plans, and you cancel at the last moment to have dinner with him. We were happy…" Myles replied as the elevator door opened.

"Myles wait, you're being irrational."

"No, I'm being honest, like you asked me to be, which is something you can't say you're being right now," Myles said getting into the elevator. Allie put her hand over the door, not letting it close.

"Please let me explain, it's not what it seems. Can I come over tonight when I'm done here?" Allie begged. "I'll tell you everything."

"I think I need a cool down period. I'll call you when I'm ready to talk about all of this. You've been different ever since we saw Lorraine, I should have known you were still angry and didn't trust me even though I told you nothing happened between us… what I don't understand is why you had to cheat on me with Ryan of all people. I thought you hated the guy, but I guess I was wrong," Myles said, pressing the close door button.

"Myles come on," Allie said.

"Good night, Allie," he replied as she moved her hand, and the doors began to shut.

****

Ryan walked out of Garrison Publishing heading towards any open flower shoppe at this hour. As he walked through rows and rows of shoppes, he pulled out his phone to call Madison. It had been a few days since he last spoke to Madison, and he missed the sound of her voice.

"Hey stranger," Madison said, answering her phone as she sat on her bed eating a bowl of cereal for dinner.

"Stranger?" Ryan asked, chuckling a bit.

"Yeah, stranger. I've barely seen you lately," Madison replied. "It's almost like you've been avoiding me."

"I'm sorry Mads. Allie and I have been going through every single letter that people mailed in, it's just led to some really late nights," Ryan replied. "I'd much rather be with you. I swear. I miss you."

"Uh huh. I don't know… getting home at one in the morning and posting about eating dinner together and going through love letters every other night? I saw her post a picture of the two of you tonight eating Italian food. It came across like a date almost," Madison admitted.

"I swear it's not a date and it was Indian food that I didn't even finish," Ryan replied.

"I know it's not, well at least I'm always hopeful it's not, but you have been distant. You would tell me if something changed right?" Madison asked.

"Of course, I would tell you and I'm calling you tonight to tell you nothing has changed except how much I miss you… which is a lot," Ryan admitted.

"If you miss me so much then how about you actually come home at a good hour tonight and I'll cook you a dinner that you'll actually finish?" Madison suggested.

"Already on my way. When will you be over?" Ryan asked, spotting a flower shoppe still open.

"Already here," Madison replied.

"Be there soon," Ryan said, entering the shoppe.

****

"Hey! That was fast!" Madison called out from the kitchen a few minutes later, as she heard the door to the apartment open and close. "I hope that spaghetti and meatballs is okay for dinner."

Madison waited for a response from Ryan for a minute before emerging from the kitchen to see Myles standing in the living room. They stared at each other for a second.

"Well, this makes sense," Myles commented, shaking his head with a chuckle.

"What are you doing here?" Madison asked.

"Oh, did Ryan not tell you that I'm his flat mate?" Myles asked, collecting some items from the desk drawer on the far side of the room.

"What are you talking about? Ryan said his roommate or flat mate, whatever you call it here, travels for work and is never here," Madison answered in disbelief.

"Classic Ryan, though that's a new lie I haven't heard before. Usually, he just tells the girl he's sleeping with that I work night shifts, so it won't be a problem if they make a lot of noise,"

Myles scoffed. "It's been a while since I needed to actually stay here seeing as I haven't been working too much down in this area of town. It's nice to know that Ryan's taken full advantage of the place though since I've been staying in Hyde Park."

Madison felt her head spinning. "I don't understand. Why would you ever be his roommate? I thought you two hated each other."

"Seems like there is a lot he's not telling you as he's currently shagging Allie at the Forever office," Myles laughed.

"That's not true and you know it," Madison retorted.

"Check out the social media pages. They've had dinner together at the office for the last couple of nights and I saw him leaving the office a little sweaty and disheveled tonight," Myles answered.

Madison closed her eyes and let out a sigh. "Myles, stop. Tell me what's really going on here."

"Look I am only here to pick up a few of my items. Go back to preparing your dinner, which I am sure you will be eating solo tonight," Myles said. "Hope this all makes betraying Allie worth it."

Madison didn't speak, watching Myles go into the second bedroom and returning moments later with another bag and a few suit jackets.

"Good night and good luck, Madison," Myles said before leaving. Madison finished making dinner and sat down on the couch with a glass of wine, waiting for Ryan to show up.

Episode 20- if you're gonna lie

"Hey! I come bearing gifts," Ryan said breathing heavy as he slid his shoes off at the front door. Madison was sitting on the couch, finishing off another glass of wine, plates of spaghetti sat on the table ice cold now. Madison didn't say a word as Ryan set down his bag and made his way to the couch handing her a bouquet of roses. Madison looked straight ahead ignoring the gesture.

"Madison, I know I haven't been around much lately, but please say you won't stay mad for too long," Ryan said, leaning in to give her a kiss on the cheek. Before his lips could touch her cheek, she pulled away. "Madison, really?"

"Met your roommate tonight," Madison said getting up from the couch. She watched as Ryan's eyes widened and he ran his fingers nervously through his hair.

"Madison let me explain…"

"Explain what? Explain that this is all been a game? I should have known better than to believe this could be real. I should have known this was all a ploy to get to Allie," Madison snapped as she started to pace the width of the living room.

"Madison it's not like that at all," Ryan tried to explain.

"Then what is it like? Why is Myles your roommate?" Madison yelled.

"It's complicated and I'm not sure how much I can actually say without putting you in danger," Ryan replied calmly.

"Putting me in danger?" Madison shook her head in disbelief. "What are you, some kind of secret spy? You know what, fine don't tell me and don't bother talking to me again," Madison said her voice trembling as she sat the wine glass down on the coffee table and headed toward the door to grab her shoes, jacket, and purse.

"Madison, stop. Please let me try to explain," Ryan said, getting up from the couch to intercept her as she struggled to put her shoes on. "Myles is my stepbrother."

"What?" Madison asked in disbelief.

"Myles is my stepbrother. Mitch McGowan is my stepdad. He owns the apartment. Myles was supposed to sell his

Hyde Park apartment and stay here, but as you know he didn't do that and that's why he's never here," Ryan started to explain.

"I don't believe you," Madison replied, continuing to put her shoes on.

"Here, look at these photos," Ryan said getting his phone out. Madison grabbed her coat from the hook near the door as Ryan hurried to find old pictures. "Look," he said, showing her a photo of a wedding, a young Ryan and Myles standing with Mitch and presumably Ryan's mother.

"That doesn't explain why you didn't tell me that he was your roommate," Madison said sliding her coat on. "Or why you brought him in to work at the magazine. Or anything really."

"I'm trying to tell you," Ryan said, getting impatient.

"Tell me then!" Madison yelled. "Why are you keeping it a secret that you two are related? Why are you staying late with Allie at work lately? What's the end game here? Why all the secrets and lies? You keep telling me it's different between us, but what I see is someone who is using people to get a promotion he thinks he deserves. It's pathetic."

"That's not what's happening. I'm not the one pulling the strings here, Mitch is and if I don't do as I'm told then my life as we know it is over," Ryan snapped.

"What does that even fucking mean Ryan? You have to hurt Allie? Me? Myles? Or what? You lose this cushy apartment and a job you'd rather not be doing?"

"He'll divorce my mom and yes, I'll lose all of this, and we will be on the street," Ryan replied. Madison dropped her bag on the floor, turning to look at Ryan. For once she could see fear in his eyes.

"I don't understand. Why would he do that?"

"I owe him a lot of money. He paid my way into and through Cambridge and some of my other debts. I couldn't get into a school on my own and so he pulled the strings to get me in and made it contingent that I pay him back," Ryan started to explain.

"Pay him back how?" Madison asked, slightly confused.

"At first, I thought it would be monetary payment, I've saved almost half of it already, but then he said he would rather have me do tasks for him. The first one was getting the job at

Forever London. Then it was bringing Myles in for the interview and so forth and so on," Ryan explained.

"But why?" Madison asked. None of this made sense to her. Was he still lying? Was he telling the truth? Her head was spinning in possibilities.

"I don't know. My instructions are clear: don't ask questions, just do what I'm told," he replied. "Sometimes it's just curating stories and posts on social media, other times it's paying people and sending them on their way."

"Or changing the dates on venue paperwork?" Madison asked as her anger started to rise again. Ryan shook his head.

"I told you, I had nothing to do with that," he said.

"So, you say, but how can I believe anything you say at this point? You've been living a double life this whole time. I don't even know who you are. Who knows what's real with you," Madison replied, her voice beginning to tremble again.

"You know me better than anyone else, I promise. I can't explain any of this, if I could, I would." Ryan took a step back from Madison.

"Just try to explain it" Madison asked, reaching down to pick up her bag.

"Madison, I can't. I don't know what to say to make this better," Ryan sighed.

"You can't, that's convenient" Madison scoffed. "You know the worst part of all of this? I was going to tell you that I love you tonight, but now I think that's the worst thing I could ever say to you, especially after this," Madison said. Ryan forced a half smile trying to comfort Madison.

"That's not the worst thing you could say, because I love you too," he said stepping towards her. Madison raised her hand signaling him to stop.

"That's too bad because I could never love someone like you," Madison said opening the door and leaving.

Madison left Ryan's flat without plan. She didn't want to go back to the townhouse this angry and then have to face Allie. She didn't want to have to lie about Myles if Allie didn't know about Ryan being his stepbrother. She didn't know whether to cry or to find something to throw. She kept walking through the streets of London as the shoppes closed and the crowds started to disappear. She wanted to run far away from the aching pain in her chest. He said he loved her, but did he mean it now or was it part of whatever game this was? Was he really the guy that kissed her at the edge of the lake, or was that part of all of this too?

Her legs started to slow as every memory came flooding in threatening to crumble her. And then she saw it, a clue to getting the information she needed, Charlie. Ryan always tried to steer her clear of Charlie. He got angry when she gave Charlie her number at Altitude. He showed up at the coffee shop the day Charlie gave Madison a tour of the city. He made sure they wouldn't have their event at Altitude and after she spotted Ryan speaking to Charlie at the relaunch party Charlie kept his distance from her. Deep down, as much as she wished it wasn't true, she knew exactly who could explain all of this to her.

****

"Let me guess, he finally told you," Charlie yelled out from behind the bar where he was drying some glasses.

"I can't believe you lied to me this whole time too! You've been collecting information and playing games just as much as Ryan has. What the hell Charlie? Were we actually friends at all?" Madison yelled, marching over to the bar.

Charlie sighed, setting a glass down before stepping out from behind the bar next to Madison. "Why don't you just calm down and I'll explain it all to you."

"Oh, so you can explain it and he can't?!" Madison yelled, her arms flailing about in anger as tears started to flow down her cheeks our frustration and feelings of betrayal.

"Madison, breathe," Charlie said trying to calm her down, his hand touching her arm.

"Don't." Madison pulled her arm away, taking a step back from him. "I don't need you to touch me. I don't even know why I came here."

"That's fair, I guess. Just listen to me please, if you just let me explain, it'll all make more sense," Charlie said, his voice soft. "It'll make it easier to forgive Ryan, I promise."

Madison drew in a deep breath. Forgiving Ryan was the last thing on her mind. She wanted answers, a reason to stop feeling betrayed and taken advantage of. "Fine," she sighed. "I'll give you twenty minutes and then I'm out of here."

"Okay. Well, I should start by telling you that anyone you meet who is part of this owes one of two men something, a debt per se. Those two men are Ken Davis and Mitch McGowan. I personally owe Ken Davis a debt. About six years ago I worked for Ken on a movie. I was part of the camera crew. We were in New York City filming the movie and I ran into a bit of trouble. Long story short, a few friends and I went out, drugs were involved, and someone died. Ken covered for me with an alibi," Charlie paused looking at the shock already crossing Madison's face.

"I didn't have a hand in the death of the person. I was honestly in the wrong place at the wrong time. Ken conditioned her help on a promise that I would owe him one day. About two years later, after I moved to London, he came to visit me. He told me about this idea that he had, an experiment of sorts that would allow them to create a new form of television or movies of sorts. He seemed really excited about it and said that it would really help Hollywood get out of its creative slump. All he needed was to cash in on some of the debts owed to him and get people to help create scenarios around someone's life, so he could start to build his storyline. The way he explained it sounded harmless. We would cause certain scenarios to play out, manipulate the environment a bit, to help create a story based on reality. This way Ken could use the real-life reactions of his test subject to create an authentic story. I signed on because it sounded like an easy way to pay my debt."

Madison nodded, listening to Charlie's story.

"What started out as a simple sort of 'research and experiment' morphed into something much larger as Ken agreed with Mitch to use their own kids, Allie and Myles, as the subjects of the story. As I'm sure you know Allie and Myles were modern day pen pals and social media friends by this point in time. Ken agreed to allow Allie to move to London and, I believe he encouraged her to take the study abroad program out here. That's where I came into play. I used my connections to get Allie a job at a local coffee shop and Myles a contract with the gallery owner,

Patrick. It didn't seem like much work, I simply pulled some strings to get two people into some great positions, and then Ken asked for something more. He asked me to recruit another person into all of this. So, I did, and things continued to progress. Every week Ken asked for something new, threatening to go to the authorities in New York about that night.

"That's where things started to spiral. The person I recruited, Colin, was to become great friends with Myles, which he did. They became drinking buddies. Allie started to feel a distance growing between her and Myles and they started fighting. The fighting started to push Myles away a bit. Colin and Myles began to hang out more and more. Colin knew some guys who held underground high stakes poker games and invited Myles to go play with them. Myles then began to gamble more than he attended his classes. Myles chased the high of alcohol and gambling and began to lose tons of money. He was losing interest in Allie, who he had months earlier claimed to be the love of his life, and anything else that used to bring him joy.

"This of course did not bode well with Mitch who decided he wanted to put an end to this whole gambling side story. Mitch stepped in and made a deal with Myles: a job at this firm that paid well enough for Myles to pay back his gambling debts in exchange for sending Allie home. You see Mitch wanted to change course. It turns out he never agreed to bring Colin in or anyone else after that. Ken got angry about the deal Mitch made with Myles, especially when Allie returned to California with a new eating disorder and her emergence onto the party girl scene.

"That's when Ken redeveloped the whole social experiment. He created a new scenario, a better controlled environment for Allie, better known as Forever London. To my knowledge, Brad Garrison is being played just as much as the rest of them. Once Mitch caught wind of what they were planning, he wanted back in. This time with Ryan, his stepson, owing him a debt. Since Myles was already working at his firm, he could then protect him and keep him out of the storyline, or so he thought. Ryan is somewhat of a loose cannon though and tends to do his own thing in life which made him a liability in Ken's eyes, so I was brought back in under Ken's normal threats to be sort of a 'handler' for Ryan. My job is to keep him from overstepping or messing everything up. Things were going fine until everyone realized Myles was sort of leading this double life and that Ryan was going to lead Myles right back to Allie. Well, that, and then you created an issue."

"What issue did I create?" Madison asked. Her mind was racing with questions while trying to process all of this information.

"Well, I realized that you intrigued Ryan in a way no other woman has. I actually realized it during our run-in with him at the coffee shop a few months back. I approached Mitch and Ken about this potential relationship, and it was agreed that I would need to do anything I could to put a stop to it before it had the change to flourish. I tried by making Altitude look double booked for the evening of the launch party, changing the date on the paperwork in what looked close enough to pass as Ryan's handwriting, and it seemed to work for a while, that it until I saw you two kissing by the lake the night of the party. Realizing that there would be no way to stop this budding romance we decided that we would need to come up with a new assignment for Ryan. One that would cause you to leave and cause Myles to split from Allie. And once again, the plan backfired, because instead of Ryan running the risk of losing you, he decided to face whatever consequences may come and tell you this secret. If Ken finds out that you know, we are all toast," Charlie finished explaining.

"I need a drink or two to process all of this," Madison said, her voice raspy.

"Good thing we are at a bar," Charlie laughed.

"True. Wait, where is everyone?" Madison asked, realizing the place was empty on a Friday night at 10PM.

"We are closed for the night. I thought something like this might happen today," Charlie answered, walking back around the bar to make Madison a drink. Madison took a seat on a barstool across from Charlie.

"What do you mean that we are all toast if Ken finds out that I know?" Madison asked, taking an old-fashioned from Charlie.

"Remember everyone involved in this owes someone a debt. Ryan owes Mitch for university tuition which is what got him into this mess. The interesting part here is that Mitch also owes Ken a debt. When this project relaunched Ken pledged money to help Mitch's firm grow. This money was based on his and Ryan's cooperation. Ken warned us all that if the integrity of the project, the sacredness of it, is breached by anyone involved, that he will makes a call on all his debts. For me that means tipping off the NYPD that I was involved that night that the man died since his case was never solved. For Mitch it means calling on the loan made to his firm and for you it could mean being pulled into all of this," Charlie explained.

"And what about Ryan?" Madison asked.

"Well Ryan's already on thin ice, so it could mean that he owes Mitch a large sum of money, or that there could be some new consequence, one that Ken creates."

"What the fuck does that mean?" Madison blurted out.

"Look everything Ken and Mitch are doing is technically illegal, so there's no telling what else Ken will do in order to keep the project going. He's obsessed with seeing this all work out."

'I'm not sure I understand his endgame here though. How can he do all of this to his own daughter? How does he expect to create a tv show or movie mirroring her life without her realizing it? And why hasn't anyone told the authorities?" Madison could feel her heart racing.

"Madison, you know as well as I do, the authorities won't do anything. These are powerful men with deep pockets. They have the money and the resources we all wish we had but will never see in our lifetimes. There's nothing someone like you and I can do in the grand scheme of this whole situation. We are replaceable minions, pawns in their overarching grasp at power," Charlie rationalized, sliding Madison another drink. "As for Ken and Allie, I'm not sure how he can do this to her. I'm not sure if he will ever actually make a movie or tv show at this point. I think the focus has shifted to something new, but there's no telling what's going on. What I do know that some people are not equipped to be parents, and Ken is one of those people."

Madison nodded, sipping her drink, slowly letting the intoxication of this night take over her. "What do I do now Charlie?"

"What do you mean?" he replied.

"I mean how do I go to the office tomorrow, knowing what I know now?"

"I'm not sure," Charlie started, pausing to walk back around the bar and sit on a barstool next to Madison. "But I do know that I go home to Patrick every night and try to make sure that our relationship stays good. I spend every moment that I can with him making sure I am living a half decent life with him. My conscious will never be fully clear, but as long as I can bring joy and love into the world through the important parts of my life, then it offsets a bit of the bad created by all of this. I try not to create any heartbreaks in the people I love, and that's how I deal with this whole unfortunate situation caused by some poor decisions made in my past."

Madison thought about Charlie's explanation for a moment and got up without a word, walking over to the windowed wall, looking down over the city. Her head was still spinning. She didn't know whether to believe everything Charlie was saying or to storm out of the room, but the first ticket back to California and leave, never looking back. But then she saw a flash of Ryan's devastated face as she told him she could never love him. She rushed out of there so fast, she didn't even have a moment to see the sincere hurt in his eyes or the roses he held dropping to the floor. Maybe this was all true.

"I call bullshit!" she exclaimed, turning around suddenly.

"What?" Charlie laughed in surprise.

"I call bullshit on this whole 'I try to do better in the rest of my life to make up for the horrible things I am doing to other people.' You can't tell me that you honestly believe that Charlie. How does being a good person to one person, to Patrick, help alleviate the pain you are causing to Allie, Myles, and Ryan? You're no better than Ken or Mitch. You- You Justify your actions with this veiled attempt to compartmentalize your life with Patrick from your life here. You've given up on actually fixing this whole situation. You've become numb to all of it and somehow, it's all just become okay to you. You've become a cog in the machine and can't see a way out. This isn't okay Charlie, none of this is okay but you are now too blind to see it." Madison scolded, slowly walking back over the bar.

"You think I don't know it's not, okay? That Ryan doesn't know this is no way to live? You think I don't grapple with the fact that there isn't a way to fix it without Ken stepping in and me going to jail. Who will that help? Use your head, Madison. You, me, or anyone else can't change this. We can't fix this without seeing everyone we love and care about ending up hurt."

"Have you even tried?" Madison asked.

"Madison," Charlies said defeatedly.

"That's what I thought," Madison replied, grabbing her purse from the bar counter. "Grow a pair Charlie and stand up for yourself," she said before exiting the bar.

****

Myles grabbed a bottle of whiskey and sat down on the couch. Allie had called a left a few messages before finally getting the message that he didn't want to talk to her still. He opened the bottle and took a swig. Someone knocked on the door. Annoyed, he got up and walked over slowly to open it. He expected to see Allie standing there with an apology but instead as he opened the door he came face to face with his father.

"I thought I made it very clear that you were to sell this place," Mitch said, stepping past Myles into the flat.

"Guess I'm not as good of a little soldier as Ryan is," Myles snickered.

"At least he's not a drunk," Mitch replied.

"I'm not drunk," Myles replied, shutting the door. "What can I do for you Mitch?"

"It's time to come back to the firm full-time," Mitch replied, running his finger along a dusty shelf in the corner of the living room. "You've had your fun taking pictures and trying to play house with Allison Davis, but play time is over."

"What makes you think I'm going to come back to the firm just because you demand it?" Myles asked, still standing by the front door.

"Because if you don't, not only will you lose this flat, but you'll also lose the one you're supposed to be living at, and I'll blacklist you from every advertising firm, gallery, magazine, print or anyone and anything that would sell your photos. Do I make myself clear?" Mitch said.

249

"What makes you think I care?" Myles scoffed.

"Because I'll also run Allie out of town again. Then what will you be left with?"

"Like you haven't already been working on putting a wedge there anyways. Dinners with Ryan sound about right? I'm sure you orchestrated those right?" Myles retorted.

"I simply told him to get her eating disorder back under control, nothing more," Mitch replied calmly.

"Her eating disorder? Allie doesn't have an eating disorder," Myles replied shaking his head. Mitch chuckled walking towards the door.

"She has an eating disorder just as much as you have a drinking problem. Maybe I won't need to run her out of town to get her out of your life. It seems there's a lot you two aren't discussing still," Mitch said, opening the front door. "I expect to see you Monday in the office, or this will all be gone." Myles watched Mitch leave, closing the door behind him. He made his way back to his bottle of whiskey screwing the lid back on as he sat down and pulled his phone out to call Allie.

Episode 21- Shake It Out

Myles knocked on Allie's door. Slowly, she got up from the couch, placing the book she was reading on the table next to her. She was nervous to see him in person after their fight, but he had called requesting to come over and talk tonight. Her heart raced as she opened the door, welcoming him inside. He walked in slowly, his face solemn. Without a word he followed her into the living room, taking a seat on the couch.

"So...." Allie said, taking a seat next to him.

"Allie, I need you to be honest with me about something," Myles began.

"I swear nothing happened between Ryan and I," Allie blurted out. Myles shook his head.

"Not that. At least, not yet. I need you to tell me if you have an eating disorder," Myles said calmly. Allie swallowed hard at the question. Her head began racing with questions, spinning at the thought of someone else knowing her secret and telling Myles.

"Who told you that?" she finally asked.

"It doesn't matter who told me. Do you have an eating disorder?" Myles asked again. Allie felt herself start to break down. The tears began to stream down her face as she nodded her head. Myles moved in closer to her, pulling her into his arms and holding her tightly.

"I should have known. I should have caught it before now. I am so sorry Allie," he whispered, his voice cracking as she began to sob in his arms. There they sat for a few minutes, Allie crying and Myles comforting her as she finally let it all out. As Allie's crying disappeared, she sat up, wiping the tears from her eyes.

"I didn't know how to tell you," she whimpered trying to catch her breath.

"When did it start?" Myles asked, holding her hand.

"After Nick left. Well, I mean the whole thing started when I left London the last time, but I swear I was better and then Nick tried to make me choose between my friendship with him or loving you and when I didn't choose him, he just left and hasn't spoken to me since. And I'm failing at the magazine. I can't do this job, I suck at it, and Madison knows it. Everyone knows it. They can all see Madison outshining me. I mean, she's way better

251

at my job than being my assistant, and—" Allie blurted out all at once, only stopping when Myles softly shushed her trying to calm her down.

"Okay, okay," Myles said trying to calm her down. "That's a lot to unpack, but let's start with the failing thing. You aren't failing. You are doing fine at the magazine."

"But I'm not. Madison is the one who came up with the idea to save the magazine. She's the one that put the launch party together. She's the one coming up with everything that Garrison loves. I suck at this job," Allie said, the tears starting to roll down her cheeks again.

"You are forgetting all the great things you've done Allison. You hired me and put your faith in me when I was a novice photographer who had yet to sell a single photo. When everything seemed to be going wrong at that first photoshoot, you showed up and changed it," Myles said. "And if it wasn't for you pushing Madison to fix her mistakes your party may have fallen flat. You are a force to be reckoned with. You push people to do their best and when you do it, they tend to shine. Sure, Madison came up with the idea to showcase the letters, but you put it into action, you got everyone to the table to do the work. Don't forget that."

Allie nodded, taking in Myles's kind words. "Thanks," she whimpered.

"Now, as to the Nick thing, what he did wasn't fair to you. I can't say that I'm surprised by it but it's still wrong to make you choose between us," Myles said, rubbing Allie's back. "I know that him and I have never gotten along but that doesn't mean you should have to choose between us."

"It's more than that," Allie managed to say, regaining her composure. "You don't understand what happened when I went home after everything that happened between us. Nick had to see me unravel and then worked hard to help put me back together. I think he was just upset about you and me because he didn't want to see me go through it again."

"I hate to ask, but how bad was it when you went back? What happened?" Myles asked softly, straightening up on the couch a bit. Allie drew in a deep breath.

"I couldn't shake the image of Lorraine's perfect body out of my head, so I started running every day. I convinced myself that if I could change my body, if I could look better, if I started to finally give in and become one of those waft thin Hollywood starlets that you would see my picture and want me back. When running didn't work I started eating less and less and working out more and more. I also started partying, hoping that maybe my pictures in tabloids and gossip columns would make their way to you." Allie paused, her hands shaking.

"One day I came in after a really long run in extremely hot temperatures, I hadn't eaten in over 24 hours, and I passed out on the floor. Nick came home and found me there and called an ambulance," Allie explained. An awkward silence fell between them.

"I haven't told anyone about that day. I mean, of course my family knew, but that was about it. I came out of rehab, did some side work with my mom's charities, and then landed an assistant's job, much like Madison's at Garrison Publishing. Brad Garrison only did it because he knew my reputation needed repair with the tabloids. I was shocked that he even gave me a job after my friends, and I crashed one of Forever's parties in L.A. and made a huge scene of it. Eventually this job became available, and I applied for it and well here we are. Nick was so pissed when I told him I was coming out here to work. I tried to shelter him from my life here and then it just boiled over. I don't blame him for being upset about us. I'm sure finding me near dead in the bathroom wasn't helpful." Allie took a breath. "Say something please."

"Allie, I need to tell you something about that day with Lorraine," Myles sighed. Allie nodded. "I asked her to help me stage what you saw so that you would leave me and leave London. I didn't know that it could cause all of that," Myles admitted.

"What do you mean stage?" Allie asked, pulling away a bit from Myles. "I don't understand how, no, understand why, you would stage something like that."

"I got into a lot of trouble hanging out with Colin and my father agreed to help me get out of it but on three conditions: one- you had to leave London; two- I had to work at his firm; three- I had to sell the Hyde Park flat and move in with my stepbrother.

Clearly, I managed to do two of those things but convince him of all three until recently," Myles explained. "I knew you wouldn't leave if I simply broke up with you. I knew I had to make you hate me or you would try to fix the issues I had and make things work between us, so I asked Lorraine to wait at the flat for you and then well, you know the rest."

"What trouble were you in?" Allie asked, her voice cold now as she tried to piece it all together in her mind.

"Colin and I gambled in some high stakes poker games, and I lost a couple million pounds," Myles said. Allie got up from the couch and started pacing back and forth in the living room. "I couldn't tell you because I really was only doing it because I knew I couldn't give you the life you deserved, the one you were giving up for me. I also knew how you felt about people like that wasting money and how much you hated Colin. I feel horrible, I mean I've felt horrible since it all happened, but now I feel even worse knowing how it affected you."

Allie shook her head. She didn't know how to feel. She didn't know what to think at this point. For years she felt like she wasn't good enough for the man sitting in front of her, to now found out that he was trying to simply cover up gambling away a large sum of money. She didn't know whether to be angry, disgusted, or simply relieved to know that after all this time the break-up wasn't because of her.

"Say something Allie," Myles begged watching her walk back and forth in front of him.

"Is that it or are there more secrets?" Allie asked.

"Well, I guess you should know, since I'm sure it is going to come out anyways, that Ryan is my stepbrother and that should about cover it," Myles replied. Allie looked over to the foyer as Madison entered the house and headed straight upstairs looking upset.

"Wait, what?" Allie asked confused. "Ryan as in Ryan Eliot? Who works at Forever?"

Myles nodded. "Remember when my father remarried for the third time? Well, it stuck, and Ryan has been my stepbrother for a while. You and I never really had much to do with my family when you were here, and well he was studying abroad that year you were out here, so you never met him."

"So, you live with Ryan?" Allie asked. "You knew he was seeing Madison?"

"I usually stay at the Hyde Park flat. I have a room at Ryan's but rarely stay there because what's the point? If Mitch came around, he would see my stuff there and not question the rest. I didn't know he was seeing Madison until tonight," Myles explained.

"Is there anything else?" Allie asked.

"No," Myles replied. "I swear there is nothing else. There are no other lies or secrets."

"Okay," Allie said sitting back down.

Myles nodded. "I promise that I will make it up to you. Even if it means I have to spend a lifetime groveling on my knees, I will make it up to you Allison Davis. I never meant to cause you so much pain. I just didn't want to entangle you further into my mess, so I found a way to make you hate me. You were willing to give up so much for me and yet I took advantage of that and squandered it all away to chase the thrill of being in rooms with powerful people and look where it got me. I promise, I swear on my life that I will make this up to you."

Allie sighed. "Let's call it a night and we can talk more in the morning."

"Okay," Myles said, getting up and heading towards the front door.

"Myles don't go. Stay here tonight," Allie said.

****

Madison sat on a bench near the Thames River, slowly sipping a cup of coffee. Her head was still spinning at the news she received the night before. She hadn't spoken to Ryan since she left his apartment. She didn't know if she wanted to talk to him again after finding out he was entangled in this mess. She couldn't imagine a future where his secret life would be okay between them. Allie was his target and Madison couldn't help but feel as if Ryan was using Madison as a tool to get closer to Allie. Allie warned her this could happen, but did Allie know what was happening too.

Madison took another sip of her coffee, letting a cold breeze tickle her face. She felt torn. She loved Ryan, hell for the

255

first time in her life, she actually loved someone deeply, but now, she couldn't trust him. She didn't know if she could continue to love the man who lived a double life, only bringing her along for half the ride.

"Madison!" a voice called out to her pulling her out of the deep thoughts rummaging around in her head. She looked up to see Ryan walking towards her. He looked rough in a pair of sweatpants and a T-shirt. His hair was messy and there were large bags under his eyes.

"I'm not ready to talk to you Ryan," she said, getting up from the bench as he approached. She turned away from him to hide the tears welling up in her eyes.

"Madison please just hear me out," he begged.

"No, I'm not ready for this conversation. I don't even know who you are anymore," she said walking away from him. He grabbed her arm trying to stop her. She yanked it away from him glaring at him.

"Madison please, let me explain it to you. Let me show you that you do know me, the real me," he begged.

"Ryan leave me the hell alone. I need time to think about this all. I need time to figure out how I can be okay with what you are doing, with what you are part of," she said. "It's twisted and sick to do something like that to another person. To manipulate and ruin their life just so someone else can profit off it."

"Madison, it's not like that. At least not for me. I'm simply trying to pay off a debt which requires me to post things on social media and sometimes cause certain situations to unfold. I don't manipulate situations; I just do as I'm told by someone else. I date and woe his client's daughters. I post the pictures he wants me to post. I do whatever I'm asked. Mitch is the one manipulating the situations, I'm just trying to keep my mom from living on the street," Ryan explained exasperated. "I don't want to lose you over this. I meant it when I said I love you."

"I know you did, but I don't know if I meant it any longer. I don't know if I can love someone who lied to me and used me like that," Madison replied.

"I never used you," Ryan said.

"Bullshit and you know it. It's all been a game with you since day one. The tricks, the lies… all of it," Madison yelled.

"I'm sure you paid the bartender to tell me that you never take girls there. Sure, you didn't change the date on the Altitude paperwork, but you are the one who gave me the information in the first place damn well knowing Charlie was involved in all of this. You manipulated me into falling for you and then got closer to Allie. You helped push me out of pitch for our latest issues. Everything you've done has been calculated and if I can't trust you then I can't love you."

"I think you know deep down inside that none of that is true. I know you felt it that first day in the lobby. You felt the intrigue, the possibility. I saw it in your eyes the first moment they met mine. Sure, I played a couple of games to make you jealous, to try and see if you were just another one of those girls that looks at me and sees a rich guy who can give you nice things, but after all was said and done, when we sat alone in Hyde Park the night you thought you were going to leave England forever, I knew you were different. I knew that you were the real deal. For once in my life, I found someone worth letting in again after Samantha...I found you. Sure, I didn't tell you everything because I was trying to protect you from this other world that I'm stuck in. I was trying to keep you from it because I feared this would be your reaction to it. And can you blame me?" Ryan asked.

Madison looked out over the river letting Ryan's words sink into her.

"I've spent all night trying to figure out how to make this better between us and then I spent most of the morning walking around hoping that maybe you'd be somewhere like this and then I could explain it," Ryan continued. "I know you are angry with me and feel betrayed, but I promise I wasn't using you. I love you more than I've ever loved anyone or anything in this world. Just let me prove it to you."

"I can't," Madison said, shaking her head as she turned to face him. "I can't promise you anything right now Ryan. I'm sorry Ryan, but I just can't." Ryan nodded, letting her disappear down a busy street and away from him.

****

"You know Ryan's mom, my stepmom, struggled with an eating disorder for a while. It makes sense that he would want to help you through your disorder, Allie," Myles said taking a bite of oatmeal. Allie sat down across from him at her kitchen table.

"He was pretty helpful. Since we are being honest though, I let him help me in hopes of making you feel jealous. After our run-in with Lorraine, I sort of snapped and started flirting with him, which the thought of now makes my skin crawl as a way to get back at you for not telling me about the event for Lorraine and Colin and as a way to get back at Madison for lying to me about dating Ryan," Allie admitted with an exaggerated shiver.

Myles laughed. "Did he flirt back?"

"Nope, it seems he is pretty committed to Madison," Allie replied. "He's so committed that I've heard the women at the office gossiping about how he's turned down every model asking him to show them a good time."

"You know, I haven't seen him committed to anyone in the past few years. Maybe Madison is good for him," Myles said, before taking another bite.

"Maybe. I just wish she hadn't lied to me about him you know," Allie said, getting up to retrieve half of a warm bagel from the toaster.

"Well, you did sort of ban her from seeing him ever again or risk losing her job. The heart wants what the heart wants." Myles shrugged.

"And what does your heart want Myles?" Allie asked, sitting back down.

"I think you know that the answer now and forever is you," Myles replied reaching across the table to grab her hand. "I just hope that after some time the same is true for you."

"Me too," Allie replied with a half-smile before taking a bite of her bagel.

****

Madison had skillfully avoided Ryan at work for a full week after their run-in at the river. Between meetings and running more errands for Allie, Madison evaded any chance Ryan could have to get her alone. She didn't answer his calls or texts and refused to open any emails she received from him that didn't appear to be about the magazine. Near the end of the week, he didn't even bother showing up to the office.

"Madison, I need to talk to you in my office," Allie said from her doorway. Madison nodded, getting up from her desk as Allie disappeared into the office. Madison quietly shut the door behind her and took a seat in front of Allie. It had practically been a week as well since they had spoken outside of meetings. Madison saw Allie and Myles at the townhouse here and there but avoided any small talk with them as she instantly headed upstairs to her room when coming home each night.

"Madison, Brad Garrison would like you to take the lead on the end of summer party. I'm not sure who told him what, but when he found out it was your idea for this party and the venue, he insisted that you were the one to plan the party. We have no doubt that it will be spectacular like the launch party. What do you say? Are you up for it?" Allie asked.

"So, you are done cutting me out of things?" Madison asked, crossing her legs, and leaning back in her chair.

"Long story short, yes," Allie replied.

Madison rolled her eyes.

"Drop the attitude, Madison. I'm trying here, okay?" Allie replied. "Do you want the job or not?"

"Fine, I'll do it. It's the least you could give me though after the past month or so," Madison replied. Allie shook her head in response as Madison stood up.

"Where's Ryan today?" Allie asked as Madison opened the door.

"I actually don't know," Madison replied disappearing back to her desk.

"I only ask because I know you two are together. It's okay you know. I talked it over with Mr. Garrison and there aren't any actual rules against here, so if you both want to date, there's nothing stopping you," Allie replied.

"It's not like I needed your permission anyways," Madison replied, leaving Allie's office. As she sat back down at her desk, a yellow sticky note was on her computer monitor.

Madison- Meet me at the bar at 7. It's
time we tried to talk again. -Ryan

She crumbled up the note tossing it in the trash can under her desk. She felt conflicted deep inside. Part of her wanted to go to him and let him explain. She wanted to believe anything he said and that he really didn't have a choice but to go along with it all, but the other part of her wanted to walk away and never speak to him again. She didn't know which part of her to trust. Which part of her was right and would keep her safe from being put into harm's way? Could she believe him? Was this all real? Was being with her part of his plan?

****

Allie dialed Nick's number as she got into the car, leaving the office, and heading home. She knew he wouldn't answer, but it was worth a try. "Hey Nick, it's me again. Look, I told Myles everything. Also, my dad told me about the wedding. Please call me back. I miss you and I love you. Call me, okay?" She hung up the phone, sliding it into her bag. She sighed heavily as the lights of the city passed by.

****

Madison paced back and forth down the alley near the bar. She was tired of being angry, but she still felt so confused by the whole situation. It was now 7:05pm and she still couldn't decide whether or not to head into the bar.

"Just go in and listen to what he has to say," a voice suggested from behind her. She turned to see Charlie standing at the corner.

"What are you doing here?" she asked.

"Making sure you go in there and give him a chance," he replied offering an encouraging smile.

"Let me guess, he called you to help him out," Madison said rolling her eyes.

"And what if he did? Are you really going to be that daft? That petty? I'm sure there are a million things you've done in life that you regret the consequences of. We all have our baggage. Some of us just have bigger bags to carry, but that doesn't mean that we don't deserve forgiveness, love, or respect. Go in there and hear him out and then decide whether or not you want to ever speak to him again. Go in there and then decide whether or not

260

you are willing to break his heart. Because I can tell you this Madison, I've known Ryan for quite some time, and I've never seen him this upset over potentially losing a woman. I've never seen him willing to put everything on the line for someone he's seeing. You can at least give him a chance," Charlie suggested. Madison nodded, rolling her eyes as she let out all the air left in her lungs. She could feel her heart sink into her stomach at the thought of breaking his heart.

Her hands started to shake as she headed to the door of the bar. She wrapped her fingers around the metal handle pulling the door open. Ryan sat alone at the bar, looking up with a hopeful twinkle in his eyes as Madison entered. He looked more put together than the last time they spoke. His hair was perfectly parted and a slight five 'o'clock shadow covered his chin. He wore a light blue button-down shirt tucked into a pair of jeans. He still looked sad and almost afraid at the power she held walking into the room.

"I didn't think you were coming or that you didn't get my note or my gift," he said, getting up from the barstool.

"So, it was you that let Brad Garrison know about the party," Madison replied. "Clearly I got your note."

"I'm glad you did. I know you're still upset with me. I know I can't explain it away or make you feel better about any of it, but Madison you have to believe me when I say I never wanted to hurt you. I didn't tell you about any of this to protect you. I swear," he said, his voice filled with a melancholy she had never heard before. She could see his eyes get misty searching hers for a sign of forgiveness and understanding.

"I love you Madison and I don't say those three words very often, if at all," he continued. Madison felt a tear escape from her eyes. She took a few steps closer, letting her purse fall from her shoulder as she wrapped her arms around him letting the warmth of his body flood into hers. She could feel his arms wrap tightly around her drawing her in even closer. He kissed the top of her head.

"I love you too," she whispered a tear rolling down her face. She held him tightly before pulling away. "I just don't know if I can forgive this."

Ryan took a step back nodding his head. "I don't blame you," he said defeatedly.

"I need more time to process it all. I need more time to know that if I choose to stay with you that I'm not going to get hurt. I need more time to know this wasn't all a trick, part of the plan. I need to know this was real, and what is still real," Madison explained.

"What can I do to show you that this is real? I know I lied. I know I hid things from you, but everything that's happened between us has been real," Ryan retorted.

"I don't know. All of this has been so much at once," Madison replied. "I want to believe you. I want to put this behind us, but I'm stuck. I just keep thinking over and over again that you are going to one day tell me that it's all been a lie. That there isn't a you and me and that there hasn't been this whole time."

"I promise you that won't happen. I promise you that I will do everything in my power to keep us together and to prove to you that this is real. Just give me a chance. I'll do anything," Ryan begged.

Madison hung her head weighing the options in her mind. "Tell me how to get you out of this," she whispered as he pulled her in to his chest.

Ryan held her close. "I wish I could."

Episode 22- you should see me in a crown

Ryan rolled over slowly rubbing his eyes. There she was sleeping soundly next to him. He rolled over onto his back staring at the ceiling, letting the memories of last night flood in.

Madison followed him into the apartment without saying a word. She slid off her shoes and sat down on the edge of the couch, tucking her feet under her. Ryan went a poured them both a glass of wine in the kitchen. He could still feel the distance between them. He headed back into the living room, handing her the glass of wine before sitting down.

"Madison, I-" He stopped as she started shaking her head no, downing the glass of wine.

"I don't want to hear about it. I just can't hear about how our relationship, this thing between us started out as a lie, a way to get to Allie. It breaks my heart to even think that all of this could be a lie still," Madison said, getting up from the couch to grab the bottle of wine.

"Madison, it may have started that way, but I will spend a lifetime proving to you over and over again that you are the one I've been waiting for, the only woman I will ever love the way I love you," Ryan assured.

"I'd love to believe that all of that is true, but what happens when Mitch tells you it's time to cut me loose? What happens when Allie finds out about all of this? What happens when you cross a line Mitch or Ken doesn't like and your life is ruined for good?" Madison asked, refilling her glass.

"It won't come to that, I promise," Ryan replied, running his hands through his hair. Madison sighed at his response.

"What if we just ran away from here? Started a life back in California or in some small town north of here or in another country like France or Germany and never looked back? What if we just ran away from here and started over?" Madison asked, settling back down on the couch. Ryan shook his head, his shoulders slumping.

"It's not that easy Madison. Believe me, Ken and Mitch would have some way of finding us or causing misfortune to us somehow. We can't just run away," Ryan replied.

"Well then how do we get you out of this? How much do you owe Mitch? Let me help pay some of it if that's what it takes," Madison retorted quickly.

"I have about half of it saved up, but even then, I know it's never going to be just about the money. I've made a good villain in Allie's story, there's no way Ken is going to just let Mitch let me go away into the night after paying him," Ryan answered.

"So, they find a new villain. I mean come on, it's not like it hasn't happened in years of television shows, movies, and literature. Once a villain exits, they find a new one...unless the issue is that you actually like playing the villain and messing with people's lives," Madison said, drawing in a deep long breath as she finished, her eyes flashing inquisitively at Ryan.

"Madison don't look at me like that. I mean don't get me wrong, it's nice to be needed, to play a pivotal role in some very twisted messed up way, but I would quit and move on if I thought there was a legitimate way to do so," Ryan explained.

"Then let's find one! Because I don't know how long I can just go along with it and act like nothing is happening," Madison snapped getting frustrated.

"How many times can I explain it to you?!" Ryan replied exasperated. "This is my life right now. It has been since before we even met... and it has nothing to do with you. So, let's stop trying to fix it and just let things settle and go back to normal between us. Can you do that please?"

Madison let a tear roll down her cheek as she nodded her head silently. "I just want to help you live the life you deserve. That's all."

Ryan got up from the couch and kneeled in front of her. Slowly he brushed the hair out of her face, kissing her lightly on the forehead. "I know you do, and one day, I promise, we will live the life we both deserve together. Just let me fix this myself."

Madison nodded, pulling him into an embrace.

Ryan sighed watching Madison breathe while she slept next to him. He hated the idea that was hurting because of him. Filled with regret, he quietly got out of bed grabbing his phone to leave the room and make a phone call. "We need to talk," he said in a hushed tone, quietly closing the door behind him.

****

Allie tried calling Nick again, getting his voicemail for the hundredth time. Frustrated, she slammed her phone down on the kitchen table.

"No luck?" Myles asked, walking into the kitchen, buttoning his shirt cuffs. His hair was a mess and still wet from his shower. Allie smirked getting up from the table.

"Where you headed to hot stuff?" Allie said, sauntering over to Myles.

"Just going to go and grab some pastries actually," Myles chuckled as Allie leaned in close to him, her lips grazing his.

"Better get some cherry ones this time," she breathed slowly pulling away without a kiss.

"You are bloody rude, you know?" Myles laughed, shaking his head at her.

"Bloody rude? Nah, I think I'm just a tad rude actually," Allie teased with a wink.

Myles wrapped his arm around her waist as she started to take a step back from him. "I don't think so," he said, pulling her in for a proper kiss.

Allie gave him a quick peck on the lips before managing to scurry back to the table as her phone dinged. Myles's shoulder slumped a bit watching her hurry to her phone. He lingered for a second more before exiting the kitchen.

"I will be back soon," he shouted from the foyer.

"Don't forget the cherry pastries!" Allie replied, her eyes glued to her phone.

****

Madison opened her eyes slowly. Her head felt heavy from the emotions of the week before. She rolled over to see that the bed was nothing but crumpled sheets. Slowly she shifted to laying on her back, staring at the ceiling above. She felt bad for being upset with Ryan, knowing that he was ultimately stuck in a world not of his own making, but she couldn't shake the feeling that all of this was the fault of the men who let their lives be controlled by Ken Davis and Mitch McGowan. She couldn't understand how Ryan could let his every move be controlled by

265

someone else. He seemed so strong and stubborn, too stubborn to take orders from someone else.

Not wanting to lay motionless while her head spun around still trying to put all the pieces together, Madison slid her legs over the edge of the bed and stood up. The air felt cold outside of the bed's blankets, so she slid her arms into one of Ryan's hoodies and headed out of the room. The apartment was quiet and still. Madison shrugged her shoulders at the sight of the empty living room and headed towards the kitchen for a water. Ryan was nowhere to be found. Sighing at this, Madison headed to the couch sitting down to wait for his return.

Madison felt restless sitting alone in the deafening sound of silence. She looked around the room for something to occupy her mind. She never really realized just how boring Ryan's apartment actually was without him. Everything seemed less grand, less exciting without him around…or maybe it was that way because she knew too much now. She knew where it all came from, that it was all produced from this world in which Ryan wasn't some mysterious, hot, self-made man. Madison got up and wandered around the perimeter of the large living room. She ran her fingers over the well-dusted shelves near the desk before running her fingers over the papers strewn about on top of the desk.

She didn't know what she was looking for, but she wanted to make sure there were no more lies. Madison slowly picked up a stack of papers off the desk and began to flip through them. Most of them were contracts from Forever, things she had seen at some point or another. She continued to flip through papers until she came face to face with herself. Madison set down the remaining papers in her hands staring into the eyes of a drawing of her.

She looked so different in his drawing than the reflection she saw in the mirror each morning. His portrait of her was breathtaking, capturing the softness of her smile, a twinkle in her eye, and as he put it a quiet but wild beauty. This wasn't just a portrait someone drew on a whim. This was a portrait drawn by a man in love.

Madison sat down on the floor letting a tear roll down her cheek and onto the drawing. The emotions of the past week finally took over and she broke out into a sob as the door to the apartment opened.

Ryan, leaving the apartment door open, set down the box of breakfast danishes on the coffee table as he rushed over to Madison on the floor behind the couch. Without a word, he dropped to his knees and pulled her into a tight embrace slowly rocking back and forth letting Madison cry in his arms.

"Madison, I hope you know I never meant to bring you into this. I've done my damnedest to shield you from it all. I swear. Everything between us is the real deal, I promise. I will spend every hour of every day, as long as you will let me, showing you, that it is," Ryan said, his voice soft. Madison didn't speak a word in return, instead she got up from where she was sitting and moved to be closer to him, resting her head on his chest as he leaned back and lay on the floor. For a moment, it all felt real to her as the world around them began to fade away and the silence of the apartment took over.

****

Allison settled in on the couch next to Myles. "What movie do you want to watch?"

Myles sighed and turned towards Allie. "Why is it so important to you that Nick calls you back? I mean I feel like you only told me about your eating disorder and everything as a way to get him back and not because you really thought that I should know. So, be honest with me, why is it so important that he calls you back?"

Allie shook her head. "Myles, stop. I told you about my eating disorder because it's important that you know about it if we are going to be together for the long haul, which is my goal. Is it not yours?"

"Of course, it is, but if you have feelings for Nick, you need to be honest with me about them," Myles replied.

"I only have feelings for you. I promise," Allie said reassuringly as she scooched in closer to kiss Myles on the lips tenderly. "Now, let's pick a movie."

Myles sighed, nodding his head as Allie laid hers on his shoulder, curling up next to him.

267

"Nothing in the horror genre please," Allie said in a silly voice. Myles chuckled in agreement and started listing off movies they could watch.

****

Madison stepped out of the bathroom, toweling off her hair from a long hot shower. Ryan was reorganizing the papers on his desk as music played from the record player in the corner. Madison smiled as Ryan hummed along to the music. The moments of her crying in his arms were only an hour ago but felt as if it was a distant memory. She could still feel the pain inside her marinating between feelings of hurt, disappointment, and outright rage, but she felt a tad more at peace with Ryan, which helped ease the tension of the pain.

"How was your shower?" he asked, looking up from the stack of papers on the desk.

"It was nice," Madison replied. "Can I ask you a question?"

"Of course," Ryan answered, taking a seat in the desk chair, and turning to fully face Madison who stood in front of him fully dressed in a pair of skinny jeans and a billowy paisley print top.

"You said you met with Mitch, and he said there was not a way to get out of your agreement, correct?" Madison asked, nervously still toweling off her wet hair.

"Correct," Ryan replied.

"Will we ever see a day where you aren't under this agreement the two of you have? Did he say how close you were to being let out of it?" Madison asked.

"I'm not sure when it will be over Mads, I tried talking my way out of it, offering him half the payment in exchange for an end date to the agreement, or even a short reprieve from it. He wouldn't budge. There's no telling how long this is going to play out, but I promise you I will make sure it ends one day and never truly affects us being together. No matter what," Ryan replied. "I love you so much Madison and it kills me to know that this has caused you pain. That my past faults and failures have caused you pain here and now."

268

"What failures? You know you deserve to be loved by a parent who doesn't hold something as trivial as paying for an education over your head right? That's not a fault nor a failure Ryan. That's just who you are. You are someone who cares deeply about others, even if you try to mask it by acting like a playboy who is anything but interested in a meaningful committed relationship. The one person who should be ashamed of all of this, who took you for granted and manipulated you into believing that you didn't deserve love, is Mitch McGowan. He's a low life coward who is willing to even sell out his own biological son to pay a debt. He's the one who should be sorry, not you," Madison ranted. "I swear if I knew of a way to pay him back for all of the hell, he's put you through, I would."

"But don't, okay? Don't get involved in this. You don't understand the power Ken and Mitch have. I'd kick myself if anything was to happen to you," Ryan interjected. "Promise me you won't do anything stupid and get involved in this whole mess."

Madison sighed out of frustration. "I promise," she said, crossing her fingers behind her back. "Anyways, I'm going to go for a walk and grab some coffee. Do you want any?"

"I'm good. Enjoy your walk, I'm going to try to get some work done for the next issue," Ryan said, turning back to the mess of papers in front of him.

"Okay, I'll be quick and then I want to show you the party details I've been working on," Madison replied, subtly skipping over to give Ryan a kiss on the cheek, before tossing the towel into the bathroom and heading out the front door. Once out in the hallway, Madison slid her cell phone out of her purse texting Charlie: "I want a meeting with Mitch McGowan, tomorrow at lunch. Make it happen."

****

The next day Madison walked into the restaurant early to get to the table before Mitch could. She was wearing a white pant suit with an emerald-green blouse, her hair straight, her make-up done with a dark lip to finish it off. The hostess showed her to the table, one table next to the one where she first encountered Mitch McGowan. She sat down looking at her watch. He would be here in five minutes if she was right in thinking he'd arrive early. She ordered a whiskey for her and a glass of red wine for him. The waiter immediately returned with the drinks and as he walked away, she spotted Mitch entering the restaurant. She watched the surprised expression cross his face as the hostess presumably told him that Madison was already at the table.

As he approached the table, Madison remained seated. Looking slightly uncomfortable, Mitch unbuttoned his suit jacket and sat down.

"I see you went ahead and ordered us drinks," Mitch said coolly.

"Let's not do the whole small talk thing. I called this meeting for a reason," Madison replied, sipping her whiskey.

"Shall we order first?" Mitch said, ignoring Madison's attempt to get to business by looking at a menu.

"No need. I had your assistant call ahead with our orders and your credit card information. Lunch is taken care of. I hope you enjoy a nice freshly made salad," Madison replied, crossing her legs, and leaning back in her chair.

Mitch McGowan chuckled to himself, a devilish grin crossing his face. "What is it that I can do for you Madison?"

"What's it going to take for you to let Ryan out of the twisted deal you made with him?" Madison asked. Mitch shifted uncomfortably in his chair. Silence fell between them as the waiter brought a steak and mashed potatoes for Madison and a salad for Mitch.

"I made it very clear to Ryan that the terms of our agreement were non-negotiable," he replied a few minutes later.

"I know he has quite a bit saved up. What if he paid half of what he owes you?" Madison suggested.

"Does he know you are here bartering on his behalf?" Mitch asked. "It's hard to believe that he does. I raised him better than that. Never let your little girlfriend fight your battles. Then again, after Samantha broke his heart with the male model I put in her life, I thought he learned the lesson to never fall in love again."

"Once again, what's it going to take to let him out of the agreement?" Madison asked, her heart racing. She could feel her confidence starting to slip at the news that Mitch was the reason

Samantha left Ryan alone in Paris. She could feel her hands start to tremble as she drew her glass back up to her lips.

Mitch watched Madison start to squirm. "I guess you didn't think that I could have that effect in his life. Samantha was a nice girl, but just like Allie did to Myles, she was making Ryan weak, too soft, so I intervened. Things were going to plan until you arrived on scene."

"So, what will it take Mitch? I'm tired of this conversation," Madison said, attempting to regain her confidence.

"You." Mitch replied bluntly, taking a bite of the salad in front of him.

"I was hoping you'd say that. Deal," Madison replied, sitting back up in her chair.

"So eager. May I inquire as to why you were willing to give in so easily?" Mitch questioned, a little shocked at Madison's answer.

"I'm your best option. Don't get me wrong, Ryan is good at what he does, but I'm better. I'm closer to Allie, hell I live with her. I have her trust, it doesn't need to be earned over and over again like it does with Ryan, and best of all, I already have Brad Garrison's trust and confidence. If you are looking to wreck Allie's life for this little project of yours, I'm a much better person for the job than Ryan ever will be," Madison said, finishing off her drink.

"Interesting," Mitch replied. "But let's sweeten the deal a little."

"Go on," Madison said leaning in.

"When I say it's time, you are going to leave and never speak to Ryan again," Mitch proposed.

Madison felt her heart drop into her stomach.

"It's either that or no deal. You had to know this would come. I'm not just going to let Ryan out of this deal so the two of you can live in your fantasy land. Ryan will be free to do whatever it is he wants to do- make children's books or whatever, but not with you by his side. Do we have a deal?"

Madison motioned to the waiter for another whiskey, biding herself some time to think about it. She wanted nothing more than to see Ryan free from this terror of a man and the horrid project he had going on with Allie's father. The waiter appeared at the table, setting down a glass and taking the empty one away. Madison took a sip, knowing that her next answer had to be yes in order to save Ryan.

"Deal," she said, setting the glass back down.

"Great!" Mitch replied. "You'll report to Charlie. He'll have directions from me. We'll let Ryan know this afternoon. Now that we have the unpleasantries out of the way, shall we enjoy a nice lunch together to mark the beginning of our business together?"

Madison stood up finishing the drink. "I think I'll pass. You can have my lunch. Wasn't hungry to begin with, but also, don't think that this discussion between us is over. Don't think I don't have my share of cards still left to play," Madison warned, tossing her napkin into her seat.

"We will see about that," Mitch chuckled as he grabbed Madison's plate from across the table as she left. As soon as she was out of sight, he grabbed his cell phone.

"That was easier than I thought it would be. She's in. Offered herself up on her own," he laughed. "I'm going to get Charlie to give her a rundown of how this all works this afternoon."

Madison exited the restaurant with her head held high but inside she could feel her heart crumbling. She made it a little over a block away from the restaurant before darting down an alley to break down into tears. Her whole body shook as she let the tears escape her eyes for a moment. Her lungs gasped for air as her mind raced to formulate a way to make all of this work. Not only was she now the servant of Mitch McGowan and Ken Davis, but she was also betraying Allie, and having to let go of the one person she loved in the whole world.

"He's worth it," she whispered to herself, trying to regain her composure. Moments later her phone dinged:

Charlie: Meet me at Altitude in an hour. The journey begins…

"Here we go," she whispered, wiping the tears from her eyes, and strongly heading out of the alley with her head held high.

Episode 23- Wildest Dreams

"So how does this work?" Madison asked, slipping off her shoes as her feet dangled above the floor as she sat on a barstool at Altitude 360.

"It's quite simple, since you don't have a direct connection with Mitch and it would be bloody odd for Allison or Myles or even Ryan to see you directly conversing with him, so all of your assignments will come through me. I tell you the assignment and you make sure it happens," Charlie explained.

"And why couldn't you tell me this over the phone instead of making me have to come here directly after work?" Madison asked, tugging at her shirt which felt a little tight.

"Because there are rules that you need to know. First, you can never tell Ryan about this. You can't insinuate that you took over his debt or that you have anything out of the ordinary to do. Second, the assignment typically is an end goal, a result in a way, and it's your job to get it there without being obvious about it. For instance, one of Ryan's assignments was to rattle Allison with a run in with Myles. He did this through getting Myles's gallery manager, my boyfriend Patrick, to send over some of the photos Myles took of her. Sure, he didn't necessarily cause them to meet, but he did manage to get a good reaction out of Allie. Are you following so far?" Charlie paused to check.

"I'm a little lost on the assignment part, I guess. I thought the whole point of this was to get video and social media posts. How did Ryan getting Patrick to send over photos get anything substantial for the overall project Ken is working on?" Madison asked.

"Pull out your phone and go to Allison's social media feed," Charlie instructed. "Alright, now scroll back to around 7 or 8 months ago. You see Allie posted some throwback photos that night which from the looks of it got a lot of likes, comments, and shares. People are already invested in her life from her party days and from the fact that Ken Davis is her father. Our job now is to help that gain traction, get her to post new videos or photos, and to help keep track of the storylines for Ken. And that brings me to rule 3, nobody is allowed to talk directly to Ken about any of this.

You will send me weekly updates and I will forward them to Mitch. Understood?" Charlie asked. Madison nodded.

"Rule 4, you don't make anything happen outside of the parameters you are given. For example, you cannot introduce someone new into the storyline unless it's approved. So, let's say you don't like Myles and Allie together, you have to live with it, don't bring in someone new or push one of them towards someone else, unless you are specifically told to do so. And lastly, rule 5, anything you post on social media is now property of the project, so choose your posts wisely. That about covers it. Any questions?" Charlie asked, wrapping up.

"What's the first assignment?" Madison asked.

"Atta girl!" Charlie laughed. "I promise that this new world isn't hard to navigate and the sting of having to report back and manipulate scenarios disappears after a while."

"Let's hope so," Madison replied.

"Anyways, part of your assignment is already in the works, you are planning the upcoming party. The other part is that you need to get Nick to the party. The goal is to cause a bit of drama between Myles and Allie and make sure you get it on video," Charlie reported.

"What kind of drama?" Madison asked, annoyed by the assignment.

"That's for you to figure out. Go big though, I think Ken and Mitch are treating this like a season finale of sorts. The bigger the better," Charlie replied. Madison sighed before sliding from the barstool.

"You know I still don't approve of any of this…just for the record," Madison said before heading towards the door.

"You don't have to approve in it! You just have to do what your told!" Charlie yelled out as Madison exited through the doors to the club.

****

Allie made her way through the office with a huge smile on her face. She spent her night curled up with Myles on the couch in his apartment. Everything felt sunny and life felt full again, even without a text from Nick.

"Morning!" Allie beamed as she passed Madison's desk.

"Morning," Madison muttered back causing Allie to stop. Allie looked inquisitively at Madison who was staring straight ahead at her computer. Allie turned to look towards Ryan's office which was once again dark.

Confused by his absence for three days in a row she looked back to Madison. "Where's Ryan?" Allie asked, lowering her voice to a whisper. "Did you guys, you know, call it quits again?"

Madison shook her head looking up at Allie incredulously. "Why would you even care if that was the case?"

"Because if you did, I would take you out for drinks to forget him once and for all," Allie replied.

"Well, we didn't break up and you don't have to be all buddy-buddy with me now that I took over party planning. Ryan's just out on a quick business trip and will be back soon," Madison lied. She knew Ryan was at home from the numerous text invites to come over that she received over the course of the last three days. She replied to each text with a well thought out excuse as she spent time learning from Charlie about her new secret life.

"Alright, someone is a little touchy today," Allie replied, rolling her eyes. "How are the party plans going?"

"I'll give you a rundown at today's meeting that takes place after your meeting with the writers. Also, you may want to go and check in on layout today as they are finalizing the last issue in this series which includes that big Hollywood romance piece too. Apparently, it's getting a lot of buzz on the internet and social media," Madison replied in a monotone voice, her eyes glued on her computer screen never meeting Allie's once. "And you have a conference call with the board in five minutes."

"Okay," Allie concluded heading into her office, lingering for a second in the doorway before closing the door behind her.

****

"So, the majority of the party will take place outdoors. We will have lanterns lining the pathways much like the launch party, but we will also have battery powered lightbulbs hanging from the trees and fairy lights wrapped around the tree trunks and branches. The main party area will have your typical dance floor and tall tables for people to gather around and eat and drink. There will be three bar areas each on a different side of the main party area. Since the venue is so big, people will be able to hashtag their photos and videos with a custom hashtag that we will then be able to pull the content from and stream it live on a huge screen in the party area. A few employees of Forever will have the ability to take live videos which will automatically link to the screen. This will mainly be used to capture who is arriving," Madison explained.

"And what about the photo op at the entrance?" Allie asked, flipping through Madison's concept book.

"We will have an area set-up much like the launch party. The carpet will be a dusty rose carpet, and we will have tall flower vases with some large bouquets," Madison explained.

"The sounds nice," Allie replied.

"My thought is that about halfway through the party, you, Allie, can address the crowd and introduce our surprise musical guest. How does that sound?" Madison asked.

"Who is our guest?" Allie inquired, looking up from the look-book.

"I will tell you right before the party," Madison answered. "Now, let's talk about what you are wearing, I had our stylist team pull four looks for you down in the closet. Shall we?" Madison motioned towards the conference room door. Allie nodded, slightly impressed, and headed towards the door. Madison grabbed the look-books and her laptop before following Allie out. She looked so serious, so uptight, so unlike her normal cheery self. Allie continued down the hall and over towards the fashion department. Madison followed quietly behind her.

"Alright, I'll leave you here to pick out your outfit while I go and finalize some minor details with the catering company," Madison said, staring down at her phone. "Oh, before I go, Olivia, will you send me the photos of each outfit? Allie, we will want to post each look on the Forever social media account and your own account and let people vote for the best one. You can wear whichever you like, but let's give them the ability to interact with you a little more before the party. Better yet, we should also have Myles try on a few different tuxes and do the same. Olivia, can you arrange a fitting for Myles?"

Olivia nodded her head. Happy with the response from Olivia, Madison disappeared around the corner before Allie could say anything. Madison stopped down an empty hallway, leaning up against the wall as she tried to catch her breath. She felt her heart racing in her chest.

"Deep breath in and out," she coached herself softly, her voice wavering. She forced air into her lungs and diaphragm and then slowly let it escape from between her lips. After a few deep breaths she started to feel calmer and started back across the office to her desk. As she sat down, she looked over to Ryan's dark office. As soon as her eyes met his door, her phone started to vibrate in her pocket.

"Of course," she whispered seeing Ryan's name on the screen. She debated for a moment whether to answer it. Over the past few days, she only vaguely text messaged him about her day. She felt guilty for avoiding him and missed him terribly. Drawing in another deep breath, she clicked the green button, picking up his call.

"I think you've been avoiding me, and I think I know why," Ryan said as soon as she put her phone up to her ear.

"What?" Madison giggled nervously.

"You are still upset over our conversation the other night and you think I've gone mad now that I haven't come into the office in a few days," Ryan answered, his voice calm yet mysterious. Madison furrowed her eyebrows. She wasn't sure how to respond to him. She was avoiding him, but not due to the reason he cited. She knew she couldn't explain it to him, but she also knew she couldn't come up with a lie to explain her behavior.

"I mean it is odd that you haven't been here. There's a lot going on with the party and everything. It would be nice to look across the office and see your face every now and again," Madison said, avoiding the question altogether.

"Well come over tonight and tell me all about it," Ryan suggested.

"Or how about you come into work?" Madison teased.

"If you come over tonight, I'll come into work tomorrow. Deal?"

Madison sighed. "Fiiiinnneee." She looked up to see Allie walking back towards her office. "I've gotta run, but I'll be over around 6."

"I look forward to it," Ryan said.

Madison put her phone away, looking back up at Allie. "That was quick," Madison said.

"I'm not sure I love any of the looks Olivia pulled for me. I think I want to wear this instead," Allie said handing her phone over to Madison to look at a photo of a long light pink dress with a tight bodice and flowy skirt made of layers of tulle with white flowers attached among the different layers.

"Who designed this dress?" Madison asked, studying the picture on the phone.

"A new designer by the name of Lacey Donahue. Can you track down a way to contact her in order to get a fitting for this dress?" Allie asked.

"Of course. Did Olivia take photos of you in the other looks?" Madison asked before handing back the phone.

"She did, they are on there. Feel free to send them to yourself. We can still do whatever your social media idea was, I just think that the Donahue dress will be better," Allie replied. "Send yourself the photos and toss my phone on my desk. I'll be right back."

Madison nodded, as Allie grabbed Clarissa and headed towards the layout room. Madison sent herself the pictures and got up to put Allie's phone on her desk like she requested. As she set the phone down, the screen dimming a bit, a picture of Allie and Nick caught Madison's eye. Madison snatched Allie's phone back off the desk, tapping the screen right before it went dark and locked her out. Madison quickly scrolled through Allie's contacts, looking for Nick's contact information. Finding his name and number, Madison searched for a piece of paper to jot it down.

"Of course, she keeps her desk pristine. Dammit," Madison hissed opening the drawers on Allie's desk searching for a sticky note or scrap of paper. Her eyes flitted over to the screen again which was starting to dim again. In a panic, Madison tapped the screen and invertedly dialed Nick's number while she continued to search for a piece of paper.

"Hello?" a groggy voice called out for the phone.

Madison's eyes opened wide as she realized her mistake. She quickly hung up the call, her mind racing to find a solution to fix this issue. In that moment she saw a pen. Picking it up, she pooped off the cap and jotted down Nick's number on the palm of her hand. Knowing Allie would be back at any moment, Madison erased the call from Allie's outgoing call list, locked the phone, and set it back on her desk, right as Allie emerged in the doorway.

"Did you get what you needed?" Allie asked.

"I did. I will work on getting you that dress. I agree, it will probably be better to go with that dress than the others," Madison replied, edging towards the doorway as Allie made her way to her desk.

"Thank you, Myles will be in the office tomorrow for his fitting. Do you need me for anything else regarding the party?" Allie inquired.

"No. I have it all under control," Madison replied.

"I will see you later then. I have some errands to run for the rest of this afternoon and then I've invited some friends over for cocktails later tonight," Allie said, grabbing her phone off the desk and her purse from her desk chair.

"Alright," Madison replied. "I may not be at the house tonight until late anyways."

"That's strange," Allie said distractedly. "Nick called me just now."

"Wh-wh-why would that be strange?" Madison asked, her heart racing.

"He hasn't answered any of my texts or phone calls since he left London a few months ago. I figured he hated me now, but maybe not," Allie said with a small chuckle. "I'll give him a call after I leave here. Have a good night, Madison."

"You too," Madison said, watching Allie grab her coat and bag.

****

"Quick, get in here!" Ryan said, pulling Madison into the apartment before she even had the chance to knock on the door. As she caught her balance from being pulled into the apartment, Madison felt her cheeks blush at the sight of the man in front of her. A smirk crossed her face as she sat down her bag, her eyes never leaving his body.

"What?" Ryan asked cheekily. "Like what you see?"

"I mean, I have some questions. First, why aren't you wearing a shirt? I mean I'm not complaining about the sight but it's just really unlike you to walk around in sweatpants and no shirt," Madison started.

"I got hot." Ryan shrugged, flashing a devilish smile.

"Fair. Though it isn't very warm in here. Second, your hair is very disheveled. No product today?" Madison inquired.

"No product in like a week," Ryan bragged, taking a step towards Madison, and wrapping his arm around the small of her back, drawing her in closer to him.

"Interesting," Madison breathed. "Third question, what is up with all of the papers on the floor?"

"It's my book," Ryan replied. "Now, are we done with the questions?"

Madison shook her head, but instead of asking another question she let herself melt into Ryan's arms, pressing her lips passionately against his. She felt consumed by him, her hands gripping onto the bare skin of his back, his hands tangling themselves in her hair. His lips now feverously pressing against her neck over and over. Madison felt herself becoming overwhelmed with emotion with each kiss. Ryan tugged at the bottom of Madison's blouse, impatiently waiting for approval to take it off. Madison reached down and pulled it off over her head. Ryan sighed, now kissing her bare shoulders. Madison shivered at his touch, longing for his lips to touch every ounce of her skin.

"Last question, shall we take this to the bedroom?" Madison asked.

"A million times yes," Ryan replied, scooping her up and carrying her towards the bedroom.

****

Allie tried dialing Nick's number again. She tried calling him back as she left the office earlier in the day, but he didn't answer. His voice rang out over the phone telling her to leave her name and number and that he would get back to her.

"Did you get lost?" Clarissa asked, heading into the kitchen.

"In my own place? I think not," Allie laughed, pushing her phone back into her pocket.

"Well, let's drink then. Olivia is getting restless and Amalia well, you know how terribly boring she can be if she is made to wait too long," Clarissa said, rolling her eyes. "I'll grab the cheese board and you grab both of those bottles of wine."

Allie laughed, complying with Clarissa's instructions. "Remind me again why we invited Amalia?"

"She overheard me talking about it to Olivia and she started fishing for an invite and Olivia being Olivia invited her along. I think she just wanted to see the inside of your amazing place," Clarissa explained in a hushed tone as they made their way back to the living room.

"Oh great, now everyone will think they can just be invited over for wine," Allie muttered with a slight chuckle following behind Clarissa as they entered the living room.

"Or they'll think that you actually like Amalia, which might be worse," Clarissa said jokingly before turning towards where Olivia and Amalia sat. "Alright ladies, we have wine, and we have cheese!" Clarissa exclaimed lifting the cheese board in her hands up in the air as she did a little shimmy.

Allie followed behind her, her mind fixated on the phone in her pocket. She set the bottles of wine down on the coffee table and sat down, drawing her phone out of her pocket first. The screen illuminated showing a picture of her and Myles, but nothing more. She sighed, resting it down next to her.

"Allie? Are you listening?" Amalia asked.

Allie shook her head. "Sorry what?" she replied.

"I asked who you were planning on wearing to the Forever party. I personally loved the red low-cut dress. I helped Olivia pick out the looks you tried on today," Amalia bragged, taking a sip of her wine. "Did you pick one?"

"I didn't choose any of them actually. I think I'm going to try out this new designer from the States: Lacey Donahue. Have you heard of her?" Allie replied coldly. Amalia furrowed her eyebrows, shaking her head in response.

"Her designs have a lot of potential. There's this pink dress that looks like a dream, perfect for the event that I am going to try and get my hands on. Madison is working on getting me a fitting with her," Allie explained.

"It's sort of risky to go with a new designer at such a big event. I guess when you are already a big name in Hollywood it doesn't matter though. The paps will love you no matter what," Amalia retorted. The room fell silent, Clarissa and Olivia exchanging awkward looks as Allie's eyes narrowed in on Amalia.

"Where is Madison?" Clarissa interjected as Allie opened her mouth to reply to Amalia.

"Oh, is she out with Ryan tonight?" Olivia mocked. "I cannot believe that out of all the people he would choose to settle down with it would be her."

"Be nice," Clarissa warned. "I think they are actually pretty good together. It's definitely calmed him about a bit."

"Well, I hope she made him get an STD panel before they hooked up. We all know that he's been around the block a time or two," Amalia laughed.

"I think Amalia is onto something. He's been with every supermodel in the UK and when he chooses to settle down with an American nobody who could stand to lose some weight if she wants to work in this industry," Olivia added.

"Ladies, I would..." Clarissa began before Allie waved her off.

"Does anyone want something stronger than wine?" Allie asked, standing up from the couch. "I think I have some margarita mix in the kitchen."

Clarissa looked at Allie confused. Allie excused herself, her fingers wrapped around her phone, as she retreated to the kitchen. She could hear Amalia and Olivia laughing. She leaned up against the counter, dialing Nick's number again. She listened to it ring and listened to his voicemail message again, this time letting it beep.

"Nick, look, I don't want to bother you, but I'm returning your call. You called me first and I guess I just want you to know that I miss you. Seeing your name pop up on my missed calls list made me realize just how much I miss you. Please call me back. I just want to know how you are." Allie paused. "Anyways, I love you and hope you are well. Call me."

✷✷✷✷

"Okay, now explain the papers all over the place and why you haven't been at work," Madison giggled, drawing circles on Ryan's bare stomach.

"That's all you have to say after what we just did?" Ryan teased, pulling her in for another kiss.

"Just tell me," Madison chuckled.

Ryan sighed jokingly. "Well, the real reason I invited you over tonight was to tell you that something amazing happened."

"Annnnnnd? What is it?" Madison asked, snuggling up to Ryan.

"Mitch called me a few days ago and released me from *our little agreement*," Ryan said in his best Al Pacino voice. Madison bit her lip, trying to hold in tears threatening to run down her face and flood the room with her secret.

"That's why I haven't been in the office. I can take a step back from Forever a bit and focus on my other passions, hence the papers everywhere. Oh, and Myles has fully moved out and I'm going to turn his room into an office slash art studio," Ryan explained excitedly. Madison silently nodded her head, turning her face away from Ryan. The joy she just felt was starting to dissipate.

"I have no idea what changed. He just called out of the blue and said the project was taking a turn and he no longer needed me. It's like the whole world is opening up," Ryan continued. With every word, Madison felt the truth of the matter sink in deeper and deeper.

"Madison, what's wrong?" Ryan asked suddenly, sitting up in the bed. "I thought you would be thrilled about this."

"I'm just so happy for you," Madison lied, wiping away a few tears from her cheeks, sniffling a bit. "I promise these are happy tears, tears of relief. I promise."

"Just think, we can take a trip up to the Lake District soon. How about right after the party? Just you and me. Think of it as a reward for throwing what I am sure will be the best party of the year," Ryan assured, rubbing Madison's arm.

284

"We will see if I survive this party," Madison trembled. "There is still so much to be done and this party has to be a million times better than my last one which is horribly overwhelming."

"I'm sorry Mads. I should be there to help. Come here," Ryan said pulling her close to him. "Let's just forget the world again and be here."

"I'd like that," Madison whimpered trying to push back any remaining tears. "I really hope you don't think I'm crying because the sex was bad, because it wasn't," she laughed.

"Thank goodness. I was really starting to develop a complex over it," Ryan teased. "I've never been told I'm bad in bed but there's always a first time for everything."

Madison rolled her eyes.

"You know, this is going to bother me now. We should do it again just make sure that you think it was good. I'm self-conscious now. I need a little reassurance," Ryan chuckled.

"Oh, do you now?" Madison asked repositioning herself to be on top of Ryan. "I guess we most definitely have to fix that."

****

"Allie, meet Lacey Donahue. Lacey, this is Allison Davis the editor-n-chief of Forever London," Madison said, leading Lacey into Allie's office. Allie stood up, coming out from behind her desk.

"It is so nice to meet you," Allie said, reaching out to shake Lacey's hand. Lacey was tall with long gorgeous copper hair. She wore a pair of dark gray cigar pants, a white boat neck sweater, and a pair of studded black and gold heels.

"It's nice to meet you too," Lacey replied, shaking Allie's hand. "It was quite the shock to hear the Allison Davis, Hollywood royalty, L.A.'s number one It Girl, wanted to fly me out to London for a fitting of one of my dresses. I swear I am still living in a dream."

Madison took the dress bag from Lacey and unzipped it removing the dress from the bag and hanging it on a rollaway rack near the seating area of Allie's office. The dress was just as gorgeous as the pictures Allie saw online.

"This dress is amazing," Allie gasped. "Absolutely gorgeous."

"I'm glad you think so. Let's get you in it and see what alterations it might require. Though I don't think you will need any at all," Lacey remarked.

Madison smiled, excusing herself out of Allie's office to finish some last-minute party details for party in two days. As she shut Allie's door, she saw Ryan wandering through the office. He was wearing a pair of jeans and a black T-shirt. His hair still didn't have any product in it and his chin now bore the makings of a full beard.

Madison smiled as she watched him weave his way to his office, turning the heads of every woman in the office as he passed by. She watched as he turned his office light on, opened the blinds, and took a seat behind his desk, putting his feet up on the edge of the corner as he leaned back in his seat. Madison shook her head as she sat down at her computer.

As she turned on her screen again, a message popped up on her instant chat:

Ryan.Eliot: Let me know what you need from me today. I'm here to help you in any way I can.
Madison.Stevens: You didn't have to come in looking like that today. There's no way I'm going to be able to get any work done now. So, distracting.
Ryan.Eliot: I'm sure there's a way to jam the door to the closet if you need a mid-afternoon pick me up.
Madison.Stevens: Don't tempt me.
Ryan.Eliot: ;)

Madison shook her head before reaching over to the files on her desk full of invoices and to do lists for the party.

"Well, he's really let himself go," Amalia whispered to Olivia in the hallway near the breakroom.

"I think he actually looks really hot this way," Olivia replied. "It's nice to see him in jeans and not a suit for once."

Madison raised her eyebrows at the two women as she passed them. She knew who they were talking about and was certain that the next gossip topic would be her. "Olivia, Amalia, it's great that I ran into you both here. I wanted to let you know that Allie will not be wearing any of the dresses you picked out, so you can return them. She decided to go with a new designer."

"We already knew she was going with a new designer. She told us about it the other night at her house," Amalia sighed.

"Speaking of that, missed you the other night," Olivia admitted. "But I'm sure you were busy with something much more pleasurable than a wine night with us. Do you have a dress picked out for the party?"

"I'm working on it," Madison replied, ignoring Olivia's obvious attempt to get information about her love life.

"I'm sure Ryan will just buy you one. He usually does for all his dates to these things. I've fitted many girls for him, though none at your size," Amalia retorted.

"He's my date actually and not the other way around. And I don't need him to buy me anything, I can afford it on my own," Madison replied cheekily. "Now, if you will excuse me, I need to grab Allie a tea and wrap up some last-minute party details."

Madison stepped around the two women, heading towards the break room. "Oh, and Amalia, I'll let Ryan know you miss his suits. I'm sure he will take your opinion into deep consideration," Madison chortled down the hall before continuing to the breakroom.

"Was that really necessary?" Ryan asked, startling Madison as she entered the room laughing to herself.

"Which part? There's no way you heard that whole conversation from here" Madison asked.

"All of it. Who cares what the Stylist's Assistant thinks?" Ryan replied. "She's just trying to get a rise out of you, and it appears to be working."

"She's harmless. I could care less what she thinks about me," Madison said, grabbing a mug from the cabinet. "And I could care even less about what she thinks regarding your style. Which, by the way, you look extremely handsome today."

"You think so? I thought about getting into my normal Ryan Eliot, Creative Director character today but decided that I would rather be myself," Ryan explained.

"I like this version of you. It reminds me of the version Ryan I met at the launch party. The Ryan that I've fallen deeply in love with," Madison said, leaning over the table in between them to grab his hand.

"I like being this version of myself with you," Ryan whispered, squeezing Madison's hand. Madison smiled, staring into Ryan's eyes as the world around them started to fade away.

"Alright you two…" Allie said appearing in the doorway of the breakroom. Madison slowly pulled her hand from Ryan's, turning back to making Allie's tea.

"Ryan, it's nice to see you in the office today. It's been a while," Allie said leaning up against the doorframe.

"Thought it was probably best to come in and hear about the media plans for the party and look at the final touches to layout in person. The team has made sure to send me virtual mock-ups through email, but I wanted to see it in person."

"We should talk about your little break from the office later," Allie suggested.

"Gladly, though I don't know if I will be around this afternoon. What if we discussed it now?" Ryan asked. Madison watched the two exchanging words as she poured the hot water of Allie's tea into the mug.

"Right now, works fine. Madison, tell Clarissa that I will need to push our meeting five minutes. Ryan, my office please," Allie said. Madison nodded, handing Allie her tea, and following her down the hall back towards her office, Ryan next to her. He made a face to Madison, rolling his eyes as they walked. Madison tried to stifle a laugh.

"I'll see you on the other side," he whispered as Madison peeled off to call Clarissa and Ryan followed Allie into her office.

****

"Yes, please let me know when the ticket is delivered. Please say it's from Allison Davis when you drop it off," Madison explained pacing back and forth on the phone outside Ryan's building. Ryan stepped out in the same jeans and black t-shirt from earlier in the day. Madison waved to him, still pacing on the phone.

"Yes. Mmhmm. Okay," she said nodding her head. "Thank you. Goodbye."

288

"Ready for dinner?" Ryan asked, leaning in to kiss Madison's cheek as she slid her phone into her purse.

"Of course," Madison replied. "Are we walking or taking a car?"

"Let's walk. It's a nice enough evening," Ryan said grabbing Madison's hand. Madison smiled, leaning into Ryan slightly as they held hands and wandered down the street passing people up and down the sidewalks. They didn't say much to each other, but Madison felt safe and alive all at the same time, until the finality of these moments crossed her mind and a deep sadness threatened to consume her. She tried to fight it, to send it packing, but she knew that at any moment she would lose this all with one simple direction given from Mitch McGowan. Madison gripped Ryan's hand tighter as they squeezed by a group of people.

She worked to memorize his silhouette, the shape of his chin, the feel of his hand in hers. She took mental pictures of his profile, his scruffy face, his broad shoulders, and his currently unkempt hair. She wanted to remember everything she could and savor every moment with him. She smiled and recorded his voice in the depths of his memory as he requested a table for them.

"What are you thinking about? You seem lost to another world," he asked, sitting down across from her.

"I'm just taking in every single moment I have with you in case one day this all slips away from us. I'm so unbelievably happy here with you," Madison confessed picking up the menu in front of her.

"I'm unbelievably happy with you too. Look, I don't have a crystal ball or the ability to tell the future, but I know for a fact that I will do everything in my power to make sure this never slips away from us. That I promise you," Ryan replied.

Madison nodded, reaching across the table for Ryan's hand. She gave it a quick squeeze and pulled her hand back.

"Want to share some naan? You'll need to carb-o-load for tonight and tomorrow," he said with a wink and devilish smile.

Episode 24- Champagne Problems

"Als, you here?" Myles called out from the door of the townhouse, trying to yell over the loud music playing.

"In here!" she yelled from the living room. Myles wandered into the crowded room full of hair and make-up people. "Sorry, it's such a mess, Clarissa and Olivia and Lizzy were over getting ready." Myles could hear Allie's voice among the people cleaning up the various mirrored stations, but he couldn't quite see her…until she stood up.

Myles let out a little gasp at the sight of her. Her hair cascaded down on one side in long waves with tiny pink flowers pinned into the waves. Her shoulders were bare as her sleeveless pink gown hugged her chest tightly giving way at her hips into a flowy gown.

"You look beyond words," Myles stuttered as she approached him. Allie laughed.

"You think so?" she asked, giving a little playful twirl.

"You always look amazing Allie," Myles replied, pulling her in for a kiss on the forehead. Allie looked up at him. He looked nervous. His green eyes shifted back and forth, focusing and un-focusing on her face as if to distract her from a secret held well within them. Allie grabbed Myles' hand, which felt balmy at her touch. Allie let go of his hand and took a step back studying his look. He went with a simple black suit, white shirt, and black tie combination. It looked sleek and understated, which would be perfect for allowing Allie's dress to shine in photos.

"You look very handsome in this suit. I'm happy our social media followers chose this one," Allie teased, trying to ease his nerves. "It looks fantastic on you."

"I could have sworn that someone posted a video asking people to choose this suit over the others," Myles laughed. "You wouldn't know anything about that would you?"

"Who would ever do such a thing? Not me," Allie said, shifting her eyes back and forth jokingly.

Myles laughed, kissing her forehead again. "It's the perfect suit for tonight. Shall we?"

Allie nodded, grabbing her clutch off the couch. She followed Myles out of the house, through the garden, and to the car. He waived off the driver and opened Allie's door allowing her to get in. As he closed the door and made his way to the other side of the car, he paused at the back, feeling for the small box in his trouser pocket.

"Did you ever think that this is where we would be after all this time?" Myles asked Allie as the car pulled away from her house.

"What do you mean?" Allie asked.

"I mean, after everything we've been through, did you ever imagine we would work together, be on the cover of a magazine together, be invited to events together, have paparazzi follow us around like we were royalty, go to parties like this, walk down red carpets, etc.? After everything we've been through, I didn't. I quite honestly never thought I would get another chance to hold your hand, to be in your life, to kiss you. I feel immensely lucky every day that you are back in my life," Myles admitted.

"Me too," Allie replied staring out the window at the cars passing by them on the road.

Madison smiled as Ryan opened the car door and held his hand out to help her out of the car. Everything was in its rightful place. A nice long blush carpet welcomed photographers and celebrities alike to stop for photos against a backdrop of romantic vines and flowers in various hues of pink.

"It looks amazing Madison," Ryan whispered in her ear as she straightened out the bottom of her dress.

"It does, doesn't it?" Madison replied taking it all in as Ryan led her to the staging area for photos. "I should go check on the inside and make sure everything looks good before Allie and Mr. Garrison arrive."

"Not without taking a picture with me first," Ryan replied.

"Ryan- I really shouldn't," Madison whispered backing up a little.

"Why shouldn't you? You work here and you put together this event. You deserve to step into the spotlight even if only for a moment," Ryan assured her. "Now come on, let's go take our first public, paparazzi crazed, event photo together. Let's unlock a new level of this relationship." Madison smiled as Ryan led her to a spot in front of the cameras.

The camera flashes started blinding Allie before she could even fully get out of the car. Myles reached for her hand as she stepped out, helping guide her onto her feet before shutting the car door behind her.

"Are you ready for this?" Allie asked. "All of this crazy fame driven chaos because of who my father is?"

"There is nothing I would be more ready for than standing next to you at events like this for the rest of my life," Myles replied. "But also, I don't think they are making such a fuss over you because of who your father is. I think you've really created a name for yourself here."

Allie smiled, squeezing Myles's hand. "Here goes nothing," she muttered as she stepped out onto the blush carpet with Myles by her side for the first time.

The inside of the venue was just as beautiful as the sketches Madison last showed the group. Ivy vines hung from the tall ceilings with a large floral arrangement hanging above the dance floor area. Rows of cocktail tables were strategically placed around the dance floor, each with an array of tall candles on gold plates in the middle. The lights were dim, letting the candles provide a romantic air of mystery in the room. A string quartet quietly played music welcoming guests into the party. A large white screen was set up behind them showing a live video stream of the carpeted entrance outside.

"This is breathtaking," Allie sighed as she entered the venue with Myles. "Madison has a way of handling a party, that's for sure."

"That she does," Myles said taking it all in. "What is the purpose of that screen though? Is it only going to show everyone entering all night? What about when everyone is here?"

"In about thirty minutes the screen will flip over to allow people to connect through this website and put up their own photos or videos. It's a new technology we are trying out," Madison explained coming up from behind Myles and Allie.

"This looks amazing Madison. Job well done," Allie said.

"Thank you. Now, as some of our guests of honor please note that in about an hour we are going to have you two come on stage and talk about your love story a bit. Now sure, people read about it in the summer issues of the magazine, but it'll mean the world to them to see your love story in person. So go and mingle for now and I'll come find you when we are ready to give the people what they want," Madison informed the two before heading in the opposite direction.

Madison left Ryan, Allie, and Myles making her way back towards the blush carpet to help monitor the arrivals of party guests. As she wandered through the enchanted gardens, she couldn't help but smile at how wonderful everything turned out. A year ago, she was serving tables at restaurants and being scolded by rich people about unnecessary garnishes or meals being too salty and here she stood in the middle of a fantastic party that she created.

"This is one of the nicer parties I've been to in a while for one of my magazines," Brad Garrison admitted walking towards Madison. "I was right to force Allie to put you in charge of this one. Hopefully she wasn't too crass with you about it."

"She was professional and thank you," Madison replied shyly. "It really was a team effort here. Allie did put in a lot of work to make this all happen. I couldn't have done it without her."

"Don't make yourself smaller for the Allies of the world Madison," Mr. Garrison advised. "You have a talent for putting on events that not only tell a story but draw people into it. I received a ton of emails from people asking how to get an invite to this event. You've created a buzz unlike any other, and that takes true talent Madison. Talent Allie does not have."

"Thank you," Madison replied.

"Maybe it's time we make you more than an assistant. Let's discuss some opportunities next week. I plan on being in London for a while, so we will set something up," Mr. Garrison said before heading into the party area.

Madison let a huge smile break out across her face as she finished her journey to the entrance. Her head was spinning with the news that she could become something more than an assistant to Allie.

"What is he doing here? Did Allie invite him?" Ryan whispered into Madison's ear.

"Don't do that!" Madison exclaimed, chills running down her spine pulling her back to reality, back to her first assignment.

"Sorry, just didn't want to yell out my questions," Ryan chuckled. "But honestly, what is he doing here?" Nick heading down the blush carpet. "I paid him a couple million dollars to stay out of London. Mitch and Ken are not going to be so happy about this."

"I'm not sure why he's here," Madison said, wringing her hands at her sides. The image of Ryan handing someone an envelope at the elevator the day of the relaunch party flashed in her mind. It all made sense. Nick's confession and abrupt departure. Nick now ignoring Allie's phone calls and text messages. He too was part of this world he warned her about before the party. This was the darkness he mentioned "This is definitely going to cause a bit of a problem. Let's go find Allie."

****

"Allie, come here," Myles said pulling Allie off the crowded pathway into a secluded alcove away from the party. Ivy vines fell over the edges of a small pergola in the tiny alcove. Myles pulled Allie in for a kiss wrapping his arms around her waist.

"Have I told you how beautiful you look tonight?" Myles whispered in her ear as she started to pull away from the kiss.

"Yes, numerous times actually," Allie giggled. "What's gotten into you tonight?"

"Well, I cannot stop myself from saying it over and over. I am one lucky man."

Madison and Ryan came up the walkway. "This party is one of the best parties I've ever attended in London," Ryan admitted, taking a glass of champagne from a waiter. Madison smiled, wrinkling her nose at him before coming to a sudden stop.

"What do you think they are doing over there?" Madison asked, nodding towards Myles and Allie off on their own.

"Hmm… maybe she is complaining about how you are upstaging her once again," Ryan teased.

"Maybe," Madison said watching the two dimly lit figures intensely.

"Well, you wanted to tell her about Nick being here, now's your chance," Ryan said taking a step forward in the direction of Allie and Myles.

Madison grabbed his arm, pulling him back a bit. "Wait. Let's not interrupt them."

"Allie, I know things haven't always been easy between us, but I am so happy with you in my life. You challenge me to be a better man every single day," Myles started. Allie smiled, looking away as she started to blush and feel her heartbeat quicken.

Ryan watched Myles start to fidget with something in his pocket. "You don't think…"

"What?" Madison asked hurriedly.

"You don't think Myles is about to ask Allison to marry him. Not here and now, right?" Ryan finished. "He's definitely got something there in his pocket."

Madison shook her head. "There's no way. Not here," she breathed as a sudden panic came over her. Even if Myles was to propose, she knew that Nick was in the main room and wouldn't be able to see it. He wouldn't be able to stop it, to cause a scene, to help her show Mitch exactly what she was capable of doing. Madison started to pat her pockets for her phone, knowing that if she could live stream on the main screen inside it would draw Nick outside.

"Give me your phone!" Madison demanded.

"What? Why?" Ryan asked, reaching into his jacket pocket for it.

"People are going to want to see this. It perfectly goes with the theme of tonight," Madison replied, snatching the phone out of his hand, and ferociously typing to link into the video streaming link. "Follow me. We need to get closer," she whispered.

"Allie, I never thought I'd get the chance to correct the past with you. I never thought we'd be able to try again and to do things right. I never should have let you go the first time. And now I hope I never have to again," Myles paused, pulling out a ring box out of his pocket. Allie's eyes filled with tears as Myles got down on one knee.

Madison was nearby but out of sight as she filmed Myles and Allie's private moment onto the big screen in the main area. Her heart was racing as Myles, now knelling, opened the ring box.

"Allison Davis, will you marry me?" Myles asked his voice certain and strong. Allie looked down at the ring, her hands shaking. It was a thin rose gold band encrusted in tiny diamonds with a large princess cut diamond in the middle.

Allie stood still, her eyes flittering away from the ring and Myles kneeling on the ground. She needed a moment to think, to take it all in. For years she dreamt of this very moment just for it to feel not as she expected. Allie's eyes locked in on a shadow of a figure in the distance walking towards the spot where she stood. Allie's mind was racing as people were stopping and now gawking at the man down on one knee and Allie standing there frozen in time.

"Allie? Did you hear me?" Myles asked in a hushed voice.

"Nick?" Allie muttered studying the way the shadow walked as it came closer.

"Allie?" Myles asked again, standing up from the ground, holding the ring box open, as Allie took a step out of the alcove.

Madison followed Allie with the camera as she made her way towards Nick leaving Myles alone in the alcove. Madison couldn't hear what they were saying, but from the look of Nick's tense shoulders and Allie's desperate grab at Nick's arm, it couldn't be good.

"Let's give them some privacy Madison," Ryan whispered into Madison's ear.

"One more second, where'd Myles go?" Madison whispered back, panning over to the alcove which was now empty. Ryan reached for his phone covering the camera as he stole it back from Madison and turned it off. He felt sad for Myles, a way he never quite felt for his stepbrother before. It was one thing to have some break up with you, it was another to have someone simply walk away from your marriage proposal.

"Let's go get a drink," Ryan suggested. "This scene is way too depressing for me to now bear sober."

"Hold on, I want to go listen to what Allie and Nick are discussing," Madison replied.

"Let them be. I'm sure they have a lot to talk about, though I am rather surprised he's here in the first place," Ryan said, placing his hand on the small of Madison's back to guide her towards the bar.

"He was on the guest list. I wonder if she said no to Myles before walking off. Why didn't we put mics in the alcoves? Hidden microphones would have been such a nice touch," Madison rambled, taking a step away from Ryan.

"Madison, let them be. You are supposed to be enjoying this event. Allie can take care of herself," Ryan replied. "Now let's get a drink and do some schmoozing and enjoy our first night out at a party like this as a couple."

"Fine," Madison sighed, turning away from Allie and Nick and following Ryan towards the bar. She took one final glance back at them before Ryan pulled her inside.

There they stood in silence. "Say something," Allie begged. "Why are you here? Why did you come back?"

Nick shook his head trying to find the words. He had them all prepared up until the moment he saw Myles start to pull the ring out of his pocket on the video screen in the main area. Before he knew it, he was walking straight out of the venue and towards the alcove.

"What did you say to him?" Nick finally asked.

Allie looked back towards the spot where she left Myles. She saw the ring, she heard the question, but the second she saw Nick she bolted. Now the alcove was empty. Myles was gone, nowhere to be seen. "I didn't answer him," she admitted, turning back to face Myles.

"You didn't even answer him?" Nick laughed incredulously. "Allison, what the fuck? That's messed up."

"What do you want me to say Nicholas?!" Allie snapped. "Why the hell are you here anyways?! You've avoided me like the plague since you left here in a huff about me being back with Myles and now here you are giving me that 'I can't believe you. I'm so disappointed' face."

"I came back to apologize. I came back to explain myself. I came back to tell you that I can't stop thinking about you! I came back to say one more time- Allison Davis, I'm in love with you, please just give me a chance. But then I saw you there with him and realized that my chance was gone. That's what you've always wanted. Myles is who you've always wanted," Nick admitted defeatedly.

Allie felt tears filling her eyes and a mixture of rage, confusion, and deep sadness filling her chest. "I don't know what I want," she admitted as the tears started to stream down her face. "I don't know what I'm even doing here or who I am anymore." Nick pulled her in, allowing her to cry in his arms. He rubbed her back trying to soothe her and shelter her from party goers passing by them trying to steal a glance.

"Allison, not here. Let's leave this party and talk," Nick whispered.

Allie took a step back, suddenly remembering where she was. "I – I- can't leave," Allie sniffled, smoothing out her hair and wiping the tears from her cheeks.

"Of course, you can't," Nick scoffed.

"Nick don't be like that," Allie replied. "I can't leave, this isn't just a party, it's work. You have to understand."

Nick stepped back from Allie. "It's always about work for you, Allie. Can't we just leave and talk about things? Can't someone else step in for you?"

"This party is about Myles and me as a couple Nick, no one can just step in for me in that," Allie retorted.

"Allison, you literally just walked away from the man's proposal without giving him an answer. You can walk away from this party too. You just aren't ready to let him go, you never have been," Nick replied, his voice low.

"Nick, how did you even know to show up here tonight? Did my dad put you up to this? Did he send you to break up things between Myles and I since he's had it out for this relationship from the start? There's no way you just showed up after all these months to tell me you love me again!" Allie exclaimed, her voice trembling. "It's not fair!"

"I called off my wedding for you Allie! After we kissed, I knew I couldn't be with Kara any longer. Not when I feel this way about you, and to be honest I thought you might have been feeling the same way and that's why you invited me here," Nick replied calmly, retrieving an invitation from the breast pocket of his suit.

Allie took the invitation from him, running her fingers over the embossed words. It was an official invitation from the magazine to attend. The same invitation that was sent to everyone here. "I didn't send this Nick…I don't know wh—"

"Allie!" Madison interjected running up to Allie and Nick in a panic. "We need you inside right this second. It's Myles."

Episode 25- Rolling in The Deep

Madison and Allie entered the main room. "He was downing drinks over at the bar. I left him with Ryan, right over—" Madison stopped in her tracks, searching the room for Ryan and Myles.

"Madison, I don't care if Myles is drinking. He is a grown man, he can make his own choices," Allie replied rolling her eyes.

"Oh, there's Ryan," Madison said taking off towards him. Allie followed, her shoulders tensing with each step. Myles was nowhere to be found. Allie felt goosebumps rise up on the back of her neck. She wanted to be outside with Nick, finishing their conversation, but the urgency in Madison's voice as she questioned Ryan about Myles' whereabouts was starting to worry.

"I don't know where he went, Madison. Mr. Garrison came by and started chatting with me about the next few issues of the magazine and Myles disappeared," Ryan shrugged.

A loud screeching sound blasted over the speakers in the room as the music cut off. Allie, Madison, and Ryan, all turned to see Myles stumbling on the stage. In one hand a bottle of whiskey and in the other a microphone.

"Shit," Madison groaned.

"Oh this will be interesting," Ryan chuckled.

Allie stood frozen watching Myles head to the center of the stage. People were starting to flood into the room.

"Is this thing working?" Myles asked, tapping the microphone. "Welcome to the event of the year…or at least… that's what I'm told it is. Either way welcome."

Allie could feel her heart pounding in her chest. She could see that Myles was drunk. Anyone could see that Myles was drunk.

"How much did he drink before you got me?" Allie whispered to Madison, not taking her eyes off the man on the stage.

"He threw back about 5 shots of tequila in less than a minute," Madison replied. "Not sure where he got the bottle of whiskey."

"I am Myles McGowan, one half of this perfect couple," Myles said, gesturing to picture of Allie and Myles on the television screens around the room. "Though, as rumor has it you all already know that this couple isn't perfect. I pro-proposed to Allison Marie Davis tonight and well she took off with another man... Yes! You heard that right, Allison Marie Davis and I are not perfect, she's a whore and well, I'm a drunk." Myles chuckled at this truth.

"The thing is, I haven't always been a drunk...but Allie... oh my dear Allie... where are you?" Myles paused to search the crowd for Allie.

"Oh, there you are! Everyone, give it up for Allie!" Myles clapped, but no one else did. Allie could feel her cheeks turning a deep shade of red. She looked around the crowd, hoping that Nick had left the party and not entered this room to see this disaster.

"Oh, my dear Allison, what my life was before I knew you. I could have been married to the actual love of my life instead of letting her go to marry someone else. I could be happy right now with children." Myles paused taking a swig of whiskey straight from the bottle. "And that is what the bloody magazine article written about us leaves out. Oh, it leaves out quite a bit actually!"

"Someone needs to stop him," Allie muttered, starting towards the stage.

"Madison, stop her from going up there," Ryan said. "This is your party; you have to get it under control." Before Madison could move, Nick made his way after Allie.

"Let's just see what happens," Madison shrugged. Madison kept her eyes on Allie as she argued with Nick who stopped her from making her way to the stage. Ryan focused in on Madison as she stared straight ahead, unmoved and unbothered by the events unfurling before them.

"Madison," Ryan said. Madison waved him off, still staring straight ahead. "Madison, what have you done?"

Her eyes met his. She opened her mouth as if to say something, but instead shook her head and shrugged her shoulders before turning back to see Allie following Nick onto the stage.

"You came to join me, how lovely, but did you need to bring him with you," Myles said, pointing to Nick.

"Myles," she hissed. "Come on."

"Not until I tell everyone the real 'love story' between us instead of this bullshit your magazine is peddling," Myles replied into the microphone. "Now gather around everyone, you've all read the article by now, it's literally plastered around this damn event, howeverrrrr, it's time for the truuuth. I met Allie through a school project. That part is true. I also did help her through some rough patchessss." Myles paused to hiccup.

Allie's heart pounded in her chest. Her eyes searched the crowd desperately for help. Ryan and Madison stood frozen where she left them. Madison wore a smirk, her eyes fixated on Myles. Ryan looked worried, his focus osculating between Allie and Madison. Myles cleared his throat and Allie turned back to look at Nick, positioning herself in between both men. Her legs felt heavy as her heart threatened to escape her chest.

"Madison, go and stop this," Ryan urged.

Madison shook her head. "Leave it alone Ryan."

Ryan sighed. "I can't."

"Ryan, let it happen. Let them figure it out on their own," Madison replied, grabbing his arm, and pulling him back to her.

"No," he said, jerking his arm away from her.

"Now what you don't know is that Allie, dear, sweet, poor Allie came to London all those years ago like a sad little puppy. She wanted an adventure, so she came to London for school and to tear my life apart," Myles let out another hiccup. "I was seeing someone when she told me she was coming to London. I knew she felt deeply for me, so I broke it off with another woman I so loved. What a BIGGGGGGGGGG mistake! Things were great with Allie at first, but then she broke me. She demanded so much from me, pushed me out of my comfort zone, pushed me to do more and to be more… she wanted so much from me that the only way I could provide the life she wanted was to start gambling… and well," Myles chuckled, looking over at Allie. "Well, to start drinking, until one day Allie left promising never to come back. Just to… get this! Just to come back and then rope me into being her good little photographer boy, alllllllll whillllllllle she was sleeeeeeeping with her best friend, who she conveniently tonight had shown up as I was proposing to her like I thought sh- sh- she wanted me too. But once a whore always a who——."

Before Myles could even finish the last word, Nick punched him in the mouth. Allie could hear the crowd gasp and through the bright lights she saw people start to leave the room. Myles stumbled back laughing a bit as Ryan hopped onto the stage.

Ryan pushed Nick back. "Go!" he demanded. Nick shook out his hand. Allie reached out to him, and he brushed her off. Taking it all in, Myles lifted the microphone up to say more.

"Enough Myles. That's enough," Ryan said grabbing the end of the mic. With one swift pull, Myles freed himself from Ryan's grip and took a step back.

"Oh, a round of applause everyone. It's another one of Allie's knights in shining armor!" Myles scoffed pulling the microphone back towards him. "Allie, did you sleep with my stepbrother? You were seeing him for a while recently."

"Myles, ENOUGH!" Ryan said pulling the microphone out of his hand. Nick stopped looking back at Allie. Seeing this she shook her head at him and stepped into the center of the stage taking the microphone from Ryan as he escorted Myles off the stage. Allie wiped a tear from her face, her hands shaking with all the eyes of the room on her.

"I'd like to apologize to everyone here about that," Allie started, her voice cracking. "Um, hmmm, how do you even follow something like that?" Allie drew in a deep breath.

"Things aren't always as they seem, and things aren't always as we tell them either. It is true, Myles and I have a rockier romance than we've led you to believe. We decided to only tell a small portion of our story instead airing our dirty laundry. I apologize for Myles's outburst here tonight. We clearly have some things to work through," Allie explained.

"Did you turn down his proposal?!" Someone from the crowd yelled out.

Allie sighed, raising the mic to her lips. "Yes, but not for the reasons he stated. I'm not romantically involved with someone else. Clearly, Myles and I have some things to work through before making that type of commitment. I apologize for this brief interruption to the event. Please feel free to grab more drinks and food. The party isn't over yet," Allie finished. As she left the stage, the crowd started yelling out questions and snapping photos. Allie ignored everyone heading towards a side door. Madison bolted through the crowd going after Allie. Madison found Allie crying in an alleyway. There sat a shell of the confident and shielded woman who welcomed Madison to London with a warm smile. She looked smaller than she did that first day. Her perfect persona cracked and was now crumbling on the ground all around her. Madison took slow small steps towards Allie until she was close enough to put a consoling hand on Allie's shoulder.

"Ladies! This is a disaster. Get it cleaned up and I expect both of you to be in the office at 8AM sharp tomorrow to discuss this," demanded the voice of Brad Garrison piercing through the darkness.

Allie turned to face Mr. Garrison, giving him a respectful nod of acknowledgment before he turned to walk away. "I hope he fires you tomorrow, because if he doesn't I will," she said turning her tears into a cold anger. "This is all your doing."

Madison took a step back. "How so?" she asked defiantly.

"This was your event. This is your problem. You invited Nick here. You let Myles get drunk. You could have stopped it at any time, instead you just stood there with a smile watching everything explode. If he doesn't fire you, you best believe I will," Allie said, smoothing out her dress as she stepped back towards the party. "Clean this up. I'm going home."

"I'm sure he will fire you first. You've made a mess of this magazine with your personal life since you started here. This was just the proof rising to the surface, Allie. Your life is a mess covered up with polite smiles and calculated appearances. This was the natural course of uncovering the truth. I stood there and watched because it was about time it all came crashing down on you. Now you get to live your truth: it doesn't matter who your dad is, how many people know your name, or how much money you have, you're human like the rest of us," Madison replied.

"You know what, don't worry about cleaning this up. I'll get someone else to do it because you're fired. You can either leave right now on your own, or I'll have security escort you out!" Allie snapped.

"You can't fire me," Madison laughed, pushing past Allie. "Good try. I'll clean up this party and see you in the morning."

Madison turned around heading back into the party. Music radiated from the speakers inside. Through the glass she could see people now dancing on the dance floor or ordering drinks at the bar. She scanned the gardens for Ryan, hoping to salvage what she could of the night with her on his arm. After walking around for a while, she found him sitting on a bench in the back, his head in his hands.

"Ryan are you okay?" she asked, rubbing his back as she sat back down next to him.

"I knew it was all too good to be true," he said, straightening up.

"What was?" Madison asked, pulling back from him, her hands falling into her lap.

"Maybe you should stay in a hotel tonight," he replied, pulling away from her. "I need some space to think."

Episode 26- Flowers

A week later, her stuff was packed ready to leave London. Every suitcase zipped up, her letters from the past packed away and her heart pieced back together, holding on by a thread. Allie was ready to go. She looked around her townhouse one last time to make sure she wasn't forgetting anything before heading back to California. The city mourned another loss with her as heavy rain pelted on the window. Allie stood frozen in the foyer listening to the rain, letting the memories wash over her.

A week ago, she stood in this spot holding Myles before heading to the party. After his outburst, Mr. Garrison personally fired Myles. A few hours after firing Myles, Mr. Garrison met with Allie, stating he had a new job assignment for her starting in a few months, enough time for her to get her shit together. She didn't even try calling Myles, letting the silence of forgotten letters and photos fall between them once again.

Allie didn't know what to do about Myles or how to help him this time. *It's all my fault.* The thought kept pushing its way to the surface. *If I never came back... if I just stayed away like he wanted me to...this wouldn't have happened.* Allie drew in a deep breath trying to stop the waves from dragging her under.

She refocused on the rain, the memory of Nick telling her how he felt in this very same spot almost six months ago. Now he was waiting for her arrival back in California to figure things out between them. After the party, he escorted her home making sure she was in good enough shape to carry on. He slept on the couch and left in the morning promising to be at the beach house when she returned.

Allie looked out the window at the sound of a car door closing. Madison was walking up the sidewalk with an umbrella. It was time to bid the city farewell once more. Madison was also being sent back to California, but to work at Garrison Publishing headquarters. Allie tried to convince Mr. Garrison to fire Madison, but he refused without giving a reason behind his decision to keep her on.

She took another look around. Another chunk of her life had passed quickly in London, teaching her how to laugh again, how to let her guard down maybe a little too much, and how to forgive but not forget the hurt caused by others. She wasn't leaving the city as a shell of a person this time. Whilst she was sad and a little heartbroken, she was stronger than the girl from all those years back who returned home devastated.

"You ready?" Madison asked, walking up behind Allie.

"How much time do we have before the flight?" Allie asked, fidgeting with a green envelope in her hand.

"You have a couple of hours," Madison responded. "Also, Mr. Garrison asked me to stay behind a couple extra weeks to help transition everything over, so if you forgot anything in your office, I'll have it mailed to you."

Allie nodded. "Let's make a small stop on our way."

Ten minutes later, Allie headed up the stairs to Myles' flat. She didn't know which felt heavier, her heart or the letter she was dropping off. Slowly she raised a fist to knock on the door, but before her knuckles touched the door, she put her hand back down to her side. She couldn't face him again, not after everything he said. She crouched down sliding the envelope under the door. Choking down some tears, she stood up slowly and headed back down the stairs. "Goodbye Myles McGowan," she whispered as his door disappeared out of sight behind her.

****

"Well, Allie is out of here," Madison said to Ryan as she walked in the door, kicking off her white sneakers. "Time to get the new guy set-up as editor-n-chief tomorrow. Man, I can't believe she's gone."

"We still need to talk," Ryan said, setting down his newspaper. Madison looked at Ryan inquisitively. For a few days after the party, she stayed in a hotel, only corresponding with Ryan via text as chaos ensued at the office. After things started to calm down, Ryan invited her back in. He was in a pair of dark sweatpants, a white T-shirt, his feet bare, and his hair poking out every which way. His eyes were sunken in a bit with dark circles under them. His chin bored some stubble, an expired 5'o'clock shadow creeping over his face.

"About what?" Madison asked.

"About the party, about things lately… I'm not okay with what you did," Ryan said. "Come sit down and let's talk about it."

307

"I didn't do anything Ryan. Myles got drunk and attacked Allie's character. That's all that happened. A lover's spat on display for all to see," Madison explained, leaning up against the wall across from the couch.

"Madison, I can't protect you from this all. I can't shield you from what comes next in this world. I can't protect you from Mitch and Ken," Ryan replied.

"Again, I don't know what you are talking about," Madison lied crossing her arms. She could feel a cold sweat forming on her neck.

"I thought it was coincidence, a happy mistake, a reprieve from this horrible life that I got to meet you, fall in love, and be released from the grip of Mitch and Ken. Then I saw you filming Allie and Myles when Nick showed up. Then I saw you trying to hide a smile when Myles was on stage making a fool of himself. It was in that moment it all made sense. I wasn't released from anything because the universe decided to finally help me out. No, you took my place, and I can't protect you any longer," Ryan said, hanging his head.

"I've never asked you to protect me, Ryan. I've never wanted you to protect me. I don't need you to protect me," Madison replied.

"You have no idea what you've gotten yourself into. They will make us break up. They will send you so far away that I will never get to be with you again. I can't stop it from happening," Ryan said, his shoulders growing tense with each word. "What you did was stupid. It was the most ignorant thing you could have done. You sentenced this relationship to death!"

"They were going to make us break-up either way. We were never supposed to be together!" Madison replied, a fury rising in her chest, spilling out in her words.

"I could have stopped it, Madison! I could have fought for this. I didn't ask you to take my place! I never asked you to step in and speak on my behalf! So, what made you do it? The validation? The need to save someone instead of working on yourself?" Ryan yelled.

Madison felt the sting of hot tears roll down her cheeks. "I did it for you. Everything I've done is for you!"

"That's hard to believe. I saw it, I saw you taking great joy in watching Allie's life unfurl in front of a large crowd," Ryan replied. "You can't tell me that was all for me."

"You deserve a life better than this Ryan! Look around and tell me that this world, this work… tell me it makes you happy. I did all of this to give you another chance at life, one where you can be free and live the life that makes you excited to be alive!" Madison snapped.

"Look me in the eye and tell me the truth Madison. Did you or did you not enjoy watching Allie fall flat on her face out there?" Ryan replied. "Tell me the truth. This wasn't all for me. This was for you to have some power in the world too. Tell me I'm wrong."

"I- I-I."

"Look me in the eyes and tell me I'm wrong Madison," Ryan repeated.

"I can't," Madison said sliding down the wall to sit on the floor. "It felt good to see her squirm up there after months of her stealing my ideas and not giving me credit. It felt good to hear her be sent back to California and for Mr. Garrison to make space on his team for me to be more than just an assistant… and all because I sent a simple set of plane tickets to Nick," Madison admitted.

"You do realize you ruined a couple lives that night too. Nick had to watch the love of his life be proposed to. Allie was called a whore and tore her apart in front of a couple hundred colleagues. Myles was fired and will most likely never get hired again because he's a drunk who went on a tirade… and I watched the woman I am so deeply in love with change into a villain before my eyes," Ryan said, letting the words fall in the space between them. "How do you think that makes me feel?"

Madison looked at Ryan as he finished speaking, her eyes searching his face for a glimmer of hope and love, but his eyes were gray like the skies outside. All of the life and love they once shared was nowhere to be found.

"You don't mean that last part," Madison said. "I'm not the villain here, you know I'm not."

"Madison, I don't even know who you are anymore. Last night you showed an ugly side to the world, a side I never dreamed that you could show. A side of yourself I was working hard to protect you from having to unleash," Ryan replied. "But now it's too late. I can't protect you now. I can't shield you from this dark world you just entered."

"Once again, I never needed you to protect me. Just love me and please say you aren't saying that you still can't do that. If that's what you are saying, then you aren't being fair. I did this for you," Madison said.

"I can try but knowing that they are going to pull us apart, that at any moment you can flop into this other version of you or that Ken and Mitch can send a simple text and you are done… that changes things for me," Ryan admitted.

"And what did you expect me to do once you told me about this world? Just accept that you would flop into this other version of yourself.? How is that fair? How is any of this fair?" Madison's head dropped into her hands. "What was I supposed to do Ryan? Watch you suffer?"

"Come here," Ryan whispered. Madison stood up slowly, making her way to the couch. Ryan sat back wrapping his arm around Madison pulling her in tightly. "You didn't have to do anything for me. Look I don't want to lose you Madison. I will try my hardest to keep you, but you are no longer mine to keep forever."

****

Myles stumbled out of bed to the kitchen to grab some water. A blue duffle was packed and sitting near the door. He looked at the clock as he poured himself a glass of water. Patrick would be here in ten minutes, and they would start their journey up north to a rehab center in the country. The weather mirrored his dreary exterior in true English fashion.

Myles finished his water, passing the door to his flat towards the bedroom. Slowly he pulled on a pair of jeans and buttoned up a dark blue shirt. He looked around the room for any remaining signs of his failed relationship with Allie to put in the box of items Patrick would dispose of. He wandered into the bathroom to brush his teeth, finding her toothbrush next to his. He picked up the little purple brush, running his fingers along the handle letting out a wobbly sigh before tossing it in the bin.

Myles brushed his teeth and grabbed his box of Allie memorabilia off the edge of his bed. He felt his phone buzz in his pocket. Patrick was downstairs. Myles gave the flat one more looks over before reaching down to grab his blue duffel bag off the floor. As he pulled the bag up and tossed its strap over his shoulder, he saw a small green envelope on the floor with his name written on the front of it.

"Allie," he whispered running his fingers over his name in her handwriting. His phone buzzed ferociously in his pocket again. He stuffed the green envelope in his back pocket and headed out of his flat carrying the box of Allie's stuff in one hand and his duffel bag over the opposite shoulder.

Myles slid the box into the back seat of Patrick's car and hopped into the front seat. He felt the envelope crunch in his back pocket.

"Ready mate?" Patrick asked before pulling away from the front of Myles' building. Myles nodded, reaching into his pocket to retrieve the envelope. As Patrick began their journey, Myles opened the envelope, pulling out a piece of paper covered in Allie's meticulous handwriting.

My Dearest Myles,

It kills me to write this letter knowing how much pain you are already in. I guess I always knew the drinking was a slight issue that began building when I lived here but wanted to overlook it because I loved and still love you so much. I am so sorry I didn't intervene sooner. I blame myself for the predicament you are now in because I didn't step in and stop it from happening. I know I pushed you back into this world. I know that I am partially to blame for all the hurt and all of the suffering you've been through throughout these years. I never meant for any of it to happen.

If I could go back and never take the position here in London, knowing what I know now, I would. I don't regret a single moment of our time together, this time or in years past. And even though I will always love you, I know now that we aren't healthy for each other. We aren't good for each other. When I left the first time, I ended up in rehab for my eating disorder. The pain of you sending me away, the cold look in your eyes that day burned into me, leaving me susceptible to anything that could give me a sense of control. I spent all these years thinking I was the only one suffering, little did I know or even imagine that you too were facing a mountain of pain.

In rehab, I found the strength to overcome my addiction, my need for control and I think that getting help could lead you down the same path. It will help you find yourself again, find that sparkle in your eye, the deep gutted laughter, the creativity in your photos… the Myles I know the world can fall in love with, because he's the man I fell in love with time and time again. It just may take letting me go, letting the idea of a future together go.

I can't wait to see your photos in print again one day and to see an article stating that you've been sober for years. I can't wait to see your face pop up on my social media feed and to see you healthier than ever. I can't wait to see all of your dreams of a family and a thriving career come true. These may be things that seem impossible now, but I promise you, they will happen. And maybe one day we will run into each other, both happy in our own lives and we will laugh about just how naïve we were in the past.

I wish you nothing but the best, Myles McGowan, and I will carry a piece of you in my heart for the rest of my life. I just need you to go and get the help you need so that I can carry that piece of you with me knowing that you are alive and thriving. Here's my one and only letter from London for you, a goodbye letter.

Love you forever and ever,
Allie

Three weeks later

Madison pulled her tablet out of her bag as she sat down to wait for boarding to begin. A small envelope fell out as she slid the tablet from its pocket, her name written on the front in Ryan's handwriting. Her chest tightened as she opened it.

Madison- I have this strong feeling that this goodbye was an actual goodbye for good. I know you can't explain it to me, and I'm not surprised. You never needed to take my place or save me from the problems I created for myself. If this is goodbye, I wish you the best of luck and please know… I will love you forever and I will see you again. -Ryan

Acknowledgements

It really does take a village to write a book. From late night texts to early morning emails and even middle of the day cry sessions, my village was the best while writing and planning and editing this book. Now, I would like to thank that village and remind you, if you actually read this part of the book, to always thank your village too.

First, to my muse, my will to live, the person that I would never ever be able to live my life without, the author of the soundtrack that makes up my very being…Taylor. Your music inspired so much of this book and these characters. Without your art this book would not exist.

Next, to my loving husband, Josh, thank you for always pushing me to work on this book before all of my other life side quests. We met when I was finishing the first draft of the book and I will always be thankful for your reminders to keep working on it even when things got hard.

Next, my OG "Letters From London" friends- Paige, Nicole, Rachel, and Lyn. When I first released this story, you were all there supporting me and now over a decade later you are each still here supporting me. No matter what adventure I decide to wander off to, you each are always there cheering me on whether you think I'm crazy or not.

To my Mom, thank you for all your endless belief that I can do whatever I set my mind to. I can only do it because you paved the way.

To Cody, Kelly, Savannah, and Stacia my advanced readers and sound boards, you are each amazing. I've bounced so many ideas off of you throughout the publishing process and I am so grateful for your feedback and ideas!

To Haley, my FANTASTIC graphic designer. We spoke for 45 minutes about the book cover for this whole series and then you and your wonderfully creative mind created the most beautiful covers I've ever seen.

And to so many others, thank you all for buying this book, for reading it, and for listening to me talk about it non-stop. I appreciate each and every one of you.

About the Author

Kristina Frankel is a first-time author. She lives in Denver, Colorado with her husband Josh and their two dogs, Claire and Amy. Kristina grew up in Las Vegas, NV and received her bachelor's degree in English from the University of Nevada-Las Vegas. Connect on Instagram: @krissunshine13